Bone Dressing

BD

Book 1 in the *Bone Dressing* Series

MICHELLE I. BROOKS

This is a work of fiction. All of the characters and events
portrayed in this novel are products of the author's imagination
or are used fictitiously.

Cover design by Novel Publicity.

ISBN: 0-615-47759-3
ISBN-13: 978-0-61547-759-6

DEDICATION

For those three amazing, magnificent creatures in
my life wise enough to call me their
Goddess of Light and Beauty ...
Dalton, Tristan, and Alex

... and to one who hasn't quite figured
that out yet, William.

CONTENTS

ACKNOWLEDGMENTS

Like most things in my life, this book couldn't have been written without the love, support and occasional whip-cracking of my friends and family. So, for everyone on both sides of the pond who has helped make my life the fantastic, wonderful, magical journey it has been, thank you from the bottom of my heart. And to those who have added some of the darker, scarier, more difficult spaces in between, thank you for helping me grow into the me I am today. I couldn't have done this without either of you.

Dalton, Tristan and Alex, thank you for taking my breath away every second of the day. You fill my life with laughter, sprinkle in just enough wild, crazy bumps to keep it interesting, and wash it all down with bucket loads of hugs and kisses. I'm so grateful you chose me to call Mom and I am so very proud of each of you, inside and out. Dalton, you are my rock with a million smiles, my biggest fan, my photographer who'll take a thousand pictures to get one good one, and my unfailing hug at the end of the day. Tristan, you are my live-in-the-moment wild man, my go-to guy, and my funny face when I can't quite remember how to smile. Alex, you are my fairy princess (of course, that makes me queen by default!), my beautiful dancer, my red-headed goddess, and my most devout, hands-on co-creator of the life and times of Syd and Bone Dressing. You three are my heroes and my inspiration, my joy and my salvation.

Thank you, Mama, for loving this little girl that lived with you, every single day of my life. I love our banana split dinners of days gone by and our margarita Fridays of days to come. Dad, thanks for all the hands-on wrestling lessons in standing up for the story and characters of Bone Dressing ... I'm ready to go to bat for them now! Mimi & Pop, thanks for always being there with a hug and a smile and supporting this crazy dream. A special thanks to Aunt Dianne for believing in me and for reading Bone Dressing before it was all nice and shiny. Thank you Tessa for having an open heart and an active keyboard! So glad I can call you friend.

And finally, to the love of my life, William, thank you for finding me, for loving me on my good days and my not so good days, for liking me just as I am without trying to fix me, and for showing me what being in love is all about. You fill my life with joy, my pages with words, and my heart with a love that grows with every breath I take. Thank you for being the someone I always knew was out there, waiting just for me.

SOUL CRACKING

I stand unmoving, but am not still,
An eddy of leaves moves not by its will,
Brushing against my face, edges rough,
Dancing in abandon, this life is not enough.
Hushed whispers echo among the blades,
Memories of white knights in the palisades,
Tripping pebbles or prancing steeds,
Of my imagination it feeds.
The Cold Breath rolls in with night's end,
To still the dawn for eyes unopened,
Arms cradling, but warmth lacking,
A shiver slides, the soul cracking.

Dalton Pigott

1 THE END OF LIFE AS I KNOW IT

The cool breeze made the hair rise on my arms, but did nothing to ease the rage boiling inside me. Instead, the seething fury within my belly redoubled its efforts to surpass the roaring flames rising from the building across the street. It was such a strange feeling, fire and ice. I felt like someone had split me into two completely separate pieces ... like I was one of those raging California wildfires all locked up tight inside one massive mountain of ice.

A shiver curled its way down my spine and my arms instinctively tightened around my legs pulling them in closer, my body desperately searching for soothing, for comfort, for warmth. As the fire raged ever stronger in the school building, I heard the crash of some unknown object as it succumbed to the blistering inferno. A huge bird, frightened by the sound, abandoned its position in a nearby tree and flew straight towards me, veering off at the last moment, screeching his fear and frustration at me for blocking his escape.

"Sorry!" I called after him. Like he could understand me! My gaze shifted back to the blazing structure. I wonder if the flames flickering in my eyes were simply a reflection of what I was watching, or something more ... a glimpse of my humanity.

Humanity! That's good! I burn down a building and the first thing that comes to mind is my own humanity!

I mean, honestly, how could I possibly be sitting on the roof of some stranger's house, in the middle of the night no less, chaos and destruction laid out in front of me, caused by me, and feel ... comforted, righteous even? Granted, Mr. Askew was a complete asshole! It really did serve him right ... the jerk! But how exactly did I end up here? How had things gotten this far out of hand? It was like I was the villain in a dramatic production someone was staging, only this was real, too real. I didn't mean for this to happen. Of course, I never meant for things like this to happen. But they always did. Maybe some part of me way down deep inside wanted them to. God, I hope not!

I barely manage to sneak up on my eighteenth birthday, and already I'm a psychiatrist's dream date, with a criminal record to boot. Or, I will have one as soon as they figure out it was me, which they will ... and fast, just because it's me. Forget DNA samples from strands of hair, I probably left my entire left pinky back there.

I looked down and grabbed hold of it just to make sure I hadn't done exactly that. No. Thank God, it was still there, gently trembling with a kind of detached dread just like the rest of me, white streak in my hair and all.

I'd found that little gift from the universe painted at my left temple earlier tonight, my reward for doing the right thing. Go figure! Other people get money, a medal, a certificate, even a kiss on the cheek. But me? God no. I get a patch of white so pure it could grace the head of Sister Theresa! Where was the justice in that?

Just then, the windows of the burning building shattered, pulling my attention back to the raging flames. Two men ran backwards away from the building dodging bits of glass that sang out in delight as they tickled the concrete and asphalt in a shower of broken pane. The men hadn't been hurt, thank God, I sure wouldn't want that to happen. But instead of feeling shocked or ashamed by setting the building on fire, like I knew I probably should, my lips twisted into a smug smile. Justice, peace, serenity even, that's what I felt. Not even the barest whisper of humility, much less guilt.

My God, where was my conscience? Shit! Why did everything always have to happen bass-ackwards for me? Wasn't this supposed to happen the other way around? Shouldn't my conscience be hunting me down and squashing me like a bug? Even Pinocchio had Jiminy Cricket yelling at him 24/7 and he was just a dumb chunk off a pine tree!

I stretched my arms, then let my hands drop behind me onto the rough shingles so I could lean back on them. "Ugh!" My left hand had landed right on top of a miss-thrown newspaper that had that wet, nasty, two-week-old slime smeared across it. Grimacing, I quickly dragged my fingers across the rough rooftop trying to get the slimy gunk off, but along with it went the first three layers of my skin. Could this night possibly get any worse? At least I still had that pinky!

Two small streams of water started to spray over the roof of the school, not the part that was burning though, the part that wasn't. Those guys were pretty smart, instead of hosing down the flaming carcass of the burning classroom in utter futility, they chose to put their energy into trying to protect all that hadn't yet been claimed by the ravenous flames.

Okay, so if my own Jiminy Cricket wasn't sounding the doomsday alarm maybe that meant setting the school on fire wasn't such a bad thing after all. Maybe it was even a good thing... under these circumstances, anyway.

Right! Great! Now I sounded like one of those idiots on death row telling everyone who's stupid enough to listen how it's not his fault he stabbed the guy fifty times. It just happened that way. The dead guy was asking for it. The convict was just minding his own business, innocently peeling an apple with a razor-sharp seven-inch blade ... and it slipped ... fifty times ... straight into the dead guy's chest. Yeah, sure, of course it happened just like that. What's not to believe?

Maybe I was conscience-challenged... from birth. Maybe the year after they electrocute my ass they'll discover that eating dill pickles and Ding Dongs with Coke after 11pm more than three times a week induces a sub-cellular shift in the conscience-retention capacity of brain cells in orphaned, lower middle-class teenagers who listen to way too much Evanescence.

Anyway, at least no one would have to deal with Mr. Askew for a while. At least not until he got a new classroom. Not as good as gone, but still an improvement.

I could just see him, our dear Mr. Asshole, holding open the door to the blazing room. Hot, blistered paint crawling off the walls and flying down around his face like Hell's personal demon-roaches. His obnoxious voice was clawing its way out of my head, repeating the words he'd thrown at me earlier that week, growling, two inches from my nose. His stench reeking past a wad of Big Red gum laced over cheap cigars, rum and Diet Coke.

"Well, Sydney? What's it gonna be? Do we tell everyone you're nothing but a filthy little thief after all? Or, do we handle this..."

He'd paused as his eyes had raked my body from head to toe. He inhaled deeply, slowly. Menacingly. Like he was drinking in my scent as if it were a physical part of my body that he could consume without even asking for my consent.

"... discreetly, with after school ... detentions?" He'd smiled sadistically at that point. Obviously, his definition of detention would be something dark and twisted, a Freddy Krueger wet-dream. Hell, it already was. He already was.

My breathing sped as my rage flared again. But the memory, unquenched, continued. "I didn't steal anything! You know that," I'd gritted out through clenched teeth. The muscles in my jaw clenched tightly, the taste of that moment curling around the back of my mouth like a spoonful of thick, sickeningly sweet cough syrup I just couldn't choke down.

Mr. Askew'd countered with quiet, slimy conviction, "Do I?" A sinister sneer played upon his lips as his cold eyes appraised me. Even the touch of his stare felt dirty, tainted. It made me feel like I'd already been eternally stained with immorality just by being in his presence.

A menacing growl that sounded nothing like me resonated from deep within my throat as my hands clenched into fists thinking about the whole nasty scene again.

Where exactly could I go from here? Where should I go from here? I couldn't tell the principal ... I still don't think he'd gotten over my orchestrating a sit-down protest against the use of animal by-products. In my defense, I'd had a geography test scheduled that day that I hadn't studied for and the protest was my ticket out of it. Of course, he'd also been pretty pissed over the bumper-to-bumper garbage cans in his office to promote recycling for a greener future ... yeah, I'd been PMSing that day. And then there were those smoke bombs in the girl's bathroom ... sheer boredom, what can I say? In any case, I wouldn't be surprised if my face graced his dartboard at this point.

Okay, the police? Huh! Right! Like they'd believe me about anything. I may have Sister Theresa's hair now, but that had to be the only thing we had in common.

The Carters then? Well, Quince and Jackie had been my foster parents long enough to know I was no picnic, but this? No, this was just one spoonful too much drama for them to handle in a single dose. Besides, I was already grounded for sneaking out last week. And for a month at that! Jesus. They'd double it at least if they so much as caught a sniff of this. And what, exactly, was their take-home message here? Spend some time working on my stealth mode to avoid detection next time around? Whatever! I'd be sure to get right on it.

Of course, I knew they were just worried about me and trying to do their best to help keep me out of trouble. So, I couldn't really blame them for taking a stand. But I sure couldn't tell them the truth, either. That was completely out of the question. My nights were mine ... only mine. The one piece of my life that nobody else could have, or share, or even know about.

Besides, it would only hurt them if I told them. Even without any more I love you's, midnight hot chocolates (heavy on the whipped cream, please), cookie batter battles (think snowball fights) and dancing in the moonlight, Mama and Daddy were still my connection to anything outside of me. When I was younger, I'd have to stop and just look down at my feet, sure that I'd catch a glimpse of their hands holding me down on the ground, keeping me from disappearing off the face of the earth in a burst of nothingness. My nights at the cemetery with them were sometimes the only thing that gave me the strength to hold it together. To make it through another day, another forced smile ... or another breath.

Dragging my lower lip between my teeth, I could almost taste the chunk of chocolate chip cookie batter I'd licked off my fingers after pelting Daddy with a wad of it just before he'd grabbed Mama from behind, lifting her off the floor. Laughing and squealing, she'd twisted around in his arms and smeared two handfuls all over his face, batter clinging to his prickly whiskers. Growling, Daddy had toppled them to the floor, grabbed her face and kissed her, waiting for her to give in to him before he rubbed his face all over her cheeks. But she'd already been won, and just started nibbling cookie dough off his jaw. When I'd sat on his back to continue the attack, Mama had just grabbed a handful of batter off the floor, slipped her hands behind him and ran it all through my hair. What a perfectly disgusting, completely insane, absolutely phenomenal night.

My parents had taught me what living actually was. My only problem was in the follow-through. I knew what I wanted out of life, I just couldn't seem to get my feet moving.

I felt around in the pocket of the trench coat I had on, pulled out an Atomic Fireball, pinched one end, popping the candy into my mouth and bit down hard ... relishing the heat as the cinnamon-hot jawbreaker slid against the inside of my cheek. I wonder if I'm anything like my parents? The fiery liquid trickled down my throat, burning its way through my body. I looked at my fingernails as I wadded the plastic wrapper before shoving it back into my pocket. I knew they were my dad's nails, strong and square, even though my fingers, long and slender, were my mom's through and through. I don't mean in physical ways like that though, that's simply genetics. I mean in how I deal with life ... how I tackle the hard candy. Mama used to say any poor shmuck could suck down cotton candy, it's nothing but a giant cloud of dreamy nothingness. The hard candy, though, that's another matter. Like when you eat an Atomic Fireball. Do you spit it right out as soon as you can't deal with it? Do you suck on it ... for like forever, suffering through the heat and pain? Or do you simply bite right on into it, risk chipping a tooth or biting your cheek or tongue, anything just so you can feel it give way beneath your teeth, reasserting your control over the minutia of your life?

Crushing the last few bits of candy before they burned a hole straight through my tongue, I swallowed hard. Yeah, usually I'm a biter. But when it comes right down to it, I do all three, it's just that my gut reaction is to chomp down. It really depends on what I'm having to choke down though. And why, the why makes all the difference.

So does the "What if?" Like, what if the ice wrapped like a blanket around me right now smothers the searing fire consuming everything real, alive and untainted inside me? Or what if this raging inferno I've got stoked to the max in my chest right now melts the glacier and evaporates any and all remaining humanity and compassion I possess? Which one should I be more concerned about? Why?

All good questions. The what-ifs and the whys are definitely my buddies for life ... absolute keepers, which is more than I can say of most of the people I know. Sad, maybe, but true.

I'm not sure how sad that really is though. People actually tend to be over-rated. It took me about sixty seconds to figure that out, maybe less. It was a little hard to tell what with all the blood and dirt flying around, not to mention the screaming. Lots of screaming. What a day that was! An entire lifetime of drama had to have been packed into that minute and it all just came busting out at the same time, kind of like one of those trick cans of nuts where a springing three-foot-long snake comes barreling out when you pop the top. Big laughs there.

Funny how they say opposites attract and that two people who are too similar would bore one another ... they usually do, too. And yet, I've been talking to myself my whole life. I certainly know myself, and I'd say I'm pretty damn similar to little old me. But I shock the hell out of myself all the time.

Maybe I really had lost it. I didn't feel like it though. I still felt like me. I just wasn't quite sure who me was yet, that's all. Yeah, okay, that's all this was. Just a case of mistaken identity. Too bad it was my own. Maybe I should post some "Missing Self" posters up around the neighborhood, with a box of Ding Dongs as the reward. What can I say, I'm still in high school, I've got very little in the way of liquid assets. On second thought, the reward should be a box of Twinkies. Gotta keep the chocolate closer to the heart.

Sirens started to peel softly in the distance, cutting through the night like a hot knife through butter. Good. The two men wouldn't be hurt, Mr. A wouldn't be able to teach, not tomorrow anyway, and the devastation was limited to necessity. Not too bad for my first felony.

My God, Syd! Focus! I have to get a grip and get out of here. Just breathe. I could do that. Nothing too complicated, just breathe. I'm sure I've done that before. Once or twice, anyway.

But even as I tried to make light of it, in that moment I felt the ground shift beneath me and the wind cut back. And, deep down, I knew this one event would change the direction of my life forever. Change me forever. Whoever the hell I was.

2 CAUGHT IN THE ACT

One week before the demise of my unconventional, inconsistent life ...

I could hear their voices as I reached the front steps. Queens and Jacks were fighting strong tonight. That was my personal nickname for Quince and Jackie, known to the IRS and the local bingo hall as Quincy and Jacqueline Carter, my legally-appointed foster parents ever since my parents died.

I knew Quince and Jackie had both always wanted me to call them Mom and Dad, but I never did. I couldn't. They were Quince and Jackie, to me. And while I did love them, well, kind of, anyway, life with them was simply a means to an end. The means being basic survival: phone, cable, food and bed; and the end being either my eighteenth birthday, just 37 days to go on that one, or life imprisonment on trumped up misdemeanor charges, whichever came first. It was going to be a close call.

Either way, Queens and Jacks were in the middle of a discussion. A loud discussion ... about me. Again. Of course. The sun was still shining, wasn't it? Hmmm, actually, it had gone down about half an hour ago. Still, it was up somewhere and my breath came just a little more easily knowing it was at this very moment shining warmly on somebody's face, even if that somebody didn't wear this particular face. Sure hope they appreciated it.

"Well, it's because you let her get away with murder," Quince grumbled. His face was that mottled beet color it always turned when he was irritated, which more often than not was about something I'd done.

"That's a bunch of crap ... she just does it anyway, no matter what I say or do," Jackie defended herself weakly.

"She wouldn't if you would step up and take control," Quince countered.

Jackie stood up and walked to stand in his face, "Control? We are still talking about Syd, right? Because you're talking like someone who doesn't even know her. She's completely blind to everything except what she wants. You would have to use a baseball bat to even try to drive an idea home long enough to stick for three seconds."

Her voice got louder as I slipped quietly through the front door. They couldn't see me from the kitchen and I tried to shut the front door and step to the side before they passed the doorway that lead into the hall.

"Yeah? Don't tempt me right now!" Quince was so mad, he was beginning to spit when he spoke. Not pretty.

12

"Quince!" Jackie practically barked out his name while she wiped her face with the back of her hand. Kind of interesting how she could kiss him until their lips turned blue, but couldn't hang with him spewing a few little drops of dribble on her face. Go figure...

Quince just turned up the heat. "Don't even start! This has got to stop. Now! She has absolutely no consideration for anyone but herself."

Jackie rebounded quickly, "Quince, I know this looks bad. It does, but maybe she has a perfectly good explanation. She's a good kid, down deep inside. I know she is. You know she is too, if you'd just stop and think about it for half a second. She's had a tough life. Much tougher than you or me."

"For God's sake, would you please stop defending her for two seconds and really take a good look at what's happening here, at what's happening today, not ten years ago?" Quince was back to pacing.

"But that's just it, Baby. We don't know for sure exactly what's happened. We only know what Principal Shell said, and he only knows what was told to him. What if he's been misinformed? It could happen." God bless Jackie.

Oh, man! They'd already heard about what had happened ... maybe I could quietly slip upstairs before they realized I was home.

"Yeah, and when I bend over stars are going to come flying out of my ass!" Man, Quince knew how to get a good mad on.

And Jackie, as sweet and tenacious as ever, still tried to smile it out of him. "Ouch! That sounds painful." Was she a saint, or just stupid? It was really hard to tell sometimes.

In any case, I'd had enough drama for one night though, what with an irreparably mangled first date with Josh, the latest boy toy to cross my path. I eased forward, but just my luck, the floorboard groaned under my foot on the next step. So much for a career as agent 00-anything. If I had a gun, I would have shot that stupid step for being the traitor it was! Actually, I'd have probably missed and shot my toe. Good thing I didn't have that gun! There, I'm counting my blessings.

"Syd, is that you?" Quince's voice boomed. Shit. He really sounded pissed. Maybe he didn't know for sure I was there yet ... if I moved quickly enough I just might make it past ...

But he knew. "Get in here. Now, Syd!"

I dragged my hands through my hair, the color of dark chocolate roots to tips, not a highlight in sight. "Yes, sir?" Man, how much do they know? Pay attention. Well, they know enough by the looks on their faces. Was Quince's lip actually sticking out a full two inches like a whiny little two-year-old brat, or what? No, Syd, don't you dare laugh! That would be bad. Really bad.

Jackie warned, "Not too hard, Quince, please?" She always tried to soften his temper. And, usually, she did a pretty good job of it. Jackie was like some kind of industrial strength insulation that slipped itself around Quince like a comfy blanket just pulled out of the dryer, all warm and soft and cuddly-smelling. Other times though, she only made things worse, just tripping Quince up, like that nice, cozy blanket had gotten all knotted up around his feet. This was one of those times.

He cut her off curtly with a sharp glance, "I'll handle it." His attention zeroed in on me as his eyes swung back like a whip, I expected to hear the crack any second now. "Syd, what the hell happened this time? Jackie spent three hours this afternoon on the phone trying to smooth things out just enough to keep your butt in school! Shell said you told one of your teachers to go to hell, after you called him a 'fucking asshole'! You practically started a riot in the middle of class."

Thank you, God. That's all they knew. "Mmm, sorry," I mumbled, relief, not regret, staining my words. I almost laughed out loud as the tension washed out of me so fast my toes curled up. Almost laughed.

"Syd, this is the third time in two months I've had to do this. Don't you have anything more to say than, 'Mmm, sorry'?" Jackie's whine just fed my own frustration and served as kindling to fan the flames of a good mad. I was supposed to care because, what, she missed her mid-afternoon rendezvous with Oprah & the Cooking Network? Honestly, who gives a shit?

The breath came out of my chest heavily as the weight of the conversation bore down on me. "Yeah, you know what? Actually, I do have more to say. Look, I appreciate all you've done for me, I do. Really. But I'm not a little kid anymore, I'm seventeen. Gonna be eighteen in just over a month. I'll be out of your hair and out of your house then! So, why not back off, just a little bit, a millimeter or two?" I held up my hand, squeezing my thumb and index finger tightly together to reiterate exactly how enormous that would be.

"Good grief, Syd. What the hell is wrong with you? Where are your God damn manners, and what the Sam Hill are you thinking?" Quince sensed my anger at his words, stopped, took a deep breath and restarted on a different note in a more concerned voice. "Okay, look, that's not what Jackie or I want. We just ..." he trailed off, searching for a way to express himself.

I wasn't in a patient mood myself though, much less in the mood to coddle either of their middle-aged neuroses. "Ungh! What?! What do you want? Blood? The life of my first unborn child? Both?" Jackie flinched and closed her eyes. I didn't like hurting her, either of them really, but I just didn't want to do this right now. Or ever, really, to be perfectly honest.

Jackie turned to me but kept her eyes on the floor as she spoke, "We want to help you however we can. We just don't know how best to do that right now, Honey." Her eyes glanced up at mine and her face was painfully sincere. She reached out and took my hand.

Jerking my hand away I blurted out, "Well, right now I just need a little more space. Room to, I don't know, to breathe."

But she continued as if I'd not reacted at all, "Syd, we certainly don't expect you to blow out your candles, rip open your presents and head straight out the door. You have time to figure things out."

Quince walked over and rested his hand on Jackie's shoulder as the first tears fell from her eyes, trying to ease her pain. That's one thing he was really good at, sponging off all of Jackie's discomforts. Problem was, he didn't just soak them up and let them go. Oh, no. He claimed ownership for each and every one and made a permanent residence for them in his personal "shit-to-stew-over-and-make-everyone-miserable-about-on-a-rainy day" data bank.

I have to admit though, Quince and Jackie really did love each other. At times like this it was most apparent. Too bad it made for a united front against yours truly.

Just then Quince looked at me and said, "I swear, sometimes you seem hell-bent on making, no, forcing everything to be so damn hard!" He threw his hands up in the air, exasperated, "My God, it's like you are your own worst enemy, Syd. I don't think you could pay someone to do a better job of screwing up your life for you."

"Yeah? Well, at least I can see me coming," I smiled ruefully.

Jackie cut her eyes up at me with a smirk on her face, "Yes, well, maybe it's time for a good pair of bifocals, Honey, or a full-length mirror ... or a new perfume. Something. Anything." She laughed shortly, not quite ready to give up on the discussion but ready for a reprieve nonetheless.

"I'm glad you two can laugh about this ..." as usual, Quince was least ready to simply let it go. Then I caught that little shift in his eyes. Quince hated to make decisions, but once he did, that was it. He wouldn't be open to discuss that particular issue ever again. And he'd just made a decision ... shit. "One month, Syd. Dishes, laundry, schoolwork. No ...," he waved his hand in the air haphazardly, "... anything, other than that."

I reeled as if he'd slapped my face hard and spluttered back, "A month? No! You've got to be kidding me. You can't do that. It might as well be a life sentence. That's ... that's forever. That's after prom."

"That's what it is. One month. This was your choice, not mine, and certainly not Jackie's." He was so damned calm all of a sudden. Quince could do that though. He could go from nuclear meltdown to all creamy and mellow in 3.5 seconds. Kind of the opposite of a Lamborghini. It really pissed me off. Now, there'd be no talking to him. It was done in his mind. Yell at Syd. Check. Sentence Syd. Check. Move on. Check.

"My choice? No way, that's bullshit! This is so unfair. You can't do this!" It irritated me that I could hear a faint whine down in there somewhere. I never whined. Bitch and moan from time to time, sure, but never, ever whine.

"Guess you just didn't see yourself coming this time, huh? Jackie may be right about those bifocals. Night, Syd." Quince helped Jackie up as she shot an eyeful of pity my way. Yeah, fat lot of good that'll do me. Sure wouldn't get me into a dress for prom.

With a tight-lipped pull on her lips that didn't quite make it to a smile, Jackie added, "Night, Honey. Sorry things worked out this way."

But Quince, her lord and protector extraordinaire was quick to intercede. "Now, stop that. You always apologize for things you didn't do. She's a big girl now, she said so herself. Let her shoulder it this time. If you want to feel bad about something, let it be that you haven't paid enough attention to me tonight. So far, anyway." Quince's arm slipped around the small of Jackie's back, pulling her body snuggly into his and burying his face in that soft, tender spot at the base of her throat.

"Quince, stop it! Syd's right here." But Jackie's protest was weakened by the smile in her eyes as she gazed up at Quince.

Even with as annoying as they could be, it always made the bitter stuff go down just a little bit better watching how completely they loved one another. Even when life was serving up nothing but fried shit sandwiches ... especially then, actually.

That was their gift, I guess. No kids, but a soul-stopping love for each other that spilled all over everyone around them, soaking them to the bone, whether they liked it or not. Life seems to be like that sometimes though, big on the give and take and just as big on neighboring spillage, good or bad. Good neighbors tend to be highly underestimated.

"Oh, you heard her. She's practically grown. And, more importantly, she's leaving. Now! Good night, Syd."

"Ungh! Night!" As I turned and began to stomp up the stairs I grumbled. "What's so god-awful good about it anyway? Being grounded? Indentured servitude? The end of life as I know it? Again. And no God damn prom! No fucking prom! What kind of bullshit is that?"

"We do love you, Honey. And, try to curb your language." Jackie's voice trailed behind me.

"Yeah, yeah. Heard it before. Maybe you should consider working on your delivery next time. Because it sucks!" I was working up to a good long mad, the kind that would take days to come down from. Thirty, to be specific.

Their words spilled out between kisses and mouthfuls of laughter this time. "We still love you."

"I know, dammit. Love you, too!" The mirror in the hall shook as I slammed my door shut. The laughter downstairs only seemed to increase in volume. Yeah, she sure didn't seem to be having a hard time swapping spit now.

Great. At least someone was having a good time here. Too bad it wasn't the only resident fun-loving minor.

3 SOUL DANCING

The door was still shaking on its hinges, threatening mutiny. I couldn't sit still. Not even if my life had depended on it. I felt trapped, caged, like the hyenas at the zoo that hover along the fence line looking so completely focused on freedom, but so utterly lost for a means to achieve it. The frantic panic of frustration and confinement pounded through my veins.

So, I did what the animals do and started to pace around the small cage that was mine to fill, my bedroom, trying to calm down. The larger the space you have to consume, the better the chance of not meeting up with yourself. Easier to face what lies outside than what threatens from within. Maybe I could outrun the beast knotting in my stomach, the one snuggling down nice and cozy, deep inside my abdomen, filling my very bones with unease and trepidation.

But instead of bringing peace, it felt like the animal filling my marrow was claiming me, taking root and feeding on my rage. After seven round trips through the jungle otherwise known as my bedroom, I was in considerably worse shape than when I'd begun. Not good. Not good at all.

But I marched on. I'm nothing if not tenacious. Pay dirt had to be just around the next bend in the carpet.

On my twelfth pass by the darkened windows, the wind outside began to pick up, lashing against the small house with a temper of its own. The night was mocking the agitation rippling off my body and consuming my mind as inconsequential and infinitesimal by comparison.

Suddenly, the exotic drums and Spanish guitars of Brio, one of Queens and Jacks signature CDs, certainly the most worn at any rate, began seeping though the walls and curling in under my door. The thunder and lightning outside started up as if on cue to the steady, sensual rhythm.

Sometimes, most times even, Brio could sooth my soul within moments, bathing me in a soft, cool spring rain. Not this time, though. This was, unfortunately for me, not anywhere near most times.

This was this time. And this time bit. Bit hard.

My room was collapsing in on me. It had to be. I know it took more time, more steps to circumnavigate my claustrophobic box. My feet stumbled over themselves in my haste, as a mild dizziness set in. Maybe if I reversed directions it would go away.

For the record, motion sickness of any kind is just that, motion sickness. Any direction works just as good as another, and the only cure is being stationary, trying to unwind it by changing directions just makes it that much worse. It would be a nice cure though, for more things than just motion sickness.

The music stepped up a pace and the thundering storm followed suit, keeping time almost as if it was being orchestrated by a cosmic conductor. Both were building in intensity, filling the air around me with an electric excitement that eased the dull nausea from my mind, but not from the pit of my knotting stomach.

All of a sudden my tenuous grasp of control snapped.

I had to get out of this room, this house. Now. If time all alone with my lonesome couldn't help, a shift in geography sure couldn't hurt.

The next blast of thunder shoved me straight into my raincoat. I had to get out before I self-imploded and made the ten o'clock news. From the sound of things, Queens and Jacks would be otherwise occupied for quite a while.

Besides, Quince specifically told me to go. Well, he did tell me to leave didn't he? Word for word. What was it? Something like, "She's leaving, now!"

So? I'll just take him at his word on that. Interpretation is all about definition, and his was unclear, or maybe too clear. Just leave. Plain and simple. So? Leaving! Now! Also simple. The suffocating bands wrapped so tightly around my chest eased off just a little.

Why don't they teach self-preservation in school? A completely practical, down-and-dirty, hands-on, no-holds-barred, this-is-how-to-live-and-grow-old happily-and-live-to-tell-the-tale-101 class. Now that's something I'd show up for, brain and all.

My reflection smiled sardonically back at me as I hastily rushed the window, unlocked the swing clamp and jerked up on the bottom pane. It usually stuck a little bit, but with the humidity from the rain, I really had to heave to get it to release. Suddenly, the panel slammed upwards freely and I had to grab it to keep it from crashing into the upper section of the window frame ... that would be some serious Eminem "window pain".

Quiet just wasn't in the cards tonight though. Of course not. That would require, gasp, cooperation from the universe on my behalf. Silly me.

Instead, my knee bumped the bottle I kept on the window sill, the one that I dumped all my loose change into. I was always saving every coin I could get my hands on for a higher purpose. At least the money I didn't need for necessities like Baskin Robbins Rocky Road ice cream. Their Peppermint Fudge Ribbon used to be my favorite, but they'd stopped making that back about the same time my parents died. Truly, a dual tragedy. Worst timing imaginable. Shame on them. But my current higher purpose was a totally ripped guitar strap I saw last month at Hancock's, where I buy most of my music gear, so Baskin Robbins hadn't seen much of me the last few weeks.

The jar fell down towards the hardwood floor in slow motion. My right leg moved forward with absolutely no coaching from me and gently rebounded it toward the rope rug by my bed. Man, Beck ain't got nothin' on me! Just call me Soccer Syd. The jar still made a moderate thuddy drop and roll, but at least no really loud fireworks. Yes!

No! Shit! Ow! God dammit! That two second pain window just kicked in and quickly reminded me exactly how heavy a jar of coins could be. It

24

felt like an elephant had jumped up and down on a pogo stick right on top of my foot.

On the plus side, no response from the rest of the house. See, life was good, a little anyway. Still, I had to get out. Now. Not quite sure what I had to get out of ... my own head, my room, my life, D, all of the above. I started through the window out onto the eave of the roof. It really didn't make any difference what I was escaping from, getting out of something, anything, was enough.

As my second foot made contact with the wet roof, I turned towards the edge, letting go of the window sill. I'd done this a thousand times before, just three small steps to the side, grab the overhanging limb of the oak tree, walk onto the lower limb, bend over and grab it with my arms, then jump down. Piece of cake.

Only not this time. On my second step, I slipped on the water and went down on my back, legs in the air over my head, bodysurfing down the rooftop, barreling towards the edge and a whole big world of pain.

My hands were clawing at the tiles with no effect whatsoever and my legs were already starting over the edge. If they went over, I went over. That was for sure. Instinctively I rolled to my left. The world should have been a blur at that speed on a stormy night. But I saw every detail. In one movement, my right leg swung over the lower branch of the oak tree and my hands found pay dirt with the rain gutter. The breath I hadn't realized I was holding in tight slid out and I quickly assessed the damage, still dangling ten plus feet above good old Planet Earth. No broken bones, not even any bad blows, just some roughed up, banged up places on my back and hands. Even my jeans were still in one piece.

For the first time, I was glad that Quince had forced me into manual labor last summer helping him put those stupid gutters up. He'd been a total pain in the ass! But Jackie had been thrilled. Now, her flowerbeds actually survived past each heavy rain. Oh, joy! We could all die a peaceful death. The flowers were safe, hallelujah! Damn! Maybe I hit my head after all.

I slid down until I could drop to the ground and let go. My knees gave some to absorb the impact, leaving me in a low crouch.

A quick check of the windows on that side of the house seemed to put me in the clear for both A.I. and P.P., not artificial intelligence and a trip to the bathroom, but adult interference and parental police, in this case one and the same. Yay for me. A two-for-one. Feeling substantially better from the adrenaline rush pounding through my veins, I slowly straightened, feeling the tension ease considerably from my neck and shoulders.

I straightened my raincoat and tightened the hood, enjoying the streams of water running off the jacket and down my arms. Turning, I started down the street. Thanks for traveling the Syd Express. Now deboarding at gate one. Please recommend us to your friends and family, especially those who like a heavy serving of terror and danger with their travel plans.

Laughter spilled out of my mouth unchecked as the rain crawled in its place. Fresh and cool. Liquid anesthetic. I tipped my head backward, closed my eyes and opened my mouth, letting the water pool inside. My body moved as if to some distant memory, my arms rising upward, my feet pulling me forward in wide arcs and circles. But my arms didn't have the freedom they needed, so I decorated an unsuspecting lawn with my raincoat as I abandoned the safety of the sidewalk for the freedom of the empty streets.

Blinking up into the rain, I gave myself completely to the overwhelming sensations surrounding me, filling me. On and on I moved, danced, feeding the storm with my essence and feasting on it in return. I gulped the energy down my throat so hard it almost hurt, like I was dying of thirst in the Gobi, so completely thirsty that my skin was drinking in the cool water through every pore of my body.

I was euphoric. It felt as if my soul had shed the confining clothing of my body and was bathing in the moonlit fall of water surrounding me. Dancing through the glistening streets was completely magical. Storms moved me, grounded me, excited me. In a way nothing else could. They always had, for as long as I could remember.

Maybe it was because my parents would wake me on stormy nights to dance in the rain in the graveyard. Or maybe it was because it was storming the day they died and took my whole world with them. But maybe it was more simple than that, more basic. Maybe it was just because I really liked water. Moving water. And nothing could beat forcefully moving water at night. It was strangely cleansing, calming and exciting at the same time. And the darkness just made it all the more magical, intoxicating, forbidden, somehow darkly captivating.

I danced and drank with no thought beyond that breath, that sip. And the water filled my soul with a promise. The promise of a purpose for me, something waiting for me, and someone somewhere, right now, waiting to do it with me. You would think it would have left me feeling only half full. But no. The promise was enough, enough for now. With those words still echoing through my head, my soul returned to me, soft and warm, filling every atom of my body to the brim. And I could breathe. For the first time in a long time, I could breathe.

As my eyes began to clear and refocus on the world around me, it was as if I was opening them for the first time. Everything was brighter, prettier. Somehow, even in the dark, the darks were darker, the lights lighter, everything more ... perfect, more striking, more captivating.

All of a sudden, I realized I was standing in the heart of the cemetery. My feet had danced their way through the wet streets for two and a half miles on autopilot. How had I managed to get here without tripping, stumbling, stepping in a manhole, playing dodge-car with a bus, body-slamming a tree, kicking a kitty, anything? I run into everything. All day, every day. The doctor should have given Mama a helmet and football pads for me the day I popped out. It would have saved a few yards of skin and a couple cases of band-aids by now. It's a really good thing I don't bruise easily, or Queens and Jacks would have had Children's Protective Services barking down their throats years ago.

But no matter how I'd gotten here. Here I was. The tombstones glittered in the rain, dark, sparkling sentinels welcoming me home.

4 BLIND DATE AT PLOT 1327-B

I loved being in the cemetery alone. Ever since my parents had died, it had been my favorite place. The place I came to hide from the rest of the world, to think things over, to cry, to try to catch my breath, but more than anything to feel. To feel anything. To feel alive. Exactly why I felt most alive in a place filled with death, I didn't question, it just worked for me.

Besides, it wasn't filled with death. Death was for hospital rooms that stank of disinfectant and sickness. Graveyards were just neighborhoods where the bones set up house.

But the cemetery at night, that was the best. Partly because I had it all to myself. Well, except for the few wild dogs that had taken up permanent residence there over the years, and the whispers and shadows of the other creatures of the night that had made this cemetery their home. But those things only seemed to bring my parents closer to me, the unspoken chatter of our little neighborhood. Given a choice, I'd take earth sounds over people sounds any day.

My hand slid along the rough stone of a monument as I slowly passed by it. Rachel Anne Kensington's gravestone, one of my favorites. Maybe favorite wasn't quite the right word, but my heart always did a funny little hiccup when I passed her. She'd died at seventeen, my age now, and a baby was buried with her, a boy who'd died the same day he was born, Jesse Alejandro Garcia de la Cruz, II. She must have died in childbirth and he beforehand. I couldn't imagine her giving up on life if she'd gazed into his eyes or heard his tiny voice, even once. She would have fought for him, I just knew it. I'd whiled away countless hours imagining who the father had been, what their lives, their love had been like, and why he, the man, was nowhere to be found, even though Rachel had loved him enough to bear his child. Had he moved away to start again, have another love, another family? Maybe, probably.

Rachel amazed me. She'd lived, loved, borne a child, died, and who knows what else, all by the time she was the exact same age I was now. An entire life, a beginning, a middle, an end, even an epilogue, to boot. And what, exactly, had I done in that same amount of time? Jack shit, that's what. Memorized the TV Guide, taught myself to play the guitar, messed around with Tai-Chi, and learned how to make one hell of a fried egg sandwich. I mean, I was okay at a lot of things, but an expert at nothing. Not one friggin' thing. Well, maybe one thing. Ruining my life to the very best of my seventeen-year-old ability. Yeah, my own worst enemy. Quince was right. Dammit!

I kept drifting through the sleeping tombstones, dragging my fingers along the odd collection of granite and marble names that now called this patch of earth home. It was as beautiful and peaceful as any park, but instead of being filled with hot, noisy, rusting playground equipment and echoing the distant refrains of the neighborhood ice cream truck, cemeteries carried the memories and promises of past lives, the ballads of lives lived and lost, some happy, some not so much, some just plain awful. How could that be depressing? If you weren't really living your own life, okay. Maybe I could understand how being around the dead would make you feel uncomfortable, guilty even. Kind of like being graded on an assignment that you kept procrastinating even starting.

Truth be told, while I spend more than half my free time happily hangin' with the dead guys, once my number's called I really don't plan on spending much time here. I'd rather be buried under an old shady oak tree on the banks of a stream in the middle of nowhere. Now that sounds quiet and peaceful. And perfect. Just the way I'd like to spend eternity. Besides, then if anyone decided to come visit, they could just picnic under the tree and go for a swim. Nice. Maybe they'd even carve their initials in the trunk from time to time. Like people will be beating a path to spend time with my cold, dried up carcass. They don't even do that now, when I'm still all warm and juicy.

I took a deep breath and my eyelids dropped as I rounded the large black marker that bordered my parents. Plot 1327-B. Home. My head rolled back and I inhaled the jasmine and magnolia that mingled together in the heavy, moist night air. I'd snuck back and planted them in the middle of the night after my parents gained resident status here. The jasmine curled and nestled along the burnished steel-colored marker that stood protectively over their bodies and the magnolia was slightly outside the boundary of the gravesite, standing on the nether-region between their patch of earth and the O'Neill's, who were parked next door. I'd never really understood the whole cut flowers thing. I needed the permanence, the life, of whole, growing plants. And these two were my favorites. Mama always had them growing by the front gate, so I figured she'd want them here.

Bending down, I kissed my fingertips and smoothed them over the engraved names of Mama and Daddy, Lily Bovay-Roberdeau and Jeremiah Rémy Roberdeau. My dad had gone by Rémy most of his life, so named by his little sister, Annalise. A twin who'd missed the starting gate by all of two minutes. "Jeremiah" just had a way of getting all tangled up in her mouth every time she tried to get it out, so she'd swapped it for his middle name. They'd been inseparable their whole lives, finishing one another's sentences. Sweet, but annoying. My mother used to joke about having married two Roberdeaus in a single day, a feat unmatched in their neck of the woods. I would've bet good money Aunt Annalise and Daddy would have died the same day too, but she'd been attacked on her way home from the university late one night and hadn't seen daybreak since. One of her students had fixated on her, three steps past bad, and had followed her home after class to profess his undying lust for her. It had been too much for Aunt Annalise, he'd really messed her up ten different shades of pain and she'd died after a couple weeks in the hospital. That had been the year before my parents joined her here. It had made the papers for three weeks running while they searched for the guy. I don't think my dad slept that whole time. The pervert's body had finally been found face down in the bayou. Strange way to off yourself, but no one questioned it. They just wrote it off as a suicide. No loss there. Annalise was buried on the other side of the cemetery in the larger family plot under the beech trees, and a month later that jerk Frankie had joined her no more than fifty feet away. Death is funny that way. You just never know who will be pulling up an eternal seat on your front porch or right next door. This cemetery even had street names, just like a sweet little district in the suburbs.

"Hi there. Ya'll enjoy the rain?" I whispered to Mama and Daddy as I leaned into a cluster of jasmine blossoms, drowning my senses in their sweet, honeyed breath.

"Hello. What brings a nice girl like you to Elm and Whitlock on a stormy Southern night like this?" A deep male voice drawled from behind me, somewhere beyond my left shoulder.

The breath jerked out of me all at once, my throat squeezed shut and my heart stopped beating. Then, with the words still itching along my spine, causing my skin to prickle all over, I spun around to face the direction the voice had come from.

"What the hell are you doing here?" I demanded, as annoyed with his presence as I was with the way his voice was still crawling in and out of my vertebrae, lingering in the spaces in between.

"Now I asked you first, chère." He was sitting on the ground leaning back on the trunk of the old oak tree that marked the perimeter of this portion of the grounds, a couple yards to my left. What looked to be straight, shoulder length dark hair was slicked back from his face, still wet from the storm, and glistening darkly in the moonlight that slipped through the branches overhead. His right leg was bent at the knee, his left leg was stretched out straight in front of him, and he was absentmindedly shifting something from one hand to the other and back again. He was perfectly at ease, as if he'd been here countless times before.

"You have to leave. You're not supposed to be here!" I knew I sounded antagonistic, or just plain bitchy, but I couldn't bring myself to care just now ... this was my space ... especially on stormy Southern nights like this.

He simply lowered his right leg, crossing the left at the ankle, laid his hands on his thighs, and leaned his head back against the tree trunk. He had absolutely no intention of clearing out any time soon.

"And you are? I mean, this is indeed a nice, quiet place, so I can certainly understand why you'd be drawn here. But at the risk of sounding rude, this is a graveyard, a city for the dead, and you are all of, what, seventeen, eighteen, with a pulse? Are you saying you call this dreamy establishment home, or is it just your home away from home?" His mouth was pulled into a half-smile and he seemed to drink all of me in, top to bottom, bones and all, without ever losing contact with my eyes. How could he do that? How did he know I thought of this as home? And why was my skin so shivery when I had a fine line of sweat running down between my shoulder blades? Besides, why, exactly, was I sweating? The rain had cooled everything down by at least ten degrees and the sun had been down for a couple of hours now.

"Yes. I mean, no, of course not!" I had to focus, sounding like a complete idiot was not up for discussion. Still, saying it and doing it are two very different things, and it took more will than I care to admit to throw up a quick wall around my raw emotions and simply squeeze out, "Who are you?" Finally, a coherent thought.

But then he spoke again, and my wall came crashing down, falling in ruins around my ankles. "I do apologize. You're quite right. I certainly have not introduced myself." He jumped up and bowed formally at the waist while he spoke softly, as if we were sharing something intimate, not a simple howdie-doodie, but a stolen moment, an exchange of some deep, personal part of ourselves. "Rémy. Jean-Rémy Beauchamps St. Claire. And who, may I ask, do I have the extreme good fortune to have crossed paths with this fine evening?"

For the first time I saw more of him than just his face and those mesmerizing eyes. His jeans were dark and clung to his body with the warm rain water they still held, defining toned, well developed legs and hard thighs. He was as soaked as I was. Nobody I knew had ever liked the feeling of bathing in Mother Nature's temper tantrums the way I did. But he did. He was perfectly at ease, sensual without any conscious intent to be so, effortlessly hypnotic, like some dark angel rising from a languorous bath in a moonlit watering hole surrounded by lush, tropical vegetation, the air thick with their sweet, pungent scent. His thin, dark blue button-down shirt was open and drying quickly, sleeves rolled up at the cuffs revealing dark, powerful forearms, the kind that only came with lots of sun and sweat. The white T-shirt underneath was still water-logged, but showed signs of drying from the heat his body was generating in areas where it pulled more tightly against his skin, the hint of muscles rolling with each movement his body made. He'd kicked off his flip-flops leaving his feet bare.

His wiggling toes told me he'd caught my perusal and brought my attention back up to his face, which was several inches above mine. I wasn't short by any means, 5'9" last fall when I'd needed a sport's physical for the track team tryouts, and I'd grown a hair since then. So, that put him at six feet, give or take a kiss. And I'd been wrong about his hair. It was longer, maybe to his shoulder blades, but he'd tied it at the back of his strong, dark neck with a leather cord. And, damn, what a neck. Strong and dark and ... oh, shit.

Wow. It took me a full minute to process all of this. All of ... him. He was a total package. Top to bottom. The real deal. It just didn't get better than this. Not in my lifetime anyway. I was so out of my league here. He had the voice, the looks, the height, and, from what I could tell the charisma, with a week's worth of leftovers to spare. I dragged a hand through my own wet locks, fighting the sensation of the earth dropping away from beneath my feet. Where were those hands holding me down to the ground when I needed them? Shit!

Somewhat reluctantly I placed my hand in his having decided to give him a quick, solid, no-nonsense kind of handshake and retrieve my hand in the shortest possible amount of time. Guinness record kind of short.

No need to worry about setting any speed records right now though. He, Rémy, was it? Great, my dad's name, just great. He was holding my hand tightly in his. Not shaking it. Not letting go of it. Just holding it, looking at me, into me ... and waiting like he was expecting something to happen.

"What?!" I managed to bark out. The rough sound of my own voice seemed to cut through the electric spell that had enveloped me with his first words. "Oh, yeah." I blinked quickly a couple of times to clear a few more of the cobwebs from my brain.

As I began to stammer incoherently, Rémy flipped my hand over and bent his mouth to it. His eyes never let go of their grasp on mine, not for a split second, and as his lips brushed the back of my knuckles I could swear the earth shifted direction. The sensations radiating from that one whispered touch, spread through my body like wildfire, destroying everything in its path, reworking all it left behind into something else, something new, something not me. And underneath that, was a feeling of sublime comfort, of ease. There was a knowing, something akin to déjà vu, but not that exactly. Something ... deeper.

"I'm Syd. Sydney Annalise Bovay-Roberdeau, but most everyone's called me Syd since I was knee-high to a tadpole." I pressed my lips tightly together and bit down on the inside of them as soon as the last syllable had slipped past my teeth so no more words could break free. Shut up, Syd! What's the matter with you? I'd have to remember to cut my tongue out later.

Slowly, much too slowly, I began to resurface. The kiss, if it qualified as that, had long since ended, but we remained ... engaged. No! Bad word choice. Focused on one another. We just remained completely focused on one another, in an involuntary, I-can't-look-away-from-you-or-I'll-turn-to-dust-and-life-will-cease-to-exist kind of way, yeah.

Once again I shook my head impatiently trying to knock things back into place, things that should never need moving. "Okay. So I'm Syd and you are apparently Rémy. Jean-Rémy Beauchamps St. Claire, to be specific, who's leaving now. Because the how do you do's are done and it's time to get back to real life."

I tugged at my hand, desperate to put some space between us, but he tightened his grip fractionally, placing my hand, knuckles down in his other hand. Softly he slid his fingers down the delicate interior skin from my fingertips to my wrist, circling the heart of my palm. Then his touch traced lightly back and forth along the delicate warmth of my wrist. It was, he was, absolutely intoxicating. Utterly decadent. And, we were just holding hands, for Christ's sake! No! Not even that. We were only shaking hands, in a manner of speaking ... just learning one another's names. How on earth could he be doing this to me? What was he doing to me exactly?

As if he could hear the confused, heated rush of emotions rambling through my mind and body, Rémy's face relaxed into a smile. "Just take it one breath at a time, Syd. How long have you played?"

"Played what?" My throat felt tight again. Surely he wasn't really reading my mind. He couldn't be. He'd better not be.

A light, playful impatience colored his words as he replied, "The guitar, Syd. How long have you played the guitar?" He still hadn't let go of my hand, ignoring my occasional tug.

"What? How did you know that?" More importantly, what the hell are you doing to me? But as I really wasn't ready for an answer to that particular question, I kept that part of the conversation for my ears only. Lesson #506 in Rules of Engagement, only ask a question you know the answer to and want to hear.

"Your hands, Syd. They tell the path of your life, to an extent anyway, and yours speak of music." His fingers circled over the thick calluses on the pads of my fingertips and thumb. "They also talk of strength and loneliness."

"Okay. No way. I get the calluses part, but you can't tell squat about the rest of that by looking at my hands." Why did every word through his lips unhinge me so terribly? Why did I care what he thought or said? So-o-o not me. Get a grip, Syd! And get your damn hand back. Now!

I started tugging again, in earnest, achieving nothing more than looking for all intents and purposes like a fisherman fighting with a rubber boot he'd managed to reel in for the dinner pot. He simply wasn't going to let go.

"Well, the muscle power you're drawing on trying to withdraw your hand from mine speaks for itself on the strength issue. As for the loneliness, I gathered that from the haunted look in your eyes. The look of someone who carries their loved ones deep down inside themselves, and has for some time now I'd guess."

"How do you do that? How can you know anything about me, much less enough to write a book on?"

"Don't know. I feel like our intro was a long time in the coming, that we've known each other much, much longer than recent history shows. Kindred spirits, perhaps."

The shock of just how much I'd have liked for that to be true brought me back to the here and now, the land of the living, in about two seconds flat. Finally, some taste of the old Syd!

"Really. Well, look, I'd apologize and tell you how I'm not usually so rude, but, yeah, honestly, I'm usually a lot worse. So, you're getting off pretty easy here all things considered. You should probably thank me. And, as far as kindred spirits go, we definitely aren't kin, and you sure don't look like any spirit I've ever seen. In my life! So, question hour's officially over and it's time for you to hit it. So, get."

"Get what, Syd? What do you want from me?" Innocent eyes gazed up at me from beneath sinfully long lashes, but the smile playing on his lips gave him away.

"Get on out of here, smarty pants. Move it. Nice to meet you. It's been a little slice of heaven. Now, goodbye. Don't let the wrought iron gate catch your soggy butt on the way out." I jerked my hand in earnest, trying albeit unsuccessfully, to break free once again.

But he just laughed. And my heart melted. "Heavens no. Not that." He twisted halfway around to catch a glimpse of his backside, showing me a side-winders' peek of it in the process. Mmm. Even in wet pants he was something else. Of course. He would be, wouldn't he? Perfect, even where the sun don't shine. "I kind of like my butt, just how it is. Misplaced spindles of raw twisted graveyard gate metal embedded in it might not be the look I'm going for. What do you think?"

"What?! What do I think? About your ass? You're asking me what I think about your ass!" Why, yes, actually I think it's perfectly delectable and can't imagine a better way to spend the next couple of hours than to sit right here and stare at it. Like I could tell Mr. Rémy St. Claire that juicy little tidbit! I'd sooner lick the sweat from the armpits of a sumo wrestler, thank you very much. Instead, I settled for, "Who the Sam Hill are you?!"

"Rémy. Could have sworn I'd mentioned it. Short memory, huh? Not into any illegal substances are you? Now, that would be a shame." My God, his eyes twinkled like chocolate-flavored diamonds.

"Oh, hell no! Not that it matters. To you, I mean. You are so leaving. Now. Go." The corners of his mouth tipped upward and his eyes sparkled even more, if that was possible. Doesn't he have a pair of sunglasses? Eyes like that should be outlawed. Entirely too distracting. They were a deep, dark charcoal gray with a starburst of gold around the pupil and a rich rim of olive green at the outer edge of the iris. And they spoke, they spoke a language all their own.

"Can't tell you how glad I am to hear it. What a relief. You really had me worried there for a minute." But he didn't sound in the least bit relieved. He sounded like someone who already knew all the answers to these questions. He definitely wasn't asking for informational purposes, but for something else ... what though? What did he want? And why on earth did he want it from me?

I braced myself for the onslaught of his next words as he began to speak. "As for leaving, that, chère, was your idea, not mine. I'm actually quite comfy right here. Besides, the view's not half bad." He pulled his arm wide to insinuate he was talking about the cemetery around us, but he wasn't looking at the view at all. Not a peek. He hadn't taken his eyes off me once yet.

"Shit, you're annoying! Do I have natural talent to thank for that or was this a learned character trait for your own twisted means of manipulating your adversaries through sheer frustration?" I choked out. I was trying for annoyed, but had to settle for flustered since I'd had to drop my eyelids just to get my mouth to function properly enough to pull the words out at all.

"Am I, Syd? Am I really? Hmmm. I'm not so sure about that. It's not annoyed that's coloring your face right now. Something closer to intrigued, or maybe even fascinated would be my take on it." Okay, his eyes were practically lit up as bright as the aurora borealis now. Smirking son of a bitch.

"You have got to be kidding me!" The audacity of this guy was absolutely staggering. "How the hell would you know what I'm thinking? You don't know me. And, even if you did, you still wouldn't have any idea at all what I was thinking, much less feeling, because you're too tanked up on yourself for there to be so much as a dark little corner left over for anyone else to fill. Now, I don't know who you are, where you came from, or why you're here. But you seem to have some small degree of sense, fleeting though it might be, so before you spend what's left of it, why don't you try to find your way home before you forget the way out of here?"

"No, Syd, I'm quite enjoying myself. As a matter of fact, I think I'm exactly where I'm supposed to be, with exactly whom I'm supposed to be. I have absolutely no intention of leaving."

"What's with the 'with'? You are not with me! We're not together! And, I am not this evening's entertainment! Besides, how can you possibly be enjoying this? Plagued with latent masochistic tendencies are you? Is your family aware of this? I hear intervention works wonders."

"I'm afraid I'll have to disagree with you there, Syd. You are standing less than three feet from me. Wherever we are, we're there together." His words resounded softly, but firmly in the quiet night air. "But perhaps you should consider leaving if my presence makes you so uncomfortable." His fingers slowly released my hand, but what should have felt like a victory left me feeling empty and cold, and all the more angry because of it.

"Enough with the polite crap!" I ground out through gritted teeth, my hands clamped tightly at my sides to control their tell-tale trembling. "Who ...," but he cut through my question like a hot knife through butter that's been left out on the counter overnight.

"I'm sorry. This was polite? Syd!" A soft chuckle rumbled dryly in his chest, melting any surviving remnants of self I'd managed to still be desperately clutching. I could drown in the sound of his laughter. I could suck it down in great gulping mouthfuls and drown myself without a second thought, without a single regret. Nothing but gratitude pumping through my veins. The most willing victim imaginable.

But not today. Today I'd still make an effort to be my own ... sweet self, no matter how bitter that might taste going down. "Don't Syd me! Who the hell are you? Because you sure aren't here by accident and you're definitely not selling Girl Scout cookies! You're not even from anywhere around here. Actually, I can't think of a single place you could be from."

Again with the smile, he was incorrigible! "Syd, have you been to the doctor recently? It may be early onset Alzheimer's. I'm still Rémy, the same Rémy St. Claire I introduced myself as just a few grumbles back. Haven't changed in the last ten minutes. Something wrong with my name? Something you don't like about it?" One eyebrow lifted as he peered up from under those amazing lashes. And the earth moved. Again.

"Ha ha. Aren't you just the town clown? I think I heard they're looking for fresh meat on SNL. Why don't you go apply? The bus station's not far from here. Just start heading north. Way, way, way-way north." I gestured in what I thought was a northerly kind of direction, but at this point I could've been waving him down to Rio for all I knew.

And he knew, too. Of course. This night just kept getting better and better! Dammit! "Mmm. I see. You've got it bad, don't you, kid? That's okay. I kind of like being around you, too. I guess we just have two very different ways of showing it." A wink punctuated the last word, and it was that wink that pushed me over the edge I'd been teetering on tenuously. My toes gripped the damp earth more tightly than the most ardent surfer dropping board in a tsunami.

"What the hell are you talking about?! I don't know you and I can absolutely guarantee I don't like you. Did you just escape from the psych ward? If so, you'd better get back quick because either your meds just ran out or you're definitely a few cards short of a full deck."

"Uh, huh. You might want to sit down." He gestured at the patch of grass beside him. It was strangely tempting even with my mad on. "You've got it worse than I thought. Can't even acknowledge the possibility, much less admit your true feelings. How well do you really know yourself, Syd? Do you even know? Well, maybe, one day, you'll allow me to supply the introductions. But not tonight. No. Tonight is for ... other things."

I circled behind the white and gray Johnson monument next door to my parents' plot and clamped my hands down on it to keep myself from taking him up on his offer. That would be the biggest mistake in a long, hard life riddled with mistakes. "Okay. You know what? You are seriously twisted. No joke. One sick little puppy. Maybe I should call the pound instead of the hospital." I glared at him, fingers tightening on the cold, hard marble just itching to let go.

"Relax, Syd. I don't bite, not without getting to know you a little better first. Besides, I just went in for my rabies booster last week." Another wink and lopsided smile from him. Another nuclear meltdown for me.

So, I retaliated. Had to. Had to put some distance between us. "How many times are you planning on saying my name? Syd, Syd, Syd, Syd, Syd! There's nobody else here! Who the hell else would you be talking to besides me?"

"Well, I suppose he could be talking to me." A little voice carried through the grounds with a soft breeze.

"Fuck!" I spun around again and faced a girl much younger than her words had implied. "Um,

45

I'm sorry. Didn't mean to talk like that in front of you. It's just a habit, that's all. A bad one, I guess. I'm trying to cut back on it." Was I, huh, news to me. "Are you with him?" I pointed jerkily towards Rémy. "Yeah. Of course you are. Why else would you be here in the middle of the night? Sorry. I'm not usually quite so slow on the uptake, but it's been one hell of a strange night."

"Oh, that's alright. I've heard worse." Somehow I doubted that. She looked like a little cherub, the kind they stick sunglasses on and print on note cards. No, those are butt-naked, except for the wings. Do wings count as clothing, or just more naked body parts? Doesn't really matter, those were just toddlers, toddlers in their birthday suits. But she was no toddler, she was at least seven or eight, maybe. More like a mini-angel, or a demi-angel. Definitely not someone exposed to the darker side of life often, or ever.

Her voice, tiny but somehow all the more powerful because of it, continued melodically. "And, yes. Rémy and I are here together. My name is Sarah," she held her delicate hand out to me trustingly.

Her bright blue eyes, hidden from the light of the full moon's reflection, were shining with an inner strength in the shadows of the trees. So much light. So much strength. She radiated it, like a beacon from a lighthouse stabbing through the darkness, illuminating the way. Just how old was this girl? I don't think I'd have that much strength of character, that much sheer force of will, blazing in my eyes if I'd live to be seven or eight hundred! Maybe she had heard worse, and then some. Things that would have me running for cover.

"Syd, this is Sarah, my baby sister. Sarah La Rosa Geneviève St. Claire. Sarah, this is Syd, Sydney Annalise Bovay-Roberdeau." His eyes tightened as they refocused on me. Hard eyes, not happy ones. But cool nonetheless, not angry. Not yet. "But then, you were saying something about your name. Is there another you'd rather be called by?"

"No. It's not that. It's just that ..." My thoughts were so unfocused and tangled in webs that my brain seized. Kind of like a real good brain freeze, but without the sweet taste of the ice cream melting in my mouth to help ease the pain.

They were just staring at me. Waiting for an explanation. How exactly was I supposed to explain what I couldn't wrap my own head around? Well, you see, you're just so damn fine that I can't get my mouth to maintain contact with my brain long enough to hold a civilized conversation. Yeah, right! Maybe he was right, maybe it was just time for me to go. Leave now and live to fight another day. Maybe. But a little hard to do when I couldn't get my feet to move!

Just then my eyes caught his and he winked with that stupid, perfect, lopsided smile again. That insipid smirk-smile he was so damn fond of. "Yeah, you've got it bad all right." That big lug was laughing at me to my face!

Ungh! This was all his fault! The muscles in my arm tightened as my fingers began to twitch. Moving on pure adrenaline, I lunged toward Rémy's smug face, my right arm pulled back ready to deliver the slap he'd been missing as a side order for all that attitude.

But before I could follow through, Rémy'd already jumped up, spun me around by my left arm that had been held out to counterbalance my turn, shifted sideways, and pulled my body tightly into the strong, warm curve of his own. "Don't move." His words were hidden in a breath that moved through the tendrils of hair that had begun to dry around my face and softly caressed my cheek.

"But ..."

"Shh, Syd. Look there." His face nudged mine in the direction he wanted me to look. And I saw it. In the trees at ten o'clock to me. But I couldn't believe what I was seeing.

A full-grown, black panther was dead-locked on us. No, not on us, on me. In full alert mode. This baby was ready to attack and take no prisoners. I sure was glad all of a sudden that I'd missed dinner. I'd have peed in my pants then and there. Or worse. All right up close and personal, next to Mr. Wonderful himself. Ewww! Maybe I need to consider skipping chow time more often. Just in case. You can't spew what you don't chew.

But "just in case" looked like something I might never need to worry about because kitty-kitty over there had just broken free of the wooded area and was crouching in the grass not ten yards away, preparing to pounce. Why hadn't I watched more National Geographic and less paranormal sci-fi? I mean, Sookie Stackhouse was great and all, but she couldn't help me much with Animal Kingdom. Or could she? There were were-panthers in her world, weren't there? Were they like normal panthers? Maybe they could only sense you if you moved. Maybe, if I just stayed really still, it wouldn't be able to see me. That didn't make sense though. I'd seen housecats stalk a mouse that had frozen in its tracks before. I was so out of luck.

And out of time. Green-gold eyes blazing in the night, the panther huddled backward in a little pre-attack shimmy-shake, then released all those wound up muscles springing into a high arc through the air, black fur gleaming in the moonlight.

Time slowed and my throat convulsed. "Oh. Shit. Don't let go."

Somehow Rémy managed to still my racing heart as he whispered in my ear, "Never. I'll never let you go, Syd. I promise." And then my world was filled with black, velvet fur and green-gold eyes.

5 REALITY BITES

The thunder of paws descending on the ground not more than three feet in front of me ricocheted up through my body as the great panther pulled himself up to the table. Really, a buffet I guess, since all three courses were still standing, the appetizer, main course and dessert. Saliva had flown from the panther's gaping jaws on impact, landing across my neck and shoulder.

Oh, my God. I'm gonna die. We're all gonna die. This is it. Oh, shit! God, I'm so sorry. For everything. For every single, stupid, selfish thing I ever did.

This could not be happening. It just couldn't be real. I squeezed my eyes shut as tight as I could and gave my head a good shake before I opened them again. Nope. It was real. Fact not fiction. And this reality was about to bite me on the ass by way of my face.

"Rémy?" I managed to squeak the word out, sounding way too similar to a rubber duck that had been squeaked one too many times.

His grip around my hips pulled me in tighter to him, trying to protect me from the inevitable. "Yeah, Syd?"

"Since I'm about to be served up here as a midnight snack, I might as well get a couple things out."

"Can it wait, Syd?" He asked as his chin stroked back and forth in my hair.

My words stumbled out quietly, but quickly. One on top of another, trying to beat Fur-butt to the punch. "Wait? Wait for what? The hereafter? I don't think we'll be doing much talking after the next few seconds. So, here goes. I love your name. Rémy is a good name. Perfect, actually. But it was my father's name."

My eyes were glued to my own reflection looking back at me from the pair of matching goldmines inches away from me. The words poured out even faster, in a mad race with death. "And, truth be told, you're so damn sexy that I can't breathe when I look at you. And I really can't call you by my dad's name when I feel my bones melt every time my eyes meet yours and all I want to do is slip into your skin and wrap myself up nice and tight in your heart. In your arms."

"Syd ..." He began, but I cut him off.

I just wouldn't have it. "No, let me finish. I might not have another chance and I can't keep this to myself for the rest of eternity. I have absolutely no idea why I feel this way, because I never do. Never have. And I just met you. But when you say my name, it pulls me. I mean, it really draws me. Like when you put two opposing magnets near one another and they slam into each other by the sheer force of nature. It's just like that. It scares the hell out of me. That, and it makes me want to jump your bones. Right now. Right here, right in the middle of the God damn cemetery." I glance towards the little girl, standing a couple of feet to my right, further from the menacing teeth. "Sorry, Sarah."

"It's okay. Told you I've heard worse." She said simply, but she was smiling softly and her eyes were warm and tender. Turning her gaze to Rémy she added, "She doesn't listen very well does she?"

"No, she sure doesn't." He tried to swallow back the escaping chuckle that slid out with it, then tipped his face back next to mine. "Syd ..." He tried again, but I still wouldn't have it.

"No. I have to get this out. I'm sorry for being so rude to you before. I just ... I ... well, I get that way when I feel threatened. And, brother, you scare the hell out of me. Because ... Because I ..."

"Syd, dammit! Let me say something!" His voice was stronger now, still low, but a couple of notches above a bona fide whisper.

But I was sick and tired of being interrupted. "God damn it! Shut the hell up, Rémy! I'm not finished yet. This is hard enough without having to fight you to get the words out! Sorry again, Sarah!" I barked out roughly.

"Yeah. Okay." Her words held no fear, just a liquid peace that spilled over my head like fresh rain. Not quite enough rain to sooth the trapped beast living inside me right now, but enough to help me finish what needed to be said.

Riding that wave of semi-collectedness, I started again. "What I'm trying to say is that I think there's a good possibility that even though I never bought into the whole love at first sight thing, and in fact, thought it was one of the most ridiculous notions I'd ever heard of, maybe, just maybe, I might have been a little hasty in making a judgment call, because you make that seem possible to me."

Silence. He said nothing. Absolutely nothing.

I waited an eternity, ten long, long seconds, at least, before adding, "Rémy?"

But still nothing. Nothing but silence responded to the single most important conversation I'd had in my entire life.

"Well!?" I semi-shouted at him and the panther tightened, preparing for the ultimate take-down, a Syd snack-down.

"Well what? Are you through now? I'm allowed to talk now? I thought I was supposed to shut the hell up." Rémy's voice slowly drawled the words, thick with frustration. And something else. What was that? Mirth? What could possibly be funny at a time like this?

"Yes, you asshole! Yeah. My bad, Sarah."

"Mm-hmm. You'd better stop talking now, Syd, you're scaring her." What? Her? Her who? Rémy was a him, a big boy him, how could I possibly be scaring him?

The four-legged terror made eye contact with me then and I knew it was game over. I watched the black pupils contract, the ripple of the jaw muscles as they pulled up, and then the forward movement. She moved slowly, knowing this battle had already been won.

The enormous paws lifted from the ground and dropped on my chest, bringing her face, those teeth, inches from my own.

"Mmm. Syd, T.J. T.J., Syd." The words came out of Rémy's mouth on a gentle roll of laughter. Then the jaws sprung open showing more ivory than a baby grand piano.

I braced myself. Every muscle in my body tightened in sheer terror as the cat's breath bathed my face, soaking me in its moist heat. How long would I be alive enough to feel the pain? Would I think as the screams were ripped from my throat? What would I taste like? Oh, yeah. Bad question. Still, I did wonder.

Hot saliva dripped down my throat as she leaned into me, her taste buds no doubt anticipating that I would indeed be tasty.

And she ... didn't bite me. She licked me. Jaw to hairline. I couldn't even scream as complete and utter confusion swamped me, instead a ragged whimper escaped my lips.

What was going on? What was I missing? Why wasn't there screaming? And blood? And pain? Lots and lots of pain. And who the hell was T.J.?

"She wants you to scratch behind her ears." Sarah's sing-song voice pushed its way through my stupor. She sounded like we were just sitting around having some kind of perverse tea party. Too bad I was the plate of cookies. And the pot of tea. And the bowl of sugar. Yeah, I was the entire fucking menu.

I ignored the gently delivered directive since I had absolutely no idea what the girl was talking about and voiced my last thought instead. "Who's T.J.? Another brother?" My own voice sounded weak, threadbare, like the knees in an old, soft, favorite pair of jeans. The ones you save for your best days and your worst days. Guess this day was both for me.

"No, silly. That's T.J." Sarah couldn't be pointing at the five foot long cat perched on my boobs could she?

Suddenly, hysteria filled my head and spilled from my mouth in wild strands of laughter. We must look like we're dancing. The three of us. Mr. Wonderful, probably featured as Mr. December in a calendar on someone's desk ... sign me up for a calendar of nothing but Decembers ... a heart-stopping, beautiful, but ferocious black panther, and little old me sandwiched right in between the two. The laughter came harder. And louder. I was really beginning to crack here.

Rémy sensed it though. "It's alright, chère. Take it easy. You're gonna hyperventilate if you don't calm down. Here, I'll walk you through it. Just breathe in ... and out ... nice and slow. That's it. A little slower now. Good, that's good, Baby." The fingers of his left hand were gently running through the dark swath of hair at my temple as his right arm continued to hold me as close to him as our bones would allow.

I felt my heartbeat slowly settle to match his, and I turned my face, laying my cheek against his warm chest. The panther reached up and licked my other cheek the same way she'd baptized the first one. Another gurgled whimper choked its way out of my trembling throat.

Immediately, Rémy slid his left hand up to my face, being careful never to lose contact with my body as he gently covered my mouth with it, his fingers splayed loosely across my nose and wet cheek. His velvety words danced along the sensitive skin of my neck and ear, and the soft whiskers of a few days growth on his own face sent a tickle chaser. "Easy, Syd. She can sense fear. And, as a natural born predator, it excites her. Entices her ... to hunt on that which fears her." His fingers brushed softly over my lips.

His touch was my buoy, his mesmerizing words my lifeline as I stood, waiting to drown in a sea of my own fear. His voice began once more, pulling me closer, reeling me in one word at a time. "So, fill your senses with something else. With something besides her. Something you're not afraid of. Me. Just feel me, Syd. Feel my arms around you. Feel my breath on your skin. My body against your back. My heartbeat beating beneath yours. My voice sliding through your head. My scent filling your senses. Fill your world with me. Only me. All of me."

The hold alone should have made me feel worse, much less the words. I was a closet claustrophobic. Didn't even like to wear my seatbelt. So, his hand over my mouth and nose should have driven me over the edge of reason. And, oh, my God. Those words. Every girl's dream, and many a girl's nightmare, all mixed-up together. Savior and perpetrator wound tightly into one gorgeous 6-foot tall thread.

But instead of feeling overwhelmed with apprehension, I felt comforted. Protected. Safe. Not alone, for the first time in a very, very long time of being alone. I turned my face even farther back into his body, my racing pulse beginning to relax once again into the warmth and security of this incomprehensibly complex man who practically consumed me, absorbing my very soul into his own as we stood facing the murderous jaws of our imminent demise.

I felt Rémy's right arm begin to subtly shift as it slid up my abdomen and then along my own arm. He gradually eased my hand up with his to caress the fur at the nape of the creature that held me trapped against the long hard body cradling mine from behind. Gently Rémy began moving my hand in long, smooth strokes down the back of the panther from the top of its head to between its shoulder blades. I wasn't so sure if it was for my benefit, or for the panther's. Either way, it seemed to be helping.

But it was definitely helping the panther faster than it was helping me. I was still battling my run-away pulse when fur darker than the darkest, pitch black hours of night thrust against my chest, a wet nose cooling the side of my chin while whiskers prickled along my check. The panther had laid the entire length of its body against mine. And then the thunder came. It didn't resonate in the sky, but within my bones. It took me a minute to realize that this homicidal predator, this vicious, cruel beast, was purring. Not only that, she was purring to save her soul. It felt like my ears were going to vibrate off any minute and splash down into one of the puddles of water still scattered around our feet.

On the one hand, that was good. Very, very good. Purring beats eating, even if it means losing some body parts to the reverberations. But on the other hand, the tips of her long fangs were resting on the soft skin just below my collarbone. And that was bad. Very, very bad. Fangs and flesh? Not good bedfellows.

"She likes you." Sarah's voice broke through the silence engulfing us, punctuated only by the continued purring from the only feline in the vicinity.

"Yes. That's a good thing, Syd. You need to control your temper a little better." Although the words were chastising, Rémy's tone was still soothing, non-judgmental.

"What?" My mind was playing catch-up but I was still definitely not Nobel prize winning material just yet.

Half of a chuckle burst from Rémy's throat. "You say that a lot. A whole lot."

"Yeah? Well, I guess that makes me smart enough to ask for additional info when I need it instead of just blundering through half-cocked like a chicken with its head cut off." I couldn't have done anything to control the sarcasm that dripped from my words if I'd wanted to.

Regardless, Rémy was the consummate gentleman. "Touché, chère, touché."

"Touché? What is that? Does it mean touchy? Are you calling me touchy? You insignificant little shit! Um, Sarah ..." Good. Anger. Something I was much more comfortable with. But honestly, I would have choked down second helpings of just about anything at that moment if I'd thought there was the slightest chance it could replace the abject fear I'd been drowning in.

"Yeah, I know, you're sorry." The words came out from Sarah in a sing-song formation. You could almost hear the smile in them.

Rémy's answer swam out on his gentle, heart-flipping laugh. "Not touchy, touché, it's French. In real life terms, it means something along the lines of you've got a good point there."

That's when it hit me. Her words brought it back. The introduction. Her introduction. This was no maniacal, bloodthirsty creature dying to rip out my throat and suck down the marrow from my bones. This was ... It was just ... No-o-o. But could this possibly be ... a house pet? "Did I hear you right? A minute ago. Did you say this beast has a name, T.J., wasn't it?"

Sarah slipped up next to the monstrous cat. "T.J. That's right. She really likes you, Syd, and she doesn't ever like anyone. Just Rémy and me. She's not a beast though, she's just protective, especially of Rémy." This sweet, poor, deluded, little girl was petting ... a panther! She was wrapping her arms around it from behind and nuzzling her rosy little cheeks in its blue-black fur, as if it was a soft, pink, fluffy bunny rabbit! I wanted desperately to jerk her away from it, to step between them and offer myself up as the midnight Scooby snack. I'd even try to find a bottle of ketchup for the bitch. But then, I remembered. I already was face-to-face with Precious.

"No way! No flipping way! Who in their right mind would take in a panther? Where on earth would you get one? By calling 1-800-atac-cat? And what do you feed them for dinner ... livestock, rodents, ill-mannered guests, your left arm? Does your cat license come with an owner brain scan to check for any latent psychoses?" Okay. Cracking accomplished. Big check there. Now we were heading for full brain separation. I was so far over the edge I couldn't tell which way was up anymore.

"Okay. Get her off. Get her off!" I was getting louder again, the fear dissipating more quickly now. "Somebody get her the hell off of me! Now, God damn it!" Stress. It does a body good. Never let anyone tell you any different.

"Come here, sweetheart. That's right. That's a good girl." Sarah was easing T.J. back down to the grass while Rémy helped release the claws that had torn through my shirt here and there. They had extended just enough to ruin the material, but not enough to hurt me. Thank you, God! Sarah sat down beside the animal, but never stopped stroking it. Crooning to it. Loving it.

At the same time Rémy warned, "Careful, Syd. T.J. doesn't respond well when she feels someone is threatening me."

Sarah chimed in happily. "Rémy's right, Syd. That's what got her going to begin with. You attacked Rémy. T.J. was just protecting him." How did they do that? Use condescending words in an easy-going, tolerant way? Damn! I hated it. They got to say their piece, but I couldn't even get a good self-righteous indignation going because they were so god-awful polite about it.

The words practically burst from my mouth like bullets from a Berretta. "Would one of you please explain to me how the Sam Hill you ended up with a fucking jungle cat as a lap kitty!"

"Syd ..." Rémy clearly wasn't pleased, but neither was I. Join the club. And just then my need to vent outweighed my need to wait patiently, quietly, on the receiving end of yet another lecture about my unending faults.

So, I trudged on, full steam ahead. "What the hell planet are you two from, anyway? No. You know what? On second thought, I don't care, don't even want to know. This, this is just too much. Way, way too much. Five damn tons too much! I came here to get away from everything, from all the drama in my life. And what do I find? Worse. First, you scare the hell out of me. Then you annoy the hell out of me. Then little sis here just materializes out of thin air."

I stopped to catch my breath while their eyes quickly shifted to one another and then back to me.

"Syd ..." Rémy started.

But I didn't wait for him to finish as I started up again pacing between the three of them in a small, tight circle. "Even that wasn't enough though, oh, no. I had to go and get molested by Bagheera over here, and spill my heart out to you."

I stopped in my tracks, my back to all of them, as my hand flew to my mouth. "Oh, shit! Oh, my God!" I whirled around to face Rémy. "Ooh! You son of a bitch! You stood there and let me tell you ... tell you ... Ungh!" I roared, my voice tight and gravelly.

"Syd ..." Sarah and Rémy both tried breaking in this time.

But I was smoking now. No stopping me. I was in a total free-fall. Flying on rage. And adrenaline. And, worst of all, self-induced humiliation. "The things I told you! Oh, my God! The things I told you!" My voice dropped an octave as I spat out each word distinctly. "And you let me. Ungh! You! You held me! You made me feel ... Shit! The things you said! Oh, God damn you! You asshole! You fucking asshole!"

"Syd! For the love of God, shut the hell up!" The deep, uncompromising pitch of Rémy's voice more than his choice of words finally managed to grab my attention. As I glared up into his face he looked pointedly at T.J. who was pacing restlessly in front of me, not looking nearly as even-tempered as she had before my unbridled tirade had ignited. A funny little rumble was emanating from her deep within her chest, not a roar, not yet anyway, but so completely not a purr.

And suddenly I felt as though someone had just doused me with a bucket of ice water.

Rémy began again, his voice deep, tight and controlled ... clearly holding a fast reign on his own anger. "Now. First, I did try to tell you. Several times, in fact."

"But you ..." I tried to break in this time, but it was my turn to be cut off at the pass.

"Shut up, Syd." The words came out in that mellow, patient way that left me standing once again in quicksand, no solid ground to fight back from. So I just stood there and blinked up at him as he resumed.

"It's my turn now. As for holding you, I had to. You know that. Or at least you would if you'd just calm your happy little ass down for half a second and think back to what happened." He gestured toward the panther, who was visibly calming down now that I'd shut my trap. Sarah was even able to gently stroke the fur along her side as Rémy continued. "T.J. was about to defend me. Against you. She only does that one way, to the death. I had to get you to calm down, fast. And to be quite honest, you, Darlin', are no Sunday picnic in the park. No offense, but trying to calm you down seems to be as easy as trying to reign in a stampede of wild buffalo with a couple of pocket poodles and a miniature pony." His mouth quirked up at the corners. "That might even be a little easier, come to think of it."

"But Rémy ..." I tried again. Thinking his mood had lightened enough from the weight of all the frustration he'd already spilled out on me. Boy was I wrong.

"Shush! I'm not done with you yet!" For the first time, he was beginning to sound irritated, not angry, but still, human. Crazy maybe, but it made me feel a little bit better. "Now, as for my words, I said what needed to be said to reach you, to bring you back down from that craggy precipice you were clinging to with both bloody hands. You were terrified." His tone softened, but only marginally. And still those eyes lost none of their intensity. "Syd, I always say what I mean, or I don't say it at all. Ever. Anything less is simply unacceptable."

I didn't even try to get in a word this time. I just waited for him to finish. And actually, his words, tough as some of them were to swallow, were soothing, calming. Okay, maybe it wasn't his words so much as his voice. Or just, him. Shit! This was bad. My stupid, audacious heart skipped a beat even as my stomach tightened with apprehension and dread.

Once again Rémy's voice had eased up, but this time his eyes followed suit, the storm clouds pulling back slightly from his still unfaltering gaze. "And finally, I know you only said ... the things you said ... because you were scared out of your mind. So, don't let that mess with your head. Not for a second. We'll just write it off as the panic attack we both know it was and let it go. No blood, no foul."

I nodded dumbly. "Okay." Great. Now I was reduced to uni-word responses. Just call me Caveman, umm, Cavewoman Syd, at your service. Perfect. I'd gone from Doctor Syd to Troglodyte Syd in less time than it takes to steam clean the carpet. Look at me ... the missing link ... but backwards. The missing God damn back-link. Just perfect. Like a regurgitating commode.

"But ...," Rémy started. Here we go. Here comes his *but*. His big, fat *but*, hanging right out there between us. And not the cushy kind either. This one had no give whatsoever, no warmth, like it had been cast in steel, with claws.

"But what?" Suspicion wrapped around me so quickly my head was reeling in its wake. The muscles in my abdomen somehow managed to tighten further than they already were and even my fearless heart faltered in anticipation. Man, it was a good thing I'd missed dinner, or we'd be peeking at the menu in reverse play right about now.

Rémy's eyes tightened in on mine. He walked up and put his hands on either side of my face, as if to guarantee his next words would find a permanent home in my head. "Sarah is my baby sister, Syd, and I'd appreciate it if you'd reign in your rather colorful vocabulary, just a hair at least. She may have indeed heard worse, still it would be nice if you'd at least make an effort."

Okay, not what I'd expected. Not at all. And as I stood there blinking up at him incoherently, trying to process his request, Sarah practically sang out a lighthearted rebuff. "Oh, Rémy. You're so serious now. I'm fine. We're all fine ... just how we are. Love you, though." And with those words Sarah circled his waist with her small arms and hugged him with her entire being the way only kids know how to do.

Rémy's eyes melted, holding nothing but a gentle love and the promise of protection for the child in his arms as he leaned over, grabbed her under the arms and spun around and around, Sarah's feet swinging out from them as her contagious giggles wracked the night air. "Love you right back, Sugar." The perfect big brother answer.

And in that instant, I felt them both slipping through the cracks into my soul. They had exactly what I wanted. What I'd been looking for all these past, long years. What I'd had, and lost. Family. A home no matter where you were as long as you were together.

And, all of a sudden, I was the odd man out. The one that didn't belong. Here, in my private place where'd I come for years. The place where I'd come to laugh, to cry, to feel. Only now, I realized that I hadn't let myself feel anyone real, anyone with a pulse, in so long that it just didn't feel ... right. It was too strong. Overwhelming. I didn't want to feel, not like this. Not this soul-wrenching pain of being utterly and completely alone. Of having nothing and no one to call my own. To ease the pain of being a one, a uni-person.

Uh uh. Don't do it, Syd. Don't break down here. Not here, not in front of them. I had to get out of here. Now!

So, I put on my best not-really-glad-to-have-met-you-but-I'll-be-nice-because-I'm-pretty-damn-glad-to-see-you-go face and tried to find a voice that matched. "Well. Sorry again, Sarah. But I don't really think I need to start wearing a muzzle just yet. We'll probably never even cross paths again."

I quickly turned, heading back to Queens and Jacks', another place where I just didn't, and wouldn't ever, belong and began to beat a hasty retreat. "Anyway, nice to meet you both. It's late and I'm shot, so best of luck. T.J., yeah, uh, many happy meals to you, hopefully of the four-legged variety. It's been a real slice of heaven, guys. Night." My eyes were stinging as I continued to distance myself from my parents and the St. Claire trio. My heart seemed to be leaking out through my sneakers leaving fresh puddles glistening in a moonlit stream behind me.

"Syd! Syd, stop! Don't go! There's more we have to say. Something we have to tell you. Something important. It's why we're here ..." Sarah's sweet voice tugged at velvet cords tethered along my ribs. When had those gotten there? Didn't matter, I couldn't stay around either of them any longer. I had to get out of there before I burned up in the light of their oneness, their belonging, their love.

I heard her voice further behind me now as I caught sight of the Richelieu mausoleum up ahead through the trees. "Stop her, Rémy. She has to hear this. Now. Tonight." Okay, no clue what that meant. And it sounded more than a little creepy, especially with her sounding so adamant about it. I had no intention of sticking around to find out, though. I'd had quite enough excitement for one night, even for me.

My steps picked up speed and I found myself jogging through the tombstones wondering how on earth my world could have changed so much since I'd entered the gates earlier this evening. My home, but now no longer my home. And all because of what, a couple of strangers and their pet kitty?

As I rounded the mausoleum I paused, leaning against the south wall of it for just a minute to catch my breath. Shit! Without the sound of my own pounding footsteps ringing in my ears, I could hear someone coming up behind me, and fast.

I thought for a second about hiding, but that sounded just too juvenile for words, even in my own mind. So, I pushed off and rounded the front side of the crypt, ready to make a mad dash for the front gate. It wasn't more than fifty yards or so up ahead ... but there I stopped short, my breath catching in my throat. My wild, hell-bent exodus stopped dead in its tracks. I'd come all this way only to be nose to nose with the local rent-a-kitty once again. Before I could even try to wrap my head around any possible Hail Mary plan of escape, Mr. Wonderful himself pulled up at the edge of the plot behind me, choosing to walk the last few yards that separated us. Probably so as not to alarm me.

Yeah, right. Whatever. A little late for that. About three heart attacks, two nervous breakdowns, one impossible, insane crush and thirty saliva-dripping, razor-sharp teeth too late, to be specific.

Alarmed? Me? Naaah. I was about as mellow as a handful of Mexican jumping beans on a patch of hot asphalt on a summer afternoon.

6 SKELETONS IN THE CLOSET

"Syd. Don't leave. Not yet, anyway. There's something we have to show you. Something you need to know." Rémy's determined gaze was locked on mine, but his body language was a blend of being studiously nonthreatening and profoundly resolute in equal doses. His voice though, was something else. Steadfast, but compassionate. Almost reluctant. What could he possibly be reluctant to tell me about?

But I was tired, too tired for any more moonlit crises. I didn't have enough strength, or resolve, for a single encore. My head and my heart were demanding an immediate rendezvous with my bed. Whether it was to escape into a dreamless sleep, to pull the covers up over my head and try to hide from the internal monsters threatening my sanity, or to cry myself a river over the sheer volume of frustrations from this endless night was still up for grabs. "So, talk. Fast. I'm tired and I want to go home. You've got exactly two minutes."

Rémy gestured with his arm for me to lead the way back towards my parents' tombstones. "Two minutes won't begin to cover it, and Sarah needs to be with us." He indicated the way with his head when my feet refused to budge.

"She's got two feet." Even in my state, I cringed inwardly as the brusque retort fell from my lips. Then guilt had me reluctantly dragging my feet back through the ghostly headstones I'd always found so comforting. Now, somehow, they seemed to be smirking, mocking me, relishing my obvious hesitation to return.

My shoulders sagged under the weight of having simply received too much. Too much drama, too much pain and fear ... too much reality, with nowhere near enough time to deal with it. Quickest way to deal? Just gag, bind, and murder the pain. Maybe not the top choice for good mental health, but it always worked for me.

I kept my eyes on the freshly mowed grass. I'd always loved the smell of the graveyard most the day the lawn was trimmed ... fresh, sweet and full of life. But tonight I couldn't smell anything but the aftermath of rain. The air was clean, but heavy still, like it couldn't let go of the last bit of moisture hanging in it, almost like two lovers dreading the coming dawn. Like Romeo and Juliet. Storms could be like that, here in the South. Violent, but sensual, with a life, a breath all their own.

My feet were heavy and slow, making the journey back take much longer than my exodus. We must have made an oddly macabre death march in the pale moonlight. Mr. Wonderful, T.J. and I traipsing through the quietly sleeping city of bones.

As we neared our destination, Sarah's soft-spoken reprimand cut through the relaxed reverie my mind had unconsciously fallen into. "I know you heard me, Syd. Why didn't you stop? I would never hurt you, neither would Rémy. And T.J., well, as long as you don't go attacking Rémy anymore, the worst she'll do to you is lick the first few layers of skin off your face with her sandpaper tongue." Okay, not only was I getting reprimanded by a mere ghost of a girl, a quarter-pint at best, but she was trying to soothe my fear? Of her? She looked just about as menacing as Shirley Temple had dancing around in her bouncing ringlets, rosy cheeks and frilly little rumba pants singing "On the Good Ship Lollipop".

But in truth she had hurt me. Both of them had. To the bone. Just by having each other, and even T.J., a family, complete with house pet. "I wasn't afraid." Shit, I sounded petulant even to me. Great! Did that mean I was emotionally younger than this ... this second grader? One more stroke to the old ego! At least you never hear that on the six o'clock news ... and today, a seventeen-year-old girl up and died from a fatal blow to her ego! Maybe I would be the first one to accomplish this fine feat. Quick, where was that number for Guinness? Since it seemed inevitable that my ship was sinking fast, maybe it wasn't too late for me to at least go down in history as it sank.

Thank God, Rémy broke through my insipid mind fart before I had a major blow-out. "This way, Syd, we're going to a different gravesite."

But as Rémy's words chased the fog of emotion and nervous chatter scrambling around my brain away, the rest of Sarah's disapproval finally decided to hit me. "And Jesus, Sarah, stop saying I attacked Rémy! I never touched him! Besides, he was laughing at me! Even if I had hit him, he had a hell of a lot more than that coming to him. He should be thanking me for showing some restraint, even if it was forced on me by a stupid black cat." The words cracked out of me like a lion tamer's whip.

We were following Rémy's lead, Sarah and I shadowing him just a step or two behind, while T.J. pulled up the rear. Sarah glanced up at me, then shifted her gaze to Rémy's back guiding our way before she responded. "Mmm. Okay, Syd. But I didn't say you successfully attacked him, just that you did indeed engage. The fact that you failed is completely irrelevant."

"My God! How old are you?" I knew my tone was accusatory, but there was nothing I could do about it right then. I think she could be old enough to be collecting Social Security, and then some.

But Sarah just smiled softly at me, and it was both cryptic and patient. Then her eyes dropped to T.J. as she rubbed along the dark furry neck, just behind the animal's left ear.

"Why T.J.?" I blurted out.

"Why T.J., what?" Rémy questioned with his left eyebrow raised.

"Just that. Why T.J.? Why that name? What does it stand for? Tear out my Jugular?" Although a soft laugh slipped out with the words, my hand fluttered nervously at the base of my throat.

"No. You really are funny, Syd." Sarah giggled that little girl giggle of hers and shook her head as she continued. "T.J. is for Tom and Jerry, of course."

"Oh, right. Of course. How stupid of me not to know that." They were both nuts. Not me, them. "Tom and freakin' Jerry? You have got to be kidding me. Ya'll named a God damn panther, a dark, menacing predator of death, after a Saturday morning cartoon? Named her after an incompetent, maniacal cat and a cute, mischievous little mouse?" Was I the only one here with a problem about that? Certainly looked that way.

Rémy tried to illuminate me. "Sarah chose the name. She thought T.J. was smart, sweet and playful, like Jerry, but also quick-tempered and a little thin-skinned like Tom."

Sarah chimed in with her two cents. "Yeah, and Tom and Jerry are always better when they're together. They bring out the best in each other. Besides, they're just so cute and funny! I love them!" Again, she hit below the belt with those God damn giggles.

"Yeah. Don't you just love slapstick! Can't beat a good healthy dose of violence in an animated shorty. I know it's what I live for. Ranks right up there with winning the lottery and ending world hunger." I paused for a minute, shaking my head, letting it sink in.

Tom and Jerry, for Christ's sake. Huh! "It's a good thing they changed their names after the first cartoon though, or T.J. would be J.J."

"Really?" Sarah was instantly curious, looking up at me without skipping a beat in petting the very kitty in question.

"Yeah. I caught part of a Tom and Jerry cartoon marathon last summer. They apparently hit the big time as Jasper and Jinx. Just doesn't have quite the same ring to it, does it?" How on earth had I pulled that out of my hat? Names?

Me? One of my many shortcomings. And this one was shorter than short, positively microscopic. I was completely and utterly name-intolerant, had been since birth. Just another wonderful piece of the genetic conundrum otherwise known as Syd. But I did have a pretty good vocabulary to make up for it. So, hey, if I couldn't quite remember someone's name, at least I could adjective the living daylights out of them!

"No. It sure doesn't." Sarah grimaced like she'd bitten into one uber-sour pickle. "But at least someone had the good sense to fix it."

I suddenly realized we'd stopped moving and immediately recognized exactly where we were standing. We were at Rachel Anne Kensington's gravesite. Hers and her baby's, Jesse Jr.

My eyes widened with surprise and quickly jumped up to Rémy's. But his stormy gray eyes, though still gorgeous, shut me out completely now. It was like a huge steel door had slammed down over them. I felt my eyelids flutter and actually had to take a step back from the sheer force of it, as if a door had literally slammed shut right in my face.

Sarah, seemingly oblivious to our silent exchange, pushed onward without hesitation as she dropped to her knees beside T.J. "Speaking of changing names, you should just call Rémy ... Beau. That's what Gigi always called him. She said ..."

But Rémy cut her off at the pass. "Syd doesn't want to know the petty, mundane clutter of our lives, Sarah. She's got enough on her plate to choke down as it is."

Ever-so-sweetly, Sarah responded, "Yes, you're probably right, Rémy. She really doesn't need to know that Gigi thought you were just too handsome to be called anything other than Beau."

Rémy groaned in mock exasperation.

And sweet little, surprisingly tenacious Sarah didn't stop there, but finished telling the tale. "You do know Beau means handsome in French? It was Pop's, Gigi's husband's, name. Jean-Luc Guillaume Beauchamps. That's where Rémy got the Beauchamps name to begin with. Gigi especially loved Rémy's eyes, how they twinkled when she caught him planning some dastardly scheme, how the storms rolled into them when he was angry, and how they swirled in deep, dark pools when he was sleepy and content."

"Sarah, we have more important things to discuss than the delusional weather patterns you and Gigi mistakenly imagine exist on my face. Syd only gave us a short time, no sense wasting it all on a bunch of useless nonsense." Rémy was sweeping around the area impatiently, the pace of his footsteps increasing with his discomfort.

"No! It's okay, Sarah." I protested, turning to give her my full attention. "I want to hear this. Don't pay him any mind at all. He's just a little grumpy right now. My schedule has suddenly opened up a bit."

"Grumpy?" Rémy muttered with narrowed eyes.

Sarah stuck her little pink tongue out quickly at Rémy, smiled warmly, and continued in a conspiratorial voice. "Well, Gigi used to say that Rémy's eyes were a lethal weapon and the day he fell in love he was going to have to pull his hat down low over his eyes and keep it there the rest of his life or else his lady love would read him just like a good book." There was clearly more spunk in Sarah than I'd given her credit for. Who would've thought? A micro-turbo-charged hellion with beautiful big blue eyes and a smile that could confound the biggest, baddest, most sadistic tyrant on the planet. It's a damn good thing the armies of the world were all too single-mindedly focused on nuclear armament to ever realize the biggest threat known to man could be delivered so easily in such a sweet, little, utterly disarming package.

"Thank you very much, Sarah. Are you quite finished now? Can we please get down to business?" Rémy, I mean Beau, was clearly back to his big, bad self, dripping fangs and all.

"Beau? Beau. Beau St. Claire. Hmmm. I think I like it. Beau. Yeah, it'll do. It'll do just fine, Beau. Thanks, Sarah, that was a great idea. Beau of the beautiful eyes. Hmm, yeah. Beau. Much better." Yup. I was rubbing it in. Rubbing it in bone deep. The look in those beautiful, stormy eyes of his, the tightening of those lips, the clenching of his jaw just egging me mercilessly on ... like throwing gasoline on a campfire.

Sarah just smiled back at me like she'd known it without my ever having said the words aloud. Boy, Rémy, I mean Beau, sure wasn't smiling now though. Nowhere near it. "God, Syd! That's enough! Now, how many times are you gonna say my name? Syd, Syd, Syd, Syd, Syd, Syd, Syd!" Rémy, woops, Beau, griped back at us while Sarah and I both dissolved into laughter, Beau's crabbiness just making it taste all that much sweeter.

Finally, I caught hold of myself enough to make some attempt at normal communication and I asked a question, the most obvious one at that. "So, anyone care to explain to me why on earth I'm standing here with the Bobbsey Twins, and one very menacing panther, in a cemetery, in the middle of the night, at a complete stranger's gravesite, instead of snuggled down deep into my nice warm bed right now?" There, that wasn't so bad. Not rude at all, really. A run-on question maybe, but I was on a roll.

"Why don't you sit down, Syd? This is gonna take a little while, so you might as well get comfortable." Although spoken with a relaxed charm, Rém ... Beau, seemed anything but relaxed. His eyes were concealed once more behind an impenetrable wall masking his emotions completely.

As I sat down facing the cold granite, drawing my feet up beside me and leaning on my hand, Sarah shifted her weight into T.J., who had stretched out beside the gravesite, her length running parallel with the grave, tail silently swishing across the marker from time to time. Sarah was using the animal's long, muscular body much like a furry black body pillow, her small legs extending across the width of the grave. The faint purr rumbling through T.J.'s upper body gained ever so slightly in volume, followed by the drooping fur-lined lids over green-gold eyes that were now more closed than open.

Ré ... Beau, on the other hand, sat with his back against the marker, his head tipped back against it and his long, muscular legs stretched out towards Rachel and me.

My fingers were absentmindedly playing with the blades of grass as Sarah and Beau exchanged a long, pointed look. Then, as if having come to some kind of silent agreement, Sarah rolled her head to look at me. She cleared her throat, nestled back into T.J. and began her tale as if it was nothing more or less than a simple campfire story.

"Syd, have you ever studied religion? Eastern religions in particular?" She paused and looked at me until I nodded my reply. Satisfied, Sarah continued. "So, you are familiar with the concepts of karma, right action and reincarnation." Although it was a statement and not a question, Sarah once again paused, waiting to continue until I confirmed her conjectured speculations with another quick nod.

"Good. Then you already understand that everything you send out, every thought, word and action, comes back around to you, good or bad, whether it's in this life or the next, or the one after that." Another pause for my agreement.

R ... Beau, was sitting quietly, his head leaning back against the dark stone, his eyes lost among the stars. He should have looked comfortable but there was a tension about him, an unease that had wrapped itself tightly around his entire being. My own lungs tightened in response and I had to look away from him to catch my breath. What was he so uptight about? It couldn't be good if it had him this stressed already. And how was I able to read his moods so easily, so quickly? Surely that took time, shared moments, some degree of common history. But somehow I knew exactly what he was feeling. Maybe not why he was feeling it, but what he was feeling, nonetheless. I felt it as if it was my own experience, my own emotion, to feel. As if we were somehow connected. Did he feel what I was feeling, too? Huh! If so, poor bastard. My feelings confused the hell out of me. How in the world could he possibly deal with them?

As my gaze shifted back to Sarah, I realized she'd been waiting for my attention before she continued. "Sorry. Go ahead. I'm listening." But now I wasn't so sure I wanted to hear any more and my vision settled on the blade of grass I was sliding between my thumb and index finger. As I reached the tip of it, I pulled downward, tearing the blade lengthwise into two separate pieces still connected at the very bottom. I felt just like that. I felt torn ... half of me, I'll admit, was pretty damn curious at this point, wanting to know where all of this was going. But there was a part of me, and it was growing quickly, that was totally in sync with what was written all over Beau, a deep, resonating apprehension. It was as if my soul was hesitating on the doorstep of some great precipice that, once seen, would change me for all time whether I plunged fearlessly headlong into the shadowy depths below or ran screaming like a lunatic in the opposite direction, diving for cover along the way.

"Syd?" Sarah quietly called, patiently waiting for me to collect the bits and pieces of my fragmented mind that seemed to be floating all around me. You'd have thought I was in some kind of ghoulish snow globe that had just been shaken up. Only, instead of little bits of Styrofoam snow floating all around me, I was standing in the center of a whirling mass of my own brain tissue, and it was slowly spiraling out of control. Oh, look there goes my right occipital lobe. And look, over there is my hypothalamus.

Stop it, Syd! I grabbed my hands, gripping them tightly together, squashing the grass mercilessly. Green juice leaked between my fingers and my knuckles turned white with the strangle of my hold. What the hell is wrong with you, Syd? Nothing has happened. Not yet, anyway. So. Get. A. Grip. And loosen your grip on the poor defenseless vegetation before your hands permanently turn the lovely color of lima beans from the sticky chlorophyll slime oozing out all over them.

I took a deep breath that was meant to be cleansing. So much for that idea. Still, it was oxygen, and oxygen was good. I took in two more lungfulls and quickly used it to glue my head back together. "Yeah, okay. I said I'm listening. So, talk already." My eyes darted with every word, not quite landing on anything long enough to completely focus all the way, just leaving me with blurred snapshots of the world around me.

"You also understand that you have many lifetimes in which to figure all this out. Different opportunities, different situations, to tackle the things you are here to learn. You'll just keep having the same issues come up until you figure out how to navigate them." She stopped for a moment and I dropped my chin in a half-nod. It seemed to suffice, because she started in again. "Well, we're here, Rémy, I mean Beau, and I, and even T.J., to help you with yours."

To help me. I'd been okay until then, but those three little innocent words did it in two seconds flat. Now I was mad. Again. I know, what's new with that? "To help me ... with my ... my what, exactly? Is something wrong with me? Are you saying I'm broken? That I need fixing? You're only what, eight years old for Christ sake?" My searing gaze shifted from her face to Beau's and I shifted, wrapping one arm around my legs and hugging them closer to my chest for stability, my other arm free and speaking right along with me as all good Southern arms do, flicking menacingly in

Beau's general direction. "And you! You're not much older than me! Ya'll don't even know me. How the hell would you know what I need or want, much less how to give it to me?" I looked over my shoulder at my backside. "Do I have a neon sign stapled to my ass saying 'This poor, screwed up fool needs your help ... now!' Maybe there's even a tickertape ad running at two in the morning on CNN flashing 1-800-HELP-SYD!" I swung my hand in T.J.'s direction, not comfortable letting even her escape my scathing rage. "And how, exactly, is a God damn alley cat supposed to do anything but scare the shit out of me? You think an enema is going to help solve my problems? Besides, who said I want help anyway?"

The vein in the hollow at the bottom of Beau's throat was twitching slightly and his jaw was clenched as he stared down hard into my eyes. "Fine. Let's take this one utterly ridiculous and completely irrational statement at a time. First, we, the three of us," he gestured in a sweeping motion that included Sarah, T.J. and himself "are here to help you because we want to and because you definitely need it, whether you choose to admit it or not. Second, no, you're not broken, not exactly, but you are beyond any shadow of any doubt clearly unable to access some of your own natural abilities for some reason. Kind of spiritually handicapped. Third, I've already told you that Sarah is a lot more experienced, a lot more mature, than what you'd guess by looking at her, I suppose you'd put me in that category as well. But even if she were only eight, she'd still have it all over you in emotional strength, hands down. At least right now. Fourth, yes, the God damn alley cat, as you so eloquently put it, is here to help you, which you would understand if you'd shut up for five seconds and let us finish explaining things to you. Fifth, while I have to admit that I might not mind seeing you shuck your pants, doing it because of a major blow-out, much less one that reeks, is just not my idea of a good time. And, finally, rather than sit there and piss and moan like a fragile little first grader, you might want to consider showing just a little appreciation for our time and interest in you rather than trying to release all of your almost eighteen years worth of pent up frustration and anger. There, questions answered. Now, back to the important issues." He turned to Sarah. "The floor's all yours, Honey."

Sarah looked at me, and it was a look of patience, acceptance and just a little trepidation. She sure stood up to bat though, and damn if she didn't swing big. "Okay. So, Syd, I'm here to help you access your past lives, specific ones. Beau will accompany you and enable you to reenact the key moments that would have been better served with different decisions on your part. And, T.J., well, she facilitates the whole process. Kind of like ..." She thought for a second before finding the words, "between now and then, between what is and what was." And she had the gall, the audacity to look perfectly peachy, as if she'd just explained away any sense of discomfort and all was right with the world.

Ri-i-i-ight. "So, let me see if I have this straight." I said, wrinkling my nose and pointing at Sarah. "You, are some grade-school, past life elevator operator working the control panel of the entire entourage of my past lives kind of like a TV programmer, or Sulu in Star Trek ... my own personal pint-size paranormal navigator." My gaze and hand shifted to Beau. "Mr. Wonderful over here is the male lead in this comedy of errors otherwise known as my life, uh, lives. Furthermore, in that capacity, he also serves as the damn cruise director." Finally, turning to T.J. I wrapped things up. "And Fluffy is the transcendental doorman, mmm, doorcat ... that or maybe some kind of furry, four-legged bouncer ... a roller coaster ride attendant, there to help get you on and off the ride, buckle your seatbelt, and remind you to keep your hands and feet inside the ride at all times? Does that just about sum things up?"

Rank sweetness was dripping so heavily on my words that I felt my nose wrinkle and my lips purse as I gazed with a smile the size of the Joker's at my fellow cemetery crashers. Yeah, and what if I just didn't want to get on this ride? What then?

Sarah looked knowingly at Beau as she scratched under T.J.'s chin, causing the black fur under her neck to stretch with a midnight blue sheen as she lifted her head to deepen the caress. Beau however, was considerably less relaxed. The muscles at his jaw were working tightly as he clearly tried to swallow some of the anger dripping from the corners of his mouth before opening his perfect lips to speak and letting it rain all over us in an enraged tirade.

Yeah, I should have backed down, been a little more patient. But I wasn't in a patient mood. I was tired, confused, frustrated, angry, emotionally spent, and still a little soggy from the rain. My curiosity, anticipation and exhilaration could take a backseat for a while. "Well?! Somebody, speak!" I barked out at them.

Finally Beau's eyes shifted slowly to me, and boy were they cold. Cold and hard. I felt a shiver snake down my spine as the temperature of his gaze permeated my body, the muscles along my shoulders and back tightening in preparation for the wrath swirling in the depths of his eyes.

He was up and pacing around us again. "Stop acting like a complete fool, Syd. It's beneath you, and it's irritating the hell out of me. Why don't you stop thinking with your head for half a second and think with your heart instead?" Now his hands were flying, punctuating his words. "What do you see? What? If I wanted to hurt you, I would have before Sarah ever joined us. Surely you don't see her as a threat, aside from being only four feet tall, if that, she's only shown you patience, trust and acceptance. That leaves T.J., who has been doing nothing but soaking up Sarah's attention for the past half hour." As he neared me this time he dropped to a squat right in front of me, his face inches from my own, his breath stirring the air across my face, ruffling my hair, whispering his scent around me, through me. His eyes locked on mine and tried as I might, I couldn't break free. "You're angry. Okay, Syd. I get that. But what, exactly, are you angry about? What?!"

"Beau ...," Sarah tried to break in, but he wasn't having it. Instead he waved his hand to silence her and just kept pushing while I could only blink up into his eyes, mesmerized by his strength, his domination. Which should have pissed me off, why wasn't it? But I didn't have time to think about it right then. Beau was too busy busting down other walls and barriers that sheltered me, keeping me in every bit as much as keeping everyone else out.

"Or are you really angry? Is all that anger there just to insulate you from the pain? A mask for all your hurt?"

"Beau ...," Sarah tried again, but with no better results.

"You son of a bitch!" I gasped on top of Sarah's words. But I too was railroaded out of the conversation. If this one-sided testosterone-fueled tirade still could be called a conversation.

"No, Sarah. It's time she faced this." I could swear I saw lightning flare in those eyes of his as he turned them back on me. "And you've said enough. So, just shut up for two seconds and listen. As Desmond Tutu would say, don't increase the volume of your voice, just improve your argument."

"Desmond Tutu? Who the hell quotes Desmond Tutu? What planet are you from?" I burst in, again.

"Syd, do yourself a favor and shut the hell up. We, the three of us, are here to help you, and to help us. This is bigger than just you, Syd. But time is not our friend anymore. I wish we could take this slowly and give you time to come to terms with it. Unfortunately, that's just not an option. You have to figure this out now, without any foreplay. Without anything to chase it down with either. But you do have us. We're here with you and we're not going anywhere." Once again he hunkered down right in front of me his nose practically kissing mine. Near miss Eskimo kisses.

Sarah piped in again. "But she doesn't have to face all of it in one night. Maybe we should give her a little time to work through it." You had to give it to her, the kid had gumption in spades, but it was the kind that left a sweet taste in your mouth, nothing bitter about it at all.

Beau still wasn't budging, but his voice, though unwavering, held a certain softness now. "Sarah, she's got to hear this. Just finish laying it out for her, Honey. She can deal with it, she'll just have to. We'll help her through it. There's no other choice."

"Enough, you two. Just spit it out already. I'm not completely incompetent." Curiosity and impatience were stretching me to the limit.

Sarah took a deep, cleansing breath and began. Again. "Well then, Syd, sometimes when we make a mess of things in one life, it sets up situations that must eventually get sorted out and cleaned up in other lives. That's what's happened with you. There are some issues that are hanging over you that have to be put right to get you back on track where you're supposed to be."

"That's just great. Not only do I have to deal with all the crap I've got going on now, but I've got past issues bearing down on me from the grave. But they're history. Right? I can just let them go. Who cares? Who will even know? I mean, honestly, Sarah, I appreciate the help, I really do, but I've got enough bullshit to deal with already. I really don't need to go looking for more. I can do my own bad just fine on my own ... no help needed there whatsoever."

"Yeah, that's just it though. You can't sweep it under the carpet, or under the tombstone. It's not going to go away. And it's going to start affecting you. Soon. In ways that might not be too comfortable for you at first ... especially on your own." Sarah's voice dropped a little with the last revelation.

"Perfect. Stormy skies are in my cosmic forecast. And you know this, how? Are you the new Channel 2 weatherman, weathergirl?"

"No, Syd. I'm ..." Sarah started to explain, but Beau cut her off at the pass.

"She's here to help you, Syd. We all are. That's really all that matters here. Other than the fact that you're running out of time. This is your last chance to figure this stuff out and fix it. It's going to take some time to do all the repair work you have to do and you don't have the luxury of tossing it around that pretty little head of yours for the next fifty years deliberating on whether or not to do it at all. Soon enough the choice won't even exist."

As he paused for an oxygen fill-up he glanced at Sarah and back at me before adding, "Besides, there are those who don't want you to accomplish any of this. And they are prepared to do absolutely anything to stop you. Whatever it takes."

"Okay. I can make this real easy for you. No. Not interested. Not today, not tomorrow, not ever. You can save yourselves some time, I'll just keep all my karma, bad as it may be, and whoever doesn't want me to do this won't get their panties in a twist. No problem." I jumped to my feet. "So, I guess we're done here. Nice to meet you ... all of you. Have a nice life, lives, however many of them you intend on having. Maybe I'll catch you the next time through."

As I turned to leave, Beau grabbed my hand. "Syd. You don't have a choice here. They're already coming after you."

I spun around, yelling in his face. "What? What do you mean, 'they're already coming after me?' What the hell did you do to me? Like I can't dig up enough trouble all on my lonesome, you thought you just had to give me a hand?"

Sarah tried to rescue him. "Syd, Beau hasn't done anything but try to help you, to protect you, for a long time now."

"Sorry, Sarah. But seeing as I've known you two the length of a good rainstorm, I don't think long time is the word of choice. You don't even know my shoe size and you've got vultures apparently closing in for the kill. Why on earth would I do anything you tell me to do? Do I look like a complete idiot?" I shook my head, pushing my hair back from my face. "No. Don't even answer that. I don't care. I'm going home. Now."

"Syd, you can't just go ..." Sarah began, but Beau took control, and for once, I was grateful.

"Sarah, let her go." Beau's voice should have sounded hollow, resigned. But even in my haste to leave, the promise in it wasn't lost on me. He had given up absolutely nothing. He was simply deferring to another time and place. This definitely wasn't over, at least in his mind.

"But Beau," the concern in Sarah's words was heavy, "we can't leave her to deal with what's coming alone. You know that better than anyone. She's in danger, even from herself."

I kept my back as straight as a board as I continued to head for the entrance, hoping it leant me a look of confidence that was completely beyond me at the moment. As a matter of fact, I was having to mentally choreograph every step I took to get me out of there. How had I made it all the way here earlier on autopilot and now couldn't so much as inhale without creating a multi-step flow chart? Man, how the mighty had fallen. And those six eyes boring holes into my back weren't helping one little bit.

"We'll keep an eye on her. And we'll be there when she needs us. We can't force this on her, as much as we'd like to. She'll just fight it all that much harder if we do." Great. Now Beau's voice not only held that godforsaken promise, but a shitload of other stuff. Like knowledge and wisdom. And conviction. He believed in what he was saying. Wholeheartedly. Dammit! That spelled trouble in a big, fat way. Belief can carry a man a thousand miles on fumes alone.

Shit! I really hate it when people standing on the opposite side of the fence from me make sense. It makes it so much harder to keep a good mad up. And, right now, I needed this mad like I needed air to breath. It was protecting me from feeling worse things. Things I just didn't even want to think about. I could think about them later. Later was good. Never was better. I'll go with never.

As I reached the gate it hit me that this was the first time in my life I'd ever wanted to leave the cemetery. And definitely the first time I was more screwed up leaving than when I'd arrived. Thanks to three very unwanted guests. Unexpected company ... what a pain in the ass. I so wished I'd never met them. Especially one Jean-Rémy Beauchamps St. Claire.

I'd known him for less time than it takes to get a good sunburn and I already felt raw. How could he do that? He was just a guy. Just another guy. There was absolutely, positively no room for a Beau of any sort. No matter how captivating his eyes were or how much I melted at the sound of his voice. My life was messy enough as is. Beau would have to go. I owed it to my own sanity to keep my world as clean as possible and that meant minimizing all the gooey, clingy floaters.

Any Beaus in the here and now would definitely belong in that basket. Yeah, when it comes to Beau, don't just say no. Say *hell* no.

Okay. I felt better. Certain disaster had been averted and my life was back in my own hands, for better or for worse. But even as I climbed back through my bedroom window and pulled back the cool, crisp white sheets to finally put this ridiculous day to rest, I knew as sure as the sun would rise in the morning that my life was about to get really, really sticky. The kind of sticky that won't just wash off but has to slowly wear away over time ... like a big blob of gum stuck to the bottom of your sneakers. Oh, joy.

7 PETTY CRIMES 101

The minute I saw Patricia's face, I realized just how much had happened last night. If my life were a book, my God, she'd be behind me by at least five or six entire chapters.

Not that it mattered right now. All Patricia cared about this second was scavenging for the low-down with my supposedly hot date the night before with Josh Pendergraft, a recent transfer student and instant hit with every female at our school. Some of the guys, too, if you believed the grapevine. I could see why, though, he looked like sex on a stick, literally. He was hot enough to scorch anybody within a ten-foot radius. Just not this particular body.

"So-o-o, tell me, tell me. How was it? Was it what you expected? I bet it was wonderful! Absolutely wonderful!" Patricia teetered somewhat precariously between a bouncy excitement and a longing wistfulness.

But for once, there were tell-tale shadows under those happy blue eyes. Guess she'd been up late studying for the big government test.

"Mr. A keep you up late?" I asked, shifting the books in my arms into a more comfortable position.

Patricia glanced up at me, then slammed into someone head-on, knocking her own books to the floor. "What?"

"Well, you obviously stayed up late. Figured it was because of Mr. Askew's test this Thursday."

"Oh. Yeah. I was. Up too late." She looked back at me as she stood up. "Now, start dishin', Syd."

I swear to God if she'd been anyone else, anyone at all, I would have smacked her. She just sort of buzzed around me like a mosquito around a twilight fire late into October. But somehow, she pulled it off. Always had. And instead of stopping her dead in her tracks, all I could do was pull a half-smile and softly shake my head, marveling at her ability to amuse my otherwise firmly dependable pessimism.

She was my best friend. Not sure why ... we were absolutely nothing alike and had completely different interests. But we were best friends, had been since second grade. Much to her parents' chagrin ... they tolerated me for her sake, but underneath all the polite frosting I could feel them screaming at me to just disappear from all their lives, or from the face of the planet, it was a little fuzzy. Either way, so long as they never had to set eyes on me again, they'd be pleased as punch.

I guess I could understand that though. I mean, I do have something of a darkness about me. Not Patricia though, she was fluffy, pink and perky. So not me. But so incredibly Patricia.

Perky. Yeah, that was Patricia in a word, perky. Something I would never, in a million years, be in danger of being mistaken for. I just don't think perky comes in my size. It sure suits Patricia though. I swear, when she wakes up in the morning, her house is immediately 500 watts brighter, bright enough to chase away the shadows ... even the ones you didn't know were there. Patricia does that. She chases away the darkness of life, and fills it with light and laughter and a profound happiness.

Not me. Oh, boy. Not me in a big, big way. For me, the light hurts. Literally. I wear sunglasses almost 24/7. I just see everything better with them, even at night. Life is just better, more digestible, seen through a filter.

Especially at dawn and dusk, sunrises and sunsets pale in comparison without my sunglasses. I'd take candles, firelight, stars and moonlight to Edison's light bulbs any day of the week. And my personal favorites were starlight and moonlight reflected off large bodies of water. It doesn't really matter what kind of water, but I'd have to say I do prefer water in motion ... oceans, rivers, waterfalls, even rain ... doesn't matter, love it all. It's sensual, mysterious and magical all tangled up together in a way that pulls on every sensation I possess, and then my imagination kicks in. Mmm. Some kind of wonderful.

"Syd, answer me! Don't just keep me hanging. Spill. Come on, give me the good stuff." Patricia was getting pretty desperate at this point. She was one of those people who needed words so much more than I ever would. And right now, I just wasn't anywhere near able to keep up with her. I was about two gallons of java too short.

"You're such a nerd." I half rolled my eyes at her.

"I know. It wears well on me though." She was absolutely right there. Most nerds were just great big walking, talking piles of uncomfortable, over-the-top-anxious, glow-in-the-dark dorkdom. Not Patricia though. She was that rare breed of I'm-not-quite-sure-I'm-comfortable-in-my-own-skin, rescue me before I faint, rosy-cheeks-in-the-morning nerd. And on her, nothing could ever look any more appealing. The perfect damsel in distress, with just a hint of Southern spitfire to add some color...

"But you are not changing the subject on me. Not this time." She handed me a tall cup of Joe and I took a good long chug, feeling the warmth slide all the way down to the pit of my stomach, soothing every single nerve ending on its way. It was sweetened just enough to cut the bite, no cream. Exactly the way I take it. Damn. Maybe that was my problem. Maybe I should be looking for a wife instead of a decent boyfriend.

Yeah. There was a reason why we worked. We both knew just how hard to push, what to give and take, and when to call it a day and simply walk away. "Now talk." Patricia's eyes glittered with a good mix of curiosity and growing impatience. God bless her, the little shit knew me just a bit too well.

We started weaving our way through the early morning rush to first period and Mr. A-fucking-mazing. I lifted my chin, took a deep breath, and stared into those absurdly clear baby blues. "It was ... short. Twenty-three minutes to be exact. Didn't even make it to dessert. Should have done the movie first. Pretty much what I expected, though. And absolutely, positively un-wonderful. Happy?"

"Oh, Syd! What did you do this time? Josh is just too perfect for words. How could you screw this one up?" Patricia tended to date second hand, through me. Actually, she tended to do most things looking through my shadow. She liked it that way. She got to feel the rush of the ride without the risk of throwing up all over herself. I was just the opposite. Don't ever ask me to just sit by and watch it being done, it screwed up my whole sense of balance. That's when I'd hurl.

"Okay. Not my fault. The idiot opened his mouth. I tried to stop him, tried to warn him, but no-o-o, he just had to talk. Had to open that perfect mouth and let words fall right out of it. That was it. He could have found something infinitely more worthwhile to do with that gorgeous set of lips of his. Don't know what I expected though. How could anyone with a name like Josh stand a chance in hell of ever making it past my dipshit radar in one piece? My mistake. But live and learn, right?"

I sucked down some instant courage with another quick breath and plowed on before I lost my momentum. When played well, momentum could almost carry you through the thick, gooey parts of life on sheer inertia alone. Hard, yes. Nauseating, sometimes. But usually, so much better than the alternatives. "Listen up because there won't be an encore performance. Queens and Jacks found out about the whole stupid mini-revolution in Mr. Asshole's room yesterday, so now I'm grounded for a month with no time off for good behavior. I instantly fell for a delicious Mr. Nobody at the cemetery after hours last night who, along with his kid sister, almost served me up as Kitty Chow to a black panther. I learned I supposedly have past lives, karma and all that unfinished business that goes along with it. Found out some majorly bad guys are supposedly stalking me as we speak. And, after much deliberation and nail-biting, decided to throw Mr. Nobody back in the water ... let him live to swim another day. It was kind of a busy night. Even for me." I took another deep breath, hoping I'd given her enough to chew on that any more questions would be slow in the coming.

Right, Syd. Like that would happen in this lifetime. Patricia wasn't about to put this conversation on hold until after class ... next month ... never. "Syd ... okay. Just give me a sec here." Bless her heart. She was reeling. Her eyes were blinking ninety-to-nothing trying to digest all that I'd belched out. I really should have gone slower for her.

But just then her eyes cleared somewhat and she managed to focus once again. "Okay. We'll come back to the whole mixed-up, pile of cow bunk you just threw at me later. Now, we'll just focus on what you were supposed to have been doing last night ... meaning, Josh. And, so help me God, I'm gonna break that stupid dipshit radar of yours if you keep this up. A black panther, Syd? Are you serious? Anyway, Josh is the third guy you've test driven this month, without taking Mr. Nobody into account. And you never even make it out of the damn car lot. It's such a waste of home-grown stud muffins, and it sounds like not only did you eject Josh from the game, but you probably ejected a perfectly innocent bystander, your Mr. Nobody, as well." It was Patricia's turn to roll her eyes at me. "And thirty days? Is that what you said? No prom?! Ahhh, dammit, Syd!"

"Stud muffins?" I grimaced at the all-together too sugary words. "Whatever. Yes, a living, breathing panther. And, I just can't kiss what I can't even stand to listen to. Call me a freak." Call me a thankful freak, I could see the door to Mr. A's room. Time was finally on my side for once. I stepped up the pace and nearly annihilated a clueless freshman bottom dweller, three steps from serenity. Funny that. Mr. A's classroom, always the subject of nightmares, could, taken in context, represent a sanctuary. Sick? Yes. Welcome to my world. "And, yes. Prom's off. Not that I'd have a date now anyway. Well, darn. Look at that. We're out of time." I glanced mock-sheepishly at Patricia as we stepped into the classroom.

"Oh, that's alright." Patricia answered with a sickeningly sweet smile wrapped around her face. "We're not done here, Sydney Annalise." Oh, man. The worst part was I knew she was dead on. Whenever she called me by more than just Syd, the pressure escalated exponentially with the number of letters involved. And this, damn, this was two out of four possible names. She was definitely nowhere near letting this one go ... not yet anyway. She'd chew on this all damn day. Man, I was tired already just thinking about it. Self-induced sleep deprivation and neurotic best friends obsessing over high school trauma-drama, not such a good mix.

"Good morning, ladies," Mr. Askew leered as we passed through the doorway. I swear I could smell the spit sliding down his canines. Disgusting. Positively puke-inspiring. "You're both looking quite lovely today." His head spun around on his neck as we passed, just like a weather vane spins in high winds ... well-oiled and completely lacking any type of brain of its own.

"Yeah. Um, thanks Mr. A." I mustered up something in the same general family as a smile, a little icy maybe but nothing overtly antagonistic. See, I could try to be pleasant. Well, I could try not to be outright offensive at any rate. That still had to count for something, right? Patricia and I both tried our best to hug the opposite door frame as we passed by the slime ball.

That's something Mr. A always did, take up half the available door space as everyone came and went. To the powers that be, I'm sure he looked like a connected, caring, interacting teacher. To those of us unlucky enough to have to cross his path on a daily basis, he was trying to interact all right, but on a whole other playing field. Somehow I just don't think trying to cop a feel should qualify him for any special merit badges. But hey, I could be wrong. Wouldn't be the first time.

And, of course, there were those girls who didn't seem to mind it, who seemed to go along with it. I don't know if they didn't get enough attention from Daddy or if they were just after an easy A. I didn't really care either way though. None of my business, I learned a long time ago to choose my battles. Even so, I still always seemed to be in the rough more than any ten people I knew.

"I certainly hope today proves to be more profitable for us than yesterday was, Sydney."

Patricia's eyes darted to mine, her body tightening with distaste. Clearly the words weren't lost on her. I deliberately kept my focus straight ahead of me speaking at the breathing sack of shit instead of to him. "Yeah. Well, it's your future, Mr. A, but I sure wouldn't hang your hopes on that one. You definitely wouldn't see a good return on your investment, because it's without a doubt a bear market out there. You know the kind I mean, the one where I can't bear to be within fifty yards of your nose-curdling stench." I turned at my desk and cocked my head, smiling innocently back up at him. I even batted my eyes for added effect. I know, color me bitch. But damn it felt good.

Patricia tried hard to swallow a laugh. She almost succeeded, too, but the snort that came out of her nose blew her out of the water and then there was just no stopping her. So she just laughed right out loud the rest of the way to her seat.

Looking up at me fairly sheepishly, Patricia said under her breath, "I am so sorry, Syd. I just couldn't help it. You could seriously be a stand-up comedian. You've definitely got a gift there. Did you see his face? I thought the vein on his neck was going to explode."

As we settled in our seats, I glanced up at the stuffed eagle on the shelf behind Mr. A's desk. With its wings spread wide it was enormous and had an uncanny way of somehow looking right back at you. As if it was trying to warn you about something. Something important.

That eagle always added an extra few layers of discomfort right up on top of my already immense distaste of being anywhere near Mr. A. I think maybe it had something to do with the way it seemed to have been caught midair. Trapped and stuffed right then and there between the clouds, mid-flight, the wind rushing through its feathers, the sun reflecting in its black, round eyes.

It really creeped me out. Big time. Made me think about the sheer agony I'd feel if my own freedom was threatened. Bet that was exactly what Mr. A liked about it. That sadistic son of a bitch!

There were some other assorted things on the shelves that collectively added up to an odd ensemble ... a branding iron, the kind you'd use to mark a cow, an old iron cross that had partially turned green, a long, curved, yellowed claw, a clay pitcher that was missing one of its two handles, a small glass jar that was empty ... well, empty except for a few dead bugs in the bottom of it ... and a large weathered piece of driftwood.

As Mr. A began to drone on about the neo-Nazi movement popular in some parts of the world, my mind began to drift back to my graveyard guests. Before I even got going though, Patricia slipped a note onto my desk. Glancing up at Mr. A to make sure the coast was clear, I scooped it up and hid it in the palm of my hand. Sure enough, his back was to the class as he scribbled frantically on the board trying to fill this heathen group of young Americans with enough knowledge to turn us all into the next generation of political movers and shakers. My God, that was a frightening thought. Surely the free world had a better pool of brain power to bank on than kids like us.

I opened the note. "So, who is Mr. Nobody and exactly how far gone are you?"

I quickly scratched back, "Great eyes, mouth made for kissing, trouble with a capitol T." Then I checked for a clear runway and flicked it back at her.

Man, now all I could think about was kissing that perfect set of lips. Shit! Thank God I didn't have to wait long before Patricia's curiosity struck home again. Now I couldn't get enough questions!

This time she was full out. "So-o-o, what gives? When are you going to see him again? By the way, love the necklace. Did you make this one too?"

I had to smile at that. So completely Patricia. She always loved my homemade body art, even though she could never wear it. We were different there, too. She was petite and all about color and patterns. Me? I was long and lean and stuck to the basics ... black, white, jewel tones and never, ever busy stuff. I just got lost in it. Not Patricia. She shined in elaborate designs brighter than a birthday cake lit with a hundred candles.

The necklace I was wearing today was a large flat chunk of rough black onyx that I'd hung on a long strap of black leather that hung almost to my waist.

I responded with, "Absolutely nothing. Absolutely never. Absolutely yes ... found it at a little resale shop on Westheimer and reworked it my way. Pretty cool, huh?"

I flicked the note back at Patricia, but she turned at that exact moment knocking the note to the floor. Of course, that was exactly when Mr. A turned to make sure we were all eager little beavers hanging on his every word.

Patricia tried to cover the evidence with her foot, but she was just a hair too slow. Even if she'd made it, her leg was twisted far enough away from her that any hope of concealment was completely out of the question.

As Mr. A reached down for the next link in my ever-growing chain of crime and punishment, he looked dead into my eyes and smiled that annoying smile of his that said exactly how pleased he was.

"My, my, my, Sydney, Patricia." His slimy gaze shifted, latching onto Patricia. "What do we have here? In-depth comments about socialist reform no doubt. Surely the rest of the class would benefit from your astute observations."

He paused to open the note, scanned it quickly, twisted his lips into a sinister grin hidden from most of the class by the tilt of his head, and cut his eyes back to me ... and my necklace. "Well, well, well. It would seem some of our students are particularly gifted at multi-tasking. Since you are so well versed on today's topic, Sydney, perhaps you'd like to paraphrase our lesson so far for those less interested in academics than you clearly are."

I stared back at him, my eyes hard and cold, my mouth tight. "Thank you very much for the offer Mr. Askew, but I think you've done such a good job of presenting the information that there really isn't any need for further clarification on my part."

His own eyes hardened at the challenge. "Very well then, Sydney. I would, however greatly appreciate you allowing me to show your fine piece of handiwork to the rest of the class. I'm sure they would love to see just what has captivated your attention, among other things. May I have it, please?" He barely tipped his head to one side, a half-smile sliding over the left side of his face.

As I hesitated, every muscle in my body tightened with anger at the extreme injustice of our unequal footing. He was the one who was constantly acting like a son of a bitch, and still, he was the one given the power to call the shots. I had to swallow back a growl as he said softly, "Now, please, Sydney." I jerked the necklace over my head and had to force my arm to extend toward him, practically throwing it into his hand, knowing even as I did so that the chances were slim to none that I'd ever see the beautiful stone again.

"Why thank you, Sydney. Something this ... lovely ... really should be allowed to be enjoyed by everyone." His wolfish half-grin returned for a moment before he turned to the other students. "Isn't it a lovely piece, class?"

I just glared at him. My fists clenched tightly. I could feel my fingernails pressing, almost cutting, into the soft tissue of my palms.

"Yeah, well, I always said she was a lovely piece, Mr. Askew, even without the sparkly little hood ornament." John Harding, quarterback for the varsity team piped in then, all his jock buds backing him up with a virtual symphony of grunts and whistles.

Mr. A chuckled under his breath. "Uh-huh. Thanks for that astute assessment, Mr. Harding. Shall I assume you haven't taken this particular model out for a test drive yet?" Mr. A glanced back down at me, clearly enjoying the direction the conversation had turned. What was the absolute fascination men had in comparing women to cars? It beat me ... unless it upped their testosterone levels by just thinking about all that oil and grit and twisted metal.

"No, sir, not for lack of effort though. But if you want to hook us up, I'd be all over it. All of her. Literally." It was John's turn to leer in my direction. He wasn't really a bad guy, just a shock jock overdosing on his own super-size ego.

103

Regardless, his band of monkeys was eating it up, the noise level in the room ratcheted upward a few decibels, overflowing with cat calls and good old boy whoops of admiration.

Pre-adult teenage boys, they just had absolutely no idea how much they sounded like a pack of hairy backed, brain dead, limp-dick Neanderthals. Yeah, and this happy little herd of soggy witted troglodytes was our hope for the future? What was I so worried about?

Right. Someone just put me out of my misery now.

But good old Johnny wasn't through just yet. "Yeah, I'm not usually into extra credit, Mr. A, but in Syd's case, I'd definitely make an exception. Hell, I'd even write a report for you, sure wouldn't be rated PG though, more like triple-X." The entire class exploded in a show of thunderous solidarity for their star QB.

What an ass. I turned my stony glare on him, but he just laughed all that much harder right into my face as he got a high five from Sam Winston, one of his tight ends.

"I heard that, my man." Sam came back laughing. "Syd's got enough going on all on her own to be an R before a word is even said. We throw you in there and the damn disc is gonna melt before they can even count the X's they'll need to rate it."

Funny how triple-X in a movie had every guy in the room salivating like Pavlov's damn dog, but the same triple-X in clothing would have them all super-gluing their zippers shut. No wonder it was so hard for most guys to read between the lines. It was because they so often thought things through with the one-eyed snake, that meant their only hope for understanding what the Sam

Hill was going on at any given time was seriously hindered by packaging.

By this point, the class had lost whatever crude resemblance it had somehow held onto that qualified it remotely as a place of learning. Now it was just a glorified locker room on a Friday night, just before the football game, minus the cleats and jock straps. Too bad Principal Shell couldn't walk by right now. Maybe Mr. Askew would finally get booted out on his slimy little ass. Nah, Mr. A'd probably just claim interference and the world would lay low for him. Boy, I hate people who can do that.

Every girl in the class started cheering as Danny Espinosa stood up and started performing his own personal, R-rated version of a touchdown dance. Hell, the guys cheered him on, too, he was that good. It was actually the very same TD boogie he used at the games. And, much as I hated to admit it, the boy definitely had some moves. I mean, come on, if you can shake your thing like that in the middle of a high school government class, just imagine the possibilities with a little good music and a little less light. Mmm, he sure did a body good.

Mr. A cleared his throat. He had a funny little look in his eyes, somehow he liked everyone getting carried away, but didn't care for not staying more at the center of attention. "Thank you, Mr. Espinosa. You may take your seat now. No doubt you'll be performing to a standing room only stadium at this Friday's game against the Wildcats."

As the class settled back down, Mr. A turned back to me for a moment. "I'll just keep this little trinket for you, Sydney. I'd hate for you to fail the test Thursday because you were distracted by it."

With that, he turned and made his way back to his desk, starting up with the ever-inspiring words of his lesson before he even reached his desk. Once there, he reached up and placed my necklace on the shelf right in between the huge claw and the branding iron. Funny, it was almost as if that spot had been waiting for it, like it belonged there. Might as well though, it was presumably the last time I'd ever lay my hands on it. Mr. A never gave anything back once he'd confiscated it. It just became his, like some sort of trophy.

Patricia touched my arm and mouthed the word, "Sorry." And she looked it, too. I just wrinkled my nose, shook my head, and sort of swatted my hand like it was no big deal. No sense in the girl stewing over things that were over and done.

"It's okay. Not your fault anyway." I breathed back, trying not to draw Mr. A's attention again. But he was making up for lost time now, writing on the chalkboard and talking as fast as the Tasmanian Devil after ten cups of java too many.

I could tell Patricia still felt bad, but tried my best to focus on the class. I really did need to do well on Thursday's test. Graduation being just around the corner didn't leave much room for stupid mistakes. And not graduating was so not an option.

It wasn't five minutes though before the bells went off for a fire drill. John and Sam slipped up on either side of me as I made my way out the door. "So, Syd. How about that extra credit? I bet I could get your mind off of losing your necklace to that shithead in no time."

"You think?" I shook my head as I glanced up at John completely unconvinced.

"Say, girl. Give my man a chance." Sam laid his arm across my shoulders as he spoke. He had a gift for making people feel at ease even as he pushed their boundaries. Never could understand quite how he did that. "He's just got a bad case of Syd fever. Have a little mercy on him, Baby. He just wants to show you a good time, that's all."

"Yeah, I'm sure that's all he wants to show me." I let my words drip with the suspicion I knew was totally valid.

"Hey, Girl. If you don't want to see what Little Johnny's got in mind for you, you just come on out with me. I'll give you a little shimmy-shake you won't ever forget." Danny glanced over his shoulder at me as his butt cheeks started to jiggle faster than should be street legal.

How the hell did he do that? I sure couldn't. I'd tried and failed, miserably. I'd immediately figured out that I looked like a tall, less curvy version of Lil Kim ... clinging to an electric fence ... in the rain. Not pretty. Pretty frightening, though. I could be a hit with the Emos, as long as they weren't too particular. If you could ignore the smell of burning tissue and hair, you were good to go.

"You need to put that thing away before you're arrested for carrying a concealed weapon, Danny." I managed to clip back.

I glanced around for Patricia. I'd expected her to be drowning me with apologies and questions and oh-my-Gods, but I didn't see her anywhere. Strange. Not typical Patricia behavior to go it alone. Maybe she'd swung by the bathroom on her way out. That was a possibility.

"Dan, shit man! Should be a sin for someone as light-colored as you to move like that. You can give a brother some serious competition." But

Sam didn't look like he felt threatened one little bit. Actually, Sam was the best dancer I'd ever seen up close and personal. And while Danny could no doubt pick up a few hundred a night in tips at the nearest male strip club, Sam could follow his feet to fame's doorstep and then blow the whole damn house down. As if to prove my point Sam jumped past me and started puttin' his moves on right there in the grass beside Danny. A cappella.

Could you call dancing without music a cappella? There should be a word for it, like there was for singing without music. Damn, I would have paid the price of my necklace just to watch Sam move like that. The way his body swung to his own rhythm, the sunlight sparkling down on him in patches through the old oak tree, the warm breeze easing its way around us was unexpectedly, mesmerizingly sensual. He held all of us in the palm of his hand, spellbound by the sway of his hips, the promise of his torment.

Shit! Was it hot out here, or was it just my stupid libido working overtime? Man, I wished the sprinklers would come on right now! If somebody didn't make him stop, we really would have a fire on our hands.

"Hey, Syd!" Patricia bounced up beside me, literally, grabbing my arm. "Here, take it." She pulled something out of her purse and quickly slipped it into my pocket before anyone else could see. Her unusually tired eyes had regained a little of their normal sparkle.

As I reached inside, I felt the cool touch of the onyx brush across the backs of my fingers and the rough leather cord slip around my thumb.

"Shit!" I groaned under my breath. "What the hell did you do, Patricia?" The whys and the wherefores were completely and absolutely irrelevant though. I had to get this back onto that damn shelf before the shit really hit the fan.

8 THE SUFFOCATING STICKINESS OF WALKING THE SPIDER WEB

Think, Syd. Figure this out now. How the hell was I going to keep Patricia's toes from roasting over this one?

"Well, I felt bad that you lost your necklace to Mr. A because of my stupidity. So, I waited until everyone was out, acted like I'd left my purse and went back in to get it. Oh, my God, Syd. That's the first time I've ever broken the rules. It felt so good! Now I have some tiny idea how you feel when you do the things you do. We need to go celebrate! Café Annie's this afternoon, my treat." Cafe Annie's had the best coffee around, and Robert Del Grande, the chef, was the greatest.

Still. "Are you fucking nuts, Patricia? I mean, thanks. But we have to put this back before Mr. A finds out it's missing or things are really gonna turn to shit fast." I was glancing around as I spoke quietly, hoping everyone was still as absorbed in Sam's dance as I'd been five seconds ago.

Seemed like it. John and Danny and about half a dozen other kids had even joined in, each somehow moving to the same rhythm. It was beginning to look like some sort of beautiful pagan ritual, but even as that thought slipped through, more girls joined in, bringing it back down to a more earthy, high schoolish scene. Too bad. A fleeting daydream concerning a fire hose knocking down girls wearing way too-high heels in soft wet grass danced through my head and before I could stop it I had to laugh under my breath. What a sight all those stupid girls would be on their asses in the wet grass, arms and legs waving in the air.

I glanced back at Patricia. Shit. She was clearly upset now. Poor thing. The one time she'd chosen to walk on the wild side and it had backfired.

She looked up at me, almost pleading with her eyes alone. "Syd, he'll never know it was me. Please. Let me watch out for you, for once. Our whole lives, you've always done the fixing. This doesn't make up for it, but at least it's something."

"Look, Patricia. I appreciate it. I really do. But think about it for just a second. Who else would take this? No one but us. If he blames me, I probably won't graduate. Not if he has his way. But if he blames you? I'd have to hurt him. Seriously, then where would we be? Neither of us would graduate and I'd be probably be facing serious jail time. Neither are very good options."

Damn, I hated having to screw up her one stab at taking a stand. But I couldn't just let her self-implode. And she would. Patricia would never be able to deal with the long term repercussions. Even if we didn't actually get caught, her guilt alone would overwhelm her ... eventually. That was just a part of who Patricia was, and it was one of the things I liked most about her.

"Dammit. I'm sorry, Syd. I was just trying to fix it and all I did was make everything a thousand times worse." Yeah, she looked like I'd just shot her dog. Actually, she looked even more pathetic than that ... more like I'd just shot a pink fluffy bunny rabbit and was standing here blowing the smoke from the end of the gun.

I put my hand on her shoulder. "It's not that bad, Shug." But it was exactly that bad. "I'll just swing by and slip it back in his room. No problem. You just relax. Everything's gonna be fine." I squeezed her shoulder to try to strengthen the point, because God only knew I had very little hope of pulling this one off. It was a well known fact that Mr. A had not one but two sets of eyes in the back of his head.

But I'd gotten myself out of messes worse than this before. Yeah, I'd also had messes not half so bad as this blow up right in my face before, too.

"Who is that hunk of raw male sin on a stick?" Patricia's mouth was practically hanging open, her eyes glazing over. I started to turn my head following her gaze, but was stopped midway as the bells started up again ringing the all clear.

I quickly wove my way back towards Mr. A's classroom. It seemed best to try to beat everyone else back and replace the evidence before any real amount of time had passed. Hopefully, if Mr. A saw me rushing he'd just assume I had to make a bathroom run. It reminded me of that Opus book by Berkeley Breathed, the one where he sideswipes a kitty and shortens a steeple. My mom read it to me a thousand times by the time I was seven, it had been one of my favorites. I wasn't exactly mowing people down, but something close to it.

As I rounded the sidewalk to his building, last temp building on the left side of the school, I saw that the lights in the room were still off. Good sign. I bolted through the door and made a bee-line for his desk. But just as I thought I had it made, I tripped over someone's backpack and came crashing down. Dammit, it was Jackie Simon's ... she always carried the whole God damn bookstore with her wherever she went. Struggling to get back on my feet and finish the job, I could hear the muffled sounds of people working their way up the path.

Shit! I felt like I was wading through water, unable to make my body to cooperate and move any faster. I jerked the necklace out of my pocket with one hand, glancing towards the door while I threw myself behind Mr. Askew's desk, catching my body with my free hand on the shelves behind it.

And then I stopped short. Steely eyes were glued to my face, a shit-eating smile fixed in place below them. Mr. A was just standing there, leaning against the doorframe watching me.

Oh, fuck me! This was gonna be bad. Big ass bad.

Mr. A cocked his head to one side. "Just put it back on the shelf, Sydney, and sit down. We'll discuss this after class." He spoke so softly I barely made out the words, but still, I could hear the triumph in his voice. He knew he'd won. Hell, I knew he'd won.

I lifted my chin higher, refusing to back down, to lose eye contact. I'd lost enough already, I'd keep my own self-esteem thank you very much. Stupid? Hell, yes. Necessary? More than air at that moment. I set the pendant down and slowly let the cord slip through my fingers without looking away from Mr. A's narrowing eyes. He didn't like to have his threat challenged. Too bad, this wasn't my week for weak and groveling. No week was my week for weak and groveling.

Patricia entered the room at the front end of the rest of the class, just in time to see the necklace drop onto the shelf. Man. This was just getting better and better. God, please don't let her open that mouth of hers and say anything stupid. I tried to stare her down with my eyes, to tell her to just stay the hell quiet and go back to her seat.

Aloud, I spoke only to Mr. A, looking back at him with the coldness that always stole over me when I'd swallowed too much of a bad thing. "Sorry, it'll have to wait until after fourth period. I've got study hall then and with finals around the corner I can't afford to miss Ms. Snyder's class."

"We'll meet right after this class, Sydney. I just don't think graduation is really a concern for you at this point. So, I wouldn't worry your sweet little head over it."

I smiled, tight-lipped. Son of a bitch! This really couldn't get any worse.

Wrong. Patricia chose that very moment to grow a spine and start babbling out what had happened. "Mr. Askew, I took the necklace. I took it right after the fire drill started. Syd just didn't want me to get in trouble, so she was trying to put it back before I got caught."

God damn it, Patricia! For the second time in less than five minutes she'd dabbled her good-hearted little fingers in my sticky mess and managed to make it even worse. Like when you walk through a monstrous spider web ... the more you wiggle and squirm, the more you just get lost in the suffocating stickiness of the spider web.

Now, Mr. A was looking at Patricia like she was a hot Butterball turkey on Thanksgiving Day. "No." I said, louder than I'd intended. "She's simply trying to save my stupid ass before graduation. Don't let her fool you, Mr. A, Patricia doesn't have the balls for something like this."

I'd deal with Patricia's hurt pride later. Right now, the priority was getting her off that little time bomb she was so innocently teetering on. God, she looked at me like I was twisting a knife in the heart of that poor little bunny I'd shot earlier. Oh well. I could deal. Attacking Mr. A's pride was my best chance of catching him off guard enough to clear Patricia, so that's where this ship was heading. Full steam ahead. So, everything was good. In a manner of speaking anyway, because it really couldn't get any worse. Of course, the last time I'd said that it had done exactly that, gotten worse. Shit.

As I refocused on Mr. A, his face morphed before my very eyes. And for the second time in as many days, I knew a decision had been reached. And I knew as sure as death visits every man, this judgment wasn't in my favor. I felt my stomach clench in anticipation of the spoken verdict, every muscle in my body tightening on my next breath.

Mr. A kept his eyes focused on me as he spoke to Patricia, waiting, watching for any hint of a response. "Well, well, well, Patricia. It would appear that we now have a third in our merry crew, wouldn't it Sydney? I look forward to seeing you both after class." His eyes tightened at the corners, angry at my lack of response. Little did he know just how hard I'd had to fight to maintain that blank, empty stare.

For once I was thankful he could be so dense. At least Patricia hadn't been locked into position as a bargaining chip. Not yet anyway. Not if I could keep that sweet, stupid mouth of hers shut.

I slowly began to walk closer to him, letting my hands skim across my thighs softly, suggestively, with every step, rolling my hips as I moved, knowing the weight of my nearness would play to my benefit in his case. Like it or not, I was a weakness for him, and damn if I wouldn't use any leverage I had at my disposal at this moment. "You can't hold two people accountable for the same crime, Mr. Askew, this was obviously a one-man job. Even Principal Shell'll cut you off at the knees on that one. So, who're you gonna pin this on? Sweet cheeks over there or yours truly?" Good. I caught the flinch in his eyes before he covered it with practiced nonchalance. He was following right where I needed him to go.

He glanced briefly back toward Patricia, then returned his otherwise immovable stare back to me. "Fine, Sydney. Have it your way. You don't like to share, that's okay. We'll keep our quality time just between the two of us. I'm all yours. Just don't forget later that this was your choice."

"Yeah. I won't forget. I have a memory that outlives elephants, Mr. A." Okay, that was a poorly concealed threat, if you could call it concealed at all. But he totally deserved it, and worse. And I was just the idiot to serve it up to him. In spades.

"I already said fine, Sydney. Be careful not to overplay your hand. I don't concede a point easily. You should take care to remember that, and respond more ... graciously." He had tired of this particular battle and was easing past me to wrap up the last fifteen minutes of class before he was required to return us to the free world. Or, at least return everyone but me.

Patricia slowly followed him, maintaining a safe distance as she pouted her way to her desk. I had to laugh to myself, I put my ass on the line for her, and where was the thanks? Lying on the cement, bleeding its guts out. Right next to the stupid rabbit.

The monotonous drone kicked in as Mr. A finally resumed class. Who would've thought I'd actually be glad he'd gotten back down to the annoying business of teaching? Not me, that's for sure, I'd have laid odds on wanting to extend the fire drill.

Five minutes later, Patricia decided to forgive me and whispered an apology with eyes that had definitely shed more than a tear or two. Damn! I really hadn't meant for her to hurt like this. But my options had been highly limited. Thanks in no small part to Patricia herself.

Finally, a virtual eternity after we'd entered class that morning, Mr. Askew asked us to start packing up for the next period. Thank you, God.

As I shoved my binder into my backpack and dropped the pen in beside it, Patricia leaned toward me, eyes pleading for forgiveness. "I am so sorry, Syd. I know I just made everything worse. I wish so bad I could undo it all."

I tried to smile reassuringly at her as I responded. "I know you do, Shug. But it is what it is now. It'll all work out one way or another."

As the late bell rang for the next class, kids started spilling out the door. Patricia, thank God, slipped through, promising to share her notes from Ms. Snyder's class with me at lunch.

Mr. A waited for the last of the students to empty from the room before he turned to me. He tipped his chin downward, the tilt of his head causing him to look up to see into my eyes. "Well, Sydney? What's it gonna be? You seem to be dealing this hand. Do we tell everyone you're nothing but the filthy little thief we've all speculated you were this whole time? Or, do we handle this ..."

He paused. His eyes slowly ravaging my body, taking his ever-loving sweet time to pass from my head all the way down to my toes and back up again, stopping from time to time as he skidded along the curves. His nose twitched as he closed his eyes and inhaled deeply. Drinking my very scent in, taking what little he knew I wouldn't offer but couldn't keep from him. And even that hit me almost as hard as if he'd already taken something from me physically without my consent. Son of a bitch.

He continued once he'd finished his fiendishly drawn-out visual attack, "... discreetly, with afterschool ... detentions?" That hideous, sadistic smile greeted me, mocking the highly precarious situation I now found myself locked into.

Well, at least I knew which of his maniacal games we were playing now. And clearly, detention in this context had absolutely nothing to do with social discipline. No. This was altogether different. This was his specialty. This would be the ugly side of dark. The side that inspired agonizing nights filled with insomnia, regrets and silent screams, and once sleep had finally stolen its way into your head, sweat-soaked nightmares that left you exhausted and paranoid.

As I let the fear wash through me, I felt the fury ignite on its heels. The nightmare had already begun. It was standing less than three feet from me, breathing the same air I was, but didn't deserve a single breath of it.

I steeled myself and managed to bite out, "I didn't steal anything, you son of a bitch! You know that." My jaw ached from the strength with which I was clenching my teeth. But everything else, students, teachers, fire drills, homework, finals, graduation, teary best friends, bleeding bunnies, frustrating Mr. Nobodies, even saber-toothed black panthers, all took a few steps into the background.

Was my comment stupid? Hell, yes! Should I have exercised some degree of caution? Probably would have been a damn good idea. Could I have stopped myself at that moment from cursing at the extreme injustice of that moment? Not only no, but *hell* no!

Mr. A only smiled that awful, godforsaken smile even more broadly. "Do I, Sydney? Do I know that?" I watched in horror as a sneer whispered unspoken promises across his lips, while his eyes stole nauseating, filthy visions of me, memorizing them to pull out later at times he was alone in the dark. His stain slowly spread, consuming me, as if I'd already committed some unforgivable sin just by remaining in his presence a moment too long.

I felt the bile in my stomach rising, threatening to further throw my world askew. Funny that. Mr. Askew was throwing my world askew. Dammit, Syd. This was so not the time to lose it. Get a hold of yourself.

But actually the laughter helped me do exactly that. The queasiness began to dissipate, slowly being edged out by the anger that always seemed to hang just a breath away from me. At first I didn't recognize the growl as coming from me when it crashed outward from deep within my throat, my entire body vibrating, resonating from the shockwaves of the guttural snarl as it erupted around me.

"I'm out of here." I somehow managed to choke the words out without allowing the vomitous contents of my stomach to escape.

"This was your call, Sydney. You renege on our deal and all bets are off. That puts sweet, little Patricia firmly back in the game. Is that what you want, Sydney? Do we play the Patricia card? Or do we keep this a private game? Between two consenting adults?"

Son of a fucking bitch. Of course, technically I wasn't an adult. Not quite yet, but this just didn't seem like the time to get drawn into a discussion over semantics. It seemed more like a time to cut my losses, agree to whatever, and regroup later to map out a surprise coup d'état. We'd learned that in French class last week ... an attack on the state.

"So very serious, Sydney. What devious schemes are running through that wild little head of yours? Hmmm? That's alright. I'll enjoy punishing you later." Once again his gaze dropped to parts of my body that held more interest for him, before returning, slowly, menacingly, to my face. "You'll enjoy it too, Sydney, much as you might like to think otherwise. As for now, though, I've got other matters that unfortunately require my attention. So, I'm afraid I'll have to postpone the first of our little sessions until tomorrow afternoon. I know what a sacrifice that must seem to you as you are so intent on sparing your dear friend from any obligation in this negotiation. Are we in agreement then? No Patricia? Just you and me?"

I jerked my head in agreement as I moved to edge past him and out the door. My anger was so volatile it was suffocating me in its intensity.

But Mr. A was enjoying this, laughing at my discomfort. "Ah, Sydney. Thank you in advance for your irascible tenacity. It will make the joy of breaking that spirit of yours all that much sweeter. And I will break you Sydney. I'll break you to my will. You'll beg me to do it, and you'll beg me for more. So very much more."

I couldn't take another second in his vicinity without hurling, so I pushed past him, ran down the steps two at a time, and slammed through the doors of the main building, gulping down the hot, sweat-soaked air that filled the non-air conditioned hallways.

9 GETTING TO KNOW YOU

As I barreled down the hall toward the girls' bathroom, the urge to continue down the hall and out the main doors nearly overwhelmed me, almost strangling me with its intensity. I dove headfirst into the bathroom, glad no one had been coming out just then or both of us would have had a severe concussion for the next day or two.

Making a bee-line for the sink, I started splashing water up onto my face, intentionally letting it run down my arms. Anything, absolutely anything to wrap my senses, my focus around was a good thing.

After a few minutes of practically bathing in the sink, I felt just a scosche better. Funny how all my body parts were still hanging on in all the right places. I felt so out of whack, I'd have laid even money on looking more like one of Picasso's renditions than anything resembling a real girl. Like maybe my left boob was stuck on the middle of my face and my nose was peeking out from my right armpit. As it was, I hardly recognized the cold, blank eyes staring back at me, boring a hole into my raw, bleeding soul. There was nothing visible of what I always saw looking back at me out of Patricia's eyes.

I liked how I looked in the reflection of Patricia's eyes. She made me feel like I was all the better for my stupid convictions and petty ideals. She was the only one aside from my parents who'd ever looked at me that way.

The teachers saw me as trouble. Queens and Jacks saw me as a responsibility, and a liability most of the time. The guys all saw me as a darkly cool, strong-willed challenge. And most of the girls saw me as too dark and strong-willed to be cool. Too close to exactly what their parents warned them not to be to ever get close enough to know me past my name, hair color and lack of fashion sense.

But Patricia saw me for me. And she liked what she saw. Lucky me. Patricia was the glue that held my sanity together. Somehow her light made my dark okay. She didn't try to chase the darkness away either, and I didn't try to diminish her light. She just let me be in my shadowed world and I simply let her shine. And it worked. It worked for both of us. Light always seems brightest in the dark and the dark always seems deepest when you can see the edges of the abyss. That was Patricia and me in a nutshell. We brought out something special in each other that would otherwise be lost.

I wasn't about to screw that up and risk her sanity, her untarnished essence by handing her over lock, stock and barrel, into the hands of some slime ball like Mr. A-fucking-skew. No way. No how. Not today, not ever. I would do anything, absolutely anything, to keep that from ever even coming up for discussion.

I stared into the mirror and took a few deep breaths to steady myself before I backed away from the wall of sinks and moved for the door.

But before I could force myself to push back through the door into the reality outside, I stopped for one last, steadying breath. Then I lifted my chin, threw my shoulders back, adjusted my backpack and shoved my way into the hall, feeling as if my reentry should pack all the heat of a NASA space capsule attempting to reestablish its position within the Earth's atmosphere.

Suddenly I found myself barreling straight into the arms of one very well-positioned, Mr. Nobody. Or maybe that actually meant he was very poorly-positioned since I'd plowed right into him. Or maybe it just depended on which body part did the plowing and interpreting. Your head, your heart, or your ... negotiables. But as the heat from his strong hands on my arms penetrated the thick haze of my mental fog, I felt my mind begin to slow down and the frantic, seething rage consuming my entire existence take a hesitant step down. Unfortunately, my level of emotional unrest didn't ease one little bit. Because, all that anger just began bleeding into the same whirl of frustrated, sexually-charged, frightened angst I'd been drowning in last night and which had been clawing at the edges of my consciousness ever since.

"What the hell are you doing here?" I spluttered. Staring at those gorgeous lips simply because I couldn't seem to lift my head past them to what I already knew were the most beautiful pair of eyes I'd ever seen in my life. The very eyes that pulled me miles inside them without even being aware of it. The kind of eyes you needed a passport to fall into because they served as a portal to other worlds, spoke a language all their own, and demanded payment in pieces of your soul. Like a moth drawn to a flame, my eyes slowly climbed up Beau's cheeks and across his nose, finally resting on the doorways to places I had yet to see.

"Well, hello to you, too, Syd. How nice to see you again. It's called the old meet and greet. See how it works? Nothing too complicated, I'm sure you can get the hang of it." He was laughing at me, only without the laughing. Usually I hated that, but this time it was oddly comforting. Why wasn't this bothering me more?

I answered in the most monotone voice I could muster as I extricated myself from his arms. "Hello back. NITSY2, that's 'nice to see you too' in text talk. Thanks, I think, for somehow managing to ground me." My lips twisted into a sardonic smile at the end of my minimalistic soliloquy.

To which, Mr. Perfectly Wonderful smiled with his entire face and out-shone the sun as effortlessly as ice cream melts on a hot summer day. "Touché, Syd. Touché."

"Again with the touchy crap. What is it with you and that? I am so not a touchy, feely kind 'a girl." I was feeling a little more like I was in the land of the living now that I'd regained my own space. "You still haven't answered me, though. What on earth are you doing here? Somehow I just don't think you're taking Home Ec." I dug into my pocket and pulled out an Atomic Fireball. "Want one?" I asked as I squeezed the wrapper, forcing the candy out the opposite end.

"Sure." I reached back in pulling out two more and handed them both over. Beau dropped one in the pocket of his trench coat and popped the other one out of the wrapper straight into his mouth. "What if I just came to keep an eye on you? You do seem to make a habit of getting yourself in over your head." Okay. Not funny. He was laughing at me, again.

I was still smiling, but there was a bite to my words. "Alright, first off, we both know damn well you're not here because of little old me. And second, how the hell would you know that? You hardly know me. The only things you've seen me struggling with in the deep end concerned you and yours, smart-ass."

Beau just laughed softly as he looked down at me with a mix of emotions playing across his face. I could make out the blend of humor and exasperation, but there were hints of other things I couldn't quite place. Worry? Anticipation? Impatience? Maybe. And, still, something else. "You seem to have no end to the names you come up with to call me in any given circumstance, Syd. Is that a natural talent or just well-practiced satire to avoid feeling too vulnerable?"

"Answer my question and I'll think about answering yours. Nothing's free anymore, or hadn't you heard? We're in the middle of a global recession." Good thing I'd paid attention here and there with Mr. A. Who would've thought it would be required reading for boy drama?

"Let's see here. If I answer your question, you'll think about answering mine? Mm-mm, that's just too easy, Syd. No deal. I don't do the short end of the stick. Ever. Global recession or no." He was still smiling down at me, but there was a glimmer of serious peeking back at me from the edges of his face.

I shrugged my shoulders, trying hard for nonchalance. "It's really more of a bat than a stupid little stick. I could just come out swinging. How do you feel about coed sports?" I could play this game of responding without answering. Hell, I wrote the book on it. "Come on out and play, Beau. Or, do you need to ask someone's permission first?" Okay. Maybe not my best effort at subtle, but at least I stood a chance of finding out if there was indeed a Mrs. Nobody waiting in the dugout.

But Beau was no beginner to this game either. "I've always bounced between shortstop and left field, so you can start swinging anytime you feel the urge, Syd. As for a girlfriend, I just haven't had the time, or the interest. And if you have any more questions about my personal life, it would be a whole lot easier if you just asked." Shit. So much for me stretching my subtle muscles. They had probably completely shriveled up from lack of use.

"Fine. I don't care why you're here. It's none of my business anyway." Just a little bit sulky sounding? Yes, just a little bit. I didn't do the short end of the stick as a rule, either. Even when you were the one doing the swinging, your hands usually came up bloody. Being too close to the action could do that.

I forced myself to turn away from him. "I have to go. Stimulating as this has been, I need to get to class. And you, you probably have some hearts to break somewhere. So, see ya."

One eyebrow raised and his eyes darkened a fraction. "Come on, Syd. Just take it as it comes." He winked at me, throwing my heart off a couple of beats, and continued talking. Thank God he seemed completely oblivious to the effect he was having on me. "Why don't you show me around your school? Class is more than half over and you haven't made it there yet. Besides, I'm sure there's at least one friendly body in the class that'll give you a rundown on any need-to-knows you might have missed." He took my arm, turning me in the opposite direction from where I'd begun to head. "Come on. We can start by grabbing a cup 'a Joe in the teacher's lounge."

Who was this guy? How could he turn my world upside down so fast? Of course, my world was always upside down. Maybe his upside down was actually my right-side up? Ouch. My head was doing somersaults now. Seriously though, how could someone follow even fewer rules than me?

As we were heading down the hall to the teacher's lounge, I finally found my voice again. "Look, I'd love to be your little hostess-slash-tour-guide, but this isn't a coffee shop. It's a school. My school. One I have every intention of graduating from in twenty-four days. So, I'm afraid mid-morning coffee breaks and romantic strolls through the stinky halls are out." I started to pull away from him.

He let my arm slide free of his hand, but still tried to convince me to redirect. "A little trust, Syd. You have to live the moment as it's meant to be lived."

"Yeah? And just let me guess. In this moment I'm supposed to wait on you hand and foot and take you wherever your heart desires." I let sarcasm dress the words heavily as I looked up at him with eyes twinkling with mischief.

"Mmm. Maybe not wherever my heart desires, but if we limit it to the confines of the school, basically. Yes. As for the hand and foot? Hmm ... body parts. Girl body parts. Yeah, that pretty much works for me. I'm a guy, I'm easy." Still laughing, his eyes darkened suddenly, taking on a more serious glint. "You really shouldn't fight fate, Syd, it tends to tempt darker things."

What the hell was he talking about now? I was about to ask him exactly that, but just then Principal Shell stepped out from the back entrance into the main suite of offices and into the hall. "I'm sorry I had to keep you waiting so long Rémy. Some days just never seem to slow down around here. Ah, Sydney. I see you've met Mr. St. Claire. He wants to take a look around Belmont and get a feel for how we do things here. He's doing some research on inner city schools for a book he's writing."

Hmm. That was interesting. Well, you couldn't get much more inner city than Belmont High, that was for sure.

Ms. Henderson, the main secretary, poked her head out the door, sweeping the hall for Principal Shell, clearly relieved when her eyes caught sight of him. "Charles. Thank goodness you haven't started with Mr. St. Claire yet. The superintendent is on line two and Manuel Rodriguez is in your office. Mr. Salazar had a surprise locker inspection and found smoke bombs again." Ms. Henderson's gaze shifted to me accusingly for a moment. "Apparently, Manuel wasn't too excited about a history test he's supposed to take during third period today so he thought he'd liven things up a bit." Under her breath she added for my ears alone, "Any idea where he came up with that plan, Syd?"

"Damn. I'm afraid I'm going to have to excuse myself once again, Rémy. Or maybe we should just try this again tomorrow? Unless ... Sydney, would you mind showing Rémy around? I'll have Ms. Henderson give you a pass for your classes. Would you mind Rémy?"

"No, not at all. I'm sure Sydney can show me everything I need to see." Mr. Shell clearly had never been seventeen. The double meaning was completely lost on him. Ten-to-one he'd walked out of the womb twenty-two years old clutching a brand spanking new college degree in his hand. The tassels on his cap and gown must have tickled dear old Mom on his way out the door. I started to laugh and had to cover it with a muddled cough.

"You alright, Syd?" Principal Shell put his hand on my shoulder and looked down at me quizzically.

I made good use of my eyelashes as a veil, keeping my eyes down and nodded, my hand still covering my mouth. "Yes, sir. I'm fine. Just swallowed some air down the wrong pipe, that's all."

"Okay. Well, take as much time as Rémy needs. This is good ... you wanted to see how things really work around here, how better than from the horse's mouth? Eh, Rémy?" Great. I was being compared to livestock. Not usually a good thing. "And Sydney's a great girl, all the kids look up to her." Better. Not exactly how I saw things, but it beat qualifying for the Kentucky Derby in a four-legged capacity any day.

"She'll be a wealth of information." Mr. Shell was laying it on thick. A good dose of guilt can do that. "Why don't you leave your coat in my office? When you're through, swing back by for it and hopefully I'll have some time to answer any questions you might have." As Beau slipped off his trench coat, Mr. Shell turned to me. "Sydney, be sure to swing by the teacher's lounge before you start and grab whatever Rémy would like ... coffee, water, a coke. Don't forget to see Ms. Henderson afterwards to pick up that pass."

"Yes, sir. I'll be sure to do that." I glanced up at Beau. How the hell had he managed this. Because I had the distinct feeling he'd orchestrated this whole thing. It was too perfect. Down to the God damn coffee, no less. But if he'd done it, he wasn't letting on. There wasn't a glimmer of trickery or guilt on his face.

I suddenly had the feeling there was an entire ocean more to Mr. St. Claire than I'd given him credit for. And, he was either really, really good, or really, really bad. My gut feeling was good, but I also had been struggling with the feeling that something big was looming up on the horizon. And not just prom, graduation, birthday and moving. Something else, something harder. Not necessarily bad, but not as sweet and definitely not nearly so easy to swallow.

Oh, well. Plenty of time to stew over that later. Right now, Beau had started towards the teachers' lounge again. Funny how he seemed to know right where it was all on his own. I had missed that earlier. My bad. I usually noticed shit like that. Time to focus, Syd.

"You seem awfully deep in thought. Care to swim to the surface for a bit? Just for a little breather, then you can dive back down." He kept his focus forward, giving me a little elbow room with my brain chock-full of thoughts.

"Yeah. Sorry. How did you do that?" My eyes slid sideways to his face accusingly then shot back to the utterly engaging worn laminate floor in front of me.

His face remained calm, not a whisper of self-reproach. "This place is surprisingly ... comfortable. You must have enjoyed your time here."

"This is it." I said as we approached the lounge. He pulled open the door, letting me enter ahead of him. As if he needed my lead.

"It's amazing what you can manage to live with when you have an ounce or two of motivation. Most people just can't seem to find enough of a reason to stick with anything, or anyone, for that matter. Guess that's why we seem to live in a disposable society these days." I stopped by the coffee setup, poured him a cup and motioned for him to add whatever incidentals he wanted.

"Please, continue. Where does the drive fit in?" He looked up at me as he added a little sugar, no cream, and stirred it around a little. Just how I took it. Interesting.

"Well, the motivation to maintain a relationship requires a desire to constantly dive deeper into one another. But that's been replaced with a drive for something that requires less effort, less substance, fast food dating, so to speak."

He'd tossed the stir stick into the garbage, rolling up the sleeves of his shirt as he turned to face me. It kind of surprised me that he seemed so interested in my take on life. Was he just really good at faking it, or could he actually be for real? I continued, hoping he was. "It applies across the board, though. Parents running away from home at middle age, kids calling it quits at fifteen, best friends on the outs because the wind changed direction, divorce, you name it. It all falls under the umbrella of relationship roulette."

I glanced around the room and suddenly realized several of the teachers were staring at me like I'd just landed from Mars.

I forced out a little laugh as I turned and headed for the door and the eternal fresh air in our hot, humid hallways. "Huh. I'm ranting. Sorry about that. Sore subject with me, I guess."

The door to the hall opened right in front of us as Ms. Pederson, the choir teacher, nearly dove into the room. Clearly she'd missed her first cup, or twelve, of coffee for the day.

"Morning, Sydney." I couldn't help but notice the trace of melancholy that shadowed her voice.

"Morning, Ms. P." I backed up to the wall, clearing the most direct line of attack for her to molest the coffee pot. God have mercy on us all if someone so much as breathed too hard in her direction before she sucked down a keg or two.

I tried to suppress a smile as she poured a couple sips of java into her cup and stopped to gulp them down, steam and all, before filling her cup to the brim. Then I stepped back out into the hall, Beau following close behind. "If the relationship's worth pursuing at all, whoever it's with, sinner or saint, then it should be worth giving a hundred percent. On both sides ... never just fifty-fifty. Anything less is just a ship waiting for an iceberg to put it out of its misery. An utter waste of time. And self. And ice, for that matter." I swallowed back a sardonic little chuckle.

Beau was holding his coffee cup with two hands and looking at me over the rim, steam blurring the space between us, haunting the footsteps just behind us. "Well said. But does that mean that you think all relationships should last forever simply by default?"

We made the bend at the end of the hall. "The science labs line this hall. Chemistry on the left, Physics and Biology on the right." I motioned toward them as I spoke.

"Absolutely not. Some people are meant to be permanent fixtures in our lives, leaving indelible marks on our soul, others are meant to be more short-term, transient, kind of like temporary tattoos." I couldn't help but smile at that ironic comparison, because it seemed like some of the most doomed relationships I'd ever seen were the very ones immortalized by permanently stamping one another's names on the other's body, like a misplaced brand. Bet they wish they'd used a peel and stick tattoo instead! "But either way, those ties will strengthen or sever without any help from us hacking away at them."

"Strengthen or sever without any help from us?" Beau looked at me skeptically out of the corner of his eye, that half tilt to his lips making me catch my breath. I dropped my eyelids immediately, refocusing on those glorious, utterly amazing, dingy old floor tiles again as his questions continued. "Does that mean you think relationships don't require any effort? That they live, breathe and die all by themselves? That we have no part in their survival, much less in their growth or direction?" He held the door to the stairwell open for me as I gestured to the case of trophies running along the wall and moved toward it.

"You're just a guy. Why are you so interested in the mechanics of love and fidelity? I thought the whole concept of commitment was taboo for ya'll. A word that should be removed from the English language. I think I even saw a petition go through my e-mail last year about that very thing." I smiled mockingly back up at him for a second before I dragged my gaze away again. I had to limit my daily intake of Mr. St. Claire. Especially up close and personal.

A mumbled half-grunt, half-laugh slipped from his throat before he tried to answer me. "Just a guy. Nice to know you have such a high opinion of my sub-standard species. I guess I should just go ahead and suck the slime off the bottom of the tank while I'm down here with the rest of the bottom-feeders?"

"Mmm. That's not a bad idea, actually. Hope you brought your toothbrush." I knew I should be more uptight around him, but damn, it was just so easy to relax into his space. Somehow, the air was fuller, more breathable when he was near. How was that even possible?

Simple. It couldn't be.

Now I was getting uptight again. Good, that was my comfort zone. Only now that I'd felt what being relaxed was like, my cozy little blankie called "hot-and-bothered" just didn't feel quite so cozy all of a sudden. Like someone had come along with one of those sweater shavers and buzzed all the soft, fuzzy spots off of it leaving it thin and a little threadbare.

"I think I'm supposed to be answering questions and showing you around." I tried to get this little train wreck of ours back on track.

But Beau wasn't going to help. "You are answering questions and showing me around."

"Somehow I don't think Principal Shell would be giving you the same highlights we're hitting."

"Yeah. You just have to love bureaucratic superintendents and smoke bombs. Especially when they both threaten to detonate at the same time." Beau's warm breath teased along my neck as he bent his head toward mine and laughed. And somehow it felt much more intimate than it should.

"That reminds me. The whole coffee girl slash tour guide thing. How did you manage to pull that off? Are you some kind of magician? Or do you just have secret mind-control powers?" Farfetched, but I was hoping to catch him off guard just enough to let something, anything slip.

No such luck. Of course. Mr. Steel Mouth, that should be his new name. I guess I did seem to reinvent his name every time the wind changed direction. Good thing we didn't live in Chicago.

Beau looked at me with eyes that were meant to be teasing, but had the dark lights of something much more serious flickering through them. "Come on, Syd, you're supposed to be paying attention here." His mouth twisted into an upside-down smile and took my heart along for the ride. "Hasn't this morning shown you anything?" He turned those dark eyes of his on me for a few heartbeats and held me within them more tightly than if I'd been gagged and bound. "Fate has a curious way of looking after itself. Fighting your own destiny? That, I'm afraid, is not only a complete and absolute waste of time, but it also creates more of the very thing you're fighting."

My lips tightened and I tried not to think too much about what he was saying. I liked choice. Freedom. And besides, this was beginning to sound just a little too preachy for my tastes. "Yeah, well, I'm not sure I'm ready to swallow that hook, line and sinker just yet, especially with my life serving as bait. Actually, I know I'm not." I glanced around, having lost track of where we were heading. And I had to smile. Score fate a big fat juicy one after all. "This is the cafeteria. You know, where everyone swallows whatever slop is dished up on their plates." I smiled sarcastically at the newly appointed defender of my destiny, enjoying the moment intensely. It was made all the better with the muted sounds of Pink's new song drifting from the cavernous kitchen.

And he just smiled down at me. Not a hint of anger or even impatience. "That's fine, Syd. I'm not asking for a commitment here." He smiled just a little too innocently at me as he said that. "All you have to do is pay attention. The rest will take care of itself." He moved toward the glass doors along the back wall.

"How!" It should have been a question, but the word practically exploded from my mouth. I'm not sure who was more surprised by it ... Mr. Wonderful or yours truly. Of course, Mr. Jackson, who'd been mop-dancing the floors a few yards from us jumped, too. I turned to him, "Sorry, Mr. Jackson. Didn't mean to ruin your tango."

"Not to worry, Syd. Everything's jus' fine. Ya'll have a good one now, you hear?" He'd already started pushing his partner around the floor again, eyes at half mast. Wonder who he was really dancing with ... the lady whose name was permanently tattooed on his arm (the love of his life) or just an imaginary someone or a fling, a peel and stick tat? Nice when you got to lead though, hands down.

I turned back to Beau who was watching me, as usual. "How, exactly does everything take care of itself? Because, let me tell you, my life hasn't exactly been a sweet little Sunday afternoon hayride through the park. And I guarantee I've paid attention to every single pile of shit I've had to shovel." My eyes rolled back to the big glass doors and suddenly I couldn't stand being inside another second.

Beau simply followed me out, but not right on top of me. I liked how he knew when to give me a little breathing space. He spoke quietly after we'd reached the trees on the opposite side of the courtyard. "Maybe you just haven't paid attention to the right things."

"Well, unless I'm going to pay attention to someone else's life, the things in my life are all there is to see. It's not like I have a choice about them. They just are what they are. And no amount of wishing is gonna change a single one of them." I half sat against the nearest table, trying not to fixate like a driveling idiot on just how well he filled out those jeans he was wearing. Or how the fabric of his T-shirt pulled across his chest under the open, button-down shirt he was wearing, the muscles of his arms extending well past the half-rolled-up sleeves. God, why couldn't I manage to keep my head straight? I'd never had such a hard time staying focused.

He spoke as if he'd read my mind. "Just breathe, Syd. And let it be. It's all good. Stop trying to control the day and just live it."

"Yeah. Carpe diem, Baby." I joked back at him, it was something my dad had always said ... every blessed day. Latin for "seize the day". It had been his own personal mantra, as if he'd known his days were numbered and didn't want to waste a single one of them. "Carpe diem."

"Come on." I rose from my wobbly little roost and started walking towards the area behind the main buildings. "The game fields and jogging track are down this way. We'll catch the tennis courts and the swimming pool on the flip side as we head back in."

We walked in silence until we padded out onto the grassy edge of the football field.

Finally, the quiet seemed to part for Beau's words as readily as the Red Sea had for Moses so long ago. As if it were as hungry for his voice as I was quickly becoming. A voice that had the uncanny ability to soothe my blistered nerves even as it awakened my senses. "The Carters seem okay. They really care about you, that much is obvious. You must have been with them quite a while now."

"Why? Is there a black furry "C" running down my back that I can't see?" I spun around as I asked, like a dog chasing after its own tail.

"Uh. Yeah, that's real attractive, Syd. You should remember that move for your wedding night. I've never seen someone so uncomfortable with acknowledging the fact that their parents love them."

"Mmmm, well. They're not my parents now, are they? And, I don't plan on ever getting married." I stopped as it finally occurred to me that I'd never spoken about Queens and Jacks to Mr. Too Perfect for Words. Shit! I was really slow today. I frowned back up at him. "And you seem to know a hell of a lot about me when you just blipped onto my radar last night. Care to explain?"

"No. Not really. Not just yet anyway. As for your foster parents, you might not see them as family, but they definitely see you as their daughter. As for the aspirations of growing up to be an old crone? Well, yeah, we'll see about that one ... good luck with it though ... it sounds very ... fulfilling." Beau couldn't resist adding with a smirk. "Maybe you should start scouting up stray cats when you see them, just in case. And what's the 'C' for ... Carter or caring?"

I shrugged my shoulders as I bit out, "Both. Neither. Maybe it's for carpe diem." I turned abruptly, ready to hightail it out of there.

"Why?" He asked falling in step beside me. I struggled to keep my eyes straight ahead of me. His eyes, though, were focused entirely on me ... tempting me, luring me to fall into the seductive trap of gazing back into them, losing myself in them. No way. Not this girl. Not today. And definitely not here. "Still hacking away at your destiny, Syd?" His right eyebrow lifted, tugging on the corner of his mouth, as he replied. I felt my fingers twitch in response, with a strange desire to reach up and touch that sinful mouth, those lips that were just a hair too full to belong to a man.

Focus, dammit, Syd! I upped my pace a little to try to outrun the desires pulling at me. Come on, Syd. You can do better than this. Just kick him out of that stupid head of yours. There's not room for him in there. Or anyone else for that matter. I could hang a "No Vacancy" sign on my butt. Maybe that would help.

Smiling once again, I risked a quick glance up at him. "No, Mr. Comedian. But I do make it a rule to head out whenever the conversation deteriorates to the point of no return. It's a good rule, serves me well."

He laughed at that, the sound tickling down my back, coming to rest at the bottom of my spine. "Well, don't let me stop you."

I grunted under my breath. One of my more feminine habits. Right, just about as feminine as hocking a loogie. But I'd save that little gem until I got really desperate.

"But ... you haven't shown me the pool or the tennis courts, and Charles did offer you up on a stick for as long as I wanted." He had a devilish smirk on his face as he repeated the principal's well-meant instructions. "He likes me, or at least he likes the idea of my using his school for inspiration in a book. Either way, we wouldn't want him to think you'd disappointed me. He just might hold that against you. And I sure wouldn't want that on my conscience." He looked at me with a face chock-full of sappy, counterfeit concern.

"Whatever you're selling, Mr. St. Claire, I'm not buying. And I'll tell them to hold your Oscar at the Will Call desk ... you deserve one after this morning's performance. Because, I know you're not writing any damn book. And I know you already know more than you probably ever should about this school, and me for that matter." I waved my hand to the side without slowing down or shifting my gaze a fraction of an inch from dead ahead. "There are the tennis courts. Exactly where you knew they'd be." You had to love a sport that scored in terms of love. Beat the hell out of keeping track of hits and tackles. Then again, maybe that just depended on how you took your love, with or without all the cream and sugar.

"Does it help, Syd?" His question caught me off guard. Which I should be getting used to around him. Everything about Jean-Rémy Beauchamps St. Claire seemed to catch me off guard. Still, it wasn't a comfortable feeling for me. Not many people in my life had managed to do it once, much less make a God damn habit of it.

All I knew was that it had to stop. It had to stop this minute. But with a sinking feeling I knew there wasn't a force on earth that would be able to make it stop.

Oh, Shit. It was becoming strikingly obvious that I was definitely in over my head here. Would I ever see the light of day the same way?

Would I ever even want to?

10 THE ICKY TOUCHY, FEELY STUFF

I had stopped walking just short of the natatorium, just a fancy word for pool building but that's what we called it here at Belmont. Still, a pool by any other name would smell ... just as much like chlorine and wet towels, unfortunately. Thank you, Master William Shakespeare. Gotta love Romeo and Juliet. He was right about the whole one-name-is-just-as-good-as-another thing. But I still didn't get it. Natatorium. Pool. Natatorium. Pool. Whatever.

I waved my arm to the left. "Pool." I announced. Sue me, natatorium sounded too much like someone was gonna be birthin' babies in there. And, let me assure you, I don't know nothin' 'bout birthin' no babies! And I intended to keep it that way for a long, long, long, long, long, long time. Thank you, Margaret Mitchell.

Gone With the Wind was practically required viewing, if not required reading, here in the South. There was even a nasty rumor that if you couldn't recite at least three quotes from it off the top of your head upon demand, you would be shipped off to New Jersey, lock, stock and barrel. Do not pass Go. Do not collect two hundred dollars. Do not stop for Tex-Mex before you cross the border. New Jersey? I wonder how Pace Picante Sauce would taste on a Philly cheesesteak? Ugh. Painful thought.

"You haven't answered me." Beau spoke quietly.

I spun around on him. "Does what help? And what exactly is it supposed to be helping?" A low growl escaped my lips, totally without my permission, which just added to my frustration. "What in God's name are you talking about this time anyway?" I demanded, staring straight into those hellaciously gorgeous eyes, feeling my stomach tighten even as my bones began to melt.

He smooshed his lips outward, then cracked that dangerous half-smile. "The anger, Syd. Does it help? Does it help mask the fear, the raw emotion?" He looked at me questioningly, as if he were really interested in the answer. But I could also see the answers sitting right there beside the questions in those dark, mysterious eyes, the answers I didn't want to know. The truths I wasn't ready to accept.

"Damn you to hell and back! God, I hate you. I wish ... I wish you'd just ... disappear. And take every memory of you with you on your way out!" But my voice had lost its own edge of truth by the end, and lacked the conviction I was so desperately counting on.

Those damn eyes of his were peeling back the thick layers of insulation I kept around my heart, around my very soul, as easily as if they were a giant snowplow pushing a deep mound of marshmallows to the side of the road. Dammit!

Somehow he saw through my walls of self-defense that had taken a lifetime to construct, past all the false bravado to the truth deep inside me. Eyes darkening dangerously, his voice hinted of cold, quiet steel as he spoke softly. "Do you, Syd? Do you want me to disappear? Is that really how you feel? Tell me to leave and this will be goodbye. But say it right here, right now, if that's what you're wanting."

All of a sudden, I couldn't speak. For the first time in my life, I was absolutely, positively speechless. Inside, I was screaming, "No! Anything but that. Anything but never being able to see your face, hear your voice, feel your breath, know you exist on the face of this earth ... with me." But my mouth couldn't form the words aloud. My head was far too busy being angry, hurt and independent. So, all I could do was stand there staring at him. Like a stupid, weak, mute little rabbit caught in the headlights of an eighteen wheeler in the middle of the night on a dark country road. Messy.

Beau reached forward and grabbed my arms just above the elbows. "Dammit, answer me, Syd! What do you want?" He jerked on my arms, not quite shaking me, but giving me a good hard wrench.

"I ... I don't know ..." I stammered out, lost in his eyes, in the potent, commanding grip of his intensity. I felt like the damn eighteen wheeler had slammed into me and flipped me in the air.

"No. Not now, Syd. You know what you want. I can see it. I know you feel it. We both know you do. Say it, God dammit! Just say it. Now! Or I walk away." He jerked on my arms again. He wasn't trying to hurt me, or scare me. He was just reeling me back in from wherever the hell I'd floated off to. Some sort of Never-hell that stood between my unfulfilling but comfortably familiar life and a frightening expanse of unknown that whispered promises of desires fulfilled and terrors confronted. Terrors confronted and overcome? Or confronted and defeated by? I couldn't tell. I only knew they'd be there, waiting for me. And only one of us would walk away at the end of the day. I didn't want to face this. Not today. Not here. Not standing in his arms. I just wanted to ... to what? Even I couldn't finish it now. Maybe I just wanted not to think right at this moment. Was that so bad? Hell, no! I didn't owe him anything. I'd just met him for Christ's sake.

"Why! You tell me why I have to answer. Why now? Why, Beau, Rémy, whoever you are? Why?" I was a breath away from tears.

But he was through talking it over. "Three, two, one." I just blinked up at him, hearing the words, but not understanding the implications. Then his hands slid away from me. "See you in the funny papers." His face was expressionless as he turned away from me and started for the double doors to the main building, roughly pushing them open.

Every cell in my body screamed out! I ran through the doors before they swung closed behind him. "No!" I cried in anguish, my voice breaking on the word. The thought of never seeing him again hitting me head-on like that fucking eighteen wheeler had pulled a U-y, you know, a u-turn, to make sure I was good and proper road kill. He stopped walking away but didn't turn to face me. "Don't go." I managed to choke out. I couldn't let him walk away. Away from me. Out of my life, forever. Because, I knew in my bones, this would be a forever kind of thing. No doubt about it.

Okay. So, damn the repercussions ... I'd face those when they came. Not today. Not in this moment. In this moment I would bring my fears to their knees through words, not superior fire power. Not superior fire power yet, anyway. "I want ..."

Shit! The bell for third period cut me off at the pass. But now, for some reason, I wanted to finish what I had to say. I had a sinking feeling the words would burn their way out of me if I didn't. Hell, I'd already resigned myself to saying it. Not saying it would bother me more than the pain of holding it inside any longer.

I took a breath, hoping for deep, but settling for rough and raspy. Then blinked once before I let the words crawl out of my mouth. "I want you around. I want you near. I want you not to go." My voice was tight with emotion. With desperation.

He still hadn't so much as moved a muscle. The sounds of doors opening and closing, hallways filling with warm, restless bodies, began to fill the air.

Why wasn't he moving? Did he need more than that? Fine! Dammit, what an asshole! "Please. Beau. I'm sorry, I didn't mean it." Still no movement from Mr. Pain-in-the-Royal-Ass. "You were right. I hide behind my anger." I was staring so hard at my feet that I thought for sure I'd find blisters on my toes when I took my tennis shoes off later. "Please. Don't go."

Risking one fraction of a glance up I found him facing me, his eyes firmly assessing my response. A single tear spilled out, staining my cheek. I looked back down in shame. And anger. Anger was always easier for me. And I started to turn away myself. I damn sure wasn't going to cry like a blubbering, dim-witted, sappy little idiot right here in front of him. Surrounded by people I knew. People I had to face every day.

But all of a sudden Beau was right there in front of me. He was all around me. Pulling me into his arms. Then pulling me quickly back outside, away from the encroaching audience. I dimly realized that it would have looked totally romantic to everyone around us, as if this tall, gorgeous man was completely unable to keep himself from pulling me to him, even in the middle of a high school hallway at rush hour. Nothing like what it really was at all ... my absurd, hideously-timed personal meltdown.

Beau crushed my body against him, keeping one arm locked around my waist and stroking my hair with his other hand as another traitorous tear slipped out, quickly followed by a third. Shit, shit, shit! I was really starting to lose it. And the more strength I felt in his hold on me, the more my guard fell. And with it, the more tears that fell. I was afraid pretty soon the flood gates were going to bust open, not my idea of a good time. What the Sam Hill had I gotten myself into this time?

But as if he knew how uncomfortable I felt with the whole water works thing, Beau quickly wiped them away with his thumb. "It's okay, Syd." He spoke so softly I could barely hear him. His eyes were filled with pain, and guilt. "I'm sorry for pushing, but it had to be done. I'm so sorry. It's okay, now. I'm right here. It's over now, Syd."

He leaned back against the building holding me tightly to his chest. If anyone did see us out here, it would still look like a lover's embrace.

I guess that was the one downside to never getting too caught up in the icky touchy, feely side of life. When it finally did catch up with you, you were an easy out. An overly-sensitized pot of goo, kind of like emotionally dysfunctional flubber. Yeah, that was me. A great big pot of deranged flubber.

Something had to give here, or I was gonna end up in one of those funny white jackets on my way to the happy little asylum. "Deep, slow breaths. Come on, Baby. You can do it." My breath choked out in a sob. Only then realizing I'd given life to the words I'd thought were only in my head.

I felt Beau's lips brush across my temple into my hair. Was it just an accident? Maybe. But somehow I didn't think so. Tired of standing there completely lifeless, spewing touchy-feely-fallout like an erupting volcano, I lifted my arms, heavy from the emotional roller coaster, and slid them around his waist. There. At least I wasn't at such a complete disadvantage now.

"That's it, Syd." Beau encouraged me, stroking one hand lightly down my back, resting it in the soft sway at the bottom. "Just breathe." Another whisper of lips across my temple. Definitely, not an accident. "Just breathe."

And I breathed. I breathed, and breathed, and breathed. It was the most effort I'd consciously put into breathing in my life. I stood there in Beau's strong, warm embrace and breathed until the hurt went away. But when the pain eased, a deep, slow ache began. The ache for him. This enigma of a man that I hardly knew, hadn't even known existed less than twenty-four hours ago. How was that even possible? How could you need the unknown? That was absolutely ridiculous. A total impossibility.

Sick and twisted. That was me. One sick, twisted little puppy. But knowing that didn't stop the burn. It just kept smoldering way down deep inside. Unhurriedly, deliberately, relentlessly it would build. Of this I was certain. Over the next days, months, years even, the heat would gradually build until it eventually consumed me. Reducing me to nothing but a small pile of ashes just waiting for the next big breeze to drive them all away.

My hands clenched the fabric of Beau's cotton, button-down shirt where it hung low on his back and I lifted up onto my toes. Leaning into him, I raised my lips toward his strong, warm neck and whispered them across that perfect arch of muscle and skin. A touch of lips that was more a promise of a kiss than it was anything physically real. My lips parted, the warm breath spilling from them and as it did, my teeth teased across his flushed skin.

I felt the arms of steel wrapped around me tighten even further as Beau pulled my body deeper into the curve of his own. I had to lift my arms higher, holding onto his muscular neck and shoulders, in order to keep from completely falling into him. But once my arms had reached their mark, Beau's silky hair began a slow torment of its own, brushing along the backs of my hands. Instantly my fingers were releasing his neck to weave their way through that luxurious hair, my body swaying strongly into his for support.

Immediately I felt Beau stiffen and I looked up into his eyes, feeling at once both deeply, intensely aroused and completely content. His stormy gray eyes told of similar thoughts and feelings. And, as I watched, his pupils dilated, the gray irises darkening almost imperceptibly. Inviting me to drown in them. To give my very life for them. Then he began to lean down into me, one hand sliding up my back, tangling in my hair, pulling gently, to tip my head back. And then his lips took mine.

His lips teased, promised, ate and drank at mine. When he gently nibbled at my lower lip, I gasped. The world tilting at a dangerous angle. Didn't he know life could end right here? Right now? But when my lips parted, Beau only deepened the kiss. Pulling me places I'd never known existed, heights beyond my wildest imagination, depths exceeding anything I'd ever thought possible.

And time stood still. The heavens stopped to listen, to watch. The simple perfection of the ideal, iconic first kiss. Only it didn't feel like a first kiss at all. It was as if my lips had been made for Beau's, and his for mine. As if we'd kissed this very kiss a thousand times before, each one as breathtakingly, impossibly perfect as this one.

It was a kiss that entire books could be written about and never begin to capture. It was a kiss that both tempted and fulfilled. It softly promised the sun, stars and never-ending smiles and yet managed to deliver the lure of darker, secret, seductive things that are not spoken of in the stark light of day.

The embrace deepened as if it had a life of its own, pulling us in with it. Stripping us both of our senses, our awareness of the world, still moving around us.

My senses were completely and utterly absorbed with Beau. His breath, his scent, the taste of his lips, of his tongue, the warmth and strength of his body against mine, the incredibly silky hair beneath my fingers, his smooth skin against my face, the sound of his groans softly vibrating in the warm depths of my mouth.

I was beyond thought, riding a wave of pure sensation with no care, no concern of any need to find solid ground, no knowledge of which direction it might lay.

All I knew was that I never wanted to leave this moment, this embrace. This life. The arms of this man with a thousand names.

11 BOOBY TRAP BAITING AND UNDERTOW WADING

But, of course, all really great moments have a beginning, a middle and an end. And that end came crashing down all over us the very next moment. Hell! Cinder-God-damn-ella got until the stroke of midnight in the magical land of Ever After and she was imaginary. I was real flesh and bones and all it got me was five minutes in the ever-delightful Belmont High at high-fucking-noon. Where was the justice in that?

"Well, well, well, Syd. Am I correct in assuming this just might be our mysterious Mr. Nobody from Patricia's note?" I spun around to face Mr. Askew, still close enough to Beau that I could feel the heat from his body warming the back of mine. Anger, frustration and a profound sense of loss filled me as I found myself staring into that hideous face, my lips still warm from Beau's kiss, arms aching for his embrace. This just should not be happening. No one should be able to taste the heady remains of heaven clinging to their lips, as they stood staring into the bottomless abyss of hell.

An exhilarated look of unspoken but highly noxious poison filled Mr. A's fleshy face, fleshy enough that he would always look soft.

His gaze swung from me to Beau, and he gave him a look that was a little too long and a little too hard. "Our 'trouble with a capitol T' with the 'great eyes' and a 'mouth made for kissing'?" Okay. I really could have done without Beau hearing that. The hair on the back of my neck rose in quiet mutiny. But Mr. A-fucking-skew wasn't through yet. Not by a long shot.

He glanced scathingly back at me. "Well, I guess you have the answer to that burning question now, don't you Sydney." His eyes refocused on Beau again, the evil slant to his lips warning of the coming bad.

His eyes widened in mock innocence, his voice carrying a sickeningly sweet lilt. "But isn't this also the very person that 'absolutely nothing' was going on with, the one that you 'absolutely never' would be seeing again?" Damn! What an asshole! I felt every muscle in Beau's body stiffen behind me. I could only imagine how cold those eyes would look right now. No hint of the warmth they'd just held.

And still Mr. Askew went on. Fucking pot-stirrer! His eyes slipped back to me, undressing me without the slightest hint of guilt. What a twisted bastard, maybe guilt wasn't even in his vocabulary.

I shifted uncomfortably. Beau must have noticed because his hand moved to rest, comforting and warm, on my back, out of Mr. A's line of sight.

156

"Well, never is such a long time, isn't it? As opposed to, oh, I don't know, tomorrow. And I have to admit Sydney, I am looking forward to our little meeting so very much. Even more so now."

Okay. If he didn't drop that ridiculous school kid, sing-song voice, I was seriously going to have to slap him. Deeper piles of shit to wade through or no.

I should just start wearing thigh-high rubber boots every day, like they were my signature accessory or something, instead of what they were, thigh-high poop boots. Speaking of which, why is it that shit floats right up front and center where you can't hide from it or even pretend it isn't there? I guess whoever said cream floats to the surface was seriously wrong ...

You know it's really gotten bad when you have to think about Mr. A just to stop thinking about the really disgusting shit. I wonder if there are two moons out there today. Or maybe Saturn slipped orbit and slammed into Neptune.

Beau slid his hand up my spine until his fingers could weave into the fringes of my hair, still out of eyesight for Mr. A. Once there, he breathed my name so that only I could hear it, and pulled gently on my hair as if he could sense my lack of direction and was trying to help me refocus.

It bothered me. A lot. Made the hair on the back of my neck prickle with rebellion ... and it comforted me, just about as much. A wash of security wrapped me in its warmth and I eased back into the curve of Beau's body to get closer to this newfound source of infinite comfort and discomfort.

Both feelings were running through me in opposite directions, which really threw my senses in a tailspin. How could this almost perfect stranger have any idea what I was going through right now when I wasn't even sure. And yet, the fact that he did notice and then did something useful with that knowledge was a powerful lure. The seduction of relying on someone else's strength rather than only on my own just upped the risk factor, like a predator sneaking up on you without your knowing there was anything to worry about.

Another little tug on my hair let me know that I'd still not answered. Why wasn't my mouth working? What the Sam Hill was wrong with me? I hardly recognized the me on the inside.

Was it just that my emotions were so screwed up because of Beau right now, that I couldn't deal with Mr. A?

Yes! My head screamed the word at me. I couldn't latch onto the anger and ride it like a surfboard through all the rough water the way I usually did because what I was feeling about Beau was too close to the opposite side of anger. The board couldn't flip both ways at the same time. Damn! I could feel the anger waiting like a lion lurking in the shadows, watching its prey, biding its time. But I needed it right here with me. In front of me. Underneath me. Inside me.

I needed to feel the brush of the lion's fur, my tongue sliding along sharp fangs, claws erupting from my own fingernails. I needed to feel that deep, raspy purr resonating inside my chest, rattling my brains from the sheer force of it. I needed to feel prey, frightened, frozen in my clutches.

What to do? Frustration was all I could grab hold of and that just wasn't enough. Not right now. Not for this. Not enough bite to hold me.

I forced myself to step further away from Beau. It was like having teeth pulled by the dentist without that pain killer, Novocain. That was how bad it hurt to move away from him. Damn, that meant there'd be no little happy-face sticker or sucker at the end. Why is it dentists hand out suckers? Building repeat business?

But I could deal with the pain. That was okay as long as the distance let the anger in. Surely, a change in geography could only help here. As much as I physically and emotionally needed to feel the comfortable warmth of Beau up close to me, I needed to feel my own strength even more. I needed to be a single unit for this. For now.

I blinked a long blink. Long enough to buy a few seconds to think, but not so long as to look weak. I tried to focus on clearing all the mushy stuff out of my heart.

Did it help? Yes, actually it had ... some. Not as much as I'd hoped, but enough to form a sticky base to build on.

I focused sharply on the divine Mr. Asshole. Right! Divinely grotesque, maybe. He was smiling, confident I was still behind in the game. As if he was playing stickman for the house in a devilish game of craps. Stickman is the guy who's in charge of the dice, pushing them across the board with, you guessed it, a stick.

Good. More anger rushed into my bloodstream, warming my body, loosening the tension, building the fire and the focus. Our dear, sweet, Mr. A had a lot to learn about craps. Best odds in the casino if you just knew when to lay down heavy odds. I did. And boy, oh boy, was I laying down maximum odds now.

"Were you a pervert from birth, or is this something you've had to work at?" I let my voice stay cool, calm.

His eyes narrowed slightly, mouth tightening into a forced smile now. "My, my, my. Tomorrow is going to be fun, isn't it, Sydney?"

Fun. Yeah. Fun would be pulling his teeth out without Novocain. Fun would be watching him squirm the way he tried to make others do. Fun might even be watching him rot in jail the rest of his fucking life, or frying on the electric chair.

Yeah. Sometimes being a Texan, born and raised, has its benefits. Cold, hard justice was just one of those perks.

I know much of the rest of the world didn't see Texas, our laws, and our sense of *good old boy* fairness the same way, much less most of the rest of the U.S., But I did. And I was who I had to be true to.

So, let 'em find their own slice of heaven. At least mine had bluebonnets and enough stars and sun to light the sky day and night. Hard to lose your way in a place lit up like that. And even if you did? Hey, at least it was one hell of a view. You could drive all day, from dawn straight through to dusk, with the most amazing sunsets and sunrises God created, and never even come close to crossing a state line, much less change countries.

Looking back up at Mr. A, I took a deep breath and rode the wave of my own living, breathing anger. "Yeah? About all that fun tomorrow ... forget it. I'll take my chances with the principal. I'm not meeting you alone anywhere, at anytime, for any reason, you sick bastard. And, furthermore, if I can manage to get you fired, it would be gravy, Baby. Icing on the God damn

160

cake." There. I hadn't even raised my voice for a single syllable. Go team.

Mr. A obviously wasn't in my personal peanut gallery cheering me on. As a matter of fact, he practically growled back at me through teeth gritted shut. "We already completed our negotiations for tomorrow, Sydney. You made your decision. The time for backing out like a skunk with its tail between its legs has passed."

"You know what they say about a girl's prerogative, Mr. A. So, just consider this skunk's changed her mind ... along with the terms of negotiation."

"You sure about this, Sydney? Thought it all the way through?" He had an uncomfortably comfortable look on his face. Why wasn't he livid? I thought he'd have at least one vein popping out on his face. But nothing. No vein popping. No ears steaming. Something wasn't right, but for the life of me I had no idea what that something was.

"As sure as shit like yours makes skunks like me smell like a bed of fucking roses, Mr. Asshole. Ooh, so sorry. I meant to say, Mr. Ass-kew, of course. Funny how they sound so similar. Almost interchangeable." I batted my eyes and smiled my best nineteenth century coquettish smile.

I think if I'd had an egg to crack on his forehead just then, it would have fried faster than Jackie could whip 'em up on a Sunday morning in her big old iron skillet with all that hot grease just a poppin' away.

Still, no flames bursting from his nostrils. In fact, no smell of burnt flesh at all. Just that hideous smile. "Fine, Sydney. Consider our previous arrangements null and void. We charter fresh waters now. Do try to keep the wind at your back, it does tend to make for smoother sailing. But I forget myself. Of course, you know what you're doing. No matter then. We'll simply handle our little ... situation through ... alternative means."

"Fine. Perfect, actually." I replied with as much confidence as I could muster at that moment. Because, it didn't feel fine, much less perfect. I was definitely missing something I had no business missing. Somehow I had the feeling I'd just set a booby trap only my boobies were the ones in the God damn trap.

"Then we save this for another day. Shall we? To fight the good fight, as they would say." He even tipped his head toward me at the end.

"Yes. Absolutely. Another day." I tipped my head back at him, but never took my eyes off his face.

"Sir." Mr. A even tipped his head at Beau, giving him another long, hard look before turning easily on his heels and heading into the main building.

"Huh! Hell of a nice guy!" Beau said with surprising sarcasm after Mr. A was inside and no longer in hearing range.

"Yeah. Sweetness and life, himself." I came back with every bit as much sincerity.

I glanced up and saw Patricia coming down the hall toward the door leading to us. Thank God she hadn't seen us yet. But just as those words formed in my head, her eyes met mine, then shifted behind me and flew wide open. She pointed at Beau and mouthed, "That's him," bouncing up and down like a little kid who'd seen a puppy in the window and just couldn't wait to get her hands on it.

Shit. I knew I had ten more pounds of questions lying in wait the next time Patricia caught up to me. Great. Just great. Like I had any answers about this. Truth be told, Beau was one big fat exciting, frustrating, walking, talking, breathing, kissing question mark for me.

Patricia's focus slid and centered just behind me again, but before I could turn, or walk away, or even speak, two strong hands pulled at my hip and shoulder, fitting me back into the curve of a body that was entirely too familiar to be uncomfortable, but positively too exquisite to be remotely relaxing. The hand on my shoulder slid to my chin, turning it to the side.

Warm breath was caressing my cheek, stroking down my neck. Promising things that sent prickly little shivers down my spine and made the day suddenly too bright, too clear. My eyes slid closed protectively, instinctively. Seeking the dark shadows and warm caresses of moonlight.

But now, suddenly, all my attention was focused on the two feet immediately surrounding me. Every scrap of my awareness was utterly consumed with everything Beau was doing and on every reaction I was having to him. I could smell the clean soap and musky cologne on his skin, see the pulse straining beneath the skin at the base of his neck at the hollow near his collar bone, hear the heart pounding strongly in his chest, and, oh God, I could feel the brush of electric heat along his skin as his cheek moved to within a breath of mine.

My own heart was thundering to a beat of its own, threatening to burst right out of my chest and into the arms of the man holding me. My brain was on overload. There were sensations coming in from nerves I'd never known I had before this moment.

It was exquisite. Perfect. Intoxicating. All-consuming. Mind-blowing and earth shattering. Yes, positively and unequivocally terrifying.

Then warm lips found mine again and all the thinking and questioning and analyzing just stopped as my head exploded with the sensations bombarding it.

All I could feel was my need to deepen this moment. To drown in it. To hold on tight to it and never let it go. My arms slid up until my hands could weave into the thick, silky hair at the back of that warm, strong neck. And I melted back into that kiss. Into those arms. A willing victim of the "Beau undertow".

The hand at my chin slid to the back of my neck, pulling me further into the kiss in a way that should have had me running for the hills. But it didn't. In fact, my fingers simply locked into his hair pulling his face closer in to mine as my toes lifted me upward. Beau's hand at my hip tightened, softly biting into my flesh and the air rushed out of my lungs, taking my last thread of sanity along with it. And I knew my next breath would pull some part of Beau into my heart, into my soul, that no surgeon would ever be able to remove.

How not to breathe?

And then the breath came. But with it came an embrace from Beau that spilled me backward over the arm that now slid around my waist and locked in place, lips never lifting from mine for even a fraction of a second. My eyes opened as if from a dream as Beau shifted over me, blanketing me from the bright sun and endless sky rising above me.

Suddenly the clouds flew across the sky, shifting into dark thunderhead clouds, settling into a sky that was similar, familiar, but completely different than it had been just a few seconds ago. The dry cool breeze blowing across me held different smells, was coming from a different direction.

And the body holding me, kissing me, consuming me, was still all I could think of, all I wanted or needed in this breath to survive until the next one. Beau. But, not Beau. Somehow this wasn't Beau. These arms that hadn't let go of me weren't his. The lips melting my soul didn't belong to that body. The warm breath spilling into me hadn't come from his lungs.

Definitely, impossibly, not Beau. Someone younger, darker-skinned, less controlled. I was, too. Sydney, but not Sydney. Not me. Someone ... someone different. Someone else. How was that even possible?

I clung tighter, my nails pricking against the tight, clean stretch of neck beneath them. My face gazed back at me, reflected in the blackest of eyes, not gray. My eyes squinted, partly because of the brilliance of the sun shining down on us, but mostly because of the unexpected transformation of Beau into ... into what? Or rather, into whom?

"Rache,"... Beau-Not-Beau, breathed into my mouth. And my heart yelled back immediately, passionately, "Jesse!" My pulse sky-rocketing with anticipation as I shifted my body as tightly as I could into that impossibly perfect form holding me, grasping me, anchoring me to him. I felt the love pouring into me from Jesse, an electric current between us that brushed along my lips, tickled my tongue, dove down my throat

165

forcing its way into my lungs, through my heart. And with each beat of blood, that electric pulse pushed through my body. Heating my senses, burying itself in my bones, muscles, flesh. It circled within me, cradled my stomach, my womb. I felt the trickle of energy as it danced up through the tissues of my hand into each fingertip. I knew if I looked down at myself, my body would be glowing with light, with this hyper-intensified rush of life. Desires, memories and feelings I hadn't known had been sleeping deep within my soul, dormant like sleeping Grizzlies in deepest winter, were awakening. And my heart ... my heart was ...

But the next moment the world turned upside down again. Going all crazy on me again ... spilling my heart and all its contents right along with it. I looked down, searching the ground frantically, as if I should be on my hands and knees gathering the misplaced pieces. But there were none to be found. Odd. Just feet, keeping the earth in place. Lifting my eyes, I found the world I'd left seconds ago. And everything was just as it had been before. Just as I'd left it.

Just Belmont High. Just this day. Just Beau. Just me. Just the perfection it had been moments before. Only somehow so much less than it had been half a second ago. Like a piece was missing that hadn't been before. A piece I'd never even noticed before. Now the perfection of that moment had been lost. Scarred and stolen from my greedy fingertips still grasping, searching for ...

For what? For who, exactly? For Beau? Or Not-Beau? For Jesse? How incredibly, insanely stupid could I possibly be today? Maybe I'd caught a twelve-hour stupid virus. Maybe if I just puked out the stupid, I'd be me again. I'd feel normal again. Well, my take on normal anyway.

My mouth still tingled from that electrically charged kiss. I glanced at my reflection in the windows of the doors in front of us, the doors leading back to normal, everyday, non-Beau life. My life. Was that really me? I focused harder on the image, on the face, as if the glass would somehow show the tiny charges dancing on my lips.

Then I turned my face back toward Beau's. My eyes tightened on his as I pushed hard against his chest with both hands. I stumbled slightly, either from the force of the movement or from the forced distance between us, I wasn't sure, as I stepped back into my own space. My own world. Sydney's world.

As if I hadn't just solved the mystery of the psycho-drama, I demanded, "What the Sam Hill was that!"

But even as the words flew out, I watched Beau's beautiful face shut down, his shields flying up right in front of me. It was as if he was a submarine batting down the hatches, preparing to submerge. Preparing for battle. Battle against who? Me? Surely not ...

Right? Right. But my little voice was all wobbly, not at all solid like what I needed right now. I needed eight-foot solid steel, not wiggle words.

"Sorry, Syd. I have to go. Now. I'll swing by Charles', Principle Shell's, office and let him know what a good job you did showing me around the place. Take care. I'm sure we'll be seeing more of one another. Bye, now." And he turned on his heels, not waiting for so much as a mono-syllabic,

167

cave man grunt from me, and walked through the doors, quickly disappearing down the hall.

"But ..." I spluttered as the blood started to reanimate my brain. Son of a bitch! What a fucking idiot I was! Dammit. Ungh!

What the hell was I supposed to do now? I'd never even had to ask myself that question before. Always so damn sure of myself and which way I wanted to go in any given moment.

But now, suddenly, here I was. The wind had moved. The earth had quaked. My heart had shattered. And what had happened? Mid-shatter the guy had made a mad dash for the escape hatch. No guy had even come close to doing that before. Not even the ones I'd wished with every godforsaken heartbeat would have. Well, basically, that pretty much meant all of them.

But this one? This one. The only one I wished wouldn't have, had run off like a scared little rabbit. Perfect. Just fucking perfect.

12 IS IT 'ONE MAN'S TRASH IS ANOTHER MAN'S TREASURE' OR ONE GIRL'S ROTTING CORPSE IS ANOTHER GIRL'S PROM DRESS?

I made it through the rest of the day keeping the bits and pieces of sanity that remained when Beau had left. I even made it through the onslaught of Patricia's twenty question bombardment. Only it had been more like a thousand and one questions. And even though I had almost no answers, she didn't really seem to notice. Maybe Beau just had the same effect on everyone else that he had on me.

No. That just wasn't possible. I mean, Patricia could at least talk without spitting or drooling or slipping into incoherent states of mass delirium. That was light years ahead of me. But at least that meant there was some glimmer of hope, didn't it?

Patricia did get just a little annoyed with my inability to stay connected to her incessant stream of Beau-babble for longer than three-and-a-half seconds at a time, but I deserved a shitload of credit for even staying in this plane of reality, didn't I?

Of course I did. And no one was going to snatch that skinny, fraying thread of success from the death-grip that my cold, aching fingers had on it no matter how truly feeble an accomplishment it might seem to them. To me, it was positively remarkable, absolutely awe-inspiring. Besides, it took every godforsaken shred of energy and gumption for me to pull it off.

"Hell's bells, Syd! Are you even listening to me? I've asked you the same flippin' question three times already." Patricia's voice nudged its way through the swirling storm of thoughts and emotions raging in my head.

"Mmm. Sorry, Patricia. I just don't know. If I had to guess, I'd have to say, yes and no. Yes, I'm pretty sure I'll see him again. And no, a big part of me just really isn't wanting that to happen. I don't see how I can possibly stop it though. Once a mountain's in motion, there really isn't much anyone can do to hold it back, is there? Even me."

"Yeah. Whatever, Syd. You could move Mount Kilimanjaro to Timbuk-flippin'-tu before sunset if you set your mind to it. And we both know that. You can do anything you decide to do. No matter how impossible everyone else on the entire planet thinks it is. You've always been that way." She looked down at her feet for a second then glanced up at me sheepishly under her long golden eyelashes. "That's why you've been my hero since I was like seven years old for Christ's sake. You always will be."

"Oh, God, Patricia. You have got to get out more often. That's for sure. I am so-o-o not hero material. You have absolutely no idea. Not a single, solitary clue."

"Shut up, Syd. I don't want to hear it."

"Oh, great. First you're yelling at me about not talking, now you're yelling at me for talking. Make up your God damn mind will you?"

Her lips pursed as her face edged closer to mine. "Sure. Right after you stop behaving like an ornery ass on ball clipping day."

Tommy Rider and Mark Matthews parked themselves on a bench a couple rows down from us on the bleachers. They had apparently overheard at least the last little bit of our conversation, because they both turned with pained expressions on their faces.

Mark's mouth was gaping in a muted shriek of agony. But Tommy slid in with, "Man, Syd, I don't know what the hell you did, but damn girl, that's some serious shit there. I'd stop it like last year if I was you."

To which Mark added with a curious little smile at Patricia, "Yeah, nobody, but nobody pisses off Patricia." Oh, man. Did he ever have it bad for the girl, or what?

I glanced sideways at Patricia. She was still clueless, lost somewhere in the middle of La-la land. Poor child. I'd have to enlighten her. Later. When Mark's ears weren't three feet away from my mouth.

I looked at them both dismissingly. "I didn't do shit. That's what she's getting all pissy about actually."

Tommy cocked his head sideways and cut his eyes back up at me under one raised eyebrow. "Well, dammit, girl. Like the Nike slut says, 'Just do it!'"

To which Mark felt compelled to add, "Shit yeah! If you're gonna do the time, might as well do the crime, Baby. 'Specially if it's fun." His eyebrows waggled with the last part.

I twizzled my finger in circles in front of me. "Yeah, I'm pretty sure you have that flipped around ten shades of backwards there. Please tell me you guys don't want to be high school counselors when you grow up. Instead of American kids being the fattest on the planet, we'll be the fastest. And not in a good way."

"Oh, it would be in a very, very good way." Mark shot back, glancing quickly at Patricia who'd finally broken into laughter.

Tommy hefted one of those guy-buddy-slaps on Mark's shoulder. You know the kind, it allows for contact between members of the male sex without threatening their testosterone production.

"Yeah, our motto could be 'Put your sexy on, America'. And in homeroom the teachers could show us really important things ..." Rising to his feet, Tommy raised his arms and did a little shimmy-shake, running his hands across his chest suggestively. "... Like how to shake your ta-ta's and give an A+ lap dance."

"Yeah, Baby! Shake it for me like it's my birthday!" Sheila Norris, one of our, drum-roll please, star volleyball players, called up as she passed the stands on her way back in from running laps.

Tommy turned to face her, putting some real effort into his little happy dance now as he belted out the words in a slow, deep voice. "Happy birthday to you! Please go with me to prom! I'll dance for you, beautiful Sheila! Happy birthday to you!" He bent over at the waist and slapped his own ass at the end, to Sheila's utter delight.

"Mmm, mmm, mmm. You're as yummy as pineapple upside-down cake." She blew him a kiss as she turned and bounced toward the locker room.

"So, is that a yes?" Tommy called back to her.

"Yeah, Baby. But remember your promise, you'll dance for me. Only me." Sheila laughed over her shoulder.

"Yes! I love you!" Tommy yelled back. Sheila gave him the look that declaration deserved. Good girl.

Tommy high-fived Mark, who was looking at him with raised eyebrows. "No offense, man, but that's just not the kind of dance I even want to think about, much less see."

A grimace passed over Tommy's face before he continued. "Ooh, wouldn't want to be sittin' in Ms. DeFranko's class for that one, huh? Uuhk!" A shiver wiggled through him as the grotesqueness of his words hit home, withered the smile on his face, and brought him right back down to his seat.

Mark grabbed his stomach and curled over it protectively. "Shit, man. Keep the visual to yourself next time. It's just plain wrong to think of all 300-plus pounds of Ms. DeFranko dripping sweat from her big old hairy pits and lap dancing at the same time." Mark looked a little green around the gills, like he was about to get a real good taste of his lunch again.

Okay. I had to laugh. Laugh and leave.

"Ya'll are so twisted. See you tomorrow, guys." I stood up and grabbed my backpack, slinging it over one shoulder, lifting my eyebrows as I smiled crookedly down at my poor little deluded hero worshiper. "Later, babe."

"Sure thing, Syd-o-ne-ey. You, just do it. Go tackle that bear. Show him who's got the big balls!" Tommy cheered me on.

Mark added, "Just be sure to keep an eyeful of where all ten of those claws are. And bring me back one if you live to tell the tale."

"Yeah, yeah, yeah. Want it dipped in silver or bronze?" I asked as I climbed down, stepping from seat to seat.

"Neither. I'll take it au natural. Some things just don't need any extra sparkles and pops to make them any more perfect." Mark answered, again with that funny little smile at Patricia. I really had to make a point of bringing her up to speed on the Mark-man's unspoken interest.

Patricia smirked at me, knowingly. "Okay, Syd. Don't worry though, I'm sure I'll have a whole Christmas list full of questions by tomorrow." She narrowed her baby blues before adding, "I just know how much you love that." Did I mention she knew me just a hair too well for comfort? Yeah. Like the whole damn head-full of hair too much.

"Right. Just call me when the game's over, let me know how it ended, and we'll call it even." Hopeful? Yes. Stupidly hopeful? Probably. But sometimes stupidity makes you try things you would never have considered before. Like mole … chicken, chocolate, chili powder and peanut butter served over rice. Voilà! A Willy Wonka dream come true in a dinner entrée of the feathered persuasion.

"Nah, where's the fun in that? You're slipping, Syd." Yeah, stupidly hopeful. Oh, well, can't blame a girl for trying. "Do you want to go look at dresses for prom later?" I noticed Mark-ster's attention shifted back to Patricia at the mention of prom. Uh-huh. He had it bad. Pretty damn bad.

"Can't. Grounded, remember?"

"Oh, that's right, dammit. What if I come by after, I could give you a call when I leave the mall and tell you if I found a dress or not." She bit her bottom lip, eyes grasping at mine for strength.

My heart tightened seeing that anxious, nervous look cloud over her face. "Sounds good. Call first though, I might call it an early night. You should think about doing that yourself. You definitely need to catch up on some Z's. You're lookin' a little pale around the edges." I really was feeling short on shut-eye, and I only slept four to six hours on a good day.

Her face eased immediately. "I will. Oh, and I'll be sure to bring the list of questions in the morning. Wouldn't want you to feel too left out, now would we?" She smiled up at me with mock innocence.

Nice to see her stretching those sarcasm muscles. We just needed to work on who she used as a guinea pig. In other words, not yours truly. Anyone else though? Fine. Line starts to the left.

"Absolutely not. Couldn't stand still waiting for that to happen," I ground out as I finally hit grass. Next time, I had to remember to just jump ... more painful physically, perhaps, but so much faster, less time for emotional shrapnel to stab its way in.

"Not with me around watching your back. See? I'm good for something. I can have big balls, too." Her sweet little sparrow voice trailed after me. I just laughed and waved in the air over my head without turning back.

I swear I started out headed straight to Jack's and Queen's. Honest. Funny how you can really mean to do the right thing, go where you know you should go, and then you look up and find yourself completely and utterly off track.

But I wasn't really upset about it. Not at all. Actually, I was quite comfortably derailed.

The first thing to catch my senses hard enough to pull me back down to Planet Earth was not any particular sound, but rather the lack of sound. That and the smell of freshly turned dirt. Lots of it. And underneath that, the smell of grass ... and life ... and death. And wrapped all around it, all around me, a nice warm blanket of comfort. Damn, all of a sudden my senses were on overdrive.

Yeah, I'd made it a full twelve hours before my own subconscious needs had kicked in, broken my sentence of house-arrest, severed my ties with the living, craved solace once again with the dead and decaying, and handed my sanity over lock, stock and barrel to my base animal senses. Never said I didn't have issues. I mean, seriously, what kind of freak makes a bee-line to the land of the lost, on autopilot no less, whenever life gets too real? Much less for the second time in as many days.

Oh, yeah, right. This kind of freak. I'm the fill in the blank here.

I should just turn right around and head my stupid little butt straight back to Queen's and Jack's. I knew that. But my feet didn't. And I just kept following them as they wove their way through the sleepy neighborhood nestled snugly beneath them. Hey, if they could get me to my safe place without any help from me two days in a row, who was I to start arguing now?

My senses took over again thankfully, stealing the reins from my over-active brain. My fingertips drank in the roughness of the tree trunks, the smoothness of cold granite, anything to strengthen the connection, the warm familiar feeling of home, of belonging.

Each step I took brought another small wave of release, another cool little sigh of relief. Suddenly, I had to feel the ground under my toes. Now. I stopped to lean on the nearest tombstone, it was one of the older ones in the cemetery. Belonged to one Jackson Talbot, beloved son and father, 1787-1852. I slipped my shoes off, stuffing the socks way down deep so they wouldn't accidentally decorate some poor shmuck's grave.

I'd always wondered about those buried with tombstones like Jackson's. Were they so unremarkable that there was nothing more to say about them? Nothing any more memorable than that? Or were the ones they left behind to blame? Maybe they were oblivious of the true life, loves and losses of the person they had buried. Or maybe they were too busy, or just too lazy to care. Pretty depressing cookie no matter how you sliced it.

I got up quickly, hooking the backs of my shoes with my left hand, not wanting to breathe another lungful of stale air standing over him. As if it would infect my life. My choices. Even my death. Right. Like someone could really do a worse job of it than I had so far? Come on, Syd. Get real.

Still, I was moving again. So much for keeping old Jackson company.

As I worked my way around the gravesites, I brushed past a wild rose bush, the greedy stems snagging at my jeans. Reaching down with my right hand, I picked one flower that seemed to be looking right at me. Then I strayed off the open grounds and wove my way through the trees, rolling the spiked stem gently between my fingers, the soft, sweet smell hovering around me. Sunlight tripping through the branches spilled in puddles of light that danced along my path. The ground wasn't as soft here. Little sticks and stones stabbed at the soft undersides of my feet. But it felt kind of good, actually. Strange, I knew somewhere deep inside that it shouldn't. But somehow it simply made me feel ... more. More real. More alive. More me. And I could do with a good dose of me right now.

The birds were revving up in the softly fading light of dusk. They could feel the breath of twilight catching under their wings, hear the hypnotic rhythm of the dragonflies and the crickets. Time for dinner and song and dance. All the standard mating rituals. Like with humans, only with no pretense, straight-up truth, more openly honest than we could ever hope to be. Had we ever been able to do that? Even as troglodytes? Or had we been screwed up on the whole sexual interaction front from the get-go?

I watched the birds, thousands of them, as they dodged and darted, soared and fell, dove fearlessly toward the ground for the kill. And I could almost feel the air sliding along my body, the cool earth rushing towards my face, the updrafts lifting me back up toward the treetops, toward freedom.

The trees thinned in front of me and I stepped out into the patch of ground that held Rachel and baby Jesse. How on earth did I end up here? Was it intentional ... just without my knowing it? Or was it simply a coincidence? Hmm. I've never been big on coincidences. But of all the places I could go, why would my feet take me here? And why today, why now?

As I stood there trying to weed out answers that wouldn't come, I realized how still my mind had become. How peaceful. I actually felt light-headed. As if all the extra baggage I'd been carting around in my mind the last couple days had weighed me down so heavily that removing it caused me to feel like I was at that place just after the highest point of the roller coaster, the penultimate. You know, the one where your stomach slides right up into your chest, lodging just behind your heart, pushing on your windpipe, and you like it. Or it shoots straight out your mouth if you don't like heights. But I did. Always had. They made me feel like I could fly.

But right now, I didn't want to fly. I wanted to lay down. Vaguely I realized I was panting. Maybe if I just sat down for a minute or two. Maybe then I'd be able to get my legs back under me. I was literally having to pull the air into my lungs at this point, struggling for each breath.

I dropped my backpack and shoes on the grass beside me and sat down on the edge of Rachel's marker, resting my arms on my knees, still twirling the flower absentmindedly. Not helping. I dropped my head down between my legs, maybe I just needed to get a little more blood to the brain. But that didn't help either. In fact, now I could hardly move. My chest felt like it had bands of steel wrapped around it. Great, now came the steel. A little late guys.

Finally, I rolled back on the gravestone closing my eyes. Still, I had to throw my arm over them to cut down on the glare from the setting sun. And then ... I could breathe.

Better. Much better. The queasiness was fading fast, too.

What was going on? Is this what exhaustion felt like? Maybe. When was the last time I'd eaten something? Couldn't remember. But just thinking of food though had my stomach rebelling in warning.

Okay, didn't need food. What else? I had been burning the candle at both ends, and in the middle here lately. But at least I felt better for the moment. I sat up ready to head straight home and jump into bed, but no sooner had I hit vertical than the world spun out of control again. My arms flew out trying to find something to brace myself against, but found nothing until they hit the gravestone. The impact crushed the stem of the rose into the tender flesh of my hand, thorns driving deep. Thick, sweet blood flowed quickly from each puncture, staining the warm granite in dark, sticky pools.

Shit! I fell backward and my head knocked against the granite like an old iron rung on a worn weathered door. Well, maybe I could lay here for a few minutes, surely that couldn't hurt. Just long enough to recoup. Yeah, just a little while ... like maybe, just one or two ... millennia.

And then there was no more thinking. No more feeling. No more roller coasters. No more Mr. A. No more Beau or Patricia. No more sun hurting my eyes. No more anything. Just quiet.

Until there wasn't.

"Syd? Syd." I felt my body jiggling without me doing the moving. Again the voice came through. A voice I knew I should recognize. "Syd. Time to wake up. Syd!" As the voice got closer I realized it was coming from my right.

Who was screwing with my quiet, dammit! I frowned at the unwelcome invader, trying to pull free but using as few muscles as possible.

"Well, at least we know she's okay." Voice number two. To my left, and lower.

Great, why don't ya'll just have a Goddamn block party right here in the middle of my piece of quiet! "Get the fuck away!" I was going for a fierce growl. The growl came, but it was all whispery, like the day after you've screamed your head off at a really great concert. Plus, with my eyes still closed, fierce definitely wasn't working for me. I think that requires eye contact. Does that mean blind people can't do fierce?

Soft fingers eased the hair back from my face at my temple. But other hands weren't so pleasant. Those were the ones biting into my upper arms. "Dammit, Syd! I asked you to watch that mouth of yours. Now, wake up." Voice number one again. But the words were more a gentle humming that, although irritating, were staying far enough away that they didn't really translate completely. It was more like my ears caught the sounds and tore them down into the bits and bobs my brain needed to make sense of them.

"Relax, Beau. She's still half asleep. At least give her time to wake up and get her bearings before you start in on her."

My eyes shot open as the name finally registered somewhere in my fuzzy brain. I tried to sit up, but those strong arms held me down. "What the hell are you doing here?" I wrenched futilely again, trying to break loose. "Let me up, God dammit!"

"I don't think that's such a good idea just yet. Why don't you try to catch your breath first?"

That would be Beau with the patronizing voice, of course. My brain was struggling to catch up. Pinching and tingling like an arm or leg that had fallen asleep.

"Get off of me, you asshole! I can breathe just fine all on my lonesome, thank you very much." I struggled to free myself from his grip, but my muscles were still pretty damn weak from sleep.

Beau looked up at Sarah. "Okay, she's her normal, fun-loving self now. Lucky us."

But Sarah was still Sarah. Sweetness and light through and through. "Syd, you really ought to stay laying down for a bit. You hit your head pretty hard by the looks of ... well, of ... things. It wouldn't be so awful to lie here and catch your breath for a little bit, would it?" Her fingers were still working their magic at my temple, gently raking through my chocolate brown hair, lifting just enough to move back to where they'd started, and repeating that easy, soothing motion. Sarah never pulled her hand back so far that I couldn't feel the warmth spilling off her fingertips, blanketing my skin with her own sweet, peaceful energy.

That's when I realized I was slightly chilled. How was that possible? It'd been warm since mid-February, we were looking at an early start to summer. I shifted my eyes back and forth, from Sarah to Beau and back again. Then all around me. The starry night. I was missing something. Something important. My eyes went back to Beau and I suddenly remembered him cradling me in his arms, blocking out the sun, leaning in to kiss me ...

Holy shit! That was it! Where was the sun? How long had I been here? Dammit! I tried to jerk myself up again. Failed miserably, of course. I felt about as useful as a limp noodle. Fan-fucking-tastic. My mad upped a couple of notches on me. So-o-o not good.

"Both of you. Get the hell off of me. Now." I managed to grit out without even biting anyone, yet. Points for Syd. Go me.

Beau's eyes tightened imperceptibly on me. "No. Not yet, Syd. You're hurt. And pretty badly, at that. You just don't feel it yet. And that's probably a good thing."

Okay. I could play big girl and admit that made me just an itty bit nervous. But admitting it and letting it rule my life were two very different things. I took a deep breath and counted to seven ... would have done ten, but seriously, if it ain't happenin' by seven, you'd have to go a whole hell of a lot higher than ten to see any results, and I just didn't have that kind of time. Or patience.

At least I could speak ... what a good little civilized homo sapien. "Look, thanks for waking me up. Your bedside manner could use a little work, still, I appreciate it. Kind of freaked that you're here ... again. But I was supposed to be home hours ago. So, have at it, enjoy yourselves. You know the way out. Just remember to lock up when you leave."

"Cute, Syd. Real cute." But that look was anything but cute. Sexy maybe. Not cute. The anger was rolling off of him in waves. Anger, along with something else I couldn't quite put my finger on. But something.

"I thought it was. Maybe you just need to loosen up a notch or two. Anyway, leaving now. So move the tush, Big Boy."

"You're telling me to loosen up? You can't be serious. You, the original Little Miss Manners, are trying to give me tips on social etiquette? You really did hit your head hard, didn't you, Syd? You do remember your name, don't you?"

"Oh, my God! I try to be all nice to you and you turn into a little shit! What the hell is your problem? You ..."

But the rest of my beautiful, decapitating speech was never heard by human ears, as Sarah cut in like a hot spoon sliding through a bowl of sinfully rich chocolate pudding. She gently slid two fingers across my lips, holding them there softly. "Syd. T.J. is here, remember what that means? We don't really want an encore, now do we? I'm sorry we surprised you again. We're not stalking you or anything. It's just that you're pretty easy for us to find. And, trust me, Syd, right now you need finding. By us, anyway."

I let a long sigh out. Feeling the tired wash through me again. But this time it really just washed through, without lingering deep down inside. "Look, Sarah, I get that you believe all this stuff about bad guys and reincarnation and whatnot. I just don't know that I do. But I do know that I have to go home. Hours ago. We can talk about all this another time. Promise. Just not now." Not bad for the original Little Miss Manners, huh?

"Okay, Beau. Help her up." Sarah stood up and took a step back from me.

It was obvious Beau wasn't exactly enthusiastic about this, but he played nice. "Fine. But you're gonna have to deal with this, Syd. Soon." He didn't stand up, just let go of my arms and leaned back a little.

Good, I shifted, preparing to sit up when my gaze finally hit T.J.'s for the first time. She'd been hidden behind Sarah and Beau up 'til then. I barely caught the tensing of the muscles along her sides as she leapt forward and landed on my chest.

What was it with this damn cat and my boobs? Ta-ta envy? She had eight for God's sake! Give me a break. But all of a sudden the ground started to shake ... what the hell? This was the Gulf Coast, we did hurricanes, not earthquakes! As my eyes widened in disbelief, the entire gravesite started to glow. The gravestone and the grass around it, as if the sun that had been missing from the sky was suddenly double-parked six feet under me. Holy fucking shit! "Get me out of here!" I yelled as calmly as I could manage staring straight into my own horrified reflection in T.J.'s golden eyes.

Out of the corner of my eye, I saw a glance pass between Beau and Sarah. The kind of glance that books were written about. "What? What was that look for? Help me, God dammit! Do the looks later, when my ass isn't about to join the hereafter."

"Um, Syd? You're not gonna like this. And we didn't do it. Just so you know." Sarah was trying to stay focused on me, but her eyes kept jumping to Beau. Which was probably for the best, because the look of fear and trepidation in her eyes wasn't helping. Not one little bit.

"What! What am I not gonna like? What didn't you do? Because somebody sure did a whole hell of a lot of something!" T.J. started to lean in closer, gazing into my eyes the way a cobra would to lull you into a false sense of security. Oh, hell no. I rolled my eyes to the first person I found. Sarah. "You know what? Scratch that. Just get me the fuck out of here. Get me out, in one piece preferably, and all is forgiven. Whoever did whatever. Complete exoneration. No blame whatsoever. Just get me out of here, now!"

"Don't be afraid, Syd. It's just T.J. She's not gonna hurt you. You know that." Sarah was shaking her head. Not what I needed to see. "But it's already begun now. Somehow, maybe all the blood, I'm not really sure, but the portal's been opened. It's accepted your entrance, and now it won't close without fulfilling the promise."

"What promise? I didn't promise anything! What the hell are you talking about? And can we please do something about Bagheera? She's starting to drool ... on my chest!" Okay. Maybe that was fair since I'd splattered her with spit, but a girl has to draw the line somewhere, right?

"I think it has something to do with what happened this afternoon." My eyes shifted to Beau, but even though he was facing me, his eyes were staring straight into the past. A funny little glassy glaze swept over them. "It somehow served as an invocation for Rachel. A prayer, a promise to complete the rite."

"Okay. Look. I don't give a good God damn what Rachel Kensington thinks happened today. She's dead. Been that way a long time now. Besides, I can't promise something I don't even understand. Get somebody else or, better yet, one of you do it. Just count me out."

Sweet little Sarah stepped in again. "Syd? It has to be you. It's about you. And, if you really want to get out of this, the quickest way is to fulfill the invocation. You just need to relive that moment in Rachel's life when things went wonky, when they veered off course, but do it right this time."

"Are you kidding me? I don't even know Rachel. I don't know a God damn thing about her, other than she's buried with a baby and had serious hots for a guy named Jesse. How the hell would I know what needs fixing, much less how to fix it? I can't even manage my own potholes without turning them into bottomless pits of fire. Now, stop standing there like a fucking bump on a log, Beau, and get me the hell out of this mess!" I really meant to stay angry. But by the end my voice had forsaken me and shifted halfway to a plea. Oh, well. I was pinned down by a black panther, on top of a grave that was glowing like a giant pumpkin on Halloween, in the middle of a patch of earth that felt like it was about to eat me faster than the damn cat could. Guess one little cry for help was allowed. Yeah. Pretty much a no-brainer. Just call me the squealer.

I saw the pain in Beau's eyes, the kind you get when someone you care about is hurting and there's nothing you can do to stop it. But when he spoke there wasn't a speck of compassion. "Why the hell are you so angry? We didn't do this to you, Syd! So stop trying to rip my head off over it." Tough love? Who the hell needs that!

"Oh. Yeah! Let's see here. Why the hell should I be upset? All my friends are out scoping the shops trying to score the perfect prom dress. Meanwhile, I'm sniffing my way through the local graveyard trying to find the perfect box of bones to play dress-up in! I may not be a ruffle and frills kind of girl, but I'm thinking partially decomposed bones are just not gonna bring out the sparkle in my eyes, and they might even leak glumpy stuff on my chest. And now, I'm stuck with a one hundred pound panther glued to my boobs until I fulfill a promise I never made to begin with. And let's not forget the ground all around me is lit up like a God damn Molotov cocktail and it feels like little old Rachel must be climbing out of her fucking grave. Did I leave anything out? Oh, yeah! Sure did. The Big Bad apparently knows what's up and wants to introduce himself to me personally. Good enough?" So, I was a little cranky. Prom only comes once. I was due.

"Okay, Syd. First of all, it's just your soul that's going to reanimate the corpse. You'll leave your body while you do it. So, no glumpy stuff on your ... on you at all." Beau really was trying to be patient, but his exasperation with my sudden girlish whining was staining the edges of his chivalry.

"Wait just one minute. Leave my body? As in dead? Are you insane? This is completely nuts. I'm going home. Now. This is just too much. Too much shit. Deal me out. Now. I fold. Have a nice life, or death, or whatever the hell it is you do."

Sarah was squatting beside me now and laid her hand on my shoulder. "Syd, I already told you T.J.'s not going to hurt you. She's just going to lure your soul out of your body."

"She's gonna do what to my soul? Suck it out of me? As in, no more Syd? Are you completely insane? No! Don't bother answering that either. I tell you what. You two just help me up and I won't have your asses thrown in jail for the rest of your lives. All one thousand of them!" I'm pretty sure I was spitting by the end because T.J.'s face was glistening in little spots in the light now.

"I'm out of here. Move it, T.J." I reached up to shove her off, I was tired of playing. But things can always get worse, and that's exactly what they did now.

Beau's hand closed around mine before I could budge T.J. an inch, and as soon as he did, all hell broke loose. The light burst out so brightly, it was like the sun was trying to shove its way out of the grave and right up my butt. At the same time, T.J. leaned into my face, touching her nose to mine, pulling the breath from my chest as easily as you'd sniff down a pumpkin pie baking on Thanksgiving Day.

"Beau, get in there. Now!" Was that Sarah's voice yelling, commanding? My hearing was fading, things were getting fuzzy around the edges, all the light was dimming.

Suddenly, I felt Beau. Warm and strong and next to me from shoulder to toe. And yelling in my ear. I could tell he was yelling from the way his face moved in my peripheral vision, but still the words barely made it to my brain. "Syd! I've got you. I'm here with you. Don't let go, Baby. Whatever you do, just don't let go!" He clamped his other hand on top of the same hand he was already holding, so that my hand was completely wrapped within his, and touched his cheek to mine.

Was he certifiably insane? Of course I wasn't letting go ... they'd have to pry his hand out of my cold dead fingers with a crowbar before I let go. Instinctively, my fingers clutched onto his, threading their way through his in a jumbled mess.

Still, this was a game I didn't want to play. The ground was buckling underneath me so violently that I knew I'd be pulled straight through to China any second! Wasn't my mom supposed to call me in for dinner right about now? Isn't that what happened in normal families? They rescued each other from shit like ... well, maybe not shit quite like this, but soft shit anyway.

Of course, I didn't have that family to hide behind. I just had me. Just the way I wanted it. Right? Of course, there were three other mammals touching me at the moment. Maybe they were more than a bag of strangers I happened across one night. More than just a pack of pot-stirring trouble-makers. They were right here with me, for me. And they were here by choice even if I wasn't. "But I really don't want to do this! What if I only make things worse? What happens then? I don't know what the hell I'm supposed to do! I'm the ruling Queen of Mass Mayhem and Destruction, remember?" I yelled out with my last bit of strength, my last shred of me, but I don't know if the words actually found sound.

Impossibly, the maelstrom of chaos jumped up the Richter scale again. Beau's grip tightened, his forehead glued to mine, our bodies melding into one. Huge chunks of dirt started shooting up around us, but there was an endless supply. More dirt just kept bubbling up as if it was being manufactured at full speed in Rachel's coffin. The light was suddenly so intense, so concentrated, I knew it could destroy everything within its reach. My eyes were wide open, aching in the blindingly bright light. Light so bright that I could practically see right through Beau, Sarah, even T.J. Turning them into ethereal guardians, eyes glowing radiantly. Hair and fur was flying in the gusts of whirling wind created by the bedlam exploding on all sides of us.

Sarah's mouth started chanting words I was sure I wouldn't have understood even if I had been able to hear them. And T.J. just kept on sucking down the damn Sydney cream pie like there was no tomorrow. And maybe, just maybe, there wasn't.

But whether there was or wasn't, wouldn't be answered. The last whisper of air was snatched from my screaming, gasping lungs, and with it my soul slipped from my body, flying down the rabbit hole.

And just like that, I was only one more lifeless collection of tissue and bones in a graveyard filled with them. The only difference was that my body was still warm, had a shitload of trouble waiting for it at home, a whole other shitload of trouble waiting for it at school, and an essay due in economics in the morning.

I would have one hell of an excuse though ... sure beats the pants off of "my dog ate my paper". I should remember to smear my homework in some of the glumpy stuff. After all, if a picture's worth a thousand words, what could beat a little show and tell? And no matter what Sarah said, when you taught a roach to play dead there was glumpy stuff, much less when you decided to play dress-up with worm-infested corpses.

Yeah, I was dressing for the occasion ... bone dressing.

I wish I'd thought to bring some paper towels, but I guess Wet Wipes would have been better anyway.

13 THE LIFE AND TIMES OF ONE JESSE ALEJANDRO GARCIA DE LA CRUZ

My eyes ached they were squeezing so tightly against the light. It was blazing. So bright, that instead of being in the dark, I was seeing everything through the blanket of bright red blood pumping in through my eyelids. I liked it though, my very own set of rose-colored glasses keeping the ugliness of the world at bay. I dragged in a lungful of dry, hot air like I'd just broken the surface of the water after going down for the third and final time.

Sensation rode down my body like a wave breaking over dry sand as my soul poured into a new body. Suddenly, I could feel each nerve ending, as if they were on hyper-drive. But I was feeling them through a different set of body parts than I had been a second ago. Legs a bit shorter, skin a little darker, heart a little ... lighter, fuller, happier.

Awkward. Still, it wasn't entirely uncomfortable. Instead, it felt strangely familiar. Like someone had taken me in at the seams, like a suit that just needed a little adjustment here, an alteration there.

I pictured one of those moving clothing racks that the dry cleaners love, my body hung in the middle of a sea of bodies moving along the ceiling rail, each with a little white ticket pinned at my shoulder. What if they lost my ticket? Was there a lost and found bin? Insurance? A 1-800 number? What if I just lost an eyeball, like a suit loses a button? Was there at least a replacement plan? Maybe a drawer full of spare parts, bits and bobs?

But I didn't really care too much. I knew this body, just as well as I knew my own. I knew how it moved, how it sounded, what it felt ... what it liked and didn't like.

More importantly, I knew what it feared more than any other thing. The one thing it couldn't live without.

I concentrated on the heart beating rhythmically in my chest, the steady rise and fall of my lungs, the pulse throbbing across my palms, down to my fingertips. The breath passing through my nose, down my throat. Hot and dry going down. Hotter, wetter coming back out.

The warm breeze grazing across my bare arms and legs distracted me, shifting my attention back to the thousands of nerves lying just under the surface all along my body. I could feel the sun baking my skin ... something I'd done a thousand times. I loved the warm kiss of sunlight on my skin. A gentle, sensual embrace straight from the heavens to me. I could lie here forever, just feeling the sun, and be perfectly and entirely content.

But, as if set to prove me wrong, sound suddenly erupted all around me. And I was the fickle one. My focus shifted immediately from my delicious solar squeeze to the lazy gurgling of the Rio Grande, the mesquite trees as they tried to capture the breeze within their branches, the lizard padding softly through the dirt a few yards off, the grasshopper chirping somewhere off to my right. A little further away I could hear the ethereal song of the hungry thrush who was eyeing that juicy chirping meal, and from high above, the predatory call of the falcon circling, watching, wanting that thrush for his own empty stomach.

Again, my mind drifted. This time it dove into my own head, my heart. I was waiting. I was waiting for him. And he was late.

Where was Jesse? He'd told me to meet him here over an hour ago, and he was always early. At least when it came to seeing me. That was one of the things I loved about him. He always made me feel like the center of his universe.

But he wasn't here. I forced myself to stay relaxed, keeping my eyes closed, breathing slowly. This was a big day. Jesse was asking my parents for my hand in marriage. I knew they would agree. Jesse was wonderful. Everything a man should be. And they knew I loved him to the depths of my soul. I pictured the handkerchief I'd embroidered his initials on, and below them, in smaller letters, the words "Te quiero con todo mi corazón, mi amor." It was written in Spanish because Jesse was half Mexican. It meant "I love you with all my heart, my love." It had taken me a month to stitch it, working by candle light each night after the house had gone to sleep. It was my wedding gift for Jesse. I'd finished it last night, working until the early morning hours, adding a small bear claw at the end. Jesse's symbol for a life well lived. I would give it to him tonight.

My mind slipped back to missing him. Needing his touch, his caress, as much as I needed the air to breathe. It bothered me that he wasn't here yet, the discomfort of it harping on my nerves, rankling like a wash of needles along my skin. What could they be talking about for so long? Surely not me. Cars maybe. Me, no.

Maybe they'd gone out back to bond over that old engine Dad had been tinkering with for months. He just couldn't seem to get the timing chain to cooperate. I could just see them, working through the late afternoon, heads bent together, shirts draped through the windows. Dad would have his undershirt pulled out of his jeans, but Jesse would be bare-chested. He loved the sun as much as I did, it just showed better on him. It darkened his skin until it glistened a rich, honeyed, coppery-brown, and only ever seemed to turn his thick, straight hair blacker and shinier. That was thanks to his mixed Cherokee-Mexican bloodline, the same cause for the color of his eyes, which were two shades darker than the color of a moonless midnight and richer than the blackest velvet.

Jesse's father had been passing through, trying to cross the Rio Grande down into Mexico, when he'd fallen head over heels for one Maria de la Cruz. The mix of genes showed in the strong, clean lines of Jesse's face, the smooth, hairless skin across his chest, and the gleam of wilder beasts than mere humans in his eyes, barely contained when he was excited.

I licked my lips, dragging the bottom one through my teeth as I did. Jesse. I needed his touch now, his strength surrounding me, cradling me. My God, how I loved him. I would do anything for him.

As if on cue, I heard those familiar footsteps as he approached. And my heart quickened, my breath caught. Even without looking, I knew his eyes would be locked on me. Wanting me with the same inescapable urgency that pulled me to him. A fire that raged between us whether we were lost in each other's arms on a warm Southern night or singing hymns at church on a bright Sunday morning.

A shadow crept over my face as he stood over me, blotting the sun from its conquest. He just stood there, for some time, not speaking a word.

"So, how long do I have to wait for our ceremony? Please tell me it's before fall. I can't bear the thought of waiting three more months to curl into your arms each night." I stretched slowly, lethargically, slowly stirring heated muscles and flesh.

"We're getting married tonight." The unsmiling severity of the words I'd been aching to hear, waiting for years to hear, caught me by surprise and my eyes flew open.

Immediately, my pulse sped at the sight of my dark love. I couldn't see him so much as the halo surrounding him, the sun so strong at his back. He reminded me of a picture I'd seen once of Michael, the Archangel. Power spilling from his body, all of heaven at his side.

"Tonight? Jesse! I never in a million years thought they'd forego their white wedding dreams. You are amazing! How did you get them to agree?" I leapt to my feet, fully alert now and threw my arms around his neck. My mouth captured his lips in a heated kiss, my hands sliding down his back as I melted into him. Warm hands clutched at the small of my back as his body folded into mine, his mouth accepting all I had to give, and then taking more. Drowning me in his need, feeding my own.

Gently Jesse eased the kiss, softening his hold, but only marginally. He pulled back just enough to stare down at me with those midnight eyes. And for the first time, I realized he was angry. Jesse didn't get angry. I'd known him my whole life and had never seem him move past irritated. Not even once. My hand slipped instinctively to his cheek.

"They said no, Rache." Anger, pain, betrayal, denial, love, possession all battled for supremacy in his sweet face. His lips were still rounded, plump from the passion of our kiss. But the muscles of his jaw were clenching, the tender flesh around his eyes tightening as rage and refusal swept over him, each vying for supremacy.

No? No to what? To this? To Jesse? To us? I felt the pain instantaneously rip a gorge as wide as the Grand Canyon between my family and me. The family I'd always loved, always trusted, always knew would be there for me, loving me, believing in me, was suddenly separated from me, torn away with a deafening finality. In that moment I knew our lives would never be the same. I blinked, trying to make sense of things that couldn't possibly make sense. "But you said ..."

Tight muscles jerked me in closer, pulling my body almost within his, desperation adding a demanding impatience to our embrace. "We will be married tonight." Resolute. Fearless. Unshakably determined. "It doesn't matter whether they agree or not. We're both old enough to decide for ourselves, Rache. It would have been nice to have their blessing, but not having it doesn't change a thing between us." He stopped briefly to press warm lips to mine, then continued. "My heart beats because you live inside me. My lungs breathe because you fill them with love. A single day without the sound of your voice, your laughter, your touch, is an eternity in hell. You are my life. You always have been. You always will be. I am yours and I will love you until the stars shower down upon us and time loses all meaning."

A cry tore from my lips as a single tear slipped down my cheek. But the coolness of it brought with it the edge of anger, and I felt the frown crease my forehead at the thought of anyone trying to stand between Jesse and me.

What was going on? How could my parents have said no? They loved Jesse. Didn't they? We'd been dancing with each other's shadows our whole lives. I didn't have a single memory of a day without him. Even when he'd spent two weeks in the hospital after fighting off that damn bear that had come out of nowhere. I'd been the idiot who just had to get closer to that adorable, fuzzy little cub ignoring Jesse's words of warning, and he'd been the one to pay the price.

And boy had he paid. That big black mama bear had missed killing him by a hair, literally. She'd ripped into the side of his chest just as he'd plunged his knife into hers. Two warriors, each set on defending the life of someone they loved. Of course, my warrior had only been sixteen at the time. I'd knocked the bear over with the biggest rock I could find, which ripped her claws out of his chest at an ugly angle, his knife tearing from hers just as inelegantly.

Both turned to me, Jesse's savage face fueled with fear for me, the bear's a mask of utter fury as she stood and roared her intent in my face. While I stared back at her, lock-kneed, body frozen in shock, Jesse knocked her out with the rock that had slipped from my fingers after my failed attempt to end the battle. He stood there a moment, blood running down his side, looking every bit the wild half-breed he was, making sure she wasn't in any shape to reengage. His first thought was my protection. Then he held his hand over her nose, a half inch from the bear's snout to make sure she was still breathing, still had a strong heartbeat. He had to know the mother and cub would survive despite us. Despite me.

I'd stayed by his side the entire time he was recouping. Keeping a constant vigil over my wild man. One claw had been ripped from the female's paw and lodged in Jesse's ribs, a memento the doctor had given him after digging it out of his side. And still he'd gone back to that spot in the woods over the months and years that had followed to catch a glimpse, leave an offering, share in the life he'd allowed to continue and the life he'd been allowed to have.

He still wore that claw on a long leather strap around his neck. A talisman he'd told me once. A promise of love and respect, a bond between us and what lies beyond. Of the unconquerable belief that life is both precious and precarious. Ours to make the most of in each moment, each breath. The sweetest moments often lying in the aftermath of the greatest defeats of our own fears, lethargy and cruelty.

"What reason did they give?" I couldn't believe I was speaking these words. I braced myself, not knowing what was coming, but feeling the pain of it already ripping through my soul.

"It seems that while it's okay for us to see each other, they have a problem with you marrying someone with my ... background." Betrayal flitted across his eyes again, sending sparks of pain from their depths.

"Your background?" The words were clear enough. I knew they were. But my mind couldn't, or maybe wouldn't, make sense of them.

"Rache, they want you to marry someone like Marcus Freemont. Live a long life and have lots of pretty, pearly white babies." His eyes dropped away from mine. An unfamiliar visitor, shame, stole his gaze, turning it down toward dark, lonely places. Places filled with nothing but pain and despair.

The color drained from my face. I knew my family, my parents and my older brother, could be prejudiced at times, but never like this. Not to this extent. Not to Jesse. Not to me. And I thought they'd been getting better about it. Outgrowing it. After all, Jesse and I had been sweethearts from the cradle. Our mothers had formed an instant bond in side-by-side beds in the single delivery room of the hospital one hot July night. They'd been inseparable for years afterward, rocking on the front porch for hours as we fed, slept, cried and played.

But ... it had always been on our front porch, never Jesse's. It had never really hit me until just then. Hypocrites! A hot surge of adrenaline moved through me. Filled me up like a dry creek bed caught in a thunderstorm. Pounding my flesh with fury. No one would steal Jesse from me. Not even my parents. I'd always done what they'd asked, what they'd expected. But not this time. This time they'd gone too far.

I looked at Jesse, and barely had to shift my gaze upward. We were almost the same height, he'd just managed to edge past me the last couple years by two inches. A big two inches to him, to me, not so much. It was the man I loved, not the length of his pants. I raised my hands to the face of my gentle warrior, cradling his cheeks in my hands, lifting his chin until he had no choice but to look into my eyes. "There's a full moon tonight. Let's go up to the Ernst Tinaja. It will be so beautiful." I smiled into that warm face inches from mine. I knew my eyes were glinting with mischief. "And it will be just us."

The pain etched into his face gave way to hope and expectation, softening his somber expression. "God, Rachel! How do you ...?" He sighed and the tension from his shoulders eased. "I was furious five seconds ago and now all I can think about is you. Kissing you. Holding you. Loving you. God, how I love you." Hunger was spilling into those dark, loving eyes, making the muscles in my stomach tighten in anticipation, but not fear. I could never be afraid of Jesse.

His thumb brushed across my lips. "There's something I need to tell you."

I slipped my fingers over his lips. "Shh. I know everything I need to know, Jesse. I know you love me. I know I love you. I know we belong together. Forever." I leaned into him and gently caressed his lips with mine.

But Jesse was hungry for more than furtive whispers of future passion. He was filled with need, longing, desires too long held in check. His rough hands tangled in my hair pulling me closer, deepening the kiss, pulling us into the warm caress of crazed ardor. My hands eased down his throat, across his broad shoulders, before clenching, nails biting through the shirt into soft flesh. Every thought silenced at his touch. Thirsting for him as desperately as he thirsted for me. Finally, I managed to let my hands fall to his chest and pushed away just enough to think again. A throaty, breath-filled laugh rippled past my lips as I looked up cautiously, playfully, into Jesse's, his own face lit with warmth from the passionate fire raging within. "I also know we need a blanket and some candles. You get those. I don't want to see my parents, or Joseph for that matter, but I need to slip into my room, get a few things and change."

The dark silhouette of despair and distrust fell over Jesse's face. "No, Rache. I don't want you going back there. It's worse than you think. I need to tell you ..."

"Jesse. I'll marry you, but I'll be damned if I'll do it in Joseph's cut-off overalls and an old undershirt. I'll sneak in my window. No one will even know I'm there. I'll meet you at the turn just past the Terlingua cut-off in an hour. Surely the rest of our lives can hold on long enough for one quick costume change."

He gave me those puppy dog eyes that always seemed to turn my knees to Jell-O and melt my heart. "Alright. But you have to stand still for just a minute and let me tell you this."

I pushed him away to arm's length. "Nothing doing. You can just put those eyes of yours back where they belong, Mister. I have a date to get married. And I don't intend on being late. And if you know what's good for you, you won't be late either, or there'll be hell to pay. I just might have to marry Marcus Freemont after all." But no sooner had the words come out of my mouth, before a tremor slithered all the way down my body and my knees buckled. "Ungh! What a disgusting thought."

Jesse was laughing, smiling down into my face, almost every trace of his earlier torment wiped away. "Somehow I don't think walking down the aisle retching in a chili pot is an improvement over this." His eyes swept down over my clothes. Then his hands slid up my thighs as his eyes locked onto mine, leaning in to capture my lips again.

"Oh, no you don't, Tiger. I told you. I have a date. And he'll be pretty pissed if you make me late. So, hands off, Buddy!" I leaned in, put my hands on his chest, and kissed him quick. Before he could even respond, I slid my leg up to the backs of his knees and pulled towards me as I pushed my arms forward. He fell straight to the ground on that great butt.

"Ow! Shit, Rache! You're gonna pay for that one! I ought to turn you over my knee and give you the spanking you deserve." Yeah, he sounded real tough with that laugh hanging at the back of his words.

But I was already yards away, running back to town. I glanced over my shoulder, then ran backwards as I laughed back at him. "Yeah? Promises, promises. It's your own damn fault it hurt. You should eat a little more, stop trying to impress every girl in the Rio Grande Valley and put some more cush on that tush."

I turned back, the wind dancing through my hair. Happier than I ever remembered being. I was getting married. Tonight! I was flying.

Jesse had gotten to his feet and was chasing behind me, catching up quickly. "You're gonna drive me crazy in the first six months! I know it."

"Well I certainly hope so, because I'm already completely nuts because of you!" I didn't look back, afraid to see how close he was now. I could hear his breathing, deep and strong, but I couldn't feel it yet. My legs were straining, muscles rebelling at how hard I was pushing them. If I could just make it a few more yards, I'd be over the rise of the hill and almost back in town. I'd win.

But all of a sudden I was flying forward and spinning upside down ... just like how a football is thrown, when it's thrown well, anyway. My brother, Joseph, was the quarterback on the varsity team. We must have spent a thousand hours throwing that stupid pigskin back and forth. But this time I was the football. Jesse had leapt through the air to tackle me, but he'd turned us midair so that he'd be the one on the bottom to catch the brunt of the fall.

"Gotcha! You little wildcat!" He swatted my rear end. "That's for taking my breath away. Next time, I won't stop with just one."

Breathless laughter spilled out of me. "You really are crazy, you half-breed!"

I lifted my head up, resting on my forearms, my entire body lying on the length of Jesse's. But as my upper weight settled onto my arms, I frowned, lifting my left hand to see why it was hurting a little.

Jesse's eyes zeroed in on the scrape at the base of my palm just as I did. He gently brushed off the dirt that was still clinging to it, then brought my hand to his mouth, my fingers splayed across his warm, smooth cheek. His warm lips caressed my palm, his tongue sliding along the soft flesh. Slowly he worked his way down to the rounded base of my hand and began softly suckling the wound, drawing out fresh blood as he did. His eyes closed as if he was in some state of euphoria. Long moments stretched as he pulled at my flesh with those warm, rosy lips. Teeth scraped gently along my skin as he lost himself in the moment. His tongue sliding across the wound, hot and demanding.

I knew it should bother me, I always knew that. But it didn't. It never had. It was intoxicating, decadent, undeniable. His touch, his hunger was lulling me into his sensual reverie. My face drawing nearer to his, my eyes softening, lips parting. I wanted to taste his lips, my warm blood clinging to them.

Some part of me realized that thought, that desire was just a little bit ... unusual. And insecurity tickled at the edges of my beautiful daydream, my dark fantasy. My eyes slowly pried themselves from Jesse's mouth and shifted to his dark eyes, still focused on my hand, glinting with unquenched hunger.

"Why do you always do that?" My voice came out soft and deep, heavy with emotion, with unfulfilled need.

His lips slid across the soft flesh of my hand, nuzzling the chaffed tissue. But those eyes. Those eyes slid up to mine and held me like a moth to a flame. "Do what, Rache? Kiss your wounds? You don't like it?" There was a hint of anger underneath all that brazen desire.

Fear knotted in my stomach. Not fear that he'd hurt me. I knew Jesse could never, would never, hurt me. But fear that he'd pull some part of him

I didn't really know away from me before I ever had the chance to meet it, to accept it.

"No!" I barked out hoarsely. I took a deep breath and continued. "I didn't say it bothered me. And it doesn't, even though it probably should. But just why? Why do you do that? Because one thing you're not doing is simply kissing my wounds. My mother has done that my whole life. And this? This definitely isn't that. It's something ..." I shook my head, waving my hand carelessly, at a loss for words to express the exquisite crumbling I felt deep inside whenever he did this.

But Jesse persisted. Tenacious little Indian. "Something, what?" His tongue slid along the scrape again. My breath caught as a shiver wove its way down my body.

"Something ... something more. Just more. A whole lot more."

He pulled back then, pressing my hand against his chest, eyes darkening. "Rache, there really is something you need to know. Before tonight. It's big. And it affects you."

Guilt washed over me, leaving a bitter taste in my mouth. "God, Jesse! I was just kidding about the half-breed thing, you know that. And this? This is nothing. It just makes me feel things I've never considered existed, much less felt. And I don't even know what it is. Or why you do it. Or why it makes me feel the way it does. But no matter what, I love you. All of you. Besides, I'm probably more of a mutt than you could ever hope to be, and I can deal with pain better than even that idiot brother of mine. So, whatever it is you think is so god-awful important can just wait. Nothing's gonna change my mind about you.

You're mine. Whether we get married tonight or not, you're still mine."

He rolled over, sliding me to the ground beneath him. Leaning over me on one arm, he slid his other hand softly along my side to my face, cradling my cheek in his palm and brushing my lips with his thumb. "God, Rache. You're so beautiful. I can't wait until tonight. There will be a tonight. And then, I'm never gonna let you out of my sight again." A gentle fire burned deep within his eyes, as he leaned forward and softly touched his lips to mine.

"Well, you'd better not. Or I'll have to beat some sense back into that thick skull of yours." I slid my arms firmly up his back, pulling him down to me when I reached his shoulders. My eyes locked on his, I kissed him deeply, parting his lips with mine, feeling my passion fuel his as my tongue tempted, teased, caressed and danced with his.

Jesse quickly resumed control of the kiss, deepening it further. But even as he did so, I was moving my hands around to his chest, pushing against him to break the soul-catching connection.

My heart in my throat, the desire burning throughout my body staining my cheeks, darkening my eyes, I stared up at him trying to catch my breath. "If we're gonna do this little thing tonight after all, you gotta let me go get ready. I want to be pretty for you, not dressed like a boy."

"Rache, if you were any prettier, I swear I'd have to keep you locked up forever, so only I could see you, be with you, be seen by you. It doesn't matter what you're wearing. All I think about is you. Your touch." His hand grazed down my cheek and neck resting on my collarbone, fingers splayed around my throat. "Your smell." Chills swept up my spine as he nuzzled closer and inhaled deeply right where my jaw line merged with my neck and ear, his cheek feathering across my own like a warm whispered breeze. "Your taste." He leaned in for a quick kiss that straddled the distance between gentleness and passion. "Your look." He lifted his head, dark eyes burning into mine as he brushed his nose against mine then tenderly kissed each eyelid, anointing me with his love.

I smiled back up into that strong, dark face and fell in love all over again. "Fine. You win. No dress." One hand had buried itself in the thick, silky hair at the nape of his neck, the other was easing along his jaw line. I let myself drown in the depths of his eyes, the warmth of his embrace, memorizing everything about him in that moment. The soft strength of his skin, the heat in his eyes, the taste of his breath as it washed over my face, the fresh, rugged smell of his body now tinged with the fever of our obsession. Finally, I slid my hand back along that jaw as I pulled him back into me for another of those intoxicating, addictive kisses, and thought no more. As the weight of my desire crashed through me, sweeping me away on a wave of bliss, my arms tightened, pulling him closer and closer, my legs weaving snugly around his, holding him so tightly to me we should have melted into one.

I felt Jesse's body melt into mine. His love poured down my throat. His passion beat along the length of my body as he tore down every hint of resistance, losing himself in the wake of my surrender. His body curved into mine possessively, craving more. His hands locked in my hair, pulling me impossibly deeper into him, the pricks of pain along my scalp that should have hurt only adding urgency to the ravishing heat storming through me. Suddenly, a groan tore from deep within his throat as he ripped his mouth from mine, loosening my grip effortlessly. "A dress? You're gonna wear a dress? You don't wear dresses."

"I told you I wanted to be pretty, girl kind of pretty." I pouted, my lips swollen from his kisses. I lifted my head to get another, hungry for more of him.

But the hands in my hair held me firmly on the ground, not giving me the freedom I needed to reach those luscious lips only inches above mine. I heard a frustrated moan wiggle its way out of my throat.

Jesse just laughed down at me. "Behave. Besides, I really want to see you in a dress. Not that you'll be wearing it for long. But it might be the only chance I get ... I've known you my whole life and only seen you in one a handful of times. Weddings, funerals, confirmations. I want to see what you'd wear just for me."

"You know I hate it when you do that."

Innocent eyes gazed back at me. Innocent my butt. "Do what, Baby? I'm giving you what you wanted. Letting you win."

"Ungh! You're giving in after I already gave in first. And furthermore, I don't need anyone to let me win anything. I do just fine all on my own." I tried my best to glare up at him, letting the fire shift from passion to annoyance.

"Well, get used to it. You won't be doing much of anything all on your own after tonight. We'll be a team. We'll do everything on our own, together."

He leaned back in to kiss me, but I shifted my weight to one side and pushed him with all my strength as I rolled out from under him and jumped to my feet. "Oh, no you don't. You said behave. We're behaving. I'll see you in an hour." I turned to finish the walk up the hill. "And don't even think about being late, or I will marry that idiot Marcus instead."

"Over my dead body, you little minx. You're mine. You always were and you always will be." He growled out before I slipped down the other side of the hill, laughing as I pictured the look I knew was plastered to his face.

"You think?" I was half running now. In a hurry to return to the arms of my hypnotic, erotic lover.

"I know." Jesse's words whispered in the breeze behind me, slipping around me in a loving, wicked embrace.

14 ALLOW ME TO INTRODUCE MR. AND MRS. JESSE ALEJANDRO GARCIA DE LA CRUZ

Forty-five minutes later, I was standing at the cut-off waiting for him. Thankfully, no one had been at home when I got there, so it had been an easy matter to quickly wash up, change, and throw some things in a bag. I'd rushed through washing my hair, the damp waves caressing my hips. As it dried, it would sit above my waist, but the weight of the water kept my hair straighter, making it seem even longer than usual now and it felt nice and cool brushing against my arms as it moved softly in the breeze.

While rubbing the soap along my arms, I'd cried out in pain as the suds bit into a gash along the tender flesh of my left forearm. I was always getting hurt, usually in my hurry to get to Jesse. My middle name should have been Clumsy Fool instead of Anne. Still, this was a really bad scratch, as wounds go, and I didn't have a clue how I'd gotten it.

Oh, well. Good thing Jesse had already agreed to marry me ... I'd tell him tomorrow he'd married just one little chunk less of me than he would have yesterday.

Dressed in an embroidered white cotton blouse, knee-length skirt and brown leather sandals, I tucked my grandmother's wedding dress in a bag to avoid any questions in case I ran into someone before I got back out of the house. I'd decided to change into that dress when we got to the canyon. Tucked inside the folds of the dress was the handkerchief I'd stitched for Jesse.

Not quite knowing when I'd be returning home, I had filled the rest of my bag with a few clothes, toothbrush, things to keep my hair in check, what little money I had, and my most treasured keepsakes. Nothing really valuable, just bits and pieces, scattered moments of my life. A picture of my mother, father, Joseph and me taken last year in Presidio, an eagle feather Jesse had given me when he first told me he was going to marry me ... we were seven years old at the time, a long strand of glittery black beads, knotted partway down that had belonged to my grandmother ... she'd only worn them on special occasions, like trips to the ballet or the opera and they'd hung all the way to her waistline, two books, both collections of stories, one by Shakespeare, the other by Poe, and a journal and pen to write my own story. The one I just hadn't gotten around to writing yet. But I would. With Jesse, I would.

I leaned back against an old oak tree and watched as a javelina nosed hungrily around a prickly pear, one of the many cacti that dotted the landscape here. I'd never understood why the colorful, rounded fruit on it was called tuna. I mean, Good Lord, we weren't anywhere near the ocean, and besides there was absolutely nothing about a prickly pear that made you think of fish. Now, nopales I got. That's what the big, spiked, padded plates that made up the rest of the plant were called. At least it was in Spanish. And pretty tasty fried with eggs and salsa. But tuna? I guess some things are just beyond comprehension. Beyond mine, anyway.

I heard horse hooves approaching and lifted a hand to shield my eyes from the sun, which although inching closer by the minute to the horizon was nonetheless relentless in its fiery blaze, staining the sky shades of yellow, pink and red. As the footsteps rounded the bend and started down the slope, Jesse's body fell between me and the sun, so that instead of the sun shining down on me, nourishing me, guiding my steps, it was Jesse. He looked like some ancient God lighting the sky with his power, his strength. The luminous sheen of his hair, glinting with deep shades of electric blue, burst across the sky above me. His dark honeyed skin was bathed in the dulcet tones of impending twilight. And below him, dust lit like golden embers billowed in stormy clouds. He stole my breath, and just as easily stole my heart.

I was captivated, speechless. His long hair was sliding like midnight silk across his back and chest, bounding in time to the pace of the hooves drumming out his approach. He had no shirt on, just two brown straps hung from his neck. The long leather cord with the bear claw that he never took off, and the new one that held eagle feathers tied on it throughout the length, interspersed with beads, gracing the smooth, taut muscles of his chest, hanging low enough that the bottom feathers brushed the tight muscles of his abdomen, gently tickling them, causing them to ripple in response.

I licked my suddenly dry lips, my fingers twitching in reaction to this perfect vision of male strength and beauty. My Jesse. My love. My life. He was magnificent.

Covering his lower body was a pair of brown suede pants that hugged his thighs and begged mercilessly to be touched, caressed. His bare feet hung at the side of Jimmy, his black mustang. He'd worked in the Mercury mines for nearly three years, saving every penny for that horse. He loved him more than most men loved their own children. Or their cars. Jesse looked every inch the Indian prince of my dreams. Strong. Proud. Breathtakingly handsome and captivatingly sincere. Innocently demanding.

As he pulled up beside me, I handed him my bag, which he quickly tied off onto the side of the horse. "Hey, Jimmy." I leaned my head against the horse's broad, coarse neck, letting my hand slide down the strong, lean line of his nose. As I reached Jimmy's mouth, his soft lips nibbled at my salty fingertips, pulling a soft giggle from me at the cool sensation. Jimmy snorted in reply, tossing his great head appreciatively, and pawed the ground in front of me.

Then Jesse's dark, mischievous eyes grabbed mine, his mouth tipped in a lopsided smile and he winked at me. Before I could so much as gasp in surprise, he'd grabbed me and pulled me up behind him over the horse. There was no saddle, just a soft dark blue blanket thrown over its back.

As his hands released my arms, I couldn't hold back another whimper, the scratch on my arm was really smarting now. Jesse looked over his shoulder at me, eyes questioning. "What? Surely that didn't hurt you?"

"Nah. I just have a little scratch. It's nothing, really. Can't even remember how in the world I got it!"

Jesse eyes sharpened on my arm, then he looked straight down into my soul. "Sure you don't remember, Rache?"

"Don't have a clue!" I half laughed back at his serious face.

That seemed to lighten his mood, because he snickered then with that lopsided smile and turned back around. "You and your war wounds! Bandages will be on every grocery list! People are gonna think I beat my wife!"

"God, that sounds wonderful!"

"Beating you sounds wonderful? Boy, we do have a problem!" I could see those gorgeous black eyes just simmering in the sunlight.

"No! Life with you sounds wonderful! Normal everyday married life ... with you." I leaned around and bit his shoulder playfully. "You are absolutely incorrigible!"

"Yeah, well, it still looks like you've got me beat. You're the cannibal."

Before my body had completely settled back into place on the horse, Jesse bit into the flanks with his heels propelling Jimmy forward. Jesse's arm slid from mine, pulling me up close behind him. My hips slid along his back until I finally nudged into place on the rocking beast. A strong, warm hand guided my thighs up close and tight, sliding them forward and tucking them just behind his own.

I moved my arms around his sides, under the teasing straps dangling from his neck, to grip the straining muscles of his abdomen. I tucked my cheek against his dark muscular back and couldn't resist nuzzling up against him, inhaling his spicy, exotic scent, before I rested my face along the sun-warmed skin pulled tightly across his shoulder blades.

Our hair caught the emotion of the night and danced together, my dark waves sliding in and out through Jesse's black, silken tresses. Our bodies moved in a synchronous rhythm, brushing, touching, mercilessly tempting, unabashedly promising.

And as we rode, the sun slowly dipped lower. Fingers of soft oranges, deep crimsons and warm burgundy slipped into the early evening sky stretching above us. Shadowed images traced along the boulders, the plants, the dirt, dancing all around us, whispering of magic worlds, of places unseen by man, places of unbelievable power, staggering beauty, eternal loves, and undying, unquenchable passions.

The cool air of twilight teased along the heated flesh of our bodies, feeding the fires already burning deep inside. We eased our way through the rough terrain. The tension within both of us built with each foot gained toward our destination. Not a tight, uneasy tension, but a tension suffused with ... anticipation. Anticipation unhindered by fear, regret or second guessing. Simply primal, hungry, loving, eager anticipation.

The volcanic landscape gradually gave way to limestone as we approached the Ernst Tinaja. Light lingering from the setting sun, slipping quickly now from the day as it dipped ever lower on the horizon, bathed the rocks in burnished shades of burgundy and violet, streaks of sapphire and midnight blue. The first hints of stars peeked down, winking at us, glittering like fairy dust sprinkled across the heavenly palette of color.

Jesse slowed the pace and slid off when we reached the lower section of the formation holding the tinaja. He reached up, placing his strong hands on my hips, lifted me from the horse, and held me over his head. My hands rested on his broad shoulders, waiting for him to lower me to the ground.

But he didn't. Instead, he just held me over him and began turning around and around. Holding me hostage with his dark, molten eyes and sinfully luscious lips.

My hands tightened on his shoulders. "Jesse! You're crazy! Put me down. I can't even think straight."

"Yes! I am crazy! Crazy for you, mi corazón!" He yelled out. "You don't need to think straight Rache. You just need to love me. To need me. I'll be your anchor." A warm laugh bellowed through him. "Your anchor and your wings!" He spun even faster, my legs flying up in the air behind me as my hands gripped his shoulders for dear life.

I couldn't help but laugh, completely exhilarated with the sensations pouring through me. "Jesse! I feel like I'm flying! I love you. I love you, Jesse!"

"Oh, you're not flying yet, Chica. But you will be. I promise you, you will be. I'll show you how. And you'll love it. You'll never want to stop." He finally let me slide down his body until my feet rested between his. "Careful, now. Wouldn't want the world to spin right out from underneath you."

I scrunched my nose and tilted my head as my eyes cut sideways up at him, a small smile playing along my mouth. "Yeah. You haven't been smoking any of that peyote with the guys, now have you? Because you're sounding a little ... out there." That was one little cactus to keep a good perimeter around. Of course, if you were Native American it wasn't illegal ... for religious use, in any case.

"Mescaline? No, there are much better ways to fly." Mescaline was the magic in peyote, the candied essence that brought about a euphoric, awakened-dream state filled with fantastically impossible visions of fantasy and whimsical reality.

"Uh-huh. You're just talking idiotic nonsense. You want to impress me? Show me something I can put my hands on."

He just laughed louder, pulling me closer. "That's just it, Rache. I have so much to show you! So much to tell you. Ungh!" He wrapped his arms around my waist and swung around in a circle again.

"Stop it, wild man! Put me down so I can change. I've got a wedding to go to. Then you can go all batty on me." I tried to sound firm. I tried and failed. It was hard to have an edge when you couldn't stop the laughter from bubbling out.

Jesse's dark brows drew together. "You just changed. You look great, Rache." He waggled his eyebrows. "Besides, I don't think what you're wearing is gonna be a problem for long."

I felt the blood rush to my cheeks, staining them a dark rose, as I tried to push away. But Jesse's arms tightened, locking me to him from the waist down. "Rache." His voice was ragged as his eyes latched onto mine. "We've waited so long. I don't ever want to let go of you again, Baby." He leaned in, brushing his lips on the tip of my nose, never letting go of my eyes. "Really, Rache. You're beautiful, mi corazón. You always are. No matter what you're wearing." His cheek grazed across my temple.

"Please, Jesse. It's important to me. I want tonight to be perfect. I want to be perfect for you. Well, as perfect as I can be. I want tonight to be a memory we'll have for all time. One we can tell our great-great-grandchildren about. And besides, you ... you look like every woman's fantasy come true, and a thousand times more." My fingers gently played along the feathers decorating his broad, tanned chest. The deepening of his eyes, the smile playing softly on his lips told me it pleased him. "Let me be that for you. Give me three minutes. That's all." Jesse's arms eased enough that I could duck under one and slip out.

"You want to be every woman's fantasy for me?" Jesse asked, eyebrows raised, feigning confusion.

"You know damn well what I mean, you smart-ass. Three minutes. You can give me three stupid little minutes." I turned and started for a rise on the left to slip behind.

"Well, I'm counting. You've got two minutes and forty-five seconds now. Just so you know. And, ready or not, when three minutes are up, you're mine. Dress or no dress. Two and a half minutes now, Rache."

I was ripping my clothes off as fast as I could, peeking over the top of the rock. "Are you always gonna be so ornery? Maybe we should call this whole thing off. I don't know if I can live my whole, entire life with a crazy, bull-headed Indian like you." Dragging the sleeveless dress from the bag, I pulled it quickly over my head, sliding my arms in before slipping the length over my body. I shimmied my hips to let the slim, beaded folds of fabric spill over them, sliding down my thighs, until the hem brushed the tops of my feet. The dress was a little long on me without shoes, but feeling the warm earth beneath my toes and the cool silk bathing the tops of my feet, made me feel beautiful, sexy, and just a little bit wanton.

"You just lost one full minute because of that smart mouth. That just leaves you thirty seconds, Rache."

"You are so-o-o mean." I pouted back, pulling the black beads on. I bent over at the waist, flipped my hair upside down to quickly finger through it, and then righted myself, hurriedly smoothing the tresses down. Reaching back into the bag, I removed the book on Shakespeare, letting the book fall open on its own in my hands. As the pages parted on Romeo and Juliet, Jesse's feather was exposed. I tucked the feather behind my ear and slid the book back in the bag.

"Yeah, and you love me just that way. You love that I can't keep my hands off you. Ten ... nine ... eight ... seven. You'd better be ready woman, because here I come. Three ... two ..."

I tucked Jesse's hankie into the bodice, glanced down one last time for a quick check and stepped out.

Suddenly, there was no more countdown. There was only the sound of our breathing and the immense silence of the desert surrounding us.

Jesse stared at me with so much emotion, the air was immediately thick with it. Love, possession, pride, definitely. Hunger, lust, need, yes. But also something much closer to fear, caution, anxiety.

The warm colors of the setting sun mixed with the cool colors of twilight lighting the beads of the dress in a myriad of colors. It clung like a silken sheath along my body, caressing it gently until the fabric flared at the knee, creating a small train at my feet. The deep "V" cut of the front was exaggerated in the back, decadently slipping below the curves of my hips. I twisted this way and that, arms slightly raised, letting the beads blaze in a mesmerizing electric display of light. "See anything you like?"

Then I turned halfway around so Jesse could enjoy that tantalizing view of the back, watching his expression over my shoulder. Loving the way his eyes were drinking me down, as captivated with me as I was with him. I slowly shifted my hips and waist in a figure eight, making the light dance across my body, before I turned back, beckoning to him with my finger.

"Now, Jesse. Now, I'm yours. Now you never have to let go of me again."

He was right in front of me before my next breath. How did he move so fast? "Not quite yet. But almost." He scooped me up in his arms, held me against his chest, and kissed me. A warm, sweet kiss filled with devotion and promise.

Then he turned and started the short climb to the tinaja.

"Jesse." I laid my palm on his cheek, pulling his face toward mine. "I want to walk. I want to know my own feet carried me here. To this night. To this place. Our place. Our personal piece of heaven."

"But your dress."

"My dress will survive." My eyes darkened with mischief before I continued playfully. "Besides, what I'm wearing isn't gonna be a problem for long, or so I've heard."

He set me down gently, reverently, almost as if he was suddenly afraid of breaking me like a china doll. He kissed me again, then stepped back so we could walk together, side by side on our private pilgrimage of love.

As we were climbing up the smooth incline, our shadows lengthened, accompanying us as silent witnesses to the binding of our souls. Quietly they swept over the layered rock walls with their naturally rich colors now magnified by the setting sun, bathed in the last brilliant breaths of red and gold spiking through the glistening velvet sky.

The cry of an eagle pierced the silence. It was a sound I cherished, and heard less frequently every day. Golden eagles were being trapped, shot and poisoned all through this area, and had been for years. Town talk was that some of the local ranchers were pushing for it. I hated it, and I knew Jesse did, too. He never really said much about it, he just got quiet and moody whenever the subject came up.

When we approached the final rise surrounding the tinaja itself, Jesse's hand gripped my arm, stopping me. "Hold up just a minute, Rache." He cocked his head to one side and took a breath, a sign that for him meant he was a little nervous. "I have a little surprise for you that the boys helped me with."

He reached behind him and pulled something from his back pocket. It was a scarf, a long, sheer, black silk scarf with little black beads all over it. Some of the beads were small and round, seed beads, that were sewn on flat against the material, but others were longer or tied in strings that moved, slipping and sliding with the slightest movement, glinting wildly, wickedly in the darkening light of sun and stars. It must have been over three feet long and was absolutely gorgeous, top to bottom.

"Mama and Lucy made this for you. I was a little worried they wouldn't finish it in time, they were tying off the last knots as I was heading out to meet you."

"My God, Jesse. I've never seen anything so beautiful. It's exquisite." My fingers traced along the tiny beads gingerly, afraid that my touch alone would make it disintegrate.

"Well, they'll be real glad to hear it. Now, turn around."

I reached out for the scarf as I began to turn.

"Ah-ah-ah." Jesse chided me. "Not just yet. Turn around." His warm hands turned me by my upper arms until I was facing away from him. "Now, close your eyes."

I did and immediately felt the brush of silk across my cheek and nose. I started to open my eyes as I asked, "What are you doing?"

"Ah! No peeking. Keep those wicked little eyes closed." As I waited, nervous excitement rushed through my veins. Jesse shifted the fabric over my eyes and tied it behind my head, blindfolding me.

He leaned in close behind me, his mouth at my ear, hot breath caressing my face. "We're gonna have to put this to good use later." As my breath caught in my throat and my knees threatened to buckle beneath me, he turned me around to check his handiwork. "Good. Now, come with me." He took my left hand in his and let his right hand rest at the small of my back, guiding me forward effortlessly. After a few steps, he briefly let go of my left hand and I heard something soft and diaphanous whisper through the air.

"Okay. Stop here, Rache." His body moved in close behind mine and he slowly loosened the scarf and slid it down from my face, letting the knot nestle along my chest as he untied it.

It took a minute for my eyes to focus, to take in what lay before me. My breath caught at the sheer beauty surrounding us, my greedy eyes sliding all around, trying to take in everything in one huge gulp.

There were candles lit everywhere. There must have been at least a hundred of them. They were clustered all around the smooth rock near the natural basin of water and tucked on narrow ledges that hung on the walls left by millions of years of erosion.

All along the ground were flowers and petals. Late spring fills the dry West Texas desert lands with a rainbow of color. The limestone basin was blanketed with large yellow flowers from the prickly pear and small fragrant ones from the huisache trees, purple blossoms from the mountain laurel, which added a grape soda scent, cobalt blue canyon sage flowers and radiant red buds from the ocotillo shrubs.

Hanging at the far side of the tinaja was a sheer white panel of fabric and as I looked over my shoulder I saw another just like it shielding the path behind us. It wasn't as if the thin panels would afford any real protection. They didn't isolate us from the land, instead they created a warm, intimate setting in the midst of the harsh landscape around us, merely a suggestion of separation. The breeze was causing the silken sheets to billow and dance, softening the light of the setting sun, subduing it, taming it. I was completely captivated by the magic, the sensuality, surrounding me. Everything, the air, the rock, the wind, Jesse, me, positively overflowed with an earthy mysticism and a spiritual eroticism, to the point that I could taste the sweetness of it with each breath, feel it fill my lungs, pound through my veins.

I felt the heated push of love, desire and overwhelming wonder and anticipation saturate my entire body, fill it to the very brim, and then spill over. But it didn't stop there, the emotion-laden energy continued to grow, to expand, consuming the space between Jesse and I, surrounding us, filling our open-air boudoir, and then expanding outward, permeating our entire world, changing it, painting it, infusing it with the desperate honeyed passion of our devotion.

I turned to Jesse, letting my hands steal up behind his neck, tears filling my eyes, and told him without words how moved I was by his act of devotion. As one tear slipped out and softly traced down my cheek, I rose up on my toes, gently pulling Jesse's face down towards mine, and laid my lips tenderly against his.

"How?" I gently shook my head in confused admiration.

"I had a little help."

"You ..." My eyes slid around us in awe before returning to Jesse. "I've never, ever seen anything so unbelievably breathtaking. I've never even imagined anything could be so perfect. This is some unearthly, wondrous, impossible dream." A shadow of doubt crossed through my mind then, forcing my gaze to drop from his. "Jesse. I don't know how to do anything like this for you. I can't ..."

"Shhh. None of that." His hand caught below my chin, slowly but determinedly lifting my face to his. "Rache. What you see here is what you give me. Every day. We make our lives what they are, ordinary or enchanting, mundane or miraculous."

"But I can't do ..." I waved my hand around me, lowering my eyes again. Lost. "... this. It isn't even in the realm of possibility for me. My God, Jesse, I wish I could. But I can't. And you deserve all of this. And more." I felt the cool track of another tear inching its way down to my jaw.

Jesse cupped my face in his strong hands, once again pulling my gaze to his. "Aah, mi corazón." He kissed the tip of my nose before he continued. "We have the rest of our lives for you to worship me and try to think up ways to convince me I chose the right girl." He winked at me wickedly and leaned in to kiss me.

I caught that full bottom lip between my teeth and nipped it. Hard enough to hurt, but not hard enough to draw blood. Jesse's laughing growl chased away the rest of my unshed tears. "Oh, you'll definitely pay for this later. Crying and biting ... on our wedding night no less. You've been one bad little girl, Rache."

"Well. You just better marry me quick before I change my mind, wild man." I pushed away from him, and he let me, but grabbed my hand and pulled me closer to the water hole, an excited gleam in his eyes.

"I thought you'd never ask!" He positioned us at one end of the natural stone well, near the edge, and I realized for the first time that there was a fire burning there in a large metal bowl that had curved handles at the top. Lying on the ground near the bowl was a white blanket covered in embroidery that Jesse picked up and draped around us both.

"Thanks, but I'm not cold, Jesse."

"Glad to hear you're not getting cold feet again." He smiled that crooked smile that I loved. "That's not really what the fire is for, though. It's a memorial to our ancestors. We're really each supposed to start with our own blue blanket and replace both of them partway through with this white one. The blue represents our past sorrows, weaknesses and loneliness. The white is for our new life of peace, happiness and fulfillment. But we only get to hold each other and kiss under the white one so we're just gonna skip to the good part." He waggled those thick eyebrows at me.

I pursed my lips and lifted my chin in mock disapproval, lifting my eyebrows to enhance the effect. "I didn't know there were blanket rules. Nobody told me. But I do know that no perverts are allowed at my wedding. So, I'm sorry, but you need to leave now."

"Leave you? Never. And a little hugging and kissing? Nah. I'll let you know when we hit perverted, Buttercup. But first things first."

He took both my hands within his and looked straight into my eyes. The playful glints of mischief faded quickly from his face, leaving a deep pool of devotion, at once both tender and passionate. The silence bloomed around us, all of nature, the world around us, held its breath in anticipation.

"Rachel Anne Kensington, I've known you my whole life, and I've loved you just as long. You are my life, mi vida. Everything I am, everything I have is yours." Warm, soft lips brushed across my fingertips. "Every gift I am blessed with I now bless you with as well." He lifted the string of feathers from his chest and placed it over my head, resting it on my own chest. "Life is a most precious gift, but it is only as special as we make it. Our lives are finite, they exist only to the extent that we allow them to breathe, to feel, to love. Rachel, you are everything precious in my life. You are my love, my soul, my equal. I will shelter you from the rain, warm you from the cold and protect you against any who would be so foolish as to threaten you. I will be your laughter in times of sorrow, your companion in times of loneliness, your lover in times of passion. My last breath is yours. I will love you until the stars shower down upon us and time loses all meaning. Our lives are one. May our journey together be a long, happy one filled with life, love and laughter. Te quiero con todo mi corazón, mi amor. Mi vida." He brushed heated lips across mine.

My heart felt as though it would explode with the force of the love flowing through it. But it was my turn now. I took a deep breath, caught myself in his eyes, and found the strength to breathe, to speak. "Jesse Alejandro Garcia de la Cruz, my heart is yours. You fill my days and my soul with magic and light. Your love showers happiness within the emptiness of my life and gives meaning to each beat of my heart. I promise to shower you with everything I am and everything I have, strength and tenderness, determination and kindness, passion, joy and delight. I withhold nothing from you, I give all of myself to you without reservation or exception. I will be our light when frustrations, difficulties and fears plague us. I will lead our way out of the storm into the break of day, to the sun that shines eternally for us and our love." I slipped the handkerchief out of my bodice, lifted Jesse's hand, sliding my fingers over his to open them, kissed his palm gently and then pressed the fabric over the warm flesh my lips had touched. "Jesse, te quiero con todo mi corazón, mi amor. I love you."

Jesse's eyes dropped to what lay in his hand, and then lingered there as if trying to memorize every stitch. His thumb moved over the needlework. Then his gaze slowly rose back up to mine, a gentle fire burning within them, within him. A small smile teased across his lips. "You made this?"

I nodded, silenced by the emotion rolling off him, unable to speak a word.

His eyes returned to what lay in his hand. "A Bear claw. Huh." He sighed again, swallowing tightly. "It couldn't be any more perfect, Rache." His gaze lifted back to mine. "I'll keep it with me always. Thank you."

Two hands cradled my face as he tipped my head tenderly back and to the side, sealing our pact, our eternal promise, with a kiss.

Leaning back in my arms, Jesse looked back at me rather sheepishly. "Okay. I need your patience for a couple last things."

He walked over to the drape on the far side, reached behind it, and retrieved a basket. Bringing the basket over to me, he set it on the ground at my feet and pulled two cotton wrapped objects from it, handing an oblong shaped one to me.

"Mama begged that we follow as much tradition as possible." He unfolded the cloth to show a piece of cooked deer meat that smelled heavenly. He pulled off one bite with his fingers. It was so tender it nearly fell to the ground. "I give you venison and promise to provide for you."

Lifting his hand to my mouth, he slipped it past my lips. The flavor attacked my taste buds as I cradled the bite in my mouth. It was exquisite.

Jesse reached over to my bundle and pulled the fabric back to reveal an ear of corn, its smell rising, mingling with the venison. He smirked as he looked back up at me, raising my hands between us. "You offer me corn to symbolize your willingness to be a good Cherokee housewife." He cleared his throat at that, but the little chuckle was still audible.

"Uh-huh." I peeked up at him through lowered lashes. "A good Cherokee housewife, huh?"

"Yeah, well, she did embroider you that scarf around your neck. It would hurt her feelings if I had to tell her you refused to give me one little ear of corn." At least he had the sense to look guilty about the whole thing.

"Alright, alright. Open up, big boy." I lifted the corn up to his mouth for him to take a bite.

"Mmmm. That's good! Let me have another bite."

"Ungh!" I groaned, but held the corn in place again.

He licked his lips. "Just one more. Pleeease, Rache."

"You better make it a big one because this good little Cherokee housewife is about to retire." Boy did he make it a good one. He bit into the corn, slid his teeth down the ear without raising his lips, slid down again, and then bit me!

"Ow!" I jerked the corn away, dropping it back onto the piece of cotton lying in the basket. "Okay. Meal time's over for you, Mister. And there'll be no dessert, either. So don't get any pretty little ideas in your head."

"Oh, come on, Rache. You know you love me, especially when I'm bad."

I raised my chin, looking off to the side. "That was before I got married, now I have to be a respectable woman. After all, I'm Mrs. Jesse Alejandro Garcia de la Cruz now. Not just some silly, little country girl." I sniffed tightly, trying my best to act as if offended.

"Oh, don't go getting all respectable on my account. I love my sweet, naughty little Rachel just the way she is, thank you very much. And if marrying her means losing that part of her, you can just consider yourself a divorced old spinster as of now."

"Too late, Mister Garcia de la Cruz." I shoved him in the chest with both hands. "You're stuck with me forever, and there's not a thing you can do about it because I'm never gonna let you go, Baby."

He grinned from ear to ear. "Is that a fact?"

"You betcha. And if you have a problem with it, I'm gonna find the best looking, biggest, strongest guy around and tell him you hurt me and he's gonna kick your ass." I punctuated the last three words with finger prods on his chest.

Jesse rolled those dark, mischievous eyes of his and sighed. "Well, if I'm really stuck with you, Señora Rachel Anne Garcia de la Cruz, whatever shall I do with you now?"

"I thought you'd never ask!" I lunged forward grabbing him around the waist. "Kiss me quick! And do it all night long."

"Hmmm. I think my pucker will tucker out if I do that all night long. We're just gonna have to think of some other things to keep us occupied. Wonder what that could be. I might have a deck of cards tucked in my bag."

"Yeah? And if you so much as think about pulling those out right now, I'm gonna put you on bread and water for a year!"

"Shit. Then I guess I have no choice but to kiss you." He leaned in as if for a kiss, but just before our lips met he let me go, wheeled around and headed to the far curtain again.

Struggling to catch my balance I glared at him. "Where are you going now, Wild Man?"

"Just a minute!" His voice rang out testily from behind the curtain. "You really are a greedy girl tonight, Rache." He returned with a pile of blankets and a couple pillows, quickly laying them out, forming a soft pallet for us.

Returning to me, he leaned back in as if to begin the kiss again. And, once again, didn't. This time though, he reached down and scooped me up, laughing at my surprised squeal.

"Consider this our front door." He said the words as he stepped to the edge of the makeshift bed. "That makes this our 'I carry you over the threshold' moment." Then he gently laid me down on the blankets and we did kiss. And boy, how we kissed! Not all night long, but pretty darn close.

As we celebrated, rejoicing in the loving bonds we had enveloped ourselves within, we explored one another's bodies. Tasting, drinking, touching, sharing, breathing one another into ourselves, we became one breath, one life, one endless, eternal love. And we gave into the sheer joy of pleasuring each other, learning one another, and learning ourselves and our own needs and desires as well.

I reveled in the hard lines, soft skin, warm breath of this man I'd known my whole life, but was truly meeting for the first time tonight. A lifetime of memories flooded my mind, overwhelming my senses as I touched each curve, caressed each muscle, learning subtle cues of pleasure, warm looks of love, the sensual grip of hungers and yearnings.

We were only two beasts lost in the desert who happened upon a watering hole, unsure if it was real or simply a mirage, too perfect to survive in the light of day. We struggled to sate addictive yearnings, insatiable yearnings, that were greedy, ravenous, uncontrollable.

I memorized every part of Jesse's perfect body; every bulge, every crevice, every shadow. And as I did so, losing myself in the sheer pleasure of it, Jesse's hands slid endlessly along my body, stroking, petting, grabbing; memorizing me just as well. Our bodies united, merging as one, and I found the missing part of me. The Jesse part. His soul penetrating into mine as surely and completely as his body did.

As our bodies finally melded into one another, the heat of our passion exploded around us. The haunting howls of coyotes sounded in the distance. Wild, heated calls into the dead of night that called to the animal within me, luring me, beckoning me, seducing me to join them in their sheer abandon. Instantly, any lingering inhibitions I had fell from my mind, slid away from my wrists, as easily as unshackling chains, chains that had been worn far too tight for far too long. As the repressed feelings of decadent, uninhibited abandon burst from the bottomless pit of my soul scorching everything in their path, the oppressive restraints forged throughout my lifetime melted away, fading into oblivion. I gave myself to Jesse, freely, completely, irrevocably.

And I was glad, so very glad, I'd had no idea what lay beyond the playful kissing and cuddling of all our yesterdays. Grateful for the restraint we'd both clung to desperately, sometimes with slipping, aching fingers, in times we'd thought were overwhelmingly passionate. For now I knew those moments had been mere glimpses, hushed whispers of the drowning, unquenchable thirst of desire that now swallowed us whole and kept us gasping for more well into the early hours of a new day. A new beginning. Our beginning.

As I lay in Jesse's arms in the early hours before dawn, warm, sated and content, I came to understand things I'd never even thought about before. Things like how pleased I was to belong to someone else. To carry someone else's love within me. The feeling of infinite possibilities in what either of us would be willing, even pleased, to do for the happiness and comfort of the other.

I finally understood why people were so hung up on weddings, formal declarations of love and all the trappings therein. Because, somehow deep, down inside those trappings I'd always thought of as bewildering and stifling, laid the kingdom of love, happiness and freedom. How was it possible to find independence and abandon through the very act of placing my heart, my soul, my life even, in the hands of another? I hadn't pretended to understand. I still didn't, I just felt it. And it felt wonderful.

My life with Jesse had finally begun. All of a sudden, my entire life up to that moment seemed to have ended. An exercise to be endured, through years of tears, laughter, lessons and joys until this day. The day I became Mrs. Jesse Alejandro Garcia de la Cruz.

As dawn finally spread her silken wings over the land, its soft golden glow spilled across our bodies. The radiance touched on a hip here, an arm there, it was impossible to tell where Jesse began and I ended, our bodies inextricably intertwined. And in the midst of tangled limbs, the white wedding blanket wove around us, between us, cradling us.

I glanced up and was immediately held captive within the loving chains of Jesse's gaze, the sun crept up, dawn breaking in his eyes. And those eyes blazed with a fire that seared my soul, branding me for all eternity. I knew in that moment that no matter what may lay ahead of us, I was his, a willing prisoner, until the end of time. Or perhaps longer still than that.

Truly, nothing mattered to me now but his smile, his happiness. And instead of fearing this, as I once would have, I felt comfort and peace within this secret knowledge. This imperative, undeniable truth.

Jesse slid out of our cozy hodgepodge, disentangling himself with reluctance, kissing me, stroking me endlessly as he did. As if he never wanted to even think of leaving my side, my bed. He slowly walked over to the curtain, tugged on his jeans, then pulled one last thing from behind it, his guitar. I adored it when Jesse played for me. He'd taught himself as a boy and not a day went by that I didn't ask him for a song.

But today, as his fingers stroked the resonating strings and his eyes held me with such devotion, he played as he never had before. While the sky slowly bled into color, the seductive, earthy song devoured me, consuming my soul note by note. His words of commitment and love, our love, our life, caressed my heart and gave wings to our love just as they gave roots to the bond that would hold us one to the other.

The soft, early morning breeze gently ruffled Jesse's hair, fingering through his black, silky strands. My fingers twitched, jealous of the casual touch. His chest and feet bare, body clothed only by the tight-fitting jeans, gave him a wild, untamed look. The look of a Cherokee man claiming his life, his love, his wife.

Instead of the notes striking out in contrast to the rocky desert around us, they merged with it, bled in and out of it, creating a singular beat, a singular pulse. The pulse, the heartbeat of time, of life, of our love.

And, in that moment, I felt the rhythm of my own heart shift. Forever replacing the Rachel I had been my entire life with the Rachel I was now. The Rachel I had been born to be. Jesse's Rachel.

15 WHO KNEW HAPPILY EVER AFTER WAS JUST A NATIONAL GEOGRAPHIC COMMERCIAL BREAK?

With the final notes of Jesse's song still gently enveloping me in their heady scent, he laid the guitar at his feet and pulled me across his lap into his strong, warm arms. His face was filled with such tenderness, such love, I could have lived that moment for an eternity and never hungered for more. I never needed to see anything other than his face, his happiness, and my own reflection in those bottomless black eyes.

The cool morning air brushed across my cheeks, whispered down my neck, slid its breathless hands down my sides. My upper body was cradled against Jesse's chest and my legs were tangled in the waves of bedding. We floated in the blankets, warm from our bodies, and they surrounded us, insulating us, protecting us from the world outside.

Jesse hugged me closely to him, my head tucking snugly into his warm, sheltering neck. Then he tipped my chin upwards, pulling my gaze to his. "Rache ..." He stopped, looking at me nervously, his focus shifting slightly, wavering, toggling between my eyes and my mouth. As if he was already trying to gage a reaction to words he had yet to speak.

I shifted the arm tucked between, sliding it around his back and letting it rest it between his strong shoulder blades. Raising my free hand, I softly cradling his cheek. It broke my heart that he could possibly feel anything other than what I was feeling, the all-encompassing love, the anticipation of our new life together. I snuggled even deeper within its filmy, but indestructible cocoon. I would have done anything to wipe that look from his face. I'd even carry it myself if I had to. Anything, just to get it off of him. My love. My husband. My everything.

"Jesse. Whatever it is, it's okay. If you don't want to talk about it, we don't have to. Nothing could keep me from loving you more tomorrow than I do today." I slid my hand behind his ear to the back of his neck, threading my fingers through his thick, cool hair, and pulled his lips to mine in a gentle, soothing kiss.

Holding him, gently refusing to release his captive lips, my gaze dove into those astonishingly dark, utterly captivating eyes. "And as long as we're together, Jesse, no one else matters. Nothing else matters. Just us. Just this. Just our love." My words swept into his mouth, my lips caressing his with each syllable.

Jesse rested his forehead against mine, slowly letting his eyelids drop. Then he just stayed there a bit, losing himself in the warm, soothing comfort of our embrace. Finally, his eyes blinked open and he looked straight into me. If I hadn't known better, I'd have said he looked straight through me and out the other side.

"No, Rache. That's just it. This has to be said. You have to know." He stopped and took one deep breath. And then another. "I just should have told you before now. I tried to. I did. I really did. But not hard enough. Not nearly hard enough." He rubbed at his forehead and looked away sheepishly.

"God, Jesse! Stop that! I love you. With all my heart. Nothing is going to change that. Ever. Nothing ever could. So..." I stopped talking, sat up straight and put both hands on either side of his face, forcing him to look at me. "Just stop worrying about what I'm gonna think and tell me. I promise you, I'll listen ... with an open heart. How could I not?"

He took another deep breath before he tried to talk. He looked away again, eyes darting nervously, so unlike the confident, self-assured Jesse I knew and loved.

Clearing his throat he cocked his head to one side and shrugged, trying for casual. Trying for nonchalant. Trying and failing terribly.

"Rache, there's ... something I need to tell you." He cleared his throat again, clenching and unclenching his fists as he did. In fact, he was clenching and unclenching them so much it looked like he was trying to milk a cow! What on earth was going on? And why were my own hands twitching? Why did I feel like I was trying to milk my own cow, a strong, black-eyed Jesse-cow, for more information?

As I sat, not exactly patiently, waiting for him to continue, his mouth moved in a little dance all its own. His jaw would shift, his lips would part, the lights in those amazing eyes would dance ... and then he'd close up again without saying a word. Not a single intonation for my hungry, anxious ears.

Finally, I reached up with both hands and wrapped them around his, stilling their nervous dance. I looked into those dark, desperate eyes of his and touched my forehead gently to his. A soft kiss of flesh. "Jesse, maybe ... well ... maybe it would be easier for you to show me. Is that possible?"

I tipped his chin and pressed my lips to his lovingly, acceptingly, holding his gaze in mine the entire time. My right hand slipped up to his cheek, gently caressing the dark, warm flesh.

Slowly he seemed to come to a decision of sorts. His mouth huffed into a small smile, and with his head tipped to one side he stared at my mouth instead of my eyes. And he finally let go.

"Okay, Rache. I'll show you. Just, please try not to be afraid. Please try." He stayed focused on my lips. Looking for all the world like a man lost at sea, eyes fixed on the only scrap of land visible in the entire world.

I just nodded, frowning slightly from the heaviness weighing in on us. Jesse's gaze finally lifted. He looked deeply into my eyes, placed his hands softly on either side of my throat and brushed his lips to mine. "I love you, Rache." The whispered words were so soft I wondered if he'd actually even said them, or if it was only my need to hear them that gave them life. Made them real.

"Now, all you have to do is watch, Rache. Don't look away. No matter what happens, just keep watching. I promise everything is going to be okay. I'll answer all your questions after I ... well, afterwards." Strong arms gently lifted me, sitting me on the bed beside him, then he disentangled himself from the bedlam of blankets surrounding us.

As he stood, he slid his jeans off, rising above me like an Indian prince and Mexican conquistador all wrapped up into one, I was mesmerized, my shallow breath failing momentarily. With the sun rising directly behind him, he had an almost ethereal glow about him, surrounding him, illuminating his skin so that he seemed to be only half human, half of this earth, the rest of him being something not quite human, not really flesh and bone, something not uniquely solid. The boundaries of his body were slightly translucent, the radiance emanating from the sun actually lighting his flesh from the inside, rather than simply illuminating the surface.

My eyes shifted from this hypnotic vision, and found Jesse's eyes locked on mine. His face was a whole stew of emotions, changing from determined to cautious, fearful to nervous, so quickly I barely had time to make one feeling out before the next slipped into place. But with each of them was excitement. A deep, fundamental, profound sense of excitement.

What on earth was my proud little half-breed up to? What could he possibly show me that I didn't already know? Especially after last night. We'd known each other our whole lives. What could possibly be left to say? What secrets could have survived all these years, could still exist between us? There wasn't enough space between our hearts, between our souls, for a single thought, much less a secret of the magnitude Jesse seemed to be carrying.

But even as that thought passed through my mind, I caught the faint trace of something different. Something unexpected.

What had happened? What, specifically, had changed? What was different in this moment than had been in the last? I couldn't put my finger on it, but I knew my eyes had picked up on something. Something small, but substantial. Definitely not something inconsequential.

My eyes began running over Jesse's face more rapidly, trying to locate what it was I'd noticed. Trying to decipher the shift that some part of me had detected. I felt the little furrow crinkle into place between my eyes at the top of my nose. The one I always got when I really studied something. My mother constantly scolded me about it, warning it would cause wrinkles.

There was a subtle shift around Jesse's eyes. They were brown. Not black. And they were harder somehow. With little golden flecks of color in them.

How was that possible? I'd studied Jesse's face, his voice, his body, my whole life. I'd made a passion of it. And never, ever had I seen those sparkling amber shards in his eyes before. Much less seen his eyes in any shade of brown whatsoever.

Some people's eyes seem to change color, not Jesse's, though. His eyes were black, blacker than black. They were the color of a great big chunk of obsidian ... in the dark ... at midnight. A patch of midnight you just couldn't clear out, no matter how bright the day. Jesse's eyes only ever changed in intensity, never color.

But now, oh my God! Even the shape of his eyes looked different. Rounder, smaller. Less ... Jesse. Less ... human. Was that even possible?

"Jesse ... what's going on?" My eyes kept shifting, focusing on one eye then the other.

Jesse didn't answer, he didn't so much as twitch one lip in response to my question. And yet, somehow I knew he'd heard me. That he was answering me. Just not with words. All I had to do to find my answers was to keep watching. But keep watching what? What was happening, exactly?

No sooner had that thought passed through my mind, than Jesse's entire face took on a translucent quality. I couldn't see through it, not really, but I couldn't quite focus on it either. It was like looking through a steamy bathroom window, only without the steam. As if an artist had come along and erased all the defining lines of Jesse's face, leaving just washes of color. Soft. Sheer. One color blending into the next.

As I glanced down, I realized his entire body looked the same way. It was all softer in some intangible way. The features and landmarks blending into one another. And into ... something else. Something still undefined ... Something ... something not quite human ...

Oh, for heaven's sake, Rache! That just wasn't possible. Stress, that's what this was. That's all this was. It sure couldn't be the complete nonsense I was busy drumming up right now.

Still, my eyes tightened in disbelief, and alarm. And as my gaze pulled down the dark, straight length of his nose, I saw it shifting, changing before my very eyes. It was curving, the color paling up near his eyes to a yellowish tint and the rest becoming a mottled grayish-black.

This was ... this was extraordinary! Magnificent! Impossible! And, yet, it was happening. Whatever it was, whatever this was, was definitely happening!

Maybe I was dreaming. Maybe the stress of running off, leaving my family to marry Jesse and find our own happiness was getting to me. That had to be it. My hands lifted up to his cheeks to reassure myself that this reality was really just a dream, just one big, fat, weird, twisted dream. That's all.

But as my hands met the sides of Jesse's face, his skin transformed. Suddenly there were feathers underneath my fingertips. Dark brown and cream tinted feathers. I felt my eyes widen in shock and disbelief.

But I was also very aware that somehow Jesse was still watching me. Waiting for my reaction. And that reaction needed to be something he could deal with. Not the stupid hysterics of a teenage girl.

So, I forced myself to take a deep breath. Then I consciously lowered the shoulders that seemed to have attached themselves to my ears. As I exhaled slowly, I raised my eyes to Jesse's, trying for everything I was worth to fill them with love, acceptance and understanding ... which was a thousand times easier said than done, since I didn't understand a damn thing that was going on here.

My vision shifted, sliding up his nose to his eyes. I saw that a beak had now firmly replaced his nose and mouth and a large rounded head stood in place of his own. My God! When had that happened? And shouldn't I have noticed it immediately? What kind of wife was I gonna be if I couldn't even tell when my husband's head changed into a bird brain!

Oh, shit! I was standing here making jokes while Jesse was changing species for Christ's sake! What the Sam Hill was wrong with me? But feathers! Shit! This was really, really bad! My better half just changed from mammal to feather-head! From ten cute little toes and a button nose to six sharp, pointed claws and a flesh-ripping beak! From Jesse to Bird-boy!

Oh, shit! Would he migrate south for the winter? Was this a permanent change? Was I going to have to sit on a nest of eggs for two months to have babies?

Oh, my God, I couldn't even take him home for Thanksgiving dinner! He's what's for dinner, for God's sake! The main course, at that!

And what on earth would I fix him for dinner? A nice worm soufflé, a mouse pie, a bowl of sunflower seeds?

Shit! How were we ever going to have sex again? I couldn't even hold his hand for God's sake!

And what about a family picture? What the hell would our kids look like? Forget that, what species would they be? What do you name baby birds? Do they get middle names?

Boy, I was definitely losing any remaining grip on sanity I possessed. I had to find a way to pull myself together. For Jesse's sake.

I forced my eyes to refocus back on Jesse. There was no long, straight black hair in sight now. Just more feathers spreading quickly down the length of his body, steadily moving just a split second ahead of my focus, replacing the skin right before my very eyes. Reaching all the way down to the powerful, yellow claws that took hold at the very bottom.

Oh, my God.

Maybe I'd eaten something bad, or something poisonous without realizing it. Maybe I was dying and this was just a momentary delirium as the blood stopped flowing to my brain.

And yet, as much as I might have wished to deny the truth of it, this was, somehow, one way or another, really and truly happening.

Jesse was one great big, beautiful golden eagle. My newly wedded husband had just turned into a bird of prey before my very eyes! What in the world was I supposed to do now? Lay eggs?

Nope. Never mind. On second thought, I just did not want to know the answer to that one. But dammit! Jesse had a hell of a lot of explaining to do! What in creation had he been thinking? How could he keep a secret like this from me all these years? How could he marry me, for Christ's sake, without discussing this minor little detail with me first?

Just a quick little, "Oh, Honey, by the way, you'll be giving birth to eaglets instead of humans." Talk about a lack of communication!

Jesse's, eagle Jesse's, body shifted suddenly and the sun caught along the beautiful colors of his feathers, sparkling in wild, iridescent hues. It captivated me, drawing me in closer. So close, in fact, that I found myself nose-to-beak with my semi-lawfully-wedded ... and feathered ... husband.

Boy, oh, boy, was I ever up the proverbial creek without a paddle! What I wouldn't have given for a nice, bat-infested cave to tuck inside of and hide for an eternity or two.

But there was absolutely nowhere to hide. Nowhere except in Jesse's eyes. In the beat of his heart. The beat that was pulsing like wildfire in his curved, feathered, chest.

Then, in a heartbeat, Jesse melted right back into his warm, brown-skinned, wonderfully human, wonderfully naked, self. I'd never been so utterly and completely happy just to be able to grab hold of someone with armpits! What a treasure! What a treat! Smelly armpits, hurray!

Jesse's strong hands slid effortlessly up my arms and around my back, clutching my body to his. Familiar black eyes poured over my face, devouring it, trying to capture what I was thinking. Drinking in my every emotion, my every thought and desire.

My heart melted inside my chest and poured out, spilling all around us. Liquid love that splashed in puddles at our feet. Even without any answers, I knew. I knew all I needed to know, all that was important.

I loved Jesse. And he loved me. And together, together we could do anything.

I took a deep breath, relaxed my shoulders, and smiled up into that tense, apprehensive face. I smiled for all I was worth, for all we were worth, hoping to show him with that small gift that my love for him was both eternal and unconditional.

I guess, for once, I accomplished my goal, because in the next instant, Jesse's hands were resting on either side of my face, cupping my cheeks with a mysterious mix of love, gratitude, fear and excitement.

"Come with me, Rache!" He grabbed both my arms and dragged me upwards until we were standing side by side.

"Just a minute, Wild man, let me catch my breath!"

But this wild man wasn't waiting for anything or anyone. He was pulling me forward, tempting me with unknown freedoms, unspoken desires.

"Come on, Rache! You're gonna love this! You're just gonna love it!"

"Love what, Jesse? What more is there? Surely nothing else compares to what you just did!?" How much more could there possibly be? "Should I be scared?"

"Hmmm. Good question, Rache. Excellent question, actually ..."

"Oh, well, that's just great, Jesse." He squeezed my hands as he continued pulling me toward his unknown destination. "Now I really am scared!"

"Oh, Rache! I love you! You're gonna be just fine! And besides, you'll have me by your side every second of the way!"

"Jesse, what in the hell are you talking about?" But his answer was to grab my face, kiss me hard and quick, and laugh as he turned away and started hurrying off, chuckles rolling over his shoulder, trailing behind him as he ran ahead. The little turkey was laughing at me! Turkey? No, eagle. Golden eagle.

Stupid Indian! Big, fat, stupid, golden eagle Indian! Just let him wait and see if I gave him a good night kiss tonight! Right! Like that was going to happen! Honeymoon or no, I had absolutely no intentions of starting my marriage off being laughed at!

"Come on! Hurry, Rache! This way!" He kept turning back his head to look at me to make sure I was still hot on his heels.

"Jesse, what is the problem? What's wrong with you? Why the big rush all of a sudden? Talk to me. I don't want to run right now. It's our first morning together, for heaven's sake. I want to enjoy it. I want to stop and smell the roses. I don't want to run a marathon! Not today. Please, Jesse."

"Oh, come on, Rache ... you're gonna go nuts over this! You're just gonna love it! And it's the perfect day for it." He skirted a small cluster of cedar trees, dodging under a couple low hanging branches as he did so. I felt the limbs tug at my hair as I rushed to keep up with him, not an altogether easy job in his current state of abject excitement.

Jesse had needed secrecy. Secrecy from even me. Why? What could possibly be so bad that he'd kept it from me our whole lives? I mean, Jesus, he'd already shown me the whole feathered side to his personality. What more could there possibly be? Exactly how far out was this going to get? I wasn't sure exactly how much more I was prepared to handle in one day. How much was left in this particular bit of reality?

I looked up just in time to refocus on Jesse half a second before I plowed into him from behind. That was a good thing, too, because I suddenly realized exactly where we were. Jesse was standing at the edge of a ravine that carved through the basin eighteen hundred feet below us at this point of the Rio Grande.

Our madcap running had carried us all the way to Mariscal Canyon. It had always been one of my favorite sections of the river. We were actually on Mariscal Mountain, overlooking the Rio Grande that was winding through the rocky desert below us. Texas spread out endlessly behind me while Mexico stretched as far as the eye could see on the other side.

The river flowed deeper here and more narrow than it did further down river, at one point spanning only eight feet between the sheer rock walls, which were absolutely breathtaking in both their height and closeness. "God, it's beautiful here, isn't it Rache?"

There were actually several beautiful stretches along this part of the Rio Grande. The Santa Elena Canyon, upriver from here was very similar to Mariscal Canyon, perhaps even more dramatic. But its wild, white-water rapids always drew more tourists.

"Yes, Jesse. It's beautiful." And it was. Truly. But my patience was wearing thin and I needed words to clear the space between us, not more running. Turning him by his shoulders to face me, I placed my hands on both of his cheeks, flushed now from our early morning race. My fingers slid back into his thick, black hair, avoiding his ears so they wouldn't muffle my voice. My eyes caught his, holding on tightly. "But you have to stop running and talk to me now. I need you to help me understand all of this."

"I know, Rache. I do. But sometimes actions really do speak louder than words. They leave so much less room for misunderstandings and miscommunication." Okay, this was getting completely too intense. Too serious.

I started to take a step back, but it was Jesse's turn to take control. He placed his hands on my cheeks. "We will talk, Baby. I promise. There's just one last thing you need to see."

"Fine, Jesse, but whatever this is, it better answer all these questions jumbling around in my head. And fast."

"Okay, Rache. It will, I promise." He kissed me softly, gently, looking into my eyes the whole time, then lowered his hands to my shoulders and turned me to face the edge of the cliff. "Clear your head now, completely. Breathe. Feel the warmth of the sun on your skin, the breeze as it moves through your hair, my body next to yours. Focus only on what is around you right now in this moment. The scent of the flowers, the sounds of the birds, of the water moving down below us, my voice in your ears."

Keeping his hands on my body, maintaining our touch, our connection, he moved behind me, then slid those strong, warm hands up my shoulder blades to my shoulders once again. "Let our love flow through you, Rache. Let it flow into your body and then back out, a giant wave crashing in upon the shoreline of your heart before washing back out to sea." His face rested, nestled, beside my own. Cheek-to-cheek we stood looking out over the Rio Grande, wholly absorbed in our own love for one another.

"Good, Rache. Now, keep feeling that, but also let in the coolness of the air as it enters your mouth with each breath, the warmth of it as it spills from your body. Just feel. Just breathe. Just be in this moment. No worries, no concerns, no thoughts. Only my voice." His cheek slid across my hair with a silken touch. "Yes. Yes, Rache. Good. That's it. Just relax into this moment. This space. Into me."

There was a lightness to me, a lightness of being, that filled me completely. As I looked out across the deep, ragged ravine I could feel the beauty, the strength, the immeasurable peacefulness of the land surrounding me as it lulled my spirit, soothing it, pulling me into itself. Into a timelessness that I'd never felt before.

I noticed, as the rock wall opposite me popped into my vision, that there was something off about my eyesight. I could see, but it was as if I was looking through someone else's eyes. I started blinking my eyes again and again trying to ease the sensation, but that didn't seem to be doing anything at all to help. Still, it didn't really seem to matter, nothing did except this moment. Jesse. Me. I was floating on an ocean of bliss.

Jesse continued, his voice echoing through my soul as he spoke in a way that touched things within me I'd never known existed. Moveable things. Strong things. Things that felt like they could overwhelm me, take over my senses in a heartbeat ... or less.

"Okay, Baby. The next time you breathe in, I want you to pull the air all the way into your fingertips. Into your toes. Straight through your body until it's released back out again through each pore of your body."

I was trembling when I finally released the last lungful of air I'd taken, pulling in what felt like it may very well be my last breath ... ever, and reversed the motion.

Suddenly, I felt parts of my body moving. Parts that shouldn't move. Not ever. Somehow it seemed like bones were shifting, but more than that. Like entire sections of my body were being remolded, as if they were little mounds of clay being squeezed and pushed into something similar, but something one hundred and eighty degrees different.

A cry was building inside me. Not so much from pain, because this wasn't uncomfortable, not exactly, but it wasn't unbearable either. Definitely not something you'd jump up and beg to do again, not if you were living in the land of the sane at any rate.

But that cry was building, gaining momentum, gaining strength, gaining volume. I had the distinct feeling this was about to go really, really badly. The only question was, could I even do anything to stop it? And if I could, would I? Did I even want to?

At that moment, with the words still floating around in my head, everything went south. My vision became even less normal, more surreal. My God, I could see a desert mouse scavenging down at the river's edge ... and that was eighteen hundred feet below us! My hearing was instantly so intense that I could hear the wings beating on a dragonfly that was circling back ten yards away.

I turned my head back to Jesse, looking at him with questions burning in my head. But when I opened my mouth to ask them, he placed his finger to my mouth and shook his head slowly, "Shhh. Don't try to talk, Rache."

Why couldn't I feel his fingertip on my lips? Why shouldn't I try to talk? Why was I hearing and seeing so clearly? Come to think of it, I could smell clearly, too. I could smell the water flowing through the ravine. Oh my God, I could even smell the dirt in the water ...

I shook my head no, but I was shaking it so fast I could practically feel my brain rattling around inside it. As it did, my chin swung around enough that I caught glimpses of myself below it.

Why did everything seem to be brown and gold? I'd put on blue jean shorts and my favorite rose-colored camisole shirt. Absolutely nothing brown or gold.

My chin began to drop and I saw Jesse trying to catch my attention, once again telling me not to. But he was too late. The cry that had been growing inside me burst out.

Only, it wasn't just your simple, ordinary, everyday, run-of-the-mill, blood-curdling scream. Oh, no. It was piercingly loud. A high-pitched cry that carried far across the desert, filling my ears with the sound of a bird ... a bird in dire distress.

A bird! A golden eagle! What?! My eyes focused on my claws digging into the ground right beside Jesse's squatting legs and feet.

My head slowly lifted, searching for Jesse's face. I needed to connect with him, to dive into those bottomless black eyes before I drowned in my own fear and confusion.

As his face filled my world, his scent filled my senses. The sound of his breath reverberated inside my own body and I saw my reflection in his eyes staring back at me as it had yesterday. Only this time, what was staring back at me wasn't even human.

Holy shit! I started to panic even as Jesse slowly shook his head yet again, smiling at me soothingly. He began to stroke his hand across the feathered length of my body from behind my head to the area just before my tail began.

My tail?! Oh, shit! My tail! I really was a bird! How? How did that happen? How was I going to change back into me? Could I even change back into me? What if I was stuck like this for the rest of my life?

I opened my mouth again to speak, but another squeal fell out instead of my pain-filled words of panic, anger and fear. And Jesse was there just shushing me again.

"Rache. Don't try to talk. Not right now. It'll just be frustrating for you." His hand slid down my back again and it was strangely comforting to me, despite my frightened, feathered state of being.

"When we gave ourselves to one another last night, through words," he smiled that lopsided smile that always melted my heart and quickened my pulse, even now, "and actions, you took a part of me, of my family, my heritage, inside you as well." He looked deeply into my eyes and I kept mine focused on that ridiculous bird staring right back at me inside his.

"My ancestors are shape-shifters. And now you are, too. By focusing on the elements around us, we can change into five different animals aside from our human form."

It was extraordinary, no, maybe it was just ... strange, to be listening to Jesse talk and being able to think about it perfectly rationally, without being able to say anything. Anything at all. Maybe that had been part of his plan ... that conniving little Indian! What a little shit! Sucker me into changing into a damn bird so he could confess his sins without letting me say a single word. Just wait. Just wait until I was back in my normal bag of bones, there'd be hell to pay, that was for sure!

But at the moment, Jesse kept on as if we were having just one of a lifetime of normal, inconsequential conversations. Conversations about absolutely nothing, no matter how important they might seem to be at the time.

"Pulling the air inside us shifts us into golden eagles. They are the light defeating the darkness, the symbol of the renewal of youth and rejuvenation, the corpse-eaters. If we turn our attention to the dirt beneath our feet, that allows us to become grizzly bears for strength, transformation and healing. Focusing on the heat, the fire within us changes us into fireflies, signifying passionate love, perseverance, the spirits of the living, and the souls of the dead. Immersing our attention in the cool depths of water brings our dolphin form, allowing for prophecy and wisdom. They also give us the ability to behave as saviors, rescuers so to speak, to carry souls places sometimes too uncomfortable for them to venture to all on their own. And finally, drawing on the sky stretching above us, particularly on the moon, turns us into wolves, warriors against the dark forces of evil, guardians of the paths traveled by the dead."

His gaze was still holding mine, my round golden brown bird eyes, intently. "We can change from one form to the next anytime we want. Just as long as no one, and I do mean no one, sees us shift. That can't happen, Rache. Ever. No matter how close you are to them. No matter how much they mean to you. Only other shifters are allowed to witness a shift. That's just about the only rule. To switch back into your human body, all you have to do is fill your heart with the love you carry for all the people in your life, Rache. Just let yourself feel your love for me. And your family. And our friends."

"So, now it's time for your first flight lesson, Rache. It's unbelievable! You're gonna love it. Trust me." Okay. He'd lost it. He was crazy. Certifiably insane. There was no way, absolutely, positively, no way in hell, I was leaving the safety and security of solid ground. Nope. That was just not happening.

But he was pushing me. Pushing me toward the edge for heaven sake! What the Sam Hill was wrong with him? Hadn't he just told me to trust him? I couldn't fly! I was just me. Just Rachel. Just a stupid, freckled girl from Texas in love with one gorgeous, shape shifting half-breed. A half-breed who happened to be pushing me toward the edge of an eighteen hundred foot drop off. Hell, I couldn't even drive yet, how on earth did he expect me to be able to fly?

And there he was pushing at me again! "Go on, Rache. You can do this. It's second nature to you. You'll do it without even having to think about it."

God, I wish he'd stop pushing me! My feet, or claws, were just a few inches from the edge of the wall's drop off. Whatever I was going to do, I'd better do it fast, or I'd be falling head over heels ... beak over claws ... whatever, down to the bottom of the ravine.

I tried to back step, but it came out as more of a back stumble. It was really hard to balance on these stupid little tripod feet. I now had a newfound respect for all my feathered friends. Tipping my head back I squawked right in Jesse's face, trying my best to sound menacing and pissed off.

Trying, and failing. His twinkling eyes and resonating laugh told me I hadn't managed to convey quite the right emotion. So, I tried the next best thing. I snapped at his hand when he reached out again trying to nudge me closer to the edge.

"Rache!" He laughed. "Stop that, you crazy woman. I'm your husband. You need to treat me with love, and respect." He flicked his finger sideways over my beak.

Love and respect, my ass. I'd been married to him for less than twenty-four hours, and already he'd turned my entire life upside down. Well, he'd better not stick that finger of his in my face again, or I'd really take a good nip at it, just enough to teach him a thing or two about respect!

"Hmmm, well, if I can't get you to jump off on your own, maybe I need to give you the right incentive ..." Okay. I so did not like the look in those pitch black eyes of his. They were dark pools of nothing but danger with just a spark of adrenaline. Not a good combination.

He stepped closer to the edge, looked around quickly, then shifted his gaze back to me. "Well, see you at the bottom, Rache." And then he took that last step towards the edge and just dove right off. Oh, my God! He dove off the side of the flipping cliff! What an idiot! What an absolute fool! I was gonna kill him! Well, I'd kill him right after I made sure he was still in one piece. Then I'd kill him. And I'd make sure it hurt like hell, too! Son of a bitch! What was he thinking? Was he even thinking? What if he ...

No! I couldn't think that! I wouldn't think that. It was the one thing I knew I'd never in a million years be able to handle. A life without Jesse in it.

I lurched toward the side of the cliff, craning my head over the edge to look for him. Hoping to see him. And hoping just as much not to see him. Either I'd see him flying past, or I'd see him lying in a puddle of bones at the bottom.

I tipped half an inch farther, just enough to actually see, and realized my eyes were closed. Come on, Rache. You can do this. Eyelids dragged back across bulbous, round eyes. It took me a minute to focus, and just as I captured his face a few feet in front of me, one unbelievable strong hand grabbed my throat and jerked me forward, lifting me off the ground and flinging me downward between the steep, rocky walls that bordered the riverbed.

Oh, I was so going to kill him! But that was okay. Black looked good on me. I could wear funeral clothes for a couple weeks at least. But right now that so was not my main problem. The big issue at this moment was how the Sam Hill I was going to stop free-falling to certain doom and destruction and start flying.

Then I felt my wings spread all on their own. The wind instantly filled them like two sails on a boat, carrying me, moving me. Absolutely unbelievable!

Oh, Jesse! How could he do this? Royally piss me off, amaze me, destroy me and remake me all at the same damn time?

Suddenly I felt rather than saw another eagle coming up close behind me. How had I known? I sure couldn't see anything, especially anything behind me. I tried to focus on my new birdie senses and realized that I could feel a shift in the air currents around me. A shift caused by his body breaking the natural wave flow created primarily by the wind, the heat and the water.

Jesse zoomed right past me, bopping my head with the tip of his tail as he thrust by inches above me. He wanted to play, did he? Fine. Two could play this game just as easily as one.

I dipped my head downward and tipped my wings forcing my body to dive into the space below Jesse. Boy did it work! Only better than I'd expected. My speed had picked up dramatically. Now I just had to figure out how to stop this nose-dive before I became nothing more than a flat, feathered pancake.

Well, if dropping my head and tipping my wings forward had sent me down here, it stood to reason that doing the opposite would reverse the effects. So, I tipped my head back just a bit, trying to keep it mild so I wouldn't overshoot my goal again, and adjusted my wings until they slanted slightly backwards.

It worked! As a matter of fact, for once my timing was impeccable. I raised up directly underneath Jesse, catching his soft, feathered belly along my back. The force of our bodies bumping into each other was strong enough that it lifted him several feet higher in the air. Smiling to myself inside, I flew a few feet off to one side and glanced smugly back over at him.

But he didn't miss a beat. He simply tilted his own head and wings and headed right back at me. Only this time he flew right up alongside me.

Then he turned his head and looked at me. And I melted from the inside out. Lock, stock and barrel. How could he possibly do that to me now? I was a bird for Christ's sake! How could I possibly feel love, want, need and desire.

And, so what if I did? What on earth could I do about it looking like this? Talk about sick.

We continued flying along through the ravine, staying about a third of the way below the tops of the rock walls that spanned the river on either side of us. I had to admit, at least to myself, he was absolutely right. It was magnificent. No words could have possibly prepared me for it.

How could this be happening? How could any of this possibly be real? But I could smell the dirt, I could feel the air rushing past my body, the coolness in it coming from the water evaporating and rising from the river, and I could see Jesse flying along my side, guiding me, sharing all of this with me. How could it not be real?

Those beautiful black eyes swung back toward me and he nodded his head downward signaling for us to drop lower.

I fell in behind him clumsily, almost crashing into him as I caught a blast of warmer air and instantly changed speed and direction. Wow, I'd have to remember to watch out for those. But exactly how do you look out for something you can't even see? Damn! Birds really are something special. I never saw them stumbling through the sky like spastic acrobats.

Suddenly, I realized Jesse had flown much farther down. Boy, did I have some catching up to do. He was almost at the riverbed itself. His head tipped up and caught sight of me immediately, waiting patiently for me to work this out. To figure out exactly how to use these new limbs, this new body. Boy, did I feel like a clumsy, gangly ugly duckling.

Shifting all my fine feathered parts, I managed to drop and hurl myself down, chunks at a time, joining him just a few feet over the rolling, churning water. It was completely different trying to fly this close to the river. The air was much thicker with water droplets. They clung to my feathers, weighting my body in a cool wet blanket.

Jesse dove down into the water and came back up with a fish in his mouth, tossed it up into the air, then caught it in his beak and gulped it down. He turned to look at me and motioned his head toward the water.

What? What did he expect me to do? I was from Texas for Christ's sake! We eat chili, bar-be-cue, fried chicken and tacos. We do not eat raw fish! I do not eat raw fish!

I did what any reasonable bird-girl would do. I shook my head no, dipped one claw into the river and splashed some water in his direction, then glared, patiently, at him. Or tried to anyway.

The patience for once was not the problem. I was a bird for Pete's sake, where was I gonna rush off to? No, the problem was trying to glare without a decent set of eyebrows, much less eyes that had corners to squint. A cool brush of water-logged air blew right into my face as I dropped down low over the river.

So, there I was, a soggy, feathered newlywed, trying my best to give my brand-spankin' new hubby the evil-eye with round, glassy, eyebrowless eyes. Yeah, I'm pretty sure I looked like a feather duster with a chronic eye twitch. Not too threatening to anything bigger than a dust ball.

Jesse nodded again toward the water, somehow managing to look menacing, dominant. How could he do that? What choice did I have? I shook my head again and looked away, obstinate to the end.

The next thing I knew he'd somehow sent a bucketful of water splashing all over me! And damn that water was cold! What a jerk!

Fine! I'd show that domineering eagle-butt a thing or two! I dove into the water, instantly feeling the river's cool, wet fingers sliding under my wings, between my feathers, tickling my hmm-hmm. But I was on a mission, dammit. A little cold water was merely an inconvenience. So. Where was a stupid, stinky fish when I needed one?

Something slipped past my feet and I looked down in curiosity. It was then that I first noticed the whole new world beneath the river's glassy surface. It was amazing. Absolutely breathtaking. Fish were swimming around everywhere, scales glistening in the light. There were boulders along the bottom with snakes tucked in underneath them. A few turtles were even scattered here and there, nipping at foliage as they swam past. I even caught sight of an eel further upstream.

A small fish slipped past right in front of me and I snapped at him with my beak. I had no idea if I'd caught him, though, because I'd hit a rougher patch of water and realized I needed to pull up fast. I was running out of air and getting too close for comfort to the underwater rocks.

Lifting my head and rolling my body like a wave turned me towards the surface. I could see Jesse through the water, flying in the air above me, protecting me, playing with me, enjoying our morning sport. My God he was magnificent! The sun sparkled off the beads of moisture clinging all over his body. His gold-spun chocolate brown eyes taking my heart for his own all over again.

Finally my body burst through the top of the water, the warmth of the sun and the brightness of the day stunning me for just a moment. Just enough that I lost my bearings, lost sight of Jesse, lost my sense of direction for a few precious seconds. The sudden flipping and flapping of the fish in my mouth had me flinging it blindly in what I thought was Jesse's direction. Hope it caught him right across the kisser, the little shit! It would sure serve him right! Of course, I'd never be that lucky. All my luck had been used up in merely getting to be with him, loving him, being loved by him. And that was just fine with me. Still, I'd give a lot to see that damn fish slap across that proud nose of his.

More likely though, it would land right in his open mouth! Some people were like that, and Jesse was one of them. Things just always worked out beautifully for him, like some grand conductor was orchestrating it all, making everything happen at just the right time, just the right place, right on cue.

Suddenly, I couldn't hear anything. Nothing, except for a deafening reverberation that rocked through my head, through my body. I know the water must have muffled the sound to some extent, but it also carried the echoing percussive blasts in waves long afterward. What on earth was that? Had a meteor hit? Had something exploded?

The next second, Jesse was there. He was everywhere. Over me, under me, in front of me, behind me, all at the same time. A gnawing sense of dread told me that he was guiding me. Guiding me and covering me from behind, protecting me, at the same time. What was happening? What was he trying to protect me from? Why couldn't I figure out what was happening?

Ooh, there was that sound again! And this time it was close enough that bits of rock from the wall showered down on us. Thick, warm drops of water fell from Jesse's body onto mine as he flew above me, leading the way. Guiding me where he wanted me to go.

Jesse glanced back over his shoulder, raking across the length of my body with his eyes, making sure I was okay, that I wasn't hurt. Desperation lit his face. I would have given a million dollars to have been able to smile at him just then. Anything to ease his pain, his discomfort, his frustration. Anything so I didn't feel like such a burden to him.

His body slid knowingly along the next bend in the rock wall, slipping up and around it as if he'd flown this very path a thousand times before. We flew into an opening in the face of the cliff I'd never noticed before. A cave right in the side of the wall of Boquillas Canyon looking out over the water over a thousand feet below. I realized immediately no one could see us here. No one would be able to find us. Maybe that was his plan. But why did we need a plan? What was going on?

As we settled onto the dirt floor, I glanced around quickly to get my bearings. There were pictures, simple and faded, but beautiful nonetheless, painted on the far wall. No doubt those had been here for hundreds of years, drawn by men and women long since chased out of their homeland.

I turned back to Jesse, surprised that he hadn't moved much. Then straightened my head and opened my eyes further, trying to focus harder on him. On his body.

Something wasn't right. What was it? My eyes were scavenging his face, searching for clues once again. But if I hadn't been able to read his human face, trying to make sense of this feathered one was just one big exercise in futility and frustration.

My gaze dropped to Jesse's body, running up and down the length of him, wondering what I was trying not to see. What I hoped not to find. But he was immersed in a pool of shadows, making it difficult to decipher what my eyes were taking in.

And then I realized what it was I was seeing. What my eyes had passed over a dozen times. Blood. Lots of blood. Jesse's blood. I looked down his chest and saw a hole near his right wing where more feathers should have been. A bullet hole. I knew that. My brothers had gotten their first bee-bee guns the Christmas they turned seven, and their first shotguns at twelve. Every year after that they went hunting with my dad. And guess who got to clean it all? Yours truly, of course. Yes, I knew bullet holes. A little too well.

And this one? This one, that was buried in my husband's chest, was a kill shot. No doubt about it.

A deep, cold dread instantly poured into my veins, filling my heart, stealing my breath. Before I could steal it back, tears began to fall from my horrified, round, brown eyes.

I moved closer to Jesse, tucking myself up next to him. Into the warmth of his body. Only he wasn't warm. He was cold. Really cold.

I felt the panic start to rise within me. The kind that you can't see through, can't breathe through, can't find your way back out of. Jesse's eyes caught mine, my tears still falling, bathing him in my sorrow, in my love.

Slowly his body started to shift back into the man I loved, the man I'd married, the man I'd agreed to share my entire life with mere hours ago. The claws and feathers all disappeared, as if they'd never even existed. As if they'd just been part of a dream, my dream, our dream. Only now the dream was over, and it was time to wake up into a never-ending nightmare.

Jesse's hands reached for my face, and although his touch was gentle, there was a fierceness to them that spoke volumes of anguish and anxiety.

"Rache." He managed to choke out. "Rache, Honey. I need you to shift back now. Right now, Baby. Can you do that for me?"

I stared back at him utterly bewildered. Well, of course I would change back. Why would he even ask that? But ... how did you do that? He'd never even told me.

As if on cue, he started to talk again. Whisper, really. I was hoping to high heaven he was only whispering so the idiot with a gun wouldn't hear us. But if I was honest with myself, I knew better than that.

"Rache, mi corazón, mi vida. Just let your heart fill with the love you have for me. You'll come right back to me as the beautiful woman you are." He swallowed hard and my stomach clenched instantly, hoping against all hope that he just needed to swallow, that was all. Plain and simple. He couldn't be choking down body fluids that were spilling from him. No. No!

This couldn't be happening! This wasn't fair! We hadn't even had lunch for God's sake!

"Rache, please, Baby, mi corazón. Please. Come to me. Now. Let go of the anger. Feel the love. Only the love. I love you, mi hija, mi vida chiquita, mi esposa bonita."

Oh, God! Not this. Ask anything of me but this. I can't do this! My baby, my little life, my beautiful wife? He couldn't ask me to open my heart at this moment, just to lose him forever. I would die a thousand deaths. Tears poured from my eyes as he captured my gaze. And my heart opened.

Every drop of love, of me, was his. His for the taking, or his for the leaving. But either way, I was his. Now and forever. I'd promised less than twenty-four hours ago to love him with everything I was and everything I had. I'd promised to hold nothing back and to give myself to him wholeheartedly.

I hung my head in defeat, my gaze dropping to his bloodied chest, and suddenly I realized my hands were resting on the sides of his body. I had shifted back. I was me again. Whoever the hell that was. And I was about to be me, all by myself. Alone. Alone for the first time in my life.

Oh, God! Don't let this happen! Please, don't! It's not fair! It's just not fair! "I love you, Jesse! I love you! I've always loved you and I always will!

Mi vida eres tú. My life is you. Only you." I pressed my lips to his body, much warmer now that he was back in his normal form. Or was this his normal form? I had no way of knowing. None at all.

There was so much I didn't know now about this man I'd thought I'd known inside out. But in this moment all the questions disappeared. All that mattered to me now, was him. His comfort. His love. His life, or what he had left of it, at any rate. And I was determined to be my best, in this moment, perhaps our last moment, for him. If this was the last memory we had together, I was going to be the best Goddamn Rachel he'd ever met. I could allow myself to regret plenty of other moments, but not this one. Not this one.

"I love you Rachel Anne Kensington. You are mi vida, my life, my beautiful, beautiful wife. I've loved you forever and I always will. Don't begrudge the time we've had. Most people never find this. Not for a single moment. It's precious. Cherish it always, cry your ocean of tears. Then pick yourself up and go out and love again. Find love again. And fly again. You will. You have to. For me."

His hand patted me weakly, but without compromise, as my lips parted in protest. "Shhh. I know, mi corazón. Not today, but one day. Promise me, Rache. You will love again. Promise me."

"Don't, Jesse. Don't make me promise things I can't do. I don't want to fly without you, and I can't love someone else when my heart belongs to you. Please, don't take that from me. Not now. It'll be ... all I have left. All I have of us. Of you. Even of me. Because you have all of me."

His eyes fluttered as he spoke again. I could hear the strain, the pain, in his voice as the words rasped through the liquid quickly filling his lungs. "I gave you every gift I'm blessed with, Rache. Use them. They will help you. You are still my life, mi vida. No matter where I am, I will be with you, always. You will never be alone, mi corazón."

He rested his hand on the string of feathers he'd placed around my neck the night before. "Life really is a gift, Rache. But you have to see it as one. You are my gift, my love, my soul. I wish I could be there to hold you, to love you the way you deserve. But I will be there, Rache. I'll be there loving you for all I'm worth. Watching over you as best I can."

The words stopped then, choked out by fitful coughs trying desperately to clear cavities that weren't meant to ever need clearing.

Suddenly I remembered it all. I was Syd. But I was Rache, too. I'd been the girl who'd lived this life. I'd been the girl who'd loved this man. The girl who'd lost this man ... and her entire world right along with him.

Jesse was dying. And no one would be able to save him. Not even me.

16 THE OVERBEARING GUILT ... OF BEING THE ONE LEFT BREATHING

The cave gradually began to fade, beginning at the edges. I realized I could no longer see Jesse's hands and feet ... they were a blur. A blur that was consuming him. Eating away at the edges of his being. The erosion of the vision continued, slowly blurring inward until nothing discernible was left to be seen, just a smoky veil.

"No! Jesse don't go!" I pulled his body up to mine and pressed my lips firmly to his ... not willing to let him go. Not again. Forcing the sensation of touch as I was losing the sensation of sight. As if by touching him, holding him, kissing him, I could hold this wonderful man, this other half of me, who was evaporating in my arms, disappearing beneath my lips, to me. I wanted to keep him with me. For just a moment longer. One more breath. Oh, who was I kidding, I wanted Jesse for one more forever. Not a second less.

"Please, Jesse! I need you! I love you! Don't go. Don't leave me. Just stay here with me. Please!" I couldn't force any more words through my throat, emotion strangling my voice, my heart.

Too many feelings were ripping through me. Tearing me into pieces. Pieces left in raw, quivering chunks strewn across the floor.

"Shh. It's okay Rache." Rache, that was me. I was both Rache and Syd. "I'll never leave you ... I can't. I'll always be there with you, just don't forget to look for me." His hand caressed my cheek so softly I wasn't quite sure he'd actually touched me at all.

"Remember. Remember all of this. But remember me most of all, and how much I love you." His beautiful voice was fading to a whisper now as his entire being was slipping away, like a thick, slow fog on a warm summer morning.

My heart was beating so hard and fast it felt like it might actually punch a hole through my chest and fly away with Jesse. Maybe that would be a good thing. Infinitely less excruciating than losing Jesse. Again. But the pounding only strengthened, redoubling its efforts. It was unbearable, intense, a thick, living, breathing agony.

My head was shaking in denial. "Please, no. Don't!" I managed to choke out, tears slipping through my lips with the words. "I can't lose you! Not again! No! No! No! I can't lose you again, Jesse! Don't leave me! Don't go! I need you! Don't go! Don't!" I squeezed my eyes closed as if that would stop the inevitable. As if not seeing would keep it from being real.

Jesse's voice answered, quietly and calmly, my eyes flew open but I could see no face. "Rache, you've always had me. And you always will. Your heart carries a part of me with you. Can't you feel it ... it beats so hard, because it beats for two, not just for one. I will love you 'til the stars shower down upon us and time loses all meaning. Remember me, my love, mi corazón, ... remember me with smiles, not tears. See you soon ..."

He winked at me with that one-sided grin filled with love and laughter, and some little secret he was passing on to me. I'd carry that last look with me until the end of time. Jesse's voice reverberated both around me and within me, hugging me, holding me, loving me, and then everything was quiet. Completely quiet. He was gone. Jesse was gone. I was alone. Again.

Then the real pain began.

I heard someone screaming in the distance, and I didn't care what their problem was, I just wanted them to shut the hell up! Now! Couldn't somebody make them shut up? Please!

Every bit of air rushed out of my lungs in a forceful gush of air as if someone had gathered me up in a bear hug and gone for a Guinness record. But the only arms wrapped around me now were my own. My own pathetic, useless arms, trying to keep what was left of me in one piece. Trying to somehow keep this bleeding, broken self from shattering into a million pieces that could never be fitted back together.

I could feel the waves of an overwhelming heartbreak ravaging my body, taking hold as if preparing to replace every part of me with an ache that could never be soothed. Somewhere in the distance I heard agonizing sobbing, sobbing too painful for a mere girl to endure. Who was that? Why were they disturbing my time of sorrow? Why hadn't someone made them shut up yet? Didn't they know? Didn't they care?

It took me another minute or two to realize that the desolate tears and wailing were coming from none other than me.

Not possible. Definitely, not possible. I wasn't a crier. I'd actually go way out of my way to avoid having to even hear someone else break down. Nonetheless, it was true.

Those heart-wrenching, soul-scarring cries were clawing their way from my own body. Jesse was gone now and I was ... wherever I was, whoever I was. Somehow, realizing that it was me doing the crying, I felt oddly ... detached for just a moment, a breath or two. As if the admission brought a momentary reprieve from the pain.

Where was my body? Where was I? Not the cave. Not anywhere I cared enough to look around and figure out the name of. It really just didn't matter where I was. It would only be where Jesse wasn't. That must be the name of this place. Not Jesse.

Still, the disconnection made me feel like I was simply watching a distant friend in pain. Only, my friend was me. I bit my lip hard and the pain was both soothing and disturbing. And both for the same reason.

I was alive. I was alive without Jesse. Again.

I had loved him, lost him, found him, remembered losing him, then lost him all over again. And all in one day. I needed a mental health day. A grimace-laced half-laugh slipped through my lips. I think I deserved a mental health year.

But in the next breath the sobbing resumed. The pain crashed over me like a tidal wave with no end, no relief in sight. And I just cried. I cried my heart out, and then I cried it back in again.

I cried for Jesse. I cried for my parents. I cried for all the times I'd never allowed myself the luxury of crying. And I cried for me ... for the pain that was yet to come. The pain that I could see lurking in the shadows before me. The pain I remembered I'd felt the first time I'd lost Jesse. The first time I'd lost my love, my life, my everything.

How could I be expected to go through this kind of unending suffering, this torture, a second time? How could this be possible? How could this be allowed? Who was getting their jollies from my overwhelming misery? Somebody had to be. Didn't they? Wasn't there supposed to be something good in everything? Even in the baddest bad, the saddest sad, the most devastating loss imaginable?

As I dove deeper into the emptiness surrounding me, filling me, I felt myself grow smaller and smaller ... until I was finally so small I could have disappeared into a void of nothingness if I'd just known how.

Not that I wanted to die. Not exactly. Just that I knew I didn't want to take the next hundred thousand breaths or so. That's all.

Slowly, time lost meaning and the world, all of it, every sound, every sight, every smell and every touch, slipped away from me, and I was left all alone, completely and entirely detached. Not even my thoughts could keep me company here. Not in this place. My only companion was my own intolerable pain. I was utterly isolated from everyone and everything. Lost here on my deserted island called Not Jesse.

I'm not sure how long I suffered like that, minutes, hours, days. I guessed hours was closer to the truth. But at some point I realized my eyes were squeezed tightly shut. I knew this first not because of the darkness, or because of the lack of lightness, but simply because I could feel again. And the first thing I felt was the pain of eyelids that had been held down for far too long.

I cautiously opened them ...

The pain of the light was overwhelming in its sheer brightness. It took too many long, breathless, disorienting minutes to count for me to make sense of the place I now found myself. But finally, this new world began to sharpen around the edges, and reality began to seep into my awareness.

I realized that the bright light wasn't really so bright. It was a soft, muted blend of moonlight and starlight. If I'd been in the right state of mind it could even have been beautiful. But for me, for now, it was just light. Well orchestrated perhaps, but still, just light. Light that wouldn't fall upon a certain head of shiny, black hair or on a certain set of dark, strong shoulders. My certain someone. My Jesse.

My body was lying on the ground. On a large, flat rock actually. At least, that's what it felt like. And there were lots of other rocks all around me. I could smell them more than see them. Strange. What was that about?

I turned my head trying to get some idea of where I was. Even with all the rock, it didn't feel like West Texas. It didn't smell the same, the animals didn't sound the same. Even the air didn't feel the same, it felt ... wetter here. Wherever here was this time around.

Slowly some of the closer rocks slipped out of the haze they'd been swallowed in. They were gravestones. I was in a cemetery. Exactly where I was supposed to be. I couldn't quite put my finger on the why, but at least I was good with the where. That was something. And, right now, a something, any something, was a million times better than a pocket full of nothings.

My eyes shifted slightly to the left and I saw a girl. She was asleep, curled up in a little ball, snuggled in close to something big and black and furry. How sweet.

Memories tickled at the edges of my mind. Sweet, little Sarah, one giant fricken' panther, Bagheera, or was it T.J.? The Big Evil, unavoidable, and after me. And something else, someone else.

A shiver shimmied its way down my spine and I burrowed deeper into the warm body wrapped around me. Strong, masculine arms tightened around my stomach, pulling me even closer before stilling quite suddenly.

I started to turn my body within the embrace. I felt torn between two opposing poles. Part of me wanted, needed, desperately to see the face, to know the person, connected to these arms. These warm, familiar arms. But another part of me didn't. Not for anything. That side just wanted to be held by them. Afraid that anything more would make the reality dissolve instantly, leaving nothing but a dream.

A sweet dream, perhaps. But in the end, nothing more substantial than just one night's fairy tale. The worst kind of nightmare.

It didn't take long though before my own stupid curiosity got the best of me and refused to be denied. I turned the rest of the way toward the man whose face I hadn't yet seen, but who had apparently been holding me, our bodies entwined on the ground in the middle of the night in a graveyard for God only knows how long.

The arms encircling me were warm and strong. But they were also alarmingly immobile. I could feel his eyes watching me, waiting for my reaction.

I took one last, long, deep breath in an effort to calm my trampled nerves, then slowly slid them up to his face, his eyes.

And I saw ... Jesse!

He was right there in front of me, looking back at me! I threw myself in his arms, crushing my body against him. In the same breath my lips found his, molding themselves to his as though they would never release him again.

And he kissed me back. Strong hands sliding up my sides to my waist, scrunching my shirt up with them. The breeze tickled across my abdomen. I melted into this kiss, placed my hands on top of his and slid them up my warm, aching skin, underneath my shirt, until they rested on the undersides of my breasts, his thumbs brushing across my swollen nipples.

"No!" Beau bellowed with a thick voice. He literally threw me aside as he yelled, "I can't do that!" I landed in a pile close to the fire. A good thing too, because suddenly I felt as cold as a side of beef in a butcher shop freezer.

My throat was so tight the words seemed to cut as they moved to my lips, "But why?!" My body began to shift, to move into a crouch ...

He was facing away from the fire, away from me, but turned his head and looked over his shoulder at my words. What was that look on his face? Disdain? Distaste? Frustration? Or just pity? As soon as I thought I had figured it out, the flickering flames would retrace the shadows on his face, subtly shifting the look. I couldn't quite keep up with the pace of his expressions to actually catch one of them before the next slid into place.

"Syd. That is just not an option for us. Now, for the love of God, pull your shirt back in place!" He stepped closer to the fire as he spoke, his face no longer unclear. It was filled with contempt. He turned away from me, but before he did I caught a glimpse, a shadow, of something else ... longing, perhaps?

Oddly, my body responded to the challenge without waiting for my head to intercede. My eyes never left his body as my feet carried me to him. I felt as if I were being drawn by sheer gravity alone. The gravity of desire. As I approached him I saw the muscles of his back stiffen, his shoulders tighten, preparing for another round. Another touch. Another rebuff.

In all honesty, this probably should have been a neon billboard screaming for me to back off. It should have been, but it wasn't. Of course it wasn't. Not for me. Not even close. In fact, the closer I came to him, the less aware I was of anything but his body and its effect on my body.

The fire was no longer warm against my back, yet I was smoldering. The heat was coming from the charge that hung in the air between us now. As if we were standing in the center of a web of electricity and every movement, every breath resonated against the strands of the web, shooting the voltage even higher.

I could feel every breath he took, could see the pulse throbbing deeply at the base of his neck. In that moment I felt like a predator utterly captivated, thoroughly enmeshed, completely intoxicated with its prey.

My body was so close to Beau's now that I could smell his heat, hear his heartbeat, see the fine sheen of desire glinting along his body in the firelight ... it was completely overwhelming. He held my senses spellbound within his power, it was impossible for me not to respond. The sheer beauty of him made my breath catch in my chest without hope of release. His glistening body, his wind-ruffled hair, held my unblinking eyes captive, refusing to let go. The taste of his silken skin tantalized my mouth and played along my tongue. Tempting. Teasing. Luring me ever closer.

I raised my hands, resting them on his broad back a breath below his shoulders. The heat radiating from Beau's body filled me and I no longer felt the need to breathe. My hands began lightly tracing down his shoulder blades as I leaned toward him, barely whispering a touch with my cheek along his back. My face began to move in time with my hands to some slow, hypnotic rhythm ... feeling, but never quite touching his skin. As my hands neared his waist, I closed the distance between us and my face moved upwards. My lips brushed along his spine, my hot ragged breath spilling out between us.

Immediately, he began to step away. "Don't move," I breathed, my body following his, not wanting to break the spell that kept him here before me.

"You don't know what you're doing!" He growled, slipping further away from me.

Suddenly I felt a chill and thought for a moment the fire had died out. But I knew instinctively that was impossible. It still illuminated his perfect body before me, making it glow with a stunningly hypnotic eroticism.

"Of course I do!" I choked out, angry and offended in equal measure, still wanting more ... needing more.

He was facing me now and I reached out for him a third time. This time I moved quickly. Hungrily pulling my body into his and grazing my teeth along the tender flesh of his throat. I dragged my hands up his back pulling him to me as my mouth quickly ascended his neck, followed the line of his jaw, and claimed his perfect lips.

But, also for the third time, he thrust me away, sending me, stumbling, to the ground. Beau was furious now. "Dammit, Syd ... it's Jesse you want! I'm just the first poor idiot you came across." He stalked away to the far side of the fire as he shot back over his shoulder, "Now please, put your hormones back in their cage and get some sleep!"

Still sitting where I'd fallen after his final rejection of me, the words slipped from my lips, "Sleep?! Where are you going? I don't want to be alone. Not right now." I felt the horror of shame wash over me at my weakness. But somehow I couldn't control it ... and maybe, just maybe, I didn't even want to ...

"Anywhere away from you," he replied so softly I wasn't sure he'd said it at all.

"Ungh! Put your own damn hormones away ... if you even have any! You want me, too! I can feel it!" My words were wasted on the dead for Beau was nowhere in sight.

That was fine with me though. Perfect, in fact. I preferred to be alone anyway ... I had ever since "the flood". That's what I preferred to call it, the car crash that had wrenched my parents out of my life forever. But I didn't want to think about them right now either.

So, why did my words sound so hollow? Nothing had changed. But then I realized that I was walking in a large circle around the fire. I had changed. Why was I acting so weird? So unlike me.

So what if I'd remembered Jesse. If that was even real. Maybe it was just some self-induced delirium, or just a dream ...

I changed direction just to make sure I could. Of course I could! What the hell was wrong with me?! Beau? No! No way! That was just ... well, just plain stupid. So, he had his own hang ups. Fine. Nothing personal. He just couldn't do the whole physical love thing. Okay. I could understand that, couldn't I? Absolutely ... no sweat!

Still, I couldn't shake that funny little ache. It hung low in my stomach, but with each breath it fluttered around in my chest. Like one of those baby birds that couldn't quite catch the wind under its wings and just hovered, sweeping and dipping, over the nest.

Alright, what if it wasn't Beau, what if it was me? What if ... I swallowed hard to clear the sudden tightness in my throat. What if Beau just didn't want me? Could I deal with that? I really wasn't sure ...

I stopped abruptly. Why was I thinking about Beau, anyway?! I turned toward the fire, grabbed my sleeping bag, and jerked it out, full-length.

Jesse. That's who I should be thinking about! What was that exactly, anyway? And where was Sarah now? She'd been here when I'd finally woken up. But she'd slipped out sometime after. Sometime while Beau and I were ... otherwise entertained.

Was it normal for her to wander off in the middle of the night? Would she be alright on her own like this? She was just a little girl, after all.

No matter what the big, bad Beau would like to believe.

On and on my mind droned for what seemed like hours, until it became a blurred, repetitious pattern. A mix of worries. Then a stream of thoughts about Jesse and Rachel ... and Beau. Again, and again, and again ...

Boy, had I ever bitten off more than I could chew. I was struggling, fighting my own hesitations and qualms. Trying to swallow this emotional mouthful down and get the dark, intoxicating flavor of Jesse out of my mouth, out of my heart, as fast as possible.

And I had to keep that soul quenching taste out of my heart, out of my mouth, out of my mind, even if it was only for a moment or two. It was just too overwhelmingly comfortable. What I wouldn't give just to be able to swallow. This whole jumbled, surreal mess had slammed my entire world sideways. And now I was trying to see it, to evaluate it from a place that no longer existed. Not even in my dreams. And I didn't think I even wanted it to.

My God, what the hell was wrong with me? I felt like I was standing at the edge of some high precipice with only a thin layer of glass under my feet. Glass that was spider-webbing with cracks as I stood there watching it, not moving a muscle for fear it would give way, sending me hurtling headfirst into a deep, dark pit of loneliness, of insanity.

Every day now seemed to bring a new challenge ... and a big one at that. I felt like I was jumping from the top of one pillar to the next, trying not to look down into the in-between. Not knowing which direction I was heading. Afraid that if I opened my eyes I'd find myself in the middle of some unnamed ocean with no way of finding my way back home. Not knowing if I even really wanted to.

Salvation by disorientation. Abandoned but not aimless. There was always a definite direction to my madness, even if I wasn't always quite sure which direction that was. I just walked the walk, no matter how dark that walk might be. I simply danced through it, alone, without inhibition or restraint, eyes closed tight to keep out all the external noise.

But either way, good or bad, these feelings just weren't going to go away. And no amount of time was going to wash them away. They were mine, whether I liked it or not. Whether I wanted them or not. They were here to stay. They were a part of me now.

New shadows on an old soul. So, how is it that they felt ancient, irrefutable, so very, very strong. Too strong for me to fight them. I felt like the helpless little newborn. Lost. Utterly powerless to the inescapable, titanic waves of change, of my own true self, threatening to pull me under. To overtake me, to change the path of my life for all time.

And these waves were so huge, so high, that if I tipped my head back far enough to see the tops of them, I knew I'd see them crashing against the moon, teasing and tickling the sun. What possible chance did I have against such a force of nature? A mere girl like me?

Fear washed over me and was quickly chased aside by anger. I was no stupid boy toy! I'd never been weak. I'd always steered my own ship, fought my own battles, chosen my own path. How could this possibly be happening to me? I was my own hero. No matter how many times a guy had wanted to be my knight in shining armor, I couldn't let him be that for me. How could I possibly be rescued by someone I could never need?

Besides, I didn't even really like horses. Jesse's was great, but I'd learned then and there that those kinds of dreams were a complete waste of time. For me, at any rate. I just wasn't hardwired the way other girls were. The girls who loved being fawned over by the likes of a Sir Lancelot or a Romeo. No, that path was lined with heartbreak, destined for ultimate and everlasting disaster if I allowed myself to be stupid enough to stroll down it.

So, why me? Why now? This couldn't be right, couldn't possibly be happening. Not to me at any rate. But knowing that, why couldn't I run ... run anywhere, just somewhere away from here. Away from this emotional avalanche crashing down all around me.

I couldn't take so much as one single step, much less circumnavigate the bottomless sandpits strewn all around me. Enclosing me. A ravenous minefield salivating over my flesh, my heart, my very soul.

The weight of the world pressed down upon me, suffocating me. The only way to get through it was to somehow remember what I never knew I was, what I never knew I wanted to be, what I nonetheless fully intended to be.

Somehow I had to latch onto the shadows of the image that had once been so vivid it had resonated brilliantly in my mind. I had to find a way to grab hold of those fading tendrils of lucidity, of slipping sanity. Otherwise, I'd be lost in the echoing desert of my own madness for all eternity.

But the only thing I could find to latch onto was Beau. He was the only constant. The only solid ground my toes could reach. The only warmth my aching fingers could manage to find, to grasp, in violent defeat and in desperate, reckless triumph.

How was that even possible? How could someone I'd known less than a week be the guardian of my heart, the captain of my ship, the path to my own salvation?

And why on earth did that knowledge bring a sense of peace with it, a stillness deep down within my soul? How could it echo with a resonating, sleepless serenity I'd never felt before, never thought existed, and now suddenly couldn't take a single breath without? Not without it. Not without him.

Because, without either one would now mean without me.

I was no longer just me. I was his me. And God help me, I would do anything, give anything, to stay that way. I had never, not for one instant, felt so alive, so free, so accepted, so cared for. Somehow this stranger, this man I'd known couldn't possibly exist, had managed to give me both wings to fly as high as I dared and roots strong enough to support that freedom. Now, the only question was what I would do with those wings ...

17 JUST HANGING WITH THE BOYS

I'd have laid good money that my busy brain would have made it impossible for my eyes to close. But as the fire faded to a quiet glow and the pre-dawn sky softly melted the darkness, I finally drifted to sleep. The last thing I felt was the blinding light of the sun as the earth cradled me in a blanket of warmth.

As tired and spent as I'd been when I'd finally given way to sleep, I would have expected it to be a deep, dreamless state. Pure exhaustion. It was anything but that.

I was floating somewhere high over the ground. Below me a group of boys was horsing around together. They were so far below me that I didn't think I'd be able to see what they were doing, much less who they were. But I could ... quite clearly, in fact. I could even hear their conversation.

What were they, 100, 200 feet below me? No, more than that ... much more. The air was thin and cool around me, even the tree tops were far, far below. A mile then? Maybe. Probably.

And I smelled something. Which was strange, because there was absolutely nothing up here but me. Was that their scent? Was I smelling them? I couldn't be sure, but somehow I thought it was. Actually, I knew it was. How odd, and yet somehow, completely natural.

I was moving in a large circular pattern. Much larger than when I'd circled the fire earlier, completely distraught. Each pass must have covered 2 or 3 miles of land below. But whereas before I'd been upset, now I could just feel the wind, my feelings were ... somewhere else. As if they'd been surgically removed and replaced with a sense of utter peace ... and protection.

Yes. And I wasn't up here by coincidence. I was watching, looking out for something ... for someone. One of those boys. Yes.

Just then, one of them tipped his chin up and looked straight at me, almost as if he could feel me there, could see me there. Impossible! But ... it was Jesse! My Jesse! He was there. He was alive! I could see him. I was watching him.

Actually I was more than watching him. I was watching him as if my life depended on it. As if his life depended on it. Depended on my protecting him. From what, though? There was no one around but his friends, our friends. Friends we'd known our whole lives. And yet the feeling of unease hung like a cold, wet blanket wrapped two shades too tight around me.

Mmm. I felt the warmth of the sun all of a sudden, as I hit a pocket of air that was hotter than the rest. Where was it? I tried to circle back to find it again, my attention momentarily diverted from the scene below.

I looked from side to side, but of course could see no difference. Hot air, cold air ... just looked the same. Just looked like air. What a surprise.

Oh well, I looked back down at the boys. They were farther away now, laughing at some stupid joke, completely oblivious to the world around them, entirely absorbed by the warmth and comfort of their friendship.

"So, Jesse, when are you gonna make a decent woman of her?" Reggie asked, catching Jesse in the ribs with his elbow.

"Huh!" Jesse half laughed. "I can never seem to pin her down long enough to ask her."

With an ear-splitting grin, Reggie chuckled back, "Oh, man! That's a shame. You better work on that stamina. Gotta learn how to make these things last, how to pin her down longer. Girls love a man with stamina!"

Sam cut his eyes sideways and offered with a smirk, "I've got a good stretch of rope in the back of the truck ..."

"Right! I'd be missing a hand if I so much as thought about that around Rache. She'd sooner die than feel like she was tied down by anyone or anything." He looked up again, smiling, glancing casually in my direction. My heart skipped a beat before it began rhythmically slamming against my chest once again.

Tommy shrugged. "Aagh, you don't need it anyway ... nothing could ever pull you two apart." His eyes filled with admiration, appreciation and longing. "It leaves a little hope for the rest of us ..."

"I guess, but ..." Jesse's voice trailed off.

"But what, man?" Sam's voice broke in, riding over the more somber tones of the conversation. "Her parents? They'll come around, and if they don't, who really cares? Rache made up her mind years ago. They can't touch that."

Jesse kicked a small brown rock distractedly, slightly nervous, as he mumbled, "Yeah, still ... But you're right, I guess." His eyes followed the stone as it bumped across the dirt, finally rolling up next to another slightly larger, reddish-colored rock. It came to a standstill as it did, almost like an embrace.

He lifted his gaze to me and all of a sudden, Jesse's sullen eyes lit up. He looked back at the group of boys and piped out with, "You know what? I'm gonna ask her tonight."

"Wow! That's great, Jess." Tommy threw his arm across Jesse's shoulders.

"Cool, man ... need that rope now? I can probably wipe most of the dirt off of it." Sam offered, laughing loudly.

"Huh! I think I'll try my luck without it this time." With that wonderful crooked smile, Jesse added, "Maybe next time, though, if she needs convincing!"

"Yeah, or for the honeymoon. Mmmm, mmm, mmm! Hey! That could be your wedding gift to them, Sam." Reggie positively glowed with dark mirth, his eyebrows waggling insidiously.

Tommy immediately ground out, "Shut up, man! That's Rache you're talking about."

"Yeah, you always did have a soft spot for her. You gonna go cry your heart out over this one?" Unrepentantly, Reggie threw one arm around Tommy's shoulders and with his other hand, pulled Tommy's head to his shoulder. He teasingly added, "Do you need a tissue? A shoulder to cry on? It's okay, man. You just let it all out. I'm here for you."

Jesse came up on Tommy's other side and bumped his bicep with the back of his hand. "Hey, um, I was thinking ... would you be my best man? I mean, if you don't want to that's cool, but ..."

Tommy quickly interrupted looking a little flushed, but happy. "No, man. I'd like that. I'd like that a lot. Sure. I'll do it."

"Great!" Jesse smiled back. "There's no one I'd rather have. And, I know it would mean the world to Rache."

"What, we're not good enough for you?" Reggie countered with feigned girlish resentment.

"Yeah, I think I need that shoulder to cry on!" Sam added with a high-pitched voice and a puppy dog face, leaning his head on Reggie's free shoulder.

"Well, come to Papa." Reggie threw his remaining arm around Sam and turned accusing eyes toward Jesse. "Now just look at that, you've gone and made a grown man cry. It's tragic! Just tragic! You should be ashamed of yourself, young man!"

All four boys burst out in unbridled laughter, walking together through the same wide open land they'd crossed a thousand times since they learned how to walk. As close and happy as four lifelong friends could ever dream to be.

Wow! This was the day Jesse was going to ask me to marry him? I'm dreaming of what happened two days ago, sixty years ago? Hmmm. I guess in some crazy way that made sense. But boy oh boy, was I fixated on this day or what?

Sam was right about my parents, though ... I didn't care at all ... either way. Now that I thought about it, I guess they'd never really managed to hide their friendly resentment towards Jesse. But nobody much trusted anyone from a different group around here, everyone pretty much stayed in their own tight little groups.

I guess that made it easier for them to just coast through life like that. I mean, no newbies meant fewer surprises along the way, fewer ups and downs. They liked him all right. Knew he was a good guy. Still, they always tried to push me to spend more time with my friends, or at church, or studying, or cleaning, or just about anything that didn't include Jesse.

The boys' conversation fell back into the light banter it had been as they cut across the stream and ducked into the woods that ran alongside it to the falls.

Pine Canyon pour-off had been the boys "spot" ever since they'd been old enough to ride their bikes out past their own streets. Instead of a club house, they had a two hundred foot waterfall on the east side of the Chisos Mountains. It took a while to get there, but they loved it and it was beautiful. Everyone in town knew it was their hangout. Just like everyone in town knew just about everything about just about everyone, except themselves and their own baggage.

As I lost sight of Jesse and the boys in the thick foliage, I began to smell something else. Someone else. Actually, somebodies ... plural. Definitely more than one. And definitely somewhere close to the falls. My feeling of unease quickly began to ramp up.

I flew on ahead to get a look-see before Jesse diverted my attention again. It would take them a good five minutes to reach the bottom of the drop off. Plenty of time for me to find out who was out there, and maybe even to see what it was they were after.

Running into people way out here was pretty rare. And when you did, it sometimes lead to trouble. Don't get me wrong. I mean, as small towns go, we were a pretty nice lot, but still, people were just people, capable of doing so much more than we ever give them credit for. The good and the bad. The great and the terrible. It's just one of those things that keep life so intensely interesting. Well, interesting as long as it wasn't spewing cow dung all over you in particular. Because, if it was, then it was pretty much just plain crappy. Literally.

I flew up to a much higher level to avoid being seen by whoever else was here. It didn't take me long to reach the waterfall, and once I had, I made a large circle around the perimeter trying to glide on the currents as much as possible to avoid catching their eye with my wing movements.

I spotted them sitting at the top of the drop off just behind some trees that lined the left edge a few yards from the water. The trees were Ponderosa Pine, very majestic, and the mountain range was filled with them. The two men had chosen a place that would be good for watching the bottom of the falls. They wouldn't be easily seen from below even though they were completely out in the open from my perspective. There was another rise to the right. I landed in some trees there so I could do some watching of my own.

There were two of them. Both were men, and both were wearing Texas Ranger uniforms. One was considerably older than the other and seemed, by definition, to be the one in charge.

As I watched them, I realized quickly that they were definitely not here by mere chance. They were here quite intentionally. They were here on a mission to find someone in particular. My someone. Jesse. My Jesse. But why? That was the question. What reason could they possibly have for wanting to find Jesse? My normal, everyday, unassuming Jesse.

I knew I still had at least a couple minutes before Jesse and the boys arrived, so I carefully shifted closer to them, limb by limb. Trying not to attract any unwanted attention, I walked along branches and dropped, using my wings only to counterbalance the pull of gravity, in order to free-fall to the branches immediately below me.

The two men were talking, whispering. Apparently they had an agenda for today. I snuggled up close to the back of the tree in front of me so that I could hear the conversation as well as I possibly could and still remain hidden behind the limbs and leaves. Ready for flight at a moment's notice.

"Whatever you do, don't shoot. Not yet." The person on the right, the one with the bigger balls, said.

The second man had hunkered down into a crouch with his rifle resting on his knees, just waiting for the boys to arrive down below. "Well, why on earth not? Why not just get rid of him now? It sure would simplify things."

I couldn't see their faces, but something was familiar about them. I knew these two men. And knew them well. But I couldn't quite make out their voices through the half-whispered words. Carefully I dropped down one more branch and silently sidled just a little further from the trunk of the tree to improve my angle. I could almost see them now. Just a little bit further.

"We need to know how far this has gotten. We have to find out if she knows anything before we kill him." He looked up and I saw a set of blue eyes so empty the sky simply sank down into them instead of being reflected back with little wispy white clouds. These were eyes unlike any others. Eyes completely disconnected to anything remotely warm, or even living. They had an overpowering darkness masked by their superficial brightness, which was only highlighted by the gleaming, slick black hair.

"She doesn't know anything. I guarantee she doesn't. She doesn't know a damn thing other than the fact that she thinks she's in love with him. All we have to do is get rid of him. She won't remember anything without him around."

"And if she already knows? Are you still prepared to finish this, Joseph? Or are you getting cold feet now that it's time?"

Joseph? Oh, God, no! Not Joseph! Not my own brother! What the hell was going on? Why on earth would Joseph want to kill Jesse? What possible reason could he have? My brain raced, trying desperately to play catch-up, to wrap itself around what was happening here.

If the man with the gun was Joseph, then the other guy must be Henry MacAfee, the Ranger that Joseph had befriended five years ago when he'd moved into town. Joseph had been fifteen at the time and he and Henry, who was about twice Joseph's age, had instantly hit it off. They'd been almost inseparable ever since.

But there was something else familiar about Henry. I couldn't put my finger on exactly what it was though. It was almost as if he reminded me of someone else. But who? I could almost see it, almost but not quite.

Joseph wasn't through trying to negotiate his way out of it. I guess that was something at least. If he didn't, that would be a lot worse. When life throws a sack of rotten potatoes your way and that's all you have to work with, then you try to pick out the less rotten ones. Joseph would just have to be my good rotten potato.

"Look, Henry. If Rachel Anne doesn't remember it all, then there's no need for a big ordeal. We just get rid of Jesse, and there won't be anything left to remind her. It's that simple."

"Nothing is ever that simple. Besides, what does it really matter if she knows anything or not? She's the wild card here. She's the one with the hand we can't see. And she's the one who can ruin us all. Are you really prepared to risk that? Just for her? What are you thinking?"

He shook his head and waved both hands in front of him as if he were warding off bad spirits. "No. You know what? I don't even want to know. Just focus. Remember exactly what's at stake here, Joseph. One stupid, insignificant girl could ruin in a single day what the church has spent over two thousand years trying to protect. Don't fall apart right when we need you the most."

"That stupid, insignificant girl is my sister, for Pete's sake! I'm supposed to just sit by and wait patiently for her to remember something that she'll die for remembering?" It was Joseph's turn to shake his head. "I don't know who you think I am, but I've watched over Rachel Anne her whole life, and I'm not about to let anything happen to her that I could have prevented."

"Dammit, Joseph! We have one goal. One. And it's a simple one. Protect the secret. At all costs. No matter how difficult that might prove to be. Besides, one less little Indian boy is always a good thing. The sooner we get them off the face of the planet, the better."

The nagging feeling of familiarity with Henry was really bothering me now. An acrid taste of discomfort and dislike hung heavily to my tongue and filled my mouth with its noxious bite.

Shit! I heard the guys coming up fast at the bottom of the drop off. How was I going to warn them? There had to be a way. There had to be a way to stop this. Think Rache! Think!

It was only a moment before Henry spoke again in a tense, muffled whisper. "Well, well, well. Be quiet now. Here they come. Be ready to fire when I say the word."

Reggie and Sam stepped out onto the side of the pool of water, having cleared the woods just ahead of Jesse and Tommy. My heart jumped, but my stomach lurched at the sight of Jesse. I'd remembered him, loved him a lifetime, married him and held him in my arms as he'd taken his last breath. All since yesterday. And here I was trying to figure out how to keep it all from happening again. But I guess again would actually mean for the third time since my memory had been the second time.

Reggie and Sam had already shed their clothes and were jumping into the water when Reggie called out to Jesse. "Hey, man, so how long do we have before you have to get back and ask permission to try on your ball and chain?"

"Yeah, Jesse, when does your life as a free man officially end?" Sam joined in once he'd splashed back up to the surface.

Tommy just cut a small, sideways smile as Jesse barked back, "Yeah, you two just keep it comin'. Your day will be here soon enough. Don't worry, I've got your back. You know me. Memory like a freakin' elephant!"

Raucous laughter from all three boys met his last words. I felt a deep ache of longing to join in with their lighthearted banter, to share these last precious stolen moments with them, but especially with Jesse. Somehow I knew this would be the last time I'd see him.

Joseph shifted and my heart jumped right up into my throat. I knew Jesse didn't die here, but still I had that uneasy feeling of impending, inevitable doom.

"Damn I can't believe he's got the nerve to ask Mom and Dad for Rachel Anne's hand. What a jackass! They'll never agree to that, not in a million years. And he knows it. He's just setting himself up for heartbreak."

Henry shushed him again, then spoke in a low, menacing voice. "They'll run off and do it anyway. You can't stop it, and you can't let that happen. You know that, as well as I do. She'll remember everything."

Joseph's chin tucked down as he contemplated the words, mulling them over in his head as if he were simply thinking of his next move in a game of chess. "Yeah. You're right. She would."

Cold blue eyes tightened on my brother, little wrinkles forming at the corners. What was it about those eyes that was so God damn familiar? Something ... but I just couldn't put my finger on it. "You have to kill Jesse now, before he ever asks them. Otherwise, the pain of losing him could be so great for Rachel it could trigger the memories of her past lives."

Slowly nodding, eyes still turned down, staring only at the space two feet from his own face,

Joseph inhaled slowly, deeply. "You're right." He agreed again.

Damn him! How could he do this to me? How could he even think about it, much less do it? He knew I loved Jesse. He knew I had my whole life. Did he honestly think it would hurt even one tear less if it happened before he asked me to marry him?

For heaven sake, in my heart I'd been married to Jesse since I was seven years old. My scoop of ice cream had fallen off the cone onto the sidewalk and he'd shared his with me. We had stood there in the sweltering heat, taking turns pushing it into each other's face as we'd licked the quickly melting scoop of vanilla, giggling as it had dripped down our chins. I'd realized right then and there Jesse would always make my downs a little more up, and make my ups right out of this world. And that I'd do the same for him. Forever. That was that. Marriage by ice cream.

And now Joseph was going to try to kill him? Not happening. Not today.

He was already aiming the long barrel as my wings cleared trees, my gaze now locked on the top of Joseph's head. A giant caw erupted from my throat as I came barreling down straight at him. I wasn't going to make it in time! Dammit! I pulled my wings in closer to my body and lengthened my neck to streamline myself, to increase my speed.

I saw Jesse's head lift toward me in slow motion as I reached my target. My ears were straining, listening for any hint of a gunshot. Just as my body passed in front of Joseph's eyes, I heard an explosion that echoed, reverberating through my entire body. I pulled up, trying to miss the tree, but couldn't lift myself fast enough and had to fly through a few of the branches, something dragging painfully across my left wing.

No-o-o! I hadn't made it in time! I'd let Jesse die, again! No! This wasn't fair! This wasn't right.

Everybody was in motion now, like the bell for a fire drill had gone off.

Joseph and Henry were making a quick retreat away from the edge, back into the woods for cover.

"Where'd that damn bird come from? Scared the ever-loving shit outta me!" Joseph was pissed! Pissed that he'd wasted a shot trying to murder Jesse!

"Shut up, you idiot! They'll hear you. We'll just have to try again later. We will succeed. Not doing so is simply not an option." Henry would obviously never let this go.

Dammit!

The boys were naked, running for cover as well at the bottom of the drop off, yelling at one another as they did, dripping water from head to toe.

"What the hell was that? Damn idiots trying to kill off the golden eagles again? Shit! Somebody needs to bend his damn rifle in half. One of these days, they really are gonna get one of us!" Sam barked out just as he ducked to miss running head-on into a low hanging pine limb.

"Yeah! What the hell? You haven't even asked to marry Rache yet and already you've got the whole town after us! Man! I sure am glad you want Tommy boy over there to be your best man and not me! It's a freakin' suicide mission!" Leave it to Reggie to try to fix this with laughter. The bigger the blood bath, the bigger the snigger as far as he was concerned.

As they continued to talk and joke, I circled three times, wanting to be absolutely positive that the two-man assassin team was done for the day, or for the moment in any case.

"You're still jealous, Reg? I promise to save one dance for you, man! So, stop leakin' everywhere! Your chest hair's gettin' all soggy from the tears! Seriously, though, that was close! Too close. Did anybody see who it was?"

Finally, when I was confident there would be no more shooting, that the men were committed to their temporary retreat, I swooped down to check on Jesse and the boys.

"Nah, man. Didn't see anyone. Matter of fact, didn't even know anyone was even up there, 'til all hell broke loose that is!" Tommy looked over at Reggie before he continued. "But hey, Reg, if you need a moment alone with Jesse, you know, just a little special, quiet time for the two of you, just let us know. We'll clear out, look the other way. No problem!"

"You asshole!" Reggie laughed, then bent over at the waist towards Tommy and shook his water-logged hair like a wild man, dousing Tommy in the downpour.

And just like that all four boys were laughing again. The drama of the moment already a mere memory.

When I got down to them, Jesse was standing there with his arm stretched out. He looked like he wanted me to use him as a perch. His eyes were watching me closely, searching my body for wounds just like mine were searching his body. Even so, I felt my heart skip a beat, my pulse increase, as my eyes slipped down the hard lines of his abdomen, stalling on his naked thighs.

I slowed, almost hovering in place as I gently let my claws wrap around his arm, trying not to let the nails bite into his flesh.

"Good girl. That's a good girl." His other hand was incredibly warm as it stroked down my body over and over, from the back of my head to the top of my tail. "Thank you. You saved my life, sweet thing."

Suddenly, his eyes hardened. He was staring at my left wing, a look of pain filling his face. "You're hurt, little one." He gently stretched my wing out. "Yeah, that's gonna leave a scar. Still, it completely missed the bones. I don't think we even need to worry about stitches. Guess it's just your lucky day, girl."

Lucky? He called this lucky? Lucky my ass. Lucky was not having your future husband shot at. Lucky was not being related to the person behind the trigger. Lucky was not beginning to feel the deep, sharp burn in my wing. And lucky was definitely not looking into the eyes of my husband, knowing he really was going to be shot tomorrow and there was absolutely nothing I could do about it.

Jesse leaned toward me and kissed the top of my head as my eyes fluttered closed. In that instant the rest of my life as Rachel Anne Kensington came crashing through my brain like a herd of buffalo being chased by a swarm of angry hornets.

Jesse's death, he hadn't died accidentally at the hands of some stupid hunter while we were flying. No, he'd risked his life, and lost it, trying to protect me. My refusal to head back home afterwards. Tommy helping me get out of here, helping me get to Houston. Finding out I was pregnant, that I carried a part of Jesse inside me.

A very special part. And finally, nine months later, Henry and Joseph catching up to us the night I gave birth.

That was bad, the night the two of them found us. I was in a park down the street from where we were staying, sitting underneath a giant magnolia tree. I'd just finished nursing my beautiful baby boy, and it was an absolutely beautiful night. Magical, but more than a little bit eerie. One of those nights filled with electricity, with the excitement of something waiting to happen. You could feel it crawling along your skin. Tommy had gone to get the two of us something to eat once he was sure the baby and I were both okay.

Henry and Joseph had both brought their hunting rifles with them. They'd shot us down like we were a couple of pirates sorting through our stolen bounty, instead of like the mother and child we were. Me begging them with my last breath to spare my baby's life. I'd been shot first and had watched, unable to move, still cradling Jesse Jr. in my arms, as Henry lowered his gun just a hair and shot him. A complicated look of intermingled pain, relief, resentment and rage had stained Joseph's troubled face. My best of the rotten potatoes.

I'd held both my Jesse's in my arms as they'd taken their last breaths on this earth. And as soon as they both had, I'd taken my own.

I can't imagine what Tommy must have gone through when he'd found us. Found us and buried us. Tommy'd decided to stay with us after burying Jesse's body on the banks of the Rio Grande, only to have to turn around and bury Jesse Jr. and me exactly nine months later. Sometime later he must have managed to have our graves marked. Wonder whatever happened to him. He couldn't have been a better friend. No one could have.

I felt the silken paths of cool tears as they caressed my cheeks. Slowly I opened my eyes, not knowing what I'd find, or where I'd be. Or even when I'd be, or who ...

The eyes that met mine were the same chocolate-flavored diamonds that had first met mine less than a week ago in the graveyard, in my graveyard.

Beau.

I was back. I was me again. Oh, yeah, I'd only been sleeping. This was just a dream. Of course I was just me.

But even if it was just a dream, now it was one I knew all the way through. And Beau knew I knew. I could see it in those dangerously captivating eyes.

Great! Just great. What could possibly happen next?

18 SECOND FIRST FLIGHT

I could hear Beau's voice reaching out to me. "It's okay. Come here. Come to me, Syd. Everything's gonna be okay. Let me sooth your pain." He was standing a couple yards away, holding his hands out to me.

I choked back the sobs that had appeared out of nowhere and threatened to spill out of me, slowly got up, and walked towards him, defeated and torn. Beau pulled me slowly, but firmly into his arms. Pulled my head to his chest and began to move slowly, rhythmically, gently rocking back and forth. It almost felt like a dance, but then not. It was nice, though, being this close to a warm body, his warm body. Not feeling him pushing me away, but holding me close instead.

It felt safe. Protected. A little bubble of sanity. And into that bubble, into Beau's chest, I started blubbering out my dream. Flying again but as me, keeping Joseph and Henry from shooting Jesse, being pregnant, Henry killing the baby and me, everything. And Beau just listened. He let me pour it all out without trying to stop me or question me or anything. He just kept running his fingers through the hair at my left temple, as if it drew his attention. His touch comforted me.

I realized we were moving now. Not in one place. We were walking, kind of. Really, it was more like a slow shuffle. Almost as if our embrace was shifting, floating in a current gently swirling all around us.

I didn't really care where we were going, but we were definitely headed in one general direction. Towards the bayou. We really weren't that far from it in this part of the cemetery, and I'd always loved that part. There was something about the water gently flowing past the garden of the dead that simply intrigued the hell out of me. It seemed cleansing. Or, maybe like it was promising to take them someplace. Or to take us someplace. I wasn't quite sure, but then again I couldn't seem to make myself care right then. I just closed my eyes and let Beau lead, trying to absorb his profound sense of ease, of strength, of conviction.

We didn't talk. Not one word. And yet, somehow, we were communicating with one another on a level I couldn't really understand. Soul talking. No, more like soul sipping. There was no formed speech, not even silently. It was more like we were tasting one another's inner selves, taking in mouthfuls of feelings, thoughts and memories without hurting, without consuming. Whatever we took seemed to immediately replace itself, never leaving an empty space.

I wanted to say I hadn't ever felt anything like it before, but somehow I knew that I had. I couldn't for the life of me remember when that could possibly have been, still I knew beyond any doubt I had.

As we slowly moved along in our dance among the dead, the sounds of the cemetery beat in a natural rhythm around us. A rhythm all their own. There was a slight breeze tickling through the branches, swishing the leaves as it slipped past. The sad call of one of Shakespeare's beloved mourning doves rode past on the gentle drafts of wind and a whole gang of Mexican Chirping Frogs picked up the beat giving it a distinct, guttural twist. Keeping time with all of this, the water in the bayou could be heard faintly, a gentle lapping against the lowest hanging limbs of the trees lining the banks. An entire ecological symphony, giving us our own private performance. Green music. Huh.

Finally, we eased up to the edge of the steep thirty-foot bank that fell away into Buffalo Bayou just past our feet. "Jump, Syd." Beau said suddenly, and I felt some of the dirt give way beneath my foot, falling down the side of the cliff.

"What?!" My head was spinning, trying to catch up with what was happening. Trying and failing. There'd just been way too much sensory input in the last twenty-four hours for my brain to process anything else.

Beau interrupted my brain freeze, "Just jump, Syd. Jump now."

"Are you crazy? I can't!" I yelled at him even though I was still in his arms.

"Yes, you can. Stop thinking about it and just do it!"

More dirt spilled down the side of the embankment and with it went what was left of any sense of calm inside my head. "You are indisputably insane! Let go of me, you lunatic!"

"I'm sorry, Syd."

"What are you sorry for, Beau? What, exactly, are you sorry for? Pulling me in, then pushing me away, only to pull me in again? Or are you sorry for scaring the hell out of me with a full-grown, bloodthirsty panther? Or for feeding me a long line of crap that ends with the biggest bad known to mankind chasing down my sorry little butt? Or maybe, just maybe, for bringing me here to the bayou and telling me to jump when I'm just too overwhelmed to do anything but follow your asinine directions?"

"No, none of that Syd. I'm sorry for this..." And that stupid, godforsaken, son of a bitch had the nerve to shove me off the edge of the bank so hard that I completely lost any and all contact with the ground under my feet, and went sailing off into thin air.

A thousand ways to remove Beau's testicles from his body flashed through my mind in an instant. And if I'd thought for one second I might actually get away with it without serious jail time, I probably would have given any one of them further consideration.

My body shifted from its forward thrust and began to drop in a horrific free-fall towards the earth that stretched out way too far below me, but much too close to me at the same time, finally my thoughts shifted to something much more practical. Namely, how to save my own sorry ass. So, I'd changed into a bird in my life as Rachel and in my dream as me. Did that mean that I could do that now? Here? All on my own?

Okay, my eyes caught a glimpse of the earth moving relentlessly closer to my face, to my entirely breakable self and suddenly my mind was racing with thoughts about animal life, and shifting. Thoughts and feelings that were supposed to open the door to such things. Golden eagle. What was the shift trigger for that one? All I could manage to focus on was the water rising quickly to meet me. Water. I didn't think that was it, but it was what filled my mind and instantly I morphed into ... a dolphin!

Oh, shit! So-o-o not good. Now I was hurtling through the air as an aerodynamic, non-limbed mammal with absolutely no hope of flying. And the earth just kept coming closer and closer by the nanosecond.

Okay! Refocus, Syd! For God's sake, think or you're gonna end up as a paraplegic dolphin entertaining kids at the one and three o'clock shows at Sea World seven days a week. What else could I see? My own body parts flying off of me? No! Stop it, Syd! You don't have time to be stupid here. Dirt. Yeah, I could see dirt. Lots of it. I could almost feel it running through my fingers.

And bam! Just like that I had shifted. I felt the wind blowing through a thick layer of fur. Dammit! I was a grizzly bear! Great! Talk about working in the wrong direction, now I was a quarter-ton, furry mammal who couldn't even swim should I be lucky enough to manage to hit the water.

Shit, Syd! Get pissed! Get stark raving mad! Blow up! Anything would be better than dying in half a second as one big chewed up, spit out fur ball!

I glanced up at the sun. Felt its heat bathe my skin. Felt the heat of my own frustration match it inside me. And a fraction of a second later? There I was ... Syd, the firefly, not a single bear hair in site! Just two sets of wings and a glowy little ass. So much for not having something to wear to the prom! I'd really light up the dance floor in this get-up!

Flitting off to the left, I managed to catch a huge gust of wind and almost got blown all the way to Timbuktu. The next updraft nearly buried me in the side of a palm tree. Whoa! Time to pay attention, Syd! I saw what looked like a cozy little nest of trees and headed for it just as fast as my little doublet wings would take me. So not fast. Not fast at all ...

So, off this little lightning bug went. Glowy itty-bitty butt and all.

Downsizing my me-ness, being me but in micro-form, gave every one of my senses a whole new perspective. It was absolutely amazing! A fantastic, exotic new world. But I hadn't really gone anywhere. This wasn't someplace new and magical. It was just the same little world I'd been living in my entire life.

In any case, this little firefly pulled up her spurs and jumped on the Sydney Express. I made my way at break-neck speed back to the school. A simple little twenty minute walk took buggy-me a mere seven hours ... two million, seven hundred, fifty thousand wing beats! My God, these little guys work hard. Of course, there had been thirty-some odd little side tracks to all sorts of amazing diversions. You know, really, truly incredible stuff, like glistening marbles, sticky candy wrappers, and soggy trash can bins. You know, fast food. Yeah. I know. Gross.

Finally, just as the sun was setting, which was pretty late this time of year, I rounded the corner two blocks from school. I'd just about made it! Too bad every conceivable bell for the day had already rung. I was late to absolutely everything. Even going home. Now that's bad.

As my little wings buzzed furiously, virtually inexhaustible, I thought I saw something familiar, so I turned back around for the umpteenth time to check it out. And sure enough, there it was. Patricia's car. Why the hell was that here at this time of night? That just didn't make a lick of sense.

I turned back around, feeling a little dazed, a little bewildered. But what the hell was new about that these days? It had practically become the norm for me the last week or so.

No sooner had I started on my way, something else caught my eye. God, what now? I buzzed back and found myself, glowy little butt and all, looking right back at me out of the window of Mr. A's car.

No way. This was just one tiny little breath too much of a coincidence to be anything but something totally uncoincidental.

No. This was totally no accident, this was calculated. Completely and sickeningly deliberate. The only question was, what exactly was this?

Mr. Asshole's face flashed in front of my eyes threatening, no promising, we'd, "... simply handle our little ... situation through ... alternative means." Instantaneously I realized what I'd been unable to see before. Unable to see because it had been here in this life that I'd known Henry ... only not as Henry. Rachel's Henry was my Mr. A.

Not looked like him. Not acted like him. No. He was him. Those horrifyingly empty blue eyes were still consumed with that same mixed-up look of pain, relief, resentment and rage. That same wolfish half-grin and that same greasy burger-joint-counter glossy black hair. That same, "Well, well, well," crap. He was simply unmistakable.

For the life of me I couldn't figure out how I'd missed it before. But then, my life as Rachel had been before this one. Maybe when I'd gone back, my current memories had stayed here with my body, with this body. Maybe.

But no matter what, Henry, Mr. Askew, had killed both my husband and my baby. And now he was threatening my best friend. My love for them, Jesse, my little boy, even Patricia, my aching yearning for them, for the comfort of their closeness, their happiness, filled my heart and soul.

Henry, Mr. A, was my Big Bad, and had been for God only knows how long ...

19 HAPPY, HAPPY, JOY, JOY ...
SCARY, SCARY

I felt the rage wash over me ... fill my body completely, top to bottom. Chasing away the sorrow, devotion, longing and joy that had instantly permeated my heart and soul with the thought of Jesse, baby Jessie and Patricia. Then, in the very next moment, I was me again. Arms, legs, Daddy's fingernails, Mama's long fingers, everything. All ten thousand screwed up parts of me. My reflection in Mr. A's car window was now that of a normal, naked, almost eighteen-year-old American teenager with normal teenage problems. Well, take out the normals and it was close enough to the truth to be acceptable.

But ... I did have a pretty bad gash on the upper part of my left arm ... and ... I leaned in closer and touched my left temple. There was a streak of white there, running down through my hair all the way to the bottom. Where had that come from? I shook my fingers in my hair right up at my scalp, trying to shake it out like it was powder, but it didn't budge. My hand slid slowly down, gripping the silken strands tightly between my fingers in an effort to pull it off, to strip it away. Still nothing. Whatever it was and whatever had caused it, it wasn't going anywhere anytime soon. Suddenly, a gentle breeze caught my hair, sliding dark chocolate strands over the streak, jerking me back to Patricia ... and my very own personal Mr. Shithead. Clothes or no clothes, black or white hair, I had to make sure Patricia was okay. But the dread sliding down my spine told me she wasn't. Not at all.

I walked. Forward. Just kept moving. If I didn't stay in any one place everything would be okay. I wasn't really aware of moving until I reached the back corner of the football field and my eyes cut across to Mr. Asshole, I mean, Mr. Askew's room. Henry's room. The Big Bad's room.

The thick, heavy taste of fury thundered through my veins. Cross it, just cross the field and keep going said that little voice deep down inside me, and so I did.

As I reached the steps leading up to the temporary building, my feet finally stopped moving. Now what? My eyes were drawn forcefully to the window and I felt myself complying without thinking about it anymore than I had during my trek here.

Oh ... my ... God.

No. No way. He had Patricia in there. One hand on her waist and one brushing the blonde hair back from her face.

Shit! What the hell was going on? Why was he touching her? Why was she letting him? And why the hell was Patricia even here, anyway?

I stood on the bottom step and leaned forward over the rail, trying to get a better look, but

Patricia's back was mostly to me, so I could only see a small slice of her cheek. Not enough to tell me anything that she might be thinking or feeling. I could see Mr. A's face just fine, those hideously empty blue eyes staring out from under that mop of glossy black hair. And what was on his face was so not good, and so perfectly clear.

The problem was Patricia was naïve enough to probably think he was concerned ... for her, no less. But I knew better. That look on his face had nothing to do with concern, especially for Patricia, or anyone else for that matter, and everything to do with what he was feeling. What he was consumed with ... lust, anger, planning. Exactly what he was planning, I so did not want to know.

As I stood there, dumbfounded, Mr. A leaned forward holding Patricia's face in his hands and ... kissed her. Granted it was her forehead, but still, it was a thousand times more than he should have been doing with his student. Besides, he was still holding her face in his hands and staring into her wide, innocent blue eyes, saying things I knew I didn't want to know, but things I wish to hell I could hear so I could nail his sorry ass in his coffin with them later.

Watching what was happening without any sound was like watching TV with the volume turned off. In silence, truth can't hide, motive rings out with a crystalline clarity. It was like the words jumbled up the truth in their hearts, in their actions.

I'd never thought about it being true in real life, though. Wow. I guess they're wrong ... you can learn something by watching too much TV. Something pretty God damn important at that.

Oh, my God. The piece of shit was trying to gain her trust.

No fucking way! My vision blurred with anger, but nothing about what I was watching got any softer. It stayed hard. Rock hard. Not a good hard either. Hard as concrete, like West Texas dirt in the middle of a drought. When it finally does rain, the water just rolls across it, never really soaking in.

Every inch of his hideous face screamed that he was happy, the son of a bitch! His face was utterly filled with joy.

Holy shit! I just realized Mr. A was staring out the window straight at me. Dammit! I still didn't have a stitch on! What to do? Shit, shit, double shit.

Wait a minute ... it's almost completely dark out here. And it's light in there. So, that should mean I'm covered. They shouldn't be able to see me, but I can see them. Still, I had the distinct feeling that he could see me, and perfectly at that. Even better than I could see him.

Actually, I wished Patricia could see me. I wished she'd turn around, look straight at me, and grow balls big enough to tell Mr. A to take a fucking leap off the God damn Ship Channel Bridge. If the fall didn't kill him, the water quality, or lack thereof, would!

"God! I wish ... Ungh! I wish you would just burn to the ground!" The words came out and I wasn't sure whether I meant Mr. A or the building. Maybe both. Maybe it didn't really matter. All that mattered was feeling clean again. Somehow getting all the bad off of me. Only I had the sinking feeling it was in me, not just on me. So, if water doesn't cut it, hell, try fire.

I glanced up and saw Mr. A's hands slide slowly down to Patricia's bottom, cupping her cheeks and pulling her up against him as he rubbed his face in her hair. The movement had shifted them so that Patricia's face was peeking around his shoulder, searching for the window, searching for the help she knew wouldn't come. Her lips parted as if there were things she wanted to say. Things that would never be heard.

What the hell was wrong with her? She was scared shitless. She looked like some tiny little bird about to be devoured by the big, bad wolf. Why hadn't she called me? Why had she come here alone? Where was her mother for God's sake? When was she going to knee him in the balls and get the hell out of there?

But as I watched, one of Mr. A's hands slid up and to the front, slipping under her shirt as it did so. As his hand reached her breast, a single tear slipped down her cheek and her eyelids dropped in defeat.

I couldn't take another second of it. I ran up the stairs taking two at a time, using the handrails to help propel myself forward.

I slammed the door open and it swung all the way back on its hinges, crashing into the wall and rebounding back towards me. Warm sticky blood began running down my arm, the gash from the bullet having ripped back open. But I was already halfway to Patricia. "What the fuck is going on here?"

Patricia's head jerked around so fast to look at me, it looked like it might just go spinning right on off her shoulders. Mr. A's sharp eyes jumped immediately to mine, but the momentary stumble in control was meticulously and surreptitiously glossed over by one of his million dollar, slicker than fried snot smiles. But this chick wasn't in the market for fried snot, thank God. Not today anyway.

I grabbed Patricia, jerking her behind me. "Get the hell out of here, Patricia. Now. Wait for me just inside the gate." I never took my eyes off of Mr. A.

Patricia mumbled something incoherently, tugging at her shirt as she stumbled towards the door. Even from the corner of my eyes I could see both panic and relief flooding over her, engulfing her with their devastating power and relentlessness, wave after wave, her expression shifting with each surge of emotion. She was in such shock, my state of undress didn't even seem to faze her at all, she was wrapped up too tight in her own little agonizing world for it to even register.

Mr. A, Henry, took a step towards me, "Well, well, well. That's quite a birthday suit, Sydney. But I think you may have misunderstood what's going on here ..."

But I pointed straight at him. "You just shut the hell up. We both know damn well what the 'well, well, well,' hell is going on here. And the game's over. You lose, Mr. A. As a matter of fact, if I were you I'd pack up my stuff and be out of here before the first bell rings in the morning because you are so done here, you fucking asshole. You will never, and I do mean never, work in this town again. Or any other if I can help it."

Raw, unadulterated rage swept over his face and lit his features with the glow of wrath and ferocity. An all-consuming blue flame that swept over his entire face instantly.

He took another step forward. I took one back. A macabre dance, a capella, and potentially lethal. At the moment, our only weapons lay within the words carefully aimed at one another.

Death by verbal skills and syntax, Mr. Webster would be so pleased.

"Sydney. What do you see happening here? Do you honestly have some naïve notion that you'll just be able to toddle off to Mr. Shell's office and make everything right with the world? Foolish girl. Do you think I care about any of this?" His hand swept around the room. "Do you think I care about her?" He motioned to Patricia. "She was a means to an end. A pleasant distraction, perhaps, but just a tool at my disposal, a tool to get to you, Sydney, and it worked. You are so beautifully predictable."

My stomach lurched at the admonishment, teeth gritting instantly, jaw tightening to its limit. But still, he went on.

"Besides, you don't really think this is the first time our sweet, innocent, little Patricia has paid me a visit, do you? She can actually be quite pleasing when she loosens that tight ass of hers up a bit." Sarcasm literally dripped from his words, pooling at his feet in a noxious puddle of smut and immorality.

My head jerked around to Patricia, who was clinging to the doorknob. Too terrified to leave, too frightened to stay, to let go of her escape hatch. To let go of me, her hero. Some hero I turned out to be.

But as my eyes captured hers, I finally saw the truth in those sad blue eyes. The truth that had escaped me for months. Her infatuation with my strength, her dependence on it, on me. Her timidity around the guys at school. Her unexplained late nights and shadowed eyes. Her audacity to take back my necklace, a cry of desperation in the hellacious darkness of her life.

My own grip on reason came slamming down around me. The guilt and shame of having failed my best friend, of not having seen something so hideous right in front of my face, struck me to the quick. I was livid, the blood pounding through my veins like a run-away freight train completely out of control.

My God, what had I done? How could I have allowed this to happen? Anyone with an ounce of common sense would have seen this coming. But not me. Not this fucking idiot! Shit! Shit, shit, shit! What the hell was I supposed to do now?

My head swung back around to the vile slab of flesh that dared call himself human. As my eyes focused on his pudgy, repugnant features, I realized he'd never stopped talking. The words finally clawing their way through my head like vultures circling a decaying carcass.

"We've played this game long enough, Sydney. You know how it ends. And it has absolutely nothing to do with anyone but you, me, and little Patricia here. You know, Sydney, if you'd simply cooperated, she would never have had to be brought into this. This was your choice." His lips twitched, tightening into a horribly unpleasant mask of amused politeness.

"You are absolutely, certifiably insane if you think for one fucking second I'm gonna let you get away with this. Much less try to lay the blame on me, you asshole. I'm gonna be sure everyone knows you for the slime bucket you are."

But Patricia was shaking her head frantically. "Syd, no ... Please ... I can't ... My parents can't ... This would kill them ..." Her words crept over me, enveloping me in their suffocating desperation. I looked at her, ready to fight to the ends of the earth for her, but the emptiness echoing throughout her, body, mind and soul, tore through me. I had the strength to fight the fight. I did. But she didn't. She just didn't have it in her. I would lose whatever was left of her if I pushed her any farther down this road. It was just too dark for Patricia. It would swallow her light and lie there begging for more.

I turned back to Mr. A. "You so much as breathe in her direction again, you fucking jerk, and so help me God, I will roast you alive, you sick bastard. It's over, Mr. As-s-s-kew. Henry." I saw his eyes darken at hearing the name. He knew. Hell, yes, he knew, the sick bastard. I lifted my chin in direct challenge to his assumed domination of the moment. "Whatever it was, it's done. You're done, you sick son of a bitch."

He just smiled and leaned back, half sitting on the table behind him. That Machiavellian shithead just stood there and smiled. "Oh, Sydney. I still don't think you understand. I play to win. I don't play to fall prey to the whims of some insipid, irrational, overly emotional little teenage slut. It doesn't matter who you go to. No one will believe you, absolutely no one. Not your parents, not the principal, not even the police, you silly, stupid girl."

He straightened back up and moved several steps closer, putting him within spitting distance if not quite within hitting distance. "Now, let me tell you how this is going to play out, Sydney. You, my dear have a choice and a big one at that. Walk away, right now, and Patricia and I will pretend you never interrupted our cozy little evening. Or, take her place and she walks away now, no strings. You are the tasty treat, the sweet little pudding, I was after all along anyway. My personal Sydney-the-slut, ready at my beck and call."

I heard a strangled sob gurgle out of Patricia's throat. Humility, anguish, disillusionment and self-loathing bleeding from her chest, pouring from her skin.

And still, Mr. Fucking Asshole went on. Like the God damn Energizer Bunny from hell. "Try to go to the principal and I'll show him years' worth of proof, like he even needs it, that you'll do anything, absolutely anything to get what you want, Sydney. Passing a class for graduation, for example, with no concern for anyone or anything but your own selfish needs. Somehow, do correct me if I'm wrong here, Sydney, but somehow, I'm thinking that you don't quite represent the pillar of social purity you'd like to make yourself out to be. As a matter of fact, there's just not much you haven't done, is there? And I've got proof of just about all of it. So, you say a word, one single word, and I'll deal your dirty little cards so fast it'll make your head spin right off its axis. And Patricia and I will continue to have our quality time together without ever missing a beat. You, my dear, lose this time. Game over."

He took a deep breath, turned and walked to his desk. "My, my, my, I do believe we're done here. I'll take that answer now please, no need to stew over it all night. After all, I sure wouldn't want to be the cause of you missing out on a goodnight's sleep." He glanced up at me as he closed his grade book. "So, will our dear, sweet Patricia be serving me this evening, or will you be returning tomorrow?"

I glanced over at Patricia. She was still shaking her head. I wasn't sure she even knew she was.

Was it no, don't tell? No, don't hurt me anymore? Or, no, don't step in and take this pain for me?

I looked back at him, our personal Dr. Jekyll and Mr. Hyde. "8pm tomorrow. But she's out of this. Forever. Effective immediately."

"Until tomorrow, then. Oh, and Sydney? No cancellations like last time. This is a one-time offer. Don't be late. I'm not a patient man. This little game of ours has gone on for far too long as it is." His eyes glinted in warning, in anticipation, his jaw tightening.

"Yeah. Whatever." I turned for the door. Patricia was fading fast. I wasn't really even sure she'd make it to the car.

Mr. A's parting words slithered across the putrid air churning around him, consuming the distance between us with an eerie precision. "It will certainly be quite a pleasure to strip you of that cocky, self-serving attitude, Sydney."

My feet stalled hauling me out of the room, anger washing over me in a heated rush. I turned my head, tight-lipped, and glared over my shoulder at the monstrous bastard behind the desk.

I regained movement within my legs, recovering the momentum of my flight for freedom. "You will never strip me ... of anything. You'll never break me. Not even in your wildest dreams. You aren't man enough for that. Not today, not yesterday, not ever." I stepped out the door with the last word, shutting the door behind me, adjusting myself to keep both hands on Patricia. She was so pale, she was practically transparent. I had to get her somewhere. Fast.

We hit the bottom of the stairs and turned towards the sidewalk leading to the parking lot. Just as it turned cornering the building, we ran headlong into Beau, Sarah and T.J. Patricia collapsed into me, practically fainting from fright at the sight of T.J.

"What the hell are you doing here!" I felt like I was at some kind of freak convention and someone had forgotten to let me know about it beforehand. That was us ... freaks gone wild. Yeah, nice. Someone should add it to next year's season on HBO.

"Your hair ... but how ..." Sarah breathed out, the words barely audible. She was staring at the streak at the side of my face. She and Beau both were. Then they looked at each other, eyes filled with unspoken words.

"Hair? I'm standing here butt-naked and you're worried about my hair? Just get her out of here." I nodded towards Patricia. "Now ... Please ... I've got something I need to do."

Beau was sliding off his trench coat, holding it up for me to slide my arms in the sleeves. "Thanks. I'll catch up with you later. Patricia?" I ran my fingers through her fine, baby blonde hair, pushing it back from her face, her eyes still glued to T.J.

"Hey, Honey. You remember Beau." I tipped her face so she could see him. "He's gonna take you home. Everything's gonna be alright. Okay, Baby? He's gonna take you right up to your front door."

I turned her face back to me. "Then you're gonna go straight to bed. You're exhausted. You need to rest. Do you understand what I'm saying?"

She nodded. "Good. That's real good, Honey. You get some sleep and call me when you wake up tomorrow. Okay?"

She nodded again. "Okay." I kissed her forehead and turned to Beau. "She lives on Bloss ..."

But he interrupted me, a bad habit of his I was coming to see. "Yeah, on Blossom Street. I know where she lives. She'll be fine, Syd. She's in good hands." He winked at me, that perfect mouth tilting up into that crooked smile that always melted my heart into puddles of pudding that dripped into my lungs filling them with a sweet, syrupy oxygen. Maybe I was a tasty little pudding after all, like Mr. A had said. Only I was for someone else's sweet-tooth.

"Thank you," I mouthed the silent words over my best friend's head. I needed Patricia out of here, someplace safe.

I turned back towards Mr. A's room, buttoned the trench coat and glanced down at my toes. I was still barefoot, but at least my naughty bits were covered. That would have to do. I had a hot date with a monster.

20 MY ITTY-BITTY, TEENY-WEENY TOWERING INFERNO

I turned back toward Mr. A's room, threw my shoulders back and prepared for battle. I absolutely abhorred him, but Mr. A was a known, one I'd had plenty of experience with. Henry was another matter, he was an unknown. How was I supposed to deal with a Big Bad that obviously didn't have a shred of morality? Didn't age? Didn't possess a heart, much less know how to operate one?

As I reached the bottom of the steps that would lead me back up to the snake's pit, I placed my hands on the two pillars that stood guard on either side of the short staircase. Taking a deep breath, meant to soothe, but only serving to feed the tension throbbing throughout my body, I let myself hang backward from my arms, preparing to use the posts to help propel myself up to the door in one fluid motion.

Just as my body began to shift forward for the thrust upward, I lifted my head and found myself face-to-face with none other than Mr. A himself. Only he looked ever so much more like Henry in this moment. A grotesque half-smile twisted his lips and his eyes seemed lit by a darkness emanating from somewhere deep inside him. He was enjoying this, the sick son of a bitch.

Let's see if I couldn't give him something to wipe that Goddamn smile off his face ...

But he beat me to the punch. "Well, well, well, Sydney. I must say, I liked your birthday suit better. Tomorrow was just too far away for you, was it? Couldn't wait that many hours to see me. I understand. Girls like you need men like me to control them. To contain them. To master them. And you know I can do that, Sydney. I will do that. Master you."

My fingers dug into the painted wood of the pillars. I hadn't let go of them. Couldn't let go of them. If I did, my last shreds of restraint would surely come crashing down around me faster than a house of cards. "Master me! You couldn't master my pet worm, much less me, you feeble-brained, nauseating excuse for a human. You wouldn't have any idea of what to do with someone who actually had some balls. And mine are big, hairy, green ones you stupid son of a bitch."

His half-smile melted instantly, contorting instead into a hostile sneer.

"You would be wise never to underestimate me, Sydney. I've been manipulating people for so long now that it's all but lost its flavor. Sweet, silly little Patricia and your pathetic brother, Joseph, included. Your balking, your frustration, your discomfort? They merely increase the pleasure for me. Haven't you realized that yet? And your odd little collection of incidentals ... Jesse, your baby, family, friends ... they merely allow me to break you, to carry out my machinations, my plans. Thank you for that. So, please, balk to your heart's content, Sydney. I really wouldn't have it any other way."

The sun had been winging down the dark side, finally slipping that last half inch on the horizon. And with it, went the switch in my head. You know the one. Everyone has one. It's usually bolted down behind three-inch thick safety glass with caution stripes painted all around it and obnoxious sirens that blare when you get too close. Spinning red lights warn you not to touch ... just stay away.

It's the button that keeps you from making those little, inconsequential decisions with devastating consequences. You know, like forgetting the border patrol has absolutely no sense of humor and telling them you have a matador, a bullfighter, tied up in the trunk. That's worth a good seven hours and a pull-a-part car with the seats and floorboards lying beside it on the gravel.

Or setting off smoke bombs in the girl's bathroom. Instant hour-and-a-half fire drill, easy and no negative backlash if you're good. Or writing fortune cookie fortunes for the monthly administration meeting at the school. You know, fortunes like "the fleas of a thousand camels will infest your armpits if you speak one word of math today", or "a close family member will die if you hand out that quiz in your briefcase". Yeah, that one's only good for a chuckle and an instant detention.

Or better yet, how to get that psychotic, slime ball of a teacher to accidentally run into your knife twenty times. Hmmm, this one is interesting, ...

The really sad part is that, except for that last little one, I'd followed through on every single one of these wonderfully, sane, well thought out ideas. Well, actually, my parents had done the whole jack-in-the-box-matador-in-the-trunk thing, but I kind of liked that one, so I didn't mind including it with my own personal idiot list. It had good company.

And, sometimes, that stupid little red button would just taunt me, teasing me mercilessly to push it. It would jump up and down, just daring me to have the balls to do whatever it was that was wanting to explode right out of my chest at that very moment.

It really was too bad I didn't seem to have a knife on me at the moment. Might actually be worth the fallout to make that last one a reality. Hmmm ... guess it's a damn good thing that we don't always get just what we think we want right when we think we want it. Probably helps to keep the prison population down at any rate. And the obit's in the Sunday paper.

My reverie was interrupted by the cruel, twisted face of the man inches from my own. "Oh, Sydney. You are going to be such a tasty little treat, and all that anger and rage you've got bottled up inside will be like a fine gravy poured on top. Something lovely to dip one's bread in. I wonder what delicious little noises you'll make for me ..."

In that moment all I could feel was my hatred for this miserable sack of oxygen. That's all he was. There was no way he could be called a man. Just a couple of useless airbags ... left and right lungs. Nothing more.

The heat of my fury thundered through my body, pounding all the way through to the tips of my fingers. It felt like a warm blanket, soothing me, comforting me.

Everywhere but at my hands. For some reason the rage was hotter there, prickling my skin. Feeling like a thousand tiny blades, as thin as needles, but with sharp, serrated edges, breaking through the soft skin of my palms. Itching them into action. Begging them to do something, something in particular. But I had absolutely no idea what that something was.

"I'm going to make you scream, Sydney. I promise you that. You were made to scream. To scream for me. I will make you scream, loudly. And then you'll beg to scream again. For more. For me, Sydney."

My fingers twitched, nails gnawing at my palms. The heat swelled inside me, threatening to engulf my entire being with the flames licking inside my stomach, clawing to get out. It was virtually unbearable. I felt like that stupid piece of wadded up newspaper used as kindling to start a fire right before it goes up in flames and the real fire begins.

Suddenly I smelled something ... something different. I couldn't put my finger on exactly what though. It kind of reminded me of campouts with my parents. Roasting marshmallows. Sitting around the campfire, talking and singing and just enjoying being together. Only this was anything but enjoyable! Why on earth would I think about that now of all times? Damn! I could almost swear I even saw little wisps of smoke curling past.

"You are positively certifiable, you insufferable, detestable shithead! And the only thing I'll ever beg for where you are concerned is that you burn in hell. You know the place, it's the one where you'll be the one doing all the screaming, you despicable jackass."

As the last words fell from my lips he lunged toward me. But before he could reach me I caught a wild light gleaming in his eyes. Flames were framing my own image in those baby blues. We both seemed to realize it at the same time turning to look at the flames that were consuming the posts, top to bottom, and even beginning to snake across the ceiling and floor boards.

My hands were still gripping the posts, but somehow they weren't burning, they weren't even sooty. It was as if a little protective force field was surrounding them. Keeping the fire from harming me. From so much as touching me. Even the strands licking across the floor seemed to curve around my feet, never actually making contact with them.

I looked up and realized that Mr. A, Henry, had taken in the same thing. Now he was staring at my hands, so I looked down at them, too. They were actually glowing in the center, in both palms. Flames licking hungrily from them, a breath above my skin. How could this be happening? What, exactly, was happening? Had I started the fire?

Impossible. But somehow I knew that was exactly what had happened. I read about people bleeding from the palms of their hands, like Jesus had on the cross. Stigmatists, I think they were called. But they bled, they didn't burn. And, really, I wasn't burning. Still, somehow, my hands had created the fire. I had created it.

Shit! I couldn't even wrap my head, warped as it was, around this one.

I looked back up at Mr. A. Warily, he took one step back. His eyes tightened on me, took in the stripe of white in my dark brown hair, the blood already seeping through Beau's trench coat from the gash on my upper arm, and those cold, heartless eyes shifted in how they looked at me. As if he'd realized something, or remembered something in that moment that altered his perception of me. And I got the definite feeling that was not a good thing. Not a good thing at all.

But just then a piece of the ceiling fell down in between us right where he'd been standing a second before. When it hit the ground, flames jumped quickly to his feet.

I looked back up at him. His focus was caught on something behind me, but I wasn't about to drag my eyes from him, from this infinitely evil, malevolent creature. I wasn't even sure I could. A deep-seated rage washed over his face as he shifted his concentration back to me.

Those furious, bottomless eyes looked at me accusingly. "You never cease to amaze me, Sydney. We'll continue this another time. Another place."

And with that, he lifted from the ground, not waiting for an answer. As his feet left the landing, he turned into a bat. It was unbelievable how effortlessly he'd done it. He'd actually lifted from the floorboards as a man. Changing into a bat had happened afterwards. How was that possible? Still trying to absorb that, I watched dumbly as he hovered briefly and stared at me with hard little black eyes, inches from my face. Then he flew off over my right shoulder, slashing his claws through Beau's coat. He dragged them across the tender flesh underneath before disappearing in the night sky.

My body pivoted automatically to follow him as he flew away and I found what had caught his attention just before he'd transformed. Beau! Beau was standing a few yards back from me. When had he gotten back here? And why? And why had he kept quiet? Why hadn't he said anything, not one flipping word?

I turned back to the burning building with the thought of trying to save it. To stop the flames from destroying the building any more than they already had. But it was immediately clear to me that there was no stopping it. It had a mind of its own. A raw, greedy hunger that demanded satisfaction.

The feelings consuming me were overwhelming. Before I let myself get swept away by them, though, I needed to get out of here before someone saw me. Still, my feet seemed to be rooted in cement. In fact, it seemed like they were cement. I couldn't get them to so much as wiggle, much less take a single step.

Beau's voice cut through the symphony of crackles and pops raging in front of me, "Syd! Come on, we have to get out of here. Now!"

But those damn legs of mine just wouldn't cooperate. Not at all. I tried to look over my shoulder at him, but I couldn't even do that, my eyes were riveted on the towering inferno glowing, growing, mere feet in front of me. If I jumped forward, I'd be standing right in the heart of the flames. Would I burn? Or would I just be me, Syd, standing in the middle of a burning building, insulated by some kind of flame-retardant protective bubble?

I heard someone yelling in the distance. Shit!

"Syd! Now! Come on!" Beau's hand landed on my left shoulder, tightening, trying to pull me out of my stupor, make me move.

He was right, I really couldn't be seen here. I knew that. I also knew I only had a few seconds before someone was gonna round that building and seal my fate.

Okay. No problem. Just turn into one of my animals. Easy. Ri-i-i-ight. Like that was working real well for me.

"I think one of the school buildings is on fire", I heard a deep male voice holler. Dammit, they were getting closer! Think, Syd, think!

Beau's other hand grabbed my upper right arm, steering clear of the torn, bleeding flesh of my shoulder. Somehow, the pain that should be wracking my body wasn't even registering. Not one little bit. I was just pissed that Beau's coat was shot to hell.

Beau leaned into me and breathed into my ear, "Shift into an eagle. Do it, Syd. Do it now!"

Okay. Eagle. Eagles flew in the air. Air. That was it. I tried to focus on the air around me. The warmth of it. The smell of burning wood hanging in it. The way it seemed to breathe against my skin. The sound of it swishing past, as if it was whispering ageless secrets to me.

The next moment, I felt the shift running through my body. I'd done it! And, I'd done it without a second to spare because as I lifted my little round feathered head, I saw two men round the sidewalk heading straight for me. Well, headed for me and the other eagle, a darker brown with streaks of gold, that had suddenly appeared.

I lifted up into the air, hung there for just a second, then flew off, the new bird on the block following close behind. Both men jumped as we took off, they'd been so focused on the fire that they were startled by the sudden movement.

"Damn! Those were big birds!" The taller man, the one I'd heard earlier yelling about the fire, said.

The smaller guy must have been a transplant, probably from New York, even though he was trying hard to mask it with a good Southern accent. In any case, Mr. Transplant seemed to know more about birds than most people. "Yeah, they are. Those are eagles. Golden eagles, if I'm not mistaken. Kind of hard to tell in this light, though."

I flew up high enough to escape his eyesight, my feathered friend hanging close to me, then I circled a few times finally landing on a rooftop surrounded by trees halfway down the block. I was close enough that I could get an eyeful, but I was far enough away that I felt safe.

Damn! Maybe I was an arsonist. I sure had picked the perfect place to watch from, just like any good, self-respecting arsonist would do. Choose a spot to sit back and revel in their own destructive force.

No! I wasn't an arsonist, dammit! It was an accident, right? Oh, who the hell did I think I was kidding? Of course I was an arsonist. I just burned down a building for Christ's sake!

My mind slipped back to what I'd walked into earlier that evening with Patricia and Mr. A. Sadness, frustration and anger washed through me, the next breath I took filling a full-size set of human, almost eighteen-year-old lungs.

A crash in the burning school building snapped my head around and suddenly, my new best friend, the huge eagle, was in my face, having flown straight at me! I ducked out of the way at the last second as he cried out, as if admonishing me. "Sorry!" It almost seemed like he'd been checking to make sure I was okay. I pulled another lungful of fresh, sweet oxygen in as deep as I could before releasing it back out into the cool night air.

As the breath slipped back out across my lips, the heat from it caught me off guard. I was burning up inside. On fire with the heat of my own emotions. But outside, outside I was cool. The gentle breezes whispered past, chasing away the warmth. But the coolness it brought slipped away just as quickly, smothered once again by the raging flames consuming my body and soul. Leaving me rocking in waves of fire and frost.

Finally, a cold, detached sensation fingered its way up my spine, stroking the nape of my neck, caressing my heart, packaging all that burning intensity smoldering inside me within a thick, frozen blanket of ice. I could see everything just as clearly, maybe even better than before because now there was some insulation to the sensations bombarding me from all sides. I knew the ice was acting like a filter of some kind, softening the world around me, muting it just enough to make it slightly more palatable, easy enough to swallow.

"Syd? Can you hear me?" Beau's voice was soft, deep, gentle. And I turned to look into those warm eyes I'd so easily lost myself in earlier, when I hadn't wanted to lose myself. I wanted to lose myself now. Big time. I wanted to forget all about the me I was and replace her with someone new, someone a little less complicated, someone a little more pleasing, a little more ... pure. Someone like Patricia.

Only, that wasn't really Patricia, was it? At least, it hadn't been for some time now. It had been a different Patricia, an artificial Patricia. Not the best friend I had known so well for so long.

Well, hell! If little Miss Lightness and Joy could reinvent herself, surely I could. Without a doubt, I could be a new me. A different me. A better me. A not me. That was the ticket. A not Sydney. A change of identity.

But would that really change what I needed so desperately to change? The gooey, slobbery stuff packed deep down inside. Thinking back about the look in Patricia's eyes, I knew the answer to that one. And it really wasn't what I wanted it to be. She hadn't really found a new self. She'd only managed to lose her old self. That was all. She'd lost herself and nobody who knew her had even missed her.

What would happen if I lost me? Would someone file a missing person's report? Would anyone notice? Would anyone even care? Once again, I knew the answer and it sucked.

I wasn't Patricia. I wasn't starting from the same place she had. I wasn't starting from lightness and brightness and the perfect little family. But maybe, just maybe, my not being all light and bright and bouncy wasn't a bad thing.

Maybe Patricia lost herself because she just didn't have the strength, the desire, the know-how ... or the help, to find herself. What if I did? How would I know for sure?

I heard an explosion and suddenly realized I was still staring into Beau's eyes as I saw the reflection of the bits and pieces of tar paper and shingles flying across the canvas of his eyes.

"What are you doing here? Why are you here?" I frowned slightly. "How are you here?"

He was looking at me cautiously, assessing me, as if he was trying to judge my ability to handle the situation and only give me as big a mouthful as he thought I could choke down right at this moment. "I'm here for you. To help you. I told you that. You know that."

My eyes shifted downward, to keep him out of my head, then they flew right back to his face. He didn't have any clothes on either! "You flew? Why didn't you tell me you could?"

He glanced away, but only away. He wasn't looking at anything in particular. He was simply not looking at me. "As for how I got here, well, I gain the powers you gain as you set things straight in your past lives. And the clothes? Don't worry, Sarah waited to make sure we got out of there alright. I passed over her on our way here. She was bringing clothes, should be here any minute."

"I set things straight? Are you kidding me? What the hell have I set straight? Jesse's dead. My baby's dead. Hell, I guess I'm dead. Or at least the me that was Rachel is." It was my turn to look away. "And Patricia, Patricia needed me and I failed her. I wasn't there for her, I didn't protect her. God! And, in trying to fix it, I only succeeded in royally pissing off one big, bad son of a bitch, lose a race with a bullet, get clawed by a bat, ruin your coat, and burn down the damn school! Somehow I just don't think felonies fall under the heading of acceptable solutions. Shit, I even managed to irreparably screw things up with you," I turned back toward the school.

"Syd. You flew. You flew again, on your own. That's what you did that you didn't do before. When Jesse died, a part of you died right there in that cave with him. Baby or no baby. But he told you to remember him, fly for him, with his dying breath he told you to look for him, that he would always be with you. You found him. You remembered him. You remembered him as Rache, but you also remember him now, as Syd. You even flew again, on your own, before he died. You saw the man responsible for his death, and yours, and your baby's." Beau's eyes flashed dangerously.

"As for Patricia, it's over. Thanks to you. No, you didn't keep it from happening. Maybe you weren't supposed to. Maybe you weren't even capable of it. Sometimes people have certain things they have to go through in life that you just can't fix for them, no matter how much you wish you could. All that matters now is that it's over. And if the damn building had to go for Patricia to find peace, it's a small price to pay." He turned back toward the blaze, laying one hand on my thigh.

"Mr. Askew, Henry, was already onto you. That's why he's been riding your back so hard these last few years. He was just trying to force you out into the open. To force your hand so he could end this once and for all. Only he hadn't expected the fire play. That one caught him completely by surprise. Thank God for that."

He looked back at me. "And as for us, we're just fine. Aren't we? Besides, who the hell else would sit on a rooftop in the middle of the night, naked, with a known felon, and try to make her feel better about herself? The coat? Wish it had been bat-proof, but I tend to be hot natured anyway, so no worries there."

My ears could hear what Beau was saying, but my head just couldn't quite wrap itself around it.

Just then, Sarah's sweet voice drifted up to us. "Hey guys! Are you still up there?"

"Sure are, and you have absolutely exquisite timing! Just toss them up ...," Beau leaned sideways on his hands and knees to look over the edge of the roof, and was hit square in the face with the trench coat he'd put on me earlier, "... here."

"Oops! Sorry, Beau!" Sarah giggled. I couldn't help but smile. How could she always be so ... light, so happy, so "in the moment"?

"Here you go." Beau draped the coat across my shoulders, pulling it around me. "See if you can hang onto it a little longer this time, huh?"

I rolled my eyes at him, "You can be such a little shit." Leaning forward I called down, "Thanks, Sarah! You're an angel!"

"Is that how it is? She's an angel and I'm a little shit?" Beau was buttoning the pants Sarah had just tossed up to him. "Give me the coat back then. If I'm gonna do the time, I might as well have a little fun with the crime!"

I pulled the front around me, locking my arms over it. "You can pry this coat out of my cold, dead fingers, or wait until I'm back in my own clothes. Makes me no difference."

Beau just smiled that insidious smile and leaned back towards the edge of the roof. "Thanks, Sarah. Wait there, I'll be down in a few minutes."

"No problem. Take your time. There's a sweet little kitty here needing some attention." Soon a deep, rumbling purr could be heard up on the roof.

Taking a deep breath to clear my head, my eyes rested blandly on the burning building across the street. "Okay. Let's assume, just for a moment here, that you're right. About all of it. That still doesn't explain how Jesse was alive and kicking to marry Rache. I mean, to marry me. He'd have died at the swimming hole with the guys earlier that day if I hadn't gone back. But I just went back. So, he couldn't have been saved back then, only just now. That means no wedding, no baby, no double grave." I rubbed the back of my hand across my eyes trying to shake some of the fog that was creeping around my brain.

"Syd, you're looking at this the only way you know how, as if time is a linear thing. But it's not." He looked off into the distance for a minute, then looked back at me. "When you went back to your life as Rachel and fixed things, saved Jesse by distracting your brother just long enough that he misfired that afternoon, you really changed it. Changed what happened back then. And everything else that's happened since then instantaneously shifted, kind of like a train that jumped over to a new track. A track laid down by you."

"Okay. But what about you and Sarah and T.J? I thought you guys had to help me, that I couldn't do this on my own?" I was still trying to play catch-up.

"I'm not sure, Syd. We didn't expect that. Somehow, when you fell asleep in the cemetery, your subconscious was able to pull you back all on its own. We'll have to figure that one out. If you can gain control of that ability when you're awake, it would be phenomenal."

That perfect half-smile slipped across his lips and was gone just as fast as it had come. "But right now, we need to get out of here, Syd. This is gonna be bad, and you don't need to be around for it. So move that stubborn little ass of yours, now. Go straight to the cemetery. Sarah and I will meet you there. Wait for us, it may be a while. Then we'll leave together. Forever. Now, get out of here. Go."

The jarring disharmony of fire truck sirens began to fill the night as I finally slid down the slope of the roof. Leaning my body into the shingles I felt for and found the tall fence line with my left foot, then pushed off to a low squat on top of the wooden fence, jumping the seven feet back down to earth. I wasn't quite sure why I felt the need to stay me, to not shift into something that would make the drop a thousand times easier. But maybe that was just it. Maybe I wasn't in the mood for easy. Sometimes hard was better. More grounding. Kept you from just floating away like a misplaced balloon, adrift in a sea of clouds.

Oh, my God! For the first time in my life, I realized it was actually me keeping me connected to the earth, not my parents. I could fly anytime I wanted to. I didn't have to stay earthbound. In that moment I felt the warmth of their love ease away from their enveloping hold around my body and slip inside me. It was my own strange way of cutting the strings, I guess. I knew I'd never need them the same way I had, but I knew they'd always be with me, watching over me, loving me.

Suddenly, I didn't want to let go of this moment. My heart felt torn in two directions, like it was still hanging onto the eave, not wanting to let go of the feeling of freedom quite yet. But in my heart there was also the achingly sweet, comforting feeling of being with my parents, of being safe and loved, of being just a kid. My stomach twisted into a knot and I tried to breathe past the lump in my throat, blinking down the tears before they fell.

So many emotions ran through me, it felt like someone had ripped open a floodgate of feelings. The energy of being alive tickled down my arms leaving a trail of goose bumps in its path. I closed my eyes and took a deep breath. Good. That helped, I leaned against the fence for a minute just breathing.

What didn't help was the thought of spending the night in juvy. My heart suddenly didn't feel quite so light. Actually, it didn't feel light at all. It felt more like it had just melted in a puddle over my intestines. So, I slipped into the shadows of the trees and made my way home, to my home, plot 1327-B. Sirens growing louder by the second.

It took everything I had not to look back. I know arsonists always watch the destruction caused by their creation. But maybe the destruction was irrelevant after all. Maybe they simply couldn't keep their eyes off the manifestation of their own power. The power we all carry within us, but rarely use. The power we're all afraid of because to actually own it we would have to accept the responsibility for our own lives. The responsibility of living a chosen life, not an accidental one.

I'd been so sure for so long that I'd want to leave this place the moment I could, and now that time had come and my feet were heavy, growing roots that extended deep down in the earth beneath my feet. I knew I would miss this place. My home. And I knew I could never look back. Not even to revel in the beauty of my own power.

But even as I accepted that truth, I felt the earth shifting beneath my feet, ever so slightly. The wind cut back, changing direction.

And, deep down, I knew this one event would change the direction of my life forever. Change me forever. Whoever the hell I was.

21 HAPPY NEVER-ENDINGS

I sat there watching the sun slowly dip below the horizon until the moon and stars filled the sky with their mystical light. I'd been here since last night. Couldn't remember the last time I'd eaten, and didn't really care, but I had cleaned up my shoulder and then slept most of the day.

What a strange, mixed-up feeling of detached purpose I found myself floating in. Only I really didn't have a clue what I was supposed to be so god-awful purposeful about. I was completely perplexed. Utterly bewildered. Just who was I? And how exactly had I ended up here?

Funny how all those little baby steps I'd taken, never seeming to move me more than a breath away from where I'd been the moment before, had somehow added up all together to carry me so far away from everything I'd ever known.

Would I ever be the Sydney I'd always thought myself to be? The "Solo Syd" who never bothered with tomorrows and certainly never bothered with getting too close to anyone. Ever. Where did that me go? And, why didn't I notice when she left? Shouldn't there have been some kind of passing off of the baton like in a relay race?

And if I wasn't me anymore, where the hell did that leave me exactly? Who was I going to be instead? Wasn't there some kind of checklist that everyone was supposed to get at times like this? You know, like one of those menus they give you in the hospital for the food you want to eat the next day. Where was mine? I'd choose a courage appetizer, an honor salad, a main course of strength with a side order of conviction, beauty for dessert and, to quench my thirst, happiness, on-the-rocks, just to make it all slide down a little easier.

I guess there just wasn't enough room on my plate for friendship and fulfillment, much less love. Oh well, my parents must have been right about that one, I guess I can't have everything on the menu. Mama used to always tell me my eyes were bigger than my stomach.

But even if she was right, I sure felt like gorging. I wanted the whole nine yards for the first time in a very long time. Longer than I could even remember.

I hadn't seen my parents in what seemed like forever, but I knew I'd miss having them near. I guess I'd just have to carry them both in my heart from here on out.

Okay, so where's the waiter when you need him? Table five is ready to order.

I looked up as Beau, Sarah and T.J. walked into the clearing. I had a thousand questions burning in my mind. But not a single one could manage to find its way out of my mouth.

So, I didn't speak. Didn't say a word. Not one syllable. I just stood up and walked over to them, silently joining their quest. Their ultimate pursuit.

After I handed Beau his trench coat, he slipped my jacket around my shoulders and handed me my guitar. I slipped my left arm and head through the strap, jerking down on it to pull it into place. Then I walked back to my parents' gravesite, squatted, and kissed the tombstone one last time. A single tear stained my cheek as I rose and turned back to my new companions. They parted just enough for me, and I slipped in step between them as we headed off to meet and greet the next bag of bones in this incredible journey called "my life."

Ahem, "lives." Plural. Yeah, can't forget that ...

To keep Syd from dressing in the bones of <u>your</u> ancestors, look for the second book in the series:

Bone Dressing

The

Dreaming

To find out more about the *Bone Dressing* series of seven novels, Syd, and their creator, Michelle, visit:

www.BoneDressing.com